RIDER'S RESCUE

THE RIDER'S REVENGE TRILOGY

Rider's Revenge

Rider's Rescue

Rider's Resolve

DEDICATION

To all my friends who've been there for me through this crazy writing journey and to the strangers who were willing to take a risk on an unknown author in the hopes of discovering a new fantasy world. Thank you.

A NOTE ON PRONUNCIATION

Members of the tribes have names that use an apostrophe after the initial consonant. For example, K'lrsa and G'van.

To pronounce these names, substitute an i or e for the apostrophe.

For example:

D'lan = Dilan

F'lia = Filia

K'lrsa = Killrisa

L'ral = Liral

M'lara = Milara

T'kar = Tikar

CHAPTER 1

K'lrsa leaned low over Fallion's neck as his powerful wings beat the air.

They were flying. Actually flying!

She'd never believed all the legends about *Amalanee* horses. How could she when she had Fallion, the only *Amalanee* in the tribes, and knew for a fact that he didn't fly?

But here they were, soaring over the plains of Toreem, leaving the Daliphate behind with every beat of his beautiful golden wings. The full moon shone upon them and her heart soared with joy.

Home. They were, finally, going home.

She took a deep breath of the crisp clean air.

And she was free. Of Toreem and its slaves and men who viewed her like a stuck pig and bound her in ridiculous layers of clothing and threatened to kill her if she so much as looked at them wrong.

She rolled her shoulders to release the foul memories. It was over and now she and Badru could start a new life together back home with her tribe.

She glanced over to where he and Garzel rode Midnight. Even though it was muted now that he was flying, Midnight's coat seemed to encompass the entire night sky, stars shining within its silky blackness.

Badru smiled and her heart skipped a beat.

Foolish, she knew.

But the times they'd spent together in the Moon Dream had felt so real—their bodies moving together in perfect harmony under the light of a full moon. With his long black hair and startling blue eyes, he'd captured her heart before they ever even met.

And now…Now she felt a pull towards him so strong it was almost physical.

Herin clutched at K'lrsa with her maimed fingers, her breath rattling in K'lrsa's ear as she leaned forward. Her breath smelled of death and decay with a cloying but ineffective amount of cinnamon mixed in.

K'lrsa fought the urge to flinch away. Too bad she wasn't riding with Badru instead, but he had as much a right to ride his Midnight as she did her Fallion. And it wasn't like she could've just left Herin behind in that field with the Daliph's soldiers closing in. (Although she had thought about it for the briefest of moments.)

After all, it was Herin and Garzel who'd known how to awaken the horses to their true nature. She shuddered at the memory of soldiers pouring out of the gates of Toreem, ready to kill them all, while Garzel calmly placed his sun stone on the tear drop mark on each horse's forehead.

At first, nothing happened. They'd stood there, knowing it was too late to run, knowing that Aran would kill them as slowly and painfully as he could. That he might even kill them and bring them back to life just so he could kill them again.

K'lrsa had thought it was over.

And then, with one shake of his head, Fallion had transformed from the magnificent golden horse she'd always known into a creature beyond her wildest imaginings. Large, magnificent wings spread from his back and his coat shone with the light of a thousand suns.

Next to him stood Midnight, just as amazing and beautiful, his coat encompassing the entire night sky.

She'd stared in awe as the soldiers raced towards them, frozen by the sheer impossibility of what had happened.

They'd had to flee, but before they did she'd touched one of those golden wings. It felt as solid and warm as his body but shimmered before her eyes like heat haze off desert sands in the middle of summer.

She turned to watch his wings beat the air.

They had to be real.

She could feel the wind they stirred. And see the lands of the Toreem Daliphate spread out far below her. The cities of Toreem and Boradol were as small as boulders, the soldiers they'd left behind no bigger than ants.

At the same time she knew this wasn't real, somehow. This wasn't her world with the rules she knew so well.

When she rode Fallion across the plains, the wind whipped at her long black hair and snatched her words away. And yet, here they were, flying faster than that, and—if she'd wanted to, which she didn't—she could've easily had a conversation with Herin who was seated behind her.

Fallion banked to the left and the mutilated stubs of Herin's fingers clutched at K'lrsa's waist. She shuddered. She'd never particularly liked the woman.

And who could blame her? Only a few days ago Herin had schemed to kill her.

She still wasn't sure Herin didn't want her gone. In Herin's eyes, it was K'lrsa's fault Badru had lost his throne.

Not like K'lrsa had forced him to free her from slavery. Or to give her back her property once he did, thereby upending hundreds of years of rules and laws.

That was all Badru.

But Herin didn't see it that way. She saw a love-sick fool destroying his life.

And maybe she was right. Because Badru had lost the Daliphate.

One foolish decision too many—this one about whether to help the Toreem Daliphate's main trading partner which would've meant turning on K'lrsa's tribe—and his grandfather Aran had revealed himself and taken back the throne.

Turns out he hadn't been as dead as everyone thought he was. She should've known, or suspected, that someone had used death walker magic to resurrect him the way Herin had Lodie.

Herin shifted behind her and K'lrsa tensed as she realized how high they were. One shove and that would be it for her.

But Herin wasn't a fool. Fallion was K'lrsa's horse. As much as Herin might want to see her gone, Herin wouldn't act now. Plus, just because Herin had wanted her dead a few days ago, didn't mean she still did.

K'lrsa was no longer the obstacle she had been. Badru had already lost his throne—and his life. Now they were united in a common purpose—save the tribes from Aran's soldiers.

K'lrsa shook her head. Herin was definitely not the sort of ally she would've chosen.

Although she did have her uses. She'd brought Badru back to life. And known how to awaken the horses.

What else did she know?

How many more secrets were locked behind those grel-like eyes?

K'lrsa glanced at Badru again.

The man of her dreams. Literally.

And the only man she'd ever actually felt was an equal.

Not perfect as it turned out. Not in real life.

But a better match than any she'd ever hoped for.

And still young, like her. She'd just reached her sixteenth summer, and Badru was only a summer or two older, if that.

They had a lifetime to grow together and form the same sort of unbreakable bond her parents had had.

He'd do well in the tribes. He was strong and skilled with a horse, and he had been the leader of the entire Toreem Daliphate. That was something. No one in the tribes would care and he couldn't tell them anyway, but the experience of being a leader and making decisions would serve him well.

And at least now he wouldn't ask her to stay in the Daliphate. He couldn't. His whole court had seen him murdered. They'd never take him back knowing he'd been revived with forbidden magic.

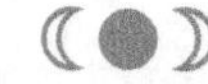

Which meant a fresh start, for both of them.

She just wished the price hadn't been so high.

She was grateful to Herin that she'd brought him back. But death walker magic demanded a life for a life. And trapped, cornered, the entire palace searching for them, they'd had no choice but to sacrifice one of their own.

Sayel. Her chief poradom. A man who'd become like a second father to her.

He'd given his life willingly, but still…

She would've stopped him if she could. He was her friend. A bit misguided at times and foolish enough to think that she'd make a good dorana when they both knew it was completely hopeless, but a friend nonetheless.

She shuddered at the memory of her days in Toreem.

Others could call it an honor to be bound with the *meza* and wear the golden *tiral*, to have poradoma there to serve your every whim, but she'd seen it for what it was.

A golden cage.

She was a Rider. A warrior and protector of her people. A proud member of the White Horse Tribe. The equal of any man.

Not some cowed songbird dressed up for display.

She'd almost lost herself in Toreem. Almost let them defeat her. But she'd persevered in the end.

And succeeded in killing the man who'd killed her father.

Not the man she'd thought it would be. Not the Daliph, but a member of the tribes.

One of her own. K'var of the Black Horse Tribe.

He'd put the lure of wealth above her father's life.

And not just his life, but all the members of the tribes. He'd come to Toreem for troops to annihilate his enemies, demanding men and weapons enough to strike down all who would stand against him.

He would've killed everyone she loved. Her mother, her brother, her younger sister. Her best friend, F'lia. Everyone she'd ever known.

Badru refused him. For her. Even though it wasn't in the best interests of the Daliphate, he'd said no.

But Badru was no longer Daliph.

Aran was. And Aran had given the order to send troops. Even now, couriers rode for the border, bearing a message of death for her people.

She had to reach them first.

She had to save them.

No matter the cost.

CHAPTER 2

As the moon dipped towards the distant horizon, full and ripe with silvery light, they flew over Boradol— the harsh, straight lines of its streets carved into the flesh of the world, its buildings reaching towards them like a clawed hand, desperate to pull them from the sky.

So far from the desert, K'lrsa could barely feel the Lady Moon's presence in that silvery glow. She was surprised to feel that much. The Daliphana were not the lands of her gods.

But soon she'd return to the plains and deserts of home, where Father Sun beat upon the earth with merciless disregard, the Lady Moon shone her benevolent gaze on all, and the Trickster wandered during the between-times, luring the unwary to their deaths.

It was a harsh land. A land of privation and struggle; unlike Toreem with its lush bounty.

But it was hers and she longed to return.

K'lrsa tensed as she studied Boradol. She'd never even seen a road before she came to the Toreem Daliphate. The tribes moved with the flow of the seasons, traveling the curves of the land. Not like those in the Daliphana who carved straight lines to their destinations through hills and over rivers with no care for what or who they destroyed.

She took a deep breath and released it slowly.

It didn't matter what those in the Daliphana did.

Because she was leaving and she was never coming back. Let them destroy their land and one another.

She was done with them.

Herin tapped her shoulder. "Land. There." She pointed towards a building in the distance, its roof sagging under the weight of the years, its sides bulging as if the whole place was about to collapse.

K'lrsa shuddered at the sight of Herin's fingers, each one missing the first joint. Even knowing it was the price Herin had paid for each failed attempt on Aran's life wasn't enough to overcome K'lrsa's aversion to such an obvious sign of weakness.

A woman like Herin would have never lasted in the tribes. She'd have given herself to the sands rather than be a burden on her family. She couldn't hunt, couldn't sew, couldn't make pottery. Couldn't even feed herself, relying instead on Garzel for that barest of necessities.

K'lrsa ignored her.

She wanted to get out of the Toreem Daliphate as soon as possible.

Herin pinched her arm, the bones at the end of her fingers pressing into K'lrsa's skin.

"Ow. What did you do that for?"

"I told you to land."

K'lrsa shrugged one shoulder. "I don't want to."

"Pzah, you foolish child. The *Amalanee* can't fly during the day. Do you want to be stranded in the middle of a field when daylight comes?"

K'lrsa pursed her lips together, loathing the old crone behind her, but she nudged Fallion towards the barn nonetheless.

As they approached the ground at a speed as fast as Fallion's fastest gallop, K'lrsa fought the urge to brace for impact.

He didn't need her to fight him. Instead, she leaned forward and pressed herself against his neck, making herself a part of him so that they moved together just like when they were racing across the plains hunting baru.

She didn't even feel the impact as Fallion's feet touched

the ground, he landed so smoothly.

And just like that, he was once more an ordinary—if an *Amalanee* could ever be considered ordinary—horse, his hooves chiming softly as he raced along a narrow dirt track, his beautiful, golden wings gone.

"Well done, *micora*," she whispered as he stopped outside the barn.

Midnight came to a stop at their side, the only other *Amalanee* horse K'lrsa had ever seen.

They were the most majestic of all horses, so rare that a person was lucky to see one in a lifetime. Faster than any other, long-legged, capable of running an entire day without rest. And extremely intelligent. When K'lrsa and Fallion hunted it was like they were one being, moving together so perfectly that no one could match them.

Badru smiled at her and K'lrsa blushed.

Even in servant's robes he was gorgeous, his long black hair pulled back into a simple club, his golden brown skin shining with health.

Too much health.

The health of one recently brought back from the dead, every wound healed as if it had never existed. He burned with the glow of Sayel's sacrifice.

She turned away, trying not to remember Badru's motionless body slung over Sayel's shoulder like so much meat, his blue eyes dulled and staring at nothing.

"K'lrsa? Are you okay?"

She nodded, but didn't look back as she dismounted.

She wobbled, holding onto Fallion's shoulder for support. It had been too long since she'd ridden a horse; her legs were no longer used to it.

Herin cleared her throat and K'lrsa reluctantly offered her a hand down. Herin harrumphed. "I don't need your help, I just need you to move so I can get down."

K'lrsa stepped back and Herin lowered herself off Fallion's back, not the least bit affected by their night's journey.

The woman might be old and withered, but she was stronger than anyone K'lrsa knew.

Badru came over to her. "K'lrsa? Are you okay?" he asked once more.

She nodded, still not quite looking at him. "Mmhm. I'm just...A lot's happened the last few days."

"I know. I'm just so glad you're safe." He pulled her close and she buried her face against his chest for a long moment, shaking with the after-effects of all she'd been through.

Tarum's attack and her trial and the fight with Balor. And then Badru's murder. And fleeing through the palace with Sayel. And Badru's resurrection and killing K'var and the horses flying and knowing that Aran had sent soldiers to slaughter her people.

She closed her eyes and took deep, calming breaths, forcing herself to focus on the moment, to center herself and put aside all emotion until she finally found the hunter's version of the Core—that heightened state of awareness that allowed her to exist in the moment separate from her feelings.

Herin shoved at them. "Come on. Sun'll be up soon. Can't have you two spotted. Especially not with her dressed like that."

K'lrsa lost the Core, returning with a snap to the real world.

She wanted to argue that what she was wearing—tight baru-hide pants and a matching vest— was perfectly normal, but she remembered her journey through the Daliphate to Toreem, and how men had stared simply because she rode a horse and how they'd reacted with horror or worse to the slightest sight of skin.

Instead, she followed Badru into the barn, her nose twitching at the dank and earthy stench of it. She was a desert child, not used to such abundance.

She settled Fallion down, stripping the small golden saddle from his back and using patches of dried grass to wipe him down. Garzel silently laid a pile of torn fresh grass at their feet and she nodded thanks, wondering what it must be like to never be able to speak.

When she was done, she stood in the broken doorway and waited until the sun colored the distant horizon with fire and cast its light on the lush, rolling green hills that surrounded them.

Somewhere birds sang, their trills of happiness filling the air, unaware that the world had shifted around them.

Even in winter, this land was more alive than her own land ever was.

Fallion nudged her with his nose and she leaned into his comforting warmth, scratching a spot behind his right ear. "We're going home, *micora*" she whispered, smiling for what felt like the first time in days.

He whinnied softly in agreement.

"Oh, how I missed you." She buried her nose against his neck and inhaled the familiar scent of him.

They'd been too long apart.

She was scared and exhausted and didn't know how on earth to defeat the men of the Toreem Daliphate, but at least she had Fallion. Steady and true.

He'd always been by her side, and never abandoned her. Even when he should have.

And she had Badru, who loved her even though it cost him the Daliphate.

And Garzel, a steady presence she knew she could count on.

And Herin, who…

Well.

Knew things. But needed close watching.

K'lrsa stepped back, reluctant to leave Fallion's sheltering warmth. "Come. Time to rest."

For now, she'd sleep and recover what energy she could.

And tonight? Tonight she'd continue her journey home.

She just hoped everyone would believe her about the Daliph's men. If they didn't, she didn't know what she'd do.

They couldn't fight, they'd have to run, and they needed enough time to do so.

Although, where they could go, she didn't know.

CHAPTER 3

K'lrsa seated herself on a bare patch of earth that looked relatively dry, and leaned against the wooden walls of the barn, looking around at their dark, dank shelter.

It still amazed her how casually the people of the Daliphana used wood. That they would leave all this wood here to rot when it could be used for a fire or to build something they could actually use.

Garzel handed her a dense bar of nuts, fat, and dried berries.

It tasted horrible—too much fat and not enough berries, but she gagged it down. It was food, after all, and a lifetime in the desert had taught her to never turn down food when she didn't know where her next meal would come from.

She choked on the last bit, wishing for water to wash it down with.

Badru, who'd settled down next to her, took a bite of his bar and spat it out.

Herin smacked him. "Pzah, boy. Don't be a fool. That's all the food we're likely to have for at least a few more days."

He shook his head. "I'll get something real to eat when I go into Boradol." He set the bar aside.

K'lrsa laughed. "What are you talking about, going to Boradol? We're going straight to the tribes." She glanced at the others. Did they know what he was talking about?

Herin pursed her lips as she glared at Badru.

Garzel was his normal unreadable self. Had he talked much before he lost his tongue? He struck her as the type to only talk when it was absolutely necessary, but maybe thirty years without a tongue had made him that way. Maybe he'd once been a gregarious, outspoken man who never shut up.

She didn't know.

And didn't have time to think about it now. Because it seemed Badru had lost his mind.

He ignored them as he dug through his small pack, setting aside items he didn't think he'd need and hefting the pack before setting aside a few more.

"Badru…" K'lrsa tried again. "You can't go into Boradol."

"I have to." He pressed his lips together in a tight line.

"What if someone recognizes you?"

His brow wrinkled as he stared at her. "That's the whole point. I need them to know I'm still alive and that I'm coming back for my throne."

K'lrsa bit her lip.

He'd died in front of everyone. Didn't he see what that meant?

Fortunately, Herin spoke up. "You can't take your throne back."

He glared at her. "Not today, maybe. I need time to build support. But I will take it back."

She shook her head. "No. You won't."

"How dare you say that?" He stood, looming over them. "I'm the rightful Daliph of Toreem. It's my birthright."

Herin cackled, almost choking. "Your birthright is it?"

"Yes. I'm the only living descendent of the last Daliph. That throne is mine by the divine right of inheritance. No one else can claim it."

"Except for the last Daliph himself, of course." Herin quirked one brow.

"Aran needs to die, Grandmother. And when he does, I'll take back my throne."

"Aran does need to die, I'll give you that. But not now. There are more important things we have to handle first."

"Like what?"

K'lrsa stared at him in surprise. "Like saving my people."

He shook his head. "They can defend themselves. This is more important. If I don't let everyone know I'm alive now, I'll never have a chance to regain what's rightfully mine."

Herin sighed. "Men and their pride."

"Pride? It's not about pride, it's about right. He took my throne."

Herin snorted. "*Your* throne?"

"Yes."

"What gives you any more right to that throne than any other man? Because you're Aran's grandson?"

He nodded. "Yes. Exactly."

"Pzah. Like I would've ever borne that man's child." She spat on the ground, the most deadly insult a member of the tribes could give. "You're no more Aran's grandson than that horse of yours is."

"What?" Badru stumbled backward. "What are you saying?"

Herin rolled her eyes. "That you're not the grandchild of the foul, loathsome human being who raped and tortured me." She narrowed her eyes as she stared up at him. "I thought you'd be pleased."

"Pleased? But that means that I'm…" He shook his head. "That I'm no one. Just a…" He frowned. "If Aran isn't my grandfather, then who is?"

Herin sighed. "Who do you think?" She nodded towards Garzel.

Badru looked back and forth between them. "But why? Why lie to me all these years?"

"To save your life. And your mother's. Do you think Aran would've let me bear another man's child? And if he had, what do you think he would've done to her if he'd known she wasn't his?"

K'lrsa shivered. She hadn't known Aran personally, but she'd heard what he'd done to Herin, Garzel, Lodie, and untold others. That's how Herin had learned death walker magic. Because Aran had killed Garzel and brought him back over and over again just to torment her.

If he'd done that to Herin's husband, what would he have done to her child?

K'lrsa shuddered at the thought.

But it seemed Badru didn't see it that way.

"So you lied?" Badru glared down at her. "You made me believe I was someone when I'm really no one?" He trembled with emotion, his entire body shaking. "But then why help me become Daliph?"

Herin laughed. "That was my proudest moment, watching them crown you Daliph. Think. All of Aran's sons and grandsons were dead. He was dead. All of them gone. No drop of his blood left on earth. And you, a child of the tribes, *my* grandchild, took his place."

She smiled, relishing the memory. "It was my final victory over him."

K'lrsa moved close enough to touch Badru's leg. "Isn't this good news, Badru? It means he's not part of you. Wouldn't you rather be Garzel's grandson than Aran's?"

He stared down at her for a long moment and then shook his head. "I don't know. I mean…Who am I if I'm not the Daliph?"

She shook her head, not understanding. "You're Badru. A strong fighter. A good man. And a member of the tribes. Like me."

"But what does that mean?" He stepped back, breaking their touch. "I need some time to think about this."

He walked to the door of the barn, and paused.

He turned back, looking at Garzel. "I am glad to know you're my grandfather."

Garzel nodded.

Next, Badru turned to K'lrsa. "And I am glad I'm a member of the tribes."

He said the words, but there was no conviction behind them. K'lrsa sat back against the wall, frowning. Did he really think so little of her and her people?

"I'm going for a walk." He turned back towards the door.

"Don't let anyone see you," Herin called after him.

After he was gone, a heavy silence fell. Finally, K'lrsa turned to Herin. "Why didn't you tell him before this?"

She shrugged. "He didn't need to know. And if thinking he was Daliph by some divine right made him a better ruler, what harm was there in it?"

Lots. Badru had not only grown up thinking himself a rightful heir to the Daliphate, he'd also grown up thinking himself the grandchild of a rapist and murderer. That had to affect how he saw himself, especially when he had no father around to counter it.

And now to find he wasn't descended from that monster…

She wanted to go after him. But would he want her there?

Herin leaned into Garzel, closing her eyes for a moment as he softly kissed her brow.

K'lrsa envied them their easy comfort.

Maybe someday she'd have that with Badru.

Someday, but not today.

CHAPTER 4

K'lrsa wanted to wait for Badru to return, but she was just too exhausted. The last few days had been a whirlwind of action and stress, and she succumbed to sleep almost as soon as her head touched the musty ground.

She found herself in the land of the moon dream, the desert sands stretching silver in every direction, undulating across the landscape. The moon hung full and ripe above her, so large it seemed to take up half the sky. The air was brisk with the bite of winter, but K'lrsa didn't feel chilled even in the diaphanous garments of the Moon Dance.

Everything was as clear as midday, including the Hidden City which loomed in the distance, its blocky spires dominating the far horizon. She knew from past experience that no matter how long she walked in its direction it would always stay just as far away from her as it was now.

She closed her eyes, relishing the feeling of home as the wind stroked her skin, the cloth strips of her outfit snapping behind her.

"My child. You return." The Lady Moon's voice was like a cool spring hidden in shade.

K'lrsa opened her eyes. The Lady was as regal and beautiful as ever, this time in the guise of the matron—an older woman, full of health and strength although wrinkles creased the corners of her eyes.

K'lrsa held the Lady's gaze, almost losing herself in the

fathomless depths of the Lady's eyes. "Yes. At last."

The Lady gestured for her to follow as she walked along the edge of a large sand dune. K'lrsa marveled at how the Lady made it look so effortless to walk in sand that sunk under K'lrsa's feet, cascading down the slope to her right.

The silence between them stretched until K'lrsa felt like she'd burst if someone didn't speak. She hustled to catch up, her feet digging deeper into the sand, struggling for every step. "The tribes are in danger. Aran, the new Daliph of the Toreem Daliphate, is sending troops to kill any who oppose the Black Horse Tribe. We need your help."

The Lady turned. Her face shifted seamlessly between a young maiden's visage, full of life and vitality, that of the matron, and that of an old crone, her face so covered in wrinkles that only her eyes were distinct.

"You need my help? But first, a question. Did you complete the vow you made to my husband?" she asked, her voice tolling like a bell.

K'lrsa backed away from that fearsome gaze, almost tumbling down the side of the dune. "Yes. The man who killed my father is dead, just as I vowed."

As the lady studied her with those eyes full of the vastness of the night, K'lrsa rushed on. "It wasn't Badru. I know I thought it was the Daliph when I set out, but it wasn't him. It was K'var. He admitted it. He's the one who killed my father."

The lady nodded. "But is that all you vowed, K'lrsa dan V'na of the White Horse Tribe?"

K'lrsa licked her lips, suddenly cold. "I…No."

Her shoulders slumped. She didn't want to go back there. She couldn't. Not right now. Not with the tribes in danger.

"What else did you vow?" the Lady asked, all warmth gone from her voice.

K'lrsa studied her feet, noticing how dirty her toenails were. Sayel would hate that.

"Well?"

"To destroy the Toreem Daliphate."

"And did you?"

K'lrsa chewed on her lip. "Well, sort of. Badru did lose his throne and they all turned on one another and…"

"No. You did not." The Lady gazed towards the distant mountains where the city of Toreem nestled. "The Toreem Daliphate is stronger than when you arrived. Aran is in power once more and he turns his gaze towards the tribes. Now more than ever, he must be defeated."

"But he's sent troops to attack the tribes. I have to warn them. I can't go back." K'lrsa's throat clenched. "Please don't make me. My people need me. If I don't warn them…"

The Lady stared at her for a long moment.

K'lrsa clenched her fists, unable to breathe, willing the Lady to let her continue on to her people.

Finally, she nodded. "Yes, your people do need you. But not just to warn them. To save them."

"Save them?" K'lrsa stared at her. "But how?"

She smiled. "You'll find a way."

K'lrsa shook her head. She couldn't stand against a trained army. Not alone.

"Don't forget, child. You bring allies with you. Look to Badru. And Vedhe."

"Who's Vedhe?" K'lrsa frowned. That wasn't a name of the tribes.

"The scarred one you saved from the slavers."

She remembered the woman. Silent. Pale-skinned, pale-haired. A slave taken for sale in Crossroads. Day after day she'd walked behind the trading caravan, never complaining, never failing, even though K'lrsa thought she'd die.

Those were her allies? A fallen leader and a scarred foreigner?

How could they possibly defeat an army?

"Who else?"

The Lady smiled, her eyes crinkling with amusement. "Herin. Garzel. Lodie."

Two old women and an old man. One who'd probably rather see her dead, one a former slave, and one without a tongue.

K'lrsa bit her lip to hide what she thought about her supposed allies.

The Lady Moon laughed softly, her voice like the tinkle of a desert spring on rocks. "You set off to challenge the entire Toreem Daliphate alone. And now you can't defeat just a few of their soldiers, even with allies by your side?"

"That was different. I didn't know any better. And my so-called allies aren't exactly warriors."

"You don't need warriors. You just need the right weapons."

K'lrsa snorted. "The right weapons? Six people can't stand against an army, no matter what weapons they have."

"Not true. There are weapons a single person could wield that would destroy an entire army."

"Really? And where are these weapons?"

The lady shook her head. "Look to your allies and you'll find the answer in time."

"But we don't have time! Aran already sent the order. His troops will be there within days."

"Then you must lead your people to the sanctuary first."

"Sanctuary? Where? We don't have great walled cities stocked with months' worth of food like Toreem."

The lady's face settled into the visage of the old crone and for a moment K'lrsa was reminded of Herin. "Must I do everything for you? You have allies. Use them."

Even old and gravelly, her voice was still beautiful, this time heavy with the weight of ages like the carvings K'lrsa had seen on some of the caves she sheltered in when caught away from the tribe overnight.

"But…"

The lady disappeared, leaving K'lrsa alone with the wind howling and the Hidden City brooding in the distance.

She paced the top of the dune. She needed to think, to let her mind find the answers to her problems. She'd never been good at that--much more inclined to act first and think later—but too much depended on her now.

She seated herself on the ground, closed her eyes, and repeated the Pattern over and over again until she finally found the Core where she could float outside of time and sensation, letting her mind drift.

But still, even there, in that place where thought was supposed to cease, she couldn't help but wonder.

What had the Lady meant?

Where was this sanctuary?

Or this weapon powerful enough to save her people?

And how was she going to find it in time?

CHAPTER 5

K 'lrsa awoke in late afternoon to a fly crawling on her face. She shooed it away and sat up, wishing for the dry heat of the plains. She felt sticky all over and the smell of the barn hadn't improved with the heat of the day.

Badru was back, but he sat alone, brooding. Herin and Garzel were seated next to each other, whispering back and forth. K'lrsa marveled that Herin could understand the grunts and hisses that were Garzel's only form of communication.

She debated telling everyone about the moon dream. On the one hand, if the Lady had wanted to talk to them, she could've. Then again, the Lady had told her to look to her allies. And what else were they going to do as they waited for the moon to rise?

So she told them what she'd dreamed as they all lolled in the late afternoon heat. Herin raised an eyebrow once or twice, but didn't interrupt. Badru continued to stare sullenly at the ground.

"So now we have to figure out where this sanctuary is before the Daliph's men arrive," she finished.

"Before *Aran's* men arrive," Badru corrected her, his jaw thrust out in a sulk.

She raised an eyebrow at that, but gave it to him anyway. "My apologies. Before *Aran's* men arrive."

Herin shrugged. "It's obvious, isn't it?"

22
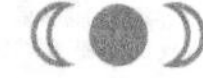

"Um, no."

"The sanctuary she mentioned must be the gathering grounds."

"What? That doesn't make any sense. That's where they're going anyway. That's where the Daliph's—Aran's—troops are headed to ambush them. They can't go there. They'll be slaughtered. There's nothing there anyway except a bunch of dirt, the central platform, and that big rock formation. How are those going to protect them?"

Herin took a bite from a travel bar, her teeth grinding it to pulp as K'lrsa waited for an answer, wanting to throttle her for taking her time.

At last, Herin swallowed. "No one can be killed while they're at the gathering grounds."

K'lrsa laughed. "Like the Daliph's troops are going to respect our ways. Or the Black Horse Tribe, for that matter."

Herin chewed for another long moment and then moved her tongue along her teeth to clean them. K'lrsa was about ready to rip that tongue right out of her mouth, when she finally answered. "They'll have no choice. You can't kill someone on the gathering grounds. It's not possible."

K'lrsa frowned at her. "How does that work? How do you know that? I've never heard that before."

Herin shrugged. "Saw it myself."

K'lrsa stared at her, waiting for some sort of additional explanation.

Garzel grunted and nudged Herin in the ribs. She glared at him for a moment, but continued, "Fine. It was the year I reached fourteen summers. I wasn't supposed to be out after dinnertime—as you know, the tribes can be pretty wild when they're all gathered together and the fermented mare's milk is flowing—but I was curious and there was a boy I wanted to see." She flicked a glance at Garzel who smiled back at her.

K'lrsa tried to picture Herin as a young girl sneaking out to meet a younger Garzel, but failed. It was impossible to think of either of them as young.

Herin squelched her lips against her teeth before she continued, the sound making K'lrsa's skin crawl. "Anyway. I snuck my way across camp to where the Riders were gathered around the fire. Two of the men were daring one another to bigger and bigger feats of daring while the others watched and laughed. I too watched as they jumped the fire over and over again as it built up higher and higher with each pass until another Rider finally pushed them away, saying it was too dangerous to continue.

"Next they juggled daggers, the blades glinting through the air, flashing with each turn of each sharpened blade. Two first, then three, then four."

Herin shook her head at the memory, a small smile on her face. "I was in awe, amazed by what they could do." She snorted. "Even I was young and foolish once."

K'lrsa smiled at the thought of a wide-eyed Herin, gazing upon the two Riders.

Herin scratched her nose with the stump of her pinky finger. "Finally, H'lar, the bolder of the two, dared the other to throw a dagger at him and said he'd catch it between his hands. Right here." She placed her hands palms together between her breasts.

K'lrsa's eyebrows rose. "Was he crazy? He actually wanted someone to throw a dagger *at* him? Right there? At his chest."

Herin shrugged one shoulder. "He was talented, but he wasn't very bright. Died hunting a desert cat a year later."

"Didn't someone stop them?"

"No. They were all drunk. Thought it was a grand idea. Gathered around to watch. Of course, none wanted to get too close to H'lar. The other Rider wasn't exactly sober by then. But I was young and foolish and eager to see his trick, so I crept as close as I could get without being seen. I was an arm's length away, maybe two."

"And?" K'lrsa leaned forward.

Herin shook her head. "And H'lar just stood there as the knife came right at his chest. Didn't try to catch it. Didn't move. Just stood there."

"What?"

Herin nodded her agreement. "The blade went right for his throat. I saw it. I was right there. It touched the skin of his throat...and then..."

K'lrsa waited for her to continue, hanging on every word.

Badru who was just as enthralled as she was, finally asked. "And then? What happened, Grandmother?"

Garzel chuckled softly. Obviously he knew the story.

"And then the knife disappeared."

"Disappeared?"

Herin nodded. "Yep. Just like that." She snapped her fingers, the sight somehow more disturbing with just her finger stumps clicking together. "The knife was gone. No one could find it. They looked everywhere. That night and the next day."

K'lrsa frowned. "So what happened?"

Herin smirked. "Well...If you listen to the men that were there that night, the dagger wasn't thrown true and someone found it in the morning and kept it to teach them a lesson."

Badru shook his head. "But that's not what happened."

"No. It's not. I asked my mother about it the next day even though I knew she'd punish me for sneaking out. And she did. I was banned from traveling for three months and had to wash all her brewing pots for the next month. But I had to know. And she was head wise woman for our tribe."

"And?" K'lrsa and Badru both asked at once.

"And she told me that no one can be killed on the gathering grounds. It's protected by the gods."

K'lrsa shook her head. "That doesn't make sense. Why would K'var demand that the Daliph's troops attack during the annual gathering if he knew that no one could be killed?"

"Because K'var was a fool who didn't believe in the gods. And it wasn't exactly common knowledge about the gathering grounds, even in my day. My mother swore me to secrecy because she knew that young men who thought themselves invincible would get into all sorts of unnecessary trouble."

Herin studied the ground for a moment. "After the Summer Spring Tribe was destroyed and most of the wise men and women with it, I suspect no one knows the secret now."

K'lrsa nodded. It made sense.

She studied Herin. How much other knowledge had they lost when Aran destroyed the wise ones? How much that was only in Herin and Garzel's heads?

She winced.

Nothing to be done about it now. "So you think as long as the tribes make it to the gathering grounds and stay there, that they'll be safe?"

Herin nodded.

"Well, that's simple enough then. They're all headed there now anyway for the annual gathering. We just convince them to move a little faster."

Herin shook her head. "If only life were that simple. What will they eat?"

K'lrsa shrugged. "The Riders can take turns hunting baru and bringing them back."

"How? They'll be surrounded by the Daliph's soldiers."

K'lrsa blinked. Herin was right. How long could the tribes last on the gathering grounds? A week? Two?

"So we get them to the gathering grounds and then we have to find the weapon right away. Within days. Is that possible? Where do you think it is?"

Herin looked at Garzel.

"Herin? Do you know where we can find the weapon the Lady mentioned?"

Herin studied her maimed hands, flexing each finger in turn.

"Herin?"

They all waited as the afternoon heat seemed to settle down upon them, chasing the air from the room.

Finally, Herin met K'lrsa's gaze, her eyes flat and black, the wrinkles on her face deepening even as K'lrsa watched. "Yes."

"Where? Where can we find it?"

Herin looked at Garzel again and he took her hand and squeezed gently as she answered. "The Hidden City."

"The Hidden City? But…Do you know where it is?"

"Yes."

Of course. She knew everything it seemed. Why hadn't the Lady just chosen her to save everyone? She certainly seemed more qualified.

"Is it far?" K'lrsa asked.

"No. Not if we take the *Amalanee*." But Herin wouldn't meet her gaze.

K'lrsa wanted to ask what she was hiding, but Herin was a snake's nest of secrets she didn't want to disturb just now.

"So we just get everyone to safety on the gathering grounds, find the Hidden City, find the weapon, bring it back, use it to destroy the Daliph's troops and then we're done? That's it."

Herin harrumphed. "Yeah. That's it."

From the way Herin and Garzel looked at each other it clearly wasn't. But no point in asking for an explanation.

Not yet at least.

CHAPTER 6

T hey flew through the next night, following the road that had brought K'lrsa to Toreem all those weeks ago. She could hardly believe what a rash fool she'd been then. Setting out to avenge her father with no more plan than to let herself be captured by a slaving caravan on the word of a god known to be capricious and cruel.

What had she been thinking?

She'd never even seen a barn before, let alone a city. Never slept under a roof. Never been surrounded by men who viewed her as no better than cattle and eyed her like a succulent piece of meat. Never had to bow her head and still her tongue or risk death.

She shuddered, glad to be done with Toreem and the Daliphate.

Hopefully forever, even if the Lady Moon didn't see it that way.

They flew until the moon touched the far horizon and then landed in a small valley just north of the road, next to a home that was clearly abandoned, its doorway yawning black and empty, the small garden outside grown over with weeds. There was a purple flower winding up the side of the house with a pungent scent that made K'lrsa want to sneeze.

As Herin and Garzel made the place habitable, chasing away a small furry creature that had nested there and clearing out a space in the main room for them to sleep,

Badru stayed with Midnight, stroking his neck softly and whispering to him.

K'lrsa stood between the house and Badru, torn between doing something useful and offering what comfort she could. Finally, she made her slow way to Badru's side. "Do you want to talk about it?"

He stepped away from Midnight, arms crossed tightly as he gazed back towards Toreem. "I don't know what to do. I don't know who I am. I don't...I was a Daliph, K'lrsa, a leader of thousands of men, and now I'm..." He shook his head, his face mottled with emotion. "No one."

"You're still you, Badru. You're a skilled warrior. I'm sure you can hunt. You have Midnight."

He shrugged one shoulder. "I'm just one of many. No one would care if I disappeared tomorrow."

"I would."

He flushed slightly at the rebuke, and K'lrsa added, "And you won't be one of many in the tribes. We aren't fighters. Hunters, yes. Fighters, no."

He scoffed. "You're just trying to make me feel better. You forget, I've fought you."

"That's hand-to-hand combat, Badru. For self-defense. But what good is Crouching Cricket against a sword? Or against a hundred trained soldiers?"

He scrunched his lips together, eyes narrowed. "What was the name of that one move you made where you swept low and kicked at my legs? That could easily disarm an attacker, even one with a sword. And that other move? Where you chopped at my arm?" He stepped closer, demonstrating in slow motion. "If you converted that into a grip, like this, you could disarm an attacker with a sword. You'd have to be fast." He shifted his stance. "Maybe more like this."

She smiled. "See? I would've never thought of that. I told you we need you."

He smiled back, the tension in his shoulders easing just a little.

"How about this afternoon, after we've slept, I show you the hundred and five attacks so you can start thinking about ways to use them to fight the Daliph's troops?"

He nodded. "I'd like that."

"Good. Now we better get some rest while we can."

As they walked towards the house, side-by-side but not touching, K'lrsa realized how few times she'd actually spent with Badru in the real world. Their bodies had learned to move together in the moon dream but they'd never learned to be together in the real world.

Here they'd only had a stolen kiss or two, a few brief moments of conversation.

She felt awkward, suddenly, wondering what happened now. The night before, Herin and Garzel had slept cocooned together, their bodies fitted to one another's with the ease of years, but Badru had returned after K'lrsa was asleep and slept by the door, alone.

Tonight, though? K'lrsa wasn't sure what to do.

She loved him. She felt drawn to him. But...How well did she really know him? Well enough to sleep next to him?

As they reached the door, she pulled away. "I better go, um, yeah." She ducked around the side of the house, her face flushed with embarrassment.

Badru paused, but then continued into the house. Through a gaping hole that had once been a window, she heard him mutter something to Herin and Garzel before settling down to sleep.

K'lrsa stayed outside, leaning against the wall of the house, as the sun slowly rose in the distance, coloring the clouds pink and purple against a pale blue sky.

A tear rolled down her cheek.

And then another.

She shook her head.

She wasn't crying because of Badru.

Or because of how scared she was to go home.

Or the dangers of finding the weapon to save her people.

No. She was crying because, more than anything in the world, she longed to talk to her father. She wanted to see his gentle smiling face and hear the soft rumble of his laughter. She wanted to know that it was all going to be alright. To hear him tell her that she could do anything, that she could make it through. That he had faith in her.

She laughed softly as she sniffed back another tear.

Maybe she didn't need him after all; it seemed she knew exactly what he would say.

She hugged herself tight and watched the sun finally break above the horizon.

Her father was gone, but life went on. Day after day. Week after week.

And at least she had this small part of him lodged in her heart, there for her in her darkest moments.

Finally, she pushed off the wall and went back inside.

Badru lay alone against the far wall, his eyes closed, his chest rising and falling in a steady rhythm. Herin snored softly off to the side, nestled in Garzel's arms.

K'lrsa watched for a long, long moment before she finally took a deep breath and made her way to Badru's side. As she lay down beside him, he opened one eye and smiled, wrapping an arm around her waist and pulling her closer. She snuggled against him, grateful for this moment of peace in the chaos.

She didn't know how long they'd have together, but she swore she wasn't going to waste it.

CHAPTER 7

They flew through each night and slept through each day as they made their way through the Daliphate. Fortunately, they always managed to find an abandoned barn or house to shelter in. K'lrsa marveled that those of the Daliphana had so much that they could simply abandon a perfectly fine building to rot and decay.

In the tribes if they'd had a large wooden structure, they would've taken every single plank and nail for use elsewhere, wood and metal being such rare commodities.

To think that her people had practically ruined themselves for the castoffs of the Daliphana.

She tried not to think about it too much as they flew in silence each night, Fallion's wings the only sound in that twilight world through which they traveled.

She honestly would've preferred to sleep outside each day rather than in some musty run-down structure in danger of collapsing on her head, but she knew the risk of discovery was too high.

A woman alone in the Daliphana? It simply didn't happen. And dressed like her? With three people in slave's robes? No.

So they slept in whatever shelter they could find while they waited for the sun to set and the moon to rise.

K'lrsa chafed at the delay, but they had no choice. The horses were fine. They'd keep going day and night. It was

the Daliphate and its stupid rules.

What was so wrong about a woman riding a horse? Or wearing comfortable clothes that allowed her full movement?

She didn't know, but she'd seen how the people of the Daliphate reacted as she rode to Toreem. One man had spat at her feet. Another had beat his daughter for talking to her.

And women had shuffled away as if she'd somehow taint them with her hedonistic ways.

It was absurd. But it was the world she was trapped in. And the last thing she needed was for someone to capture her and keep her from warning her people.

Finally, at least a day later than she would've liked, as the moon was about to set, they reached Crossroads, a small border town that consisted of auction houses for trading slaves, and brothels and bars for fleecing traders of their newly acquired riches.

Trading caravans camped around the town's perimeter, their slave goods penned like so much cattle.

They landed on a small rise to the north of the city, behind a tall copse of trees.

The wind shifted and K'lrsa grimaced at the stench of so much dirty humanity clustered in such a small space. To think that the Black Horse Tribe had willingly led some of these traders across the desert to obtain their human cargo. It disgusted her and made her burn with an anger so deep she felt ill with it.

There was a part of her that wanted to see them all destroyed, each and every man who'd spent his time and energy ripping others from their homes, killing those too weak for the journey, and chaining and selling the rest.

They all, every one, deserved the worst fate she could give them.

But another part of her just wanted to get home.

Let someone else right this wrong. Surely she wasn't the only one who saw how vile it was.

She stepped through the trees, careful not to leave their shelter, and looked down upon Crossroads. It looked more crowded than the last time she'd been there, but she didn't know what was normal. Maybe she'd passed through during a lull.

Or maybe the fires were soldiers, massed together, ready to set out in the morning and attack her people.

"Herin," she called, softly.

Herin came to stand by her, their de facto leader now.

"There are a lot of camps down there. There weren't near this many when I came through on my way to Toreem."

She nodded and turned back to Badru and Garzel. "Go into Crossroads. Find out what's going on."

Badru gestured at his rough-spun brown robe—the slave's garment they'd found for him when they fled the slaughter in the throne room. "Can't in this. There's bound to be one or two men that've made it as far as Boradol and would know it for slave garb."

Herin glared at him through slitted eyes. "Then find something else to wear."

"Like what? We didn't pack spare clothes."

"Then steal some. Or sneak around in alleys so no one sees what you're wearing." She turned away, rolling her eyes in disgust.

Badru pressed his lips tight together. "Fine. But Garzel stays here. I don't need to explain him, too."

Herin raised an eyebrow, but didn't argue. "I suggest you go now, then."

K'lrsa cast a nervous glance at the horizon. The moon was gone but the sun not yet risen. "Shouldn't he wait?"

"For what?" With her malevolent gaze and hunched shoulders, Herin looked just like a grel waiting for its prey to die.

"It's not safe. It's the Trickster's time."

Herin harrumphed. "We're not in the desert, girl. Your gods have no power here."

"Don't you mean *our* gods?"

"No." Herin turned away, ending the conversation.

But K'lrsa wasn't having it. As Badru stomped out of camp, making far too much noise for comfort, K'lrsa followed Herin. "How can you turn your back on the gods? You know they're real."

"They're real, but they aren't all-powerful. And they've never done much for me. Or my sister. Or Garzel." She smirked at K'lrsa. "They didn't even save you, did they? Just sent you off to get yourself killed."

K'lrsa touched the moon stone around her neck. Lodie's stone, not the one she'd grown up with. It felt like wearing an outfit that had belonged to someone else. It fit, but not comfortably. She'd made peace with the stone, but it was an uneasy peace and she longed to have her own stone back.

"But I didn't die, did I? And I did kill the man who killed my father just like Father Sun promised."

"Well, then. Seems you should worship them and do whatever they want, no matter the cost."

"I didn't say that. But you'd be a fool to turn your back on them."

"Would I?" Herin shook her head. "Ah, the simplicity of youth. May you never come to understand that you're nothing to your gods but a piece in a game of strategy so vast you can't even see the game board. An expendable piece, I might add."

She turned away again and this time K'lrsa let her go.

K'lrsa huddled in the midst of three tree trunks, hoping it would be enough to shelter her from any casual glances, as she waited for Badru to return. A bush to her right had a sharp peppery scent that tickled the back of her throat; she ignored it as best she could.

Soon she'd be home. Back to the plants and animals she knew. Back where things made sense and with people she trusted.

She smiled as she imagined what it would be like to see her little sister M'lara again. How much had she grown in the months since K'lrsa had been gone?

And her best friend, F'lia. Sun-bright and full of happiness. Her smile faltered.

Did F'lia know that L'ral was dead? That he'd died with her father?

Did she know he was the one who'd betrayed her father to his death? Had she been part of it?

And what about K'lrsa's mother and brother?

They had to know her father was dead. She'd left the markings for the next traveler to find. And her mother's moon stone had surely told her the moment he'd died.

They'd be angry with her, for leaving like she had, she knew that.

Her brother would lecture her on how irresponsible she was. Her mother would probably punish her with icy silence.

But hopefully they'd also welcome her back. Be glad to see her whole and safe once more.

Hopefully.

She shivered as she stared into the gray of early morning, wondering where Badru was, craving the simple comfort of his presence.

CHAPTER 8

B adru returned just as the sun was rising, coloring the sky in oranges and yellows. He darted away from the closest camp, hunched low to the ground, looking far too much like an escaped slave. Fortunately, no one noticed and he made it to the shelter of the trees without incident.

"What did you find out?" Herin demanded as K'lrsa extricated herself from her shelter.

"We need to move." Badru grabbed Midnight's slim silver saddle and flung it over his back.

He turned to where they still stood, watching him in surprise. "Now. Get your stuff so we can get out of here."

"Badru, it's daylight. We can't ride during the day."

"We have to. Most of those camps are soldiers. And they'll find us if we don't. I heard a few of the commanders talking about how they were going to prowl for new recruits in the neighboring hills today. We can't be caught up in that."

Without another word, they packed up the rest of the camp—there wasn't much to pack—and were mounted on their horses and already over the next hill by the time the sun fully rose.

K'lrsa urged Fallion next to Midnight. "Badru, how did they get here so fast?"

"They're a well-trained, disciplined army." Badru's jaw was clenched as he stared ahead over Midnight's ears. "My army."

She winced at his anger. "But it's only been a handful of days."

"Which is why they aren't on the march yet. Couriers probably reached the border the day after I was attacked with orders to gather in Crossroads. It's the point that makes the most sense if you want to go after the tribes."

"But how could the couriers get here so fast?"

"They don't have to rest, K'lrsa. Change horses in every major city. Pass the message to a fresh courier if the old one gets tired. I could have an order to any place within the Toreem Daliphate within a day."

"But how did all the soldiers gather so fast? Surely they can't travel as fast as a courier."

He flicked a glance at her. "That's only three garrison's worth. There are ten along the border."

She clutched Fallion's reins as she swayed in the saddle. "How many soldiers is that?"

"One thousand." He scanned the horizon, his shoulders tensed for battle.

K'lrsa couldn't breathe. She tried to picture a thousand armed, trained men attacking her people. Including all the men, women, and children, the tribes weren't much bigger than that. Her tribe had maybe two hundred and the other five tribes were about the same size.

"That's almost a soldier for every single member of the tribes," she breathed.

Badru nodded, his expression grim.

K'lrsa slumped. "How can we defeat them?"

"Pzah, child." Herin smacked her on the hip. "The weapons in the Hidden City are more powerful than a thousand soldiers. More powerful than ten thousand soldiers. Those weapons could destroy the world."

K'lrsa shivered.

She didn't want to destroy the world.

She just wanted her family and friends to be safe.

But if the only way to save them was to kill those soldiers?

She chewed on her lip.

She didn't want to hurt *anyone*.

But to save the ones she loved, she'd do what she had to.

CHAPTER 9

They spent a restless day sheltered in a dry, dead space nestled between two small hills, waiting for the Daliph's soldiers to crest the rise. This close to the plains, the land was more flat than near Toreem. And more sparsely populated—with no conveniently empty barns or houses to hide them.

As soon as the sun set, they flew back towards Crossroads. K'lrsa had to see for herself how many soldiers there were. Their ranks seemed to have doubled in one day.

Badru pointed to signs that they were ready to leave—supply wagons heaped with grain and dried meat, the fact that all the soldiers were already asleep, only a handful of guards left to patrol.

Herin muttered darkly as they turned the horses towards the tribes.

K'lrsa ignored her until she finally had to give in to her curiosity. "What's wrong, Herin? Why are you so upset?"

"I didn't want us to fly very far tonight, but now we're going to have to."

"Why?" K'lrsa craned her head around to see Herin, but quickly turned back around when she felt herself slipping off of Fallion's back.

"We shouldn't stop in the barren lands. I thought we'd be able to camp on the edge and fly over tomorrow night."

"You mean that stretch of dead land between here and the tribes?"

"Yes."

K'lrsa shrugged. "I didn't like it, but we camped there on the way here and were fine. We have plenty of food. As long as we don't drink the water we should be safe."

"It's not the food or water I'm worried about." Herin's tension was almost palpable.

"Then what is it?"

But Herin wouldn't say more. She just sat there, oozing distress, her fingers clutching painfully at K'lrsa's waist as they flew onward.

It was true, the barren lands hadn't been pleasant the first time she'd crossed them with Harley and his caravan. He'd certainly been unhappy that they'd had to stay there for a night. And something definitely was off about the place. K'lrsa had had horrible nightmares the night they camped there. And she wasn't the only one.

But it wasn't dangerous. Just unpleasant.

Herin sitting behind her full of anxiety was far worse.

As they reached the edge of the barren lands, K'lrsa could see that it stretched far to the left and right, like some giant knife had slashed through the earth from top to bottom.

There was nothing living in the barren lands. No plants, no animals. And the few pools of water were so dark and stagnant she'd have never dared try them.

They soon left the fertile green lands of the Toreem Daliphate behind until ahead and to each side all they could see was death.

It was worse from the sky.

When she'd ridden through before she'd imagined it was just a narrow strip of destruction they were passing through. That in the distance, just a little ways away, it was normal, dry ground.

But from above she could see the truth of it.

This was destruction on a scale she could barely fathom. What had once lived here? People? Baru?

How many plants had once thrived on the now-dead ground?

As they flew onward, catching the occasional whiff of charcoal—as if the ground below them still burned—K'lrsa felt the despair of the place sink into every pore, weighing her down, bringing out the worst thoughts and feelings, the ones she usually managed to keep at bay.

Herin was right, they couldn't land in this place.

They had to get past it before morning.

She leaned over Fallion's neck. "Faster, *micora*," she urged.

She knew he was already going as fast as he could, but she silently willed him forward, begging him to take them past this place of sorrow.

The moon crept lower and lower in the sky.

And still there was no sign of the other side.

K'lrsa had a panicked moment when she wondered if maybe they'd turned the wrong way and would be forever trapped in this place.

But, finally, she glimpsed the plains ahead, a faint lightening of the darkness. Dry and flat, they might be, but they were alive in a way the barren lands would never be again.

"Ha! See! We're going to make it." K'lrsa laughed, full of joy.

But even as she laughed, Fallion dove for the ground.

"Fallion, don't. Keep going."

But nothing would keep him from landing. Midnight was right there, trailing in his wake.

As their hooves touched the blackened ground, the moon disappeared below the horizon and once more they were just two normal horses—beautiful, but nothing more than that.

She glanced back at Herin. "We can keep going. The horses aren't tired."

"No, we can't."

"Why not?"

"It's the Trickster's time." Herin slid from Fallion's back, stumbling as her feet touched the ground.

"But you said the gods have no power here."

Herin shook her head. "They had no power in the Daliphate. But we're not in the Daliphate anymore."

"We're not in tribal lands either."

"Yes. We are."

"This? This isn't part of our lands." K'lrsa shook her head in denial.

"Who do you think made this place? *Your* gods. They did it to protect the tribes from the Daliphana. Only in this one place is it narrow enough to cross."

K'lrsa stared around. To her left was the withered stump of a tree and what looked like the bones of some small animal. She'd seen something like it once, when a fire had spread across the plains, burning everything in its wake.

"When did they do this?"

"Four hundred years ago. When the tribes agreed to protect the Hidden City."

"And nothing's grown back since? That doesn't seem right." The burn area she'd seen was now one of the most fertile areas she knew of. This should've long ago returned to what it was before.

"How can you be so ignorant of our history? Were you too interested in horses and arrows to pay any attention to your wise one? Just because you wanted to be a Rider is no excuse."

K'lrsa crossed her arms across her chest and glared at Herin. "I learned everything our wise man could teach me. But it wasn't much. He knew nothing of this place. Or if he did, he didn't speak of it."

"What kind of a wise one was he?"

"All that was left after the Summer Spring Tribe disappeared. Aran didn't just kill your family, Herin, he killed all of the head wise men and women. They'd gathered for the decennial gathering with their chosen successors. After that, all we had left were a handful of second tier apprentices, none fully-trained, and maybe a few family members who knew some of the lore."

"Why were they with the Summer Spring Tribe? They should've been at the gathering grounds."

K'lrsa shrugged. "I don't know."

Herin shook her head. "I should've known it was about more than punishing me."

"What was?"

"Aran's attack on my tribe. I thought he'd killed them to punish me. But he attacked because he saw a chance to eliminate the wise ones." She glanced at Garzel who'd been listening silently. "It's a good thing he never realized how much Lodie and I knew or he would've likely killed us, too."

Garzel nodded.

K'lrsa finally dismounted. She'd put it off for as long as she could, but she couldn't stay on Fallion's back until dawn. That wasn't fair to him. "What do you know that he'd want to kill you for?"

"Until your moon dreams, did you think the Hidden City was real?"

K'lrsa shrugged. "I guess. I knew it was our sacred trust to protect it, but no one I knew had ever been there or even knew where it was."

"Did you or anyone know what it contains?"

"No."

"Or why it needed protecting?"

"No."

Herin nodded. "Exactly. And who would protect what they don't know needs protecting?" She snorted. "I underestimated him." She paced back and forth glaring out at the dark gray sky and cussing under her breath, her hands clenching and unclenching.

"Herin? Are you okay?"

Badru joined them, throwing Midnight's saddle to the ground, sending up a plume of thick black dust.

Herin stopped dead. "Aran must be killed."

"Now? We're on our way to warn the tribes. We can't go back." K'lrsa crossed her arms. The others could go back if they wanted, but she was staying right where she was until the sun rose and then she was continuing on to her tribe.

Herin narrowed her eyes, glaring at the ground like it had personally harmed her. "No. You're right. We have to protect the tribes first so they can protect the city. But then Aran must die. You have to kill him."

"Why do I have to do it? You can kill him just as easily as I can."

Herin was silent for a long, long moment.

"Herin?"

"Hm? Oh, right. Of course I can." She turned away. "Get some rest. We ride again at first light."

She joined Garzel and they spoke softly back and forth, only the frantic gestures they made showing how heated their conversation was.

K'lrsa watched, wondering what it was they were keeping from her.

Why did she have to be the one to kill Aran? Why couldn't it be Herin? Or even Badru?

She turned away.

It didn't matter.

Not like they could force her to do it.

She was a Rider. She made her own choices.

CHAPTER 10

K'lrsa lay down to sleep with Badru's arm thrown protectively around her waist, his body nestled against hers the only bit of warmth in that miserable wasteland. On another night she might've been more interested in the feel of his strong body pressed against hers, but the death in the soil seemed to leech through her skin right to her soul, weighing her down with undefined fears and sorrow.

As soon as she closed her eyes, she found herself in the moon dream.

But it wasn't like the last time.

The Lady Moon was nowhere to be seen either in the desert or the sky. Neither was Father Sun. It was twilight, the in-between time, everything hazy and cold. The Trickster's time.

She could see, but everything was gray, muted as if all life had been drained, leaving just a shell behind.

She started to walk, needing to move to remind herself she was alive, but every grain of sand cut her bare feet, digging into the crevices of her skin and burning like hot coals.

A bitter wind whipped the sand into a fine dust that choked and blinded her, keening of loss and death.

She curled in on herself, trying to hide from the relentless attack, but it was no use. She couldn't escape the

wind and sand. So she pushed forward, hoping to find shelter against the side of a nearby sand dune, but with every step the dune seemed farther and farther away.

She fought her way forward, screaming her defiance. The wind snatched her words away and flung them back into her face.

And then, suddenly, it stopped.

K'lrsa's ears echoed with the memory of the wind's howl. She slowly drew her arm away from her eyes and looked around.

She stood at the top of a sand dune. Below her, in a hollow trough between dunes, lay row after row of bodies, staked to the ground, bellies sliced open, eyes gouged out.

Just like her father, the day she'd found him.

Except, instead of one body, it was hundreds. Hundreds tortured, mutilated, and left to die. The sounds of their moans reached her. A man on the end twitched, bright red blood flowing from his torn palm.

She struggled not to be sick as she stared at the carnage below. Grel arrived in a squawking flock and descended towards the bodies, their beaks already glistening red with the blood of their prey, their heavy bodies lumbering through the air.

She screamed for them to go away, but no sound came.

She tried to run down the slope, but her feet wouldn't move.

She watched in horror as they landed and began to feed.

She collapsed to her knees, keening, her hands clutched tight before her, as she watched the macabre scene below.

The grel walked among their bounty, feasting on the bodies, pulling at tender flesh, fighting one another over the most prized bits.

As she watched, unable to look away or help, she realized something.

She knew these people.

There, in the first row center, was her mother—her long black hair spread above her head like a fan.

And, there, in the second row on the left side, was her brother—his hawk nose the same as their father's.

And next to him poor little M'lara—barely out of girlhood, her gangly limbs stretched tight between metal stakes.

K'lrsa screamed and struggled, but it was no use. No sound came. And she stayed right where she'd fallen.

Laughter filled the air, cruel and vicious. The laughter of a child who loves to torment.

She turned to see a fat little boy with a big belly and a sly smile watching her.

The Trickster. Vile imp. Bane of all.

She snarled at him.

His laughter deepened, a roaring, boisterous noise that belied his size. "Oh ho. They told me you had spirit, K'lrsa dan V'na of the White Horse Tribe." He tilted his head to the side and studied her. "What would you do? If I let you go right now?"

She still couldn't move, but now she could speak. "I'd save them."

"But you're too late. They'll die no matter what you do." He tsked as he stared down at them. "I guess you could kill them like you did your father…Give them that final mercy?"

She glared at him. "Then I'd kill you. I'd throttle your skinny little neck."

He rocked back and forth on his feet, his lips quirked into a slight smile. "Is that any way to talk to a god? Do you talk to my mother that way? Or my father?"

She found herself lost in the depths of his eyes, unable to pull free. Where the Lady Moon's were as vast and deep as the night sky and Father Sun's were like banked coals, the Trickster's were brown like the desert sands, constantly shifting, a restless maze with no exit.

"What do you want with me?" she whispered.

He waved his hand and the bodies disappeared. The dunes, too.

They stood alone on blackened earth like that where she slept.

"Are they really dead?" she asked, her stomach hollow with fear. "Was that a true vision? Or just a prank?"

"What? Those people?"

"Yes."

He thought about it for a moment. "No. One might die tonight, it's not yet clear, but the others still live."

"Then why show that to me?" she screamed.

He slowly transformed until he looked like a young man about her age, his brown hair flopping into his eyes, a mischievous expression on his face. Seemingly harmless, but she knew the truth. He was vicious and cruel no matter what guise he wore.

"Tell me, K'lrsa dan V'na of the White Horse Tribe. What would you give to never see that happen?"

"What?"

"What would you give? To save all those people?"

She shook her head. "I don't understand what you're asking me. Is that going to happen?"

"That?" He thought about it a moment. "No."

He smiled slyly. "The Daliph's men aren't that creative. Such a shame." He shook his head.

She glared at him, wishing she could wrap her hands around his neck and squeeze, but knowing it was hopeless. "Do you really care so little for the living?"

He shrugged. "See one man kill another, you've seen them all. Except for the few rare exceptions who try to make it exciting." He sighed. "Of course, the most interesting ones we had, K'var and G'van, are now dead thanks to you."

"And they deserved it, too." She stepped away from him. "Do you really enjoy watching men die?"

"No more than I enjoy watching them live. Most people are as boring in death as in life and in life as in death. You really are a tediously dull lot." He eyed her sideways and she was reminded of a desert cat she'd once watched play with its prey before making the final kill.

She crossed her arms. "What do you want from me? Why am I here?"

He shrugged. "I thought you might become interesting with proper encouragement."

"Proper encouragement."

"Yes. I figured if I reminded you what's at stake…"

"I already know what's at stake."

"Do you?" His eyes flashed golden for a moment.

"Yes. I'm already headed towards the tribes. I'm going to get them to the gathering grounds and then find this weapon and defeat the Daliph's troops."

"Is that so?"

"Yes."

He stared at her with his maze-like eyes. "Hm. Even knowing what it will cost? Interesting…Or perhaps you don't know the cost?" He smiled his wicked little smile. "I hope it's the latter. So much more fun that way."

"What are you talking about?"

But he was gone before the words had left her mouth.

She awoke, shivering, as the first rays of the sun touched the distant horizon.

"Everything okay?" Badru mumbled, still mostly asleep.

"Yes. But it's time we got out of this place."

The sooner she could forget her dream and this awful place, the better.

CHAPTER 11

They made it onto the plains long before midday, the horses as eager to leave that dead, barren place behind as the humans.

K'lrsa smiled to see her home once more. The brown sere grass, the wide open spaces stretching in every direction with a few straggly trees in the distance.

She took a deep breath, inhaling the scents of sage and dust.

They found a small stream she remembered from the journey to Toreem, barely wide enough for a person to stand in, and shallow, but pure, clean water nonetheless. Stripping out of her Rider's leathers which were covered in grime after so much time in the saddle, she knelt in the middle of the stream and poured handfuls of water over her skin, rinsing away the worst of the dirt and dust of travel.

Before she'd left for Toreem she would've never thought to bathe in water—it was too scarce a resource. She would've been happy to go weeks without even a sweat bath, only giving in when her mother started commenting that Fallion smelled better than she did. She'd never really cared about her appearance or being clean or presentable.

Seemed the Daliphate had changed her.

Just a little.

Now she reveled in the feel of the cool, clear water coursing over her body, washing away all traces of the

Daliphate and the Trickster's land. She ducked her head in the stream, scratching her scalp clean, her mind flashing back to Mistress Hawthorne and her absolute horror when she'd had to wash K'lrsa's hair that first time.

Poor woman. The man she loved was dead and she'd probably never even know it.

K'lrsa flung her hair back, spraying water everywhere as it slapped against her bare back. It was almost to her waist now. She'd have to trim it soon.

Badru stood on the bank, goggle-eyed, his mouth half-open as he watched her.

"What?" She stood, sluicing the water from her skin with her hands.

"You're naked."

"Yes. And?" She wished she had one of the soft linen wraps the poradoma had used. She didn't feel like putting her hunting leathers back on just yet. But they were all she had.

"Someone could see you." He pulled the servant's robe off and threw it at her. "Cover up." He glanced around as if expecting hundreds of men to come running from the barren, empty plains around them.

She snorted and threw it back at him. "I'm just naked, Badru. What's the big deal?"

He flushed. "Just naked? No respectable woman…" He trailed into silence as she raised an eyebrow.

She was about to give him a piece of her mind about Toreem and its view on respectable women and how that wasn't what she would consider worth emulating, when Herin stripped off her own clothes and waded into the stream upriver from K'lrsa.

"Grandmother!"

"Pzah, boy. We're not in Toreem anymore. You want to live in the tribes, you'd best get used to a little nudity."

Garzel stripped down and joined her.

Badru's eyes bulged. He turned away.

Herin laughed. "When we reach the tribes men and women will be traipsing around naked all over the place."

Badru turned slightly—enough so he wouldn't have to

see Herin and Garzel, but could still see K'lrsa. "Is that true? Do you all run around naked all the time?"

She laughed. "No." She beat the dust out of her hunting leathers, scraping away the worst bits of muck with a small rock. "But if it makes more sense to not wear clothes, then we don't. Easier to wipe a little dirt off your skin than off your hunting leathers."

She'd never really thought about it, but at any given time there was probably at least one adult running around naked. Or almost naked. And there were always children running around naked. So much easier than trying to keep them *and* their clothes clean.

Herin came back out of the stream, using one of the servant's robes to dry herself.

"So, now what?" K'lrsa asked, putting her clothes back on.

"Now we find your tribe and warn them." Herin handed the robe off to Garzel and rebraided her hair.

"And then the others."

"It may be too late for them."

"What do you mean?"

Badru walked down the bank until he was almost out of sight before finally stripping out of his clothes and stepping into the stream. K'lrsa admired his lean, muscular frame until he saw her and turned away, which only served to give her a good look at the back of him, which was just as nice.

Herin cleared her throat, drawing K'lrsa's attention back to the conversation. "Your tribe is the closest to the gathering grounds. They'll be able to get there ahead of the Daliph's troops as long as we reach them in the next few days and they actually listen to what we have to say. But the other tribes won't have time." She flung the slave's robes on again, grimacing.

"They might if we hurry."

Herin shrugged, clearly not agreeing.

"Then we warn them not to come. The Daliph's troops won't track them down, will they? Especially not when they can flee into the desert."

Herin narrowed her eyes. "No, not likely they could follow. But if the tribes don't come, you lose anyway."

K'lrsa, whose attention had been drifting back towards Badru, turned back. "What? Why?"

"Because they won't be there to vote."

K'lrsa tilted her head in question.

"Wasn't it your father who was proposing a vote to expel the Black Horse Tribe?"

"Yes."

"Well, how do you think that works?"

K'lrsa shrugged. She'd never paid much attention to the adult business at the gathering. All she'd ever cared about was seeing her friends and competing against the other Riders.

Herin rolled her eyes. "At any tribal gathering, anyone can make a proposal. And then any member of the tribe *who is there* can vote on it. If they're not there, they can't vote."

"Okay. So, if they don't go, then the Black Horse Tribe isn't expelled. So what? There's always next year."

"What if the vote is to expel the White Horse Tribe?"

"What? No! That's not…"

"Why not? The Black Horse Tribe can propose expulsion of your tribe as easily as you can propose expulsion of them. While you're both still members of the tribes, you each have a say in the direction the tribes take."

K'lrsa shook her head. "But that's not fair. They want to destroy our way of life. Betray our sacred trust. *Kill* people."

"And if enough people agree with them, then that's the way the tribes will go." Herin shrugged. "You, on the other hand, want to hold your people back and deny them the benefits of trade. Medicines. Money. Weapons. All the things that could make life on the plains easier. There might be a fair number of people who vote against you."

K'lrsa chewed on her lip. "Then shouldn't we go after the tribes that are farthest away first so we can have as many votes as possible?"

"It's too late."

"Then it's too late for all of us, Herin. The tribes farthest away are the ones most likely to be our allies. We have to get them to the gathering grounds or we'll lose."

"Let's solve one problem at a time. First step, we find your tribe and convince them to hurry their preparations. Then we'll worry about the others. So. Where are they?"

K'lrsa turned towards the plains as if that would somehow give her the answer. "I'm not sure. They should have moved camp closer to the desert when winter came, but there are a few possible camps they could be at and I don't know which one they chose. If my dad were still alive, I think I know where they'd be, but with him dead..."

Herin poked her in the chest. "Use your moon stone."

K'lrsa grimaced. "It doesn't like me."

The stone contained the knowledge of all its former bearers and, since it was Lodie's, it was like being surrounded by someone else's close family, one that didn't particularly like her.

K'lrsa reached for the cord around her neck. "Here. You use it."

Herin took a step back. "No."

"Because you're not a first-born?"

"That. And other things. Just ask the stone and get it over with."

K'lrsa touched the stone and felt a vague vibration, a grudging awareness. "But how? What do I ask it?"

"How should I know? I've never had one of the things."

K'lrsa thought of her mother and brother and sister, of the camps along the edge of the desert where they'd likely be. She asked the stone for guidance, help in figuring out where they might be.

Nothing but the mental equivalent of a sullen shrug.

She shot back at it with the thought that if it helped her find Lodie it could go back to her and they'd finally be done with one another.

At that, she felt a spark of interest. And a definite tug towards the far edge of the White Horse Tribe lands and a camp they hadn't used since she was barely able to walk. The tug grew stronger until it was practically dragging her forward.

She resisted, wondering if that's where her tribe was or if that's where Lodie was. Why would they use that camp?

The tug of the moon stone became so insistent she took an involuntary step forward.

"Okay, okay. I'm going." She flung herself onto Fallion's back and held a hand out for Herin to join her.

"It told you where they are?"

K'lrsa fought the urge to leave without her. "I don't know," she said, gritting her teeth to resist the call of the stone.

"What do you mean, you don't know?" Herin hoisted herself up behind K'lrsa.

K'lrsa managed to hold off until she saw that Garzel and Badru were ready and then the pull of the moon stone was too much. She urged Fallion to a gallop.

"Slow down." Herin gasped as they pelted across the plains. "You can't exhaust the horses like this."

But K'lrsa had no choice. The moon stone was driving her forward, demanding that she reach her destination.

Now.

Right now.

The last time that had happened, she'd found her father dying in the desert.

She hoped this time was different and that the stone just really, really wanted to get rid of her.

CHAPTER 12

Fortunately, Fallion and Midnight were not normal horses, because there was nothing K'lrsa could do to stop the compulsion of the moon stone. They rode through the heat of the sun, sweat pouring off their bodies, dust clogging their noses and throats. They didn't eat, they didn't stop for water.

The just rode and rode and rode until the sun was about to set, casting shadows before them with the remainder of its light.

And then it was finally, thankfully over. They stumbled to a halt just outside a baru-hide barrier, the peaks of tents peeking out above it.

K'lrsa tried not to think about what would've happened if twilight had set before they found the camp. Would the stone have cared? Or would it have driven them right on into the Trickster's grasp?

She fell from the saddle, grasping at Fallion's side to keep from collapsing.

At least it was a camp and not a solitary tent or an old woman out in the wild by herself. She'd been worried all day that the stone was driving her to Lodie and that she'd taken off on her own.

Even though K'lrsa had made Lodie a sister of her blood, it didn't mean K'lrsa's mother would actually welcome her with open arms. (The only person K'lrsa's

mother had ever welcomed with open arms was K'lrsa's father. Him she'd loved with her entire being. Maybe it was why she had so little room for anyone else.)

K'lrsa approached the camp, noting all the changes, big and small. The barrier was new. And no longer did the tents sprawl far and wide in small groups. Now they huddled close together in the center of the ringed space, all except one tent that looked like it was trying to escape.

Two Riders stood guard. One had a bow drawn, the arrowhead pointed at her chest.

The other's hand clutched the knife on his belt, but didn't draw. It was D'lan. Her brother. Tall and proud, with the same hawk-nose as their father. Seven years older than her, he'd always been more like a disapproving father than brother.

She stepped closer, half-smiling, unsure of her welcome. D'lan tightened his grip until his knuckles were white, staring at her with black eyes.

She stopped, glancing between him and the other Rider, both men she'd known her whole life. "D'lan?" She asked, half-laughing. "Don't you recognize your own sister?"

She knew she'd gained some weight in the Daliphate, but surely not that much.

"Get V'na. Now." D'lan jerked his head at the other guard.

The guard took off running for their mother while K'lrsa took another step closer. Why had he sent for her mother like that?

Badru and Garzel dismounted behind her.

"Stay where you are," D'lan growled, dropping into a fighting stance.

"D'lan." K'lrsa took another step closer.

"I said, stay where you are." He spoke through gritted teeth, his eyes flat with menace.

K'lrsa stopped.

What was going on here? He'd always been harsh with her, but he'd never treated her like this before.

Like an enemy.

Badru came to stand by her side, lacing his fingers in

hers. D'lan watched him with that flat gaze, hatred burning through every line of his body.

She squeezed Badru's hand, never taking her eyes from D'lan. "Go back," she whispered.

"No. I'm with you to the end."

"Where's Lodie?" She asked as she heard a commotion coming from the center of camp.

D'lan glared at her. "So you did send that slave here?"

"There are no slaves in the tribes. And, yes, I sent her. She has my moon stone to prove it."

D'lan cracked his jaw, but didn't respond.

"D'lan. Where is she? Did you harm her? She's a sister of my blood." The moon stone at her neck flared red as she took a half-step forward.

D'lan pulled his knife from its sheath, his hand trembling. "Stay where you are."

"D'lan!" This was ridiculous. What had she done to warrant this type of distrust?

Her mother strode up to the entrance, trailing what looked like half the tribe behind her. Gone were the soft robes she'd once worn. Now she was dressed in the leathers of a Rider, her arms lean and sinewy, baked by the sun. She looked like someone had boiled all the flesh from her bones and then strung skin across what was left.

Her eyes were like charred bits of wood, sunken deep in her face. There were lines on her forehead and cheeks that hadn't been there before. She drew her dagger and thrust it towards K'lrsa. "How dare you come back here. Did you think we wouldn't know what you'd done?" she spat.

"What are you talking about?" K'lrsa looked back and forth between the stony faces of her family and past them to the crowd. Not a single friendly face looked back at her.

She stepped closer, keeping an eye on the blade in her mother's hand, Badru right behind her. "Mom. D'lan. What is wrong?"

Her mother nodded to two Riders. "Seize her."

K'lrsa backed up a step and bumped into Badru. "Seize me? For what?"

Badru stepped around her and dropped into a fighting stance, balanced lightly on the balls of his feet. A Rider leveled an arrow at Badru's heart.

"Badru. No." K'lrsa tried to push him aside, but he blocked her path, intent on staying between her and danger. "I can handle this. They're my family. Get out of my way."

"No. Get on Fallion. I'll hold them off until you're free."

The two Riders who'd been ordered to seize her approached, one from the left, one from the right, their hands raised, ready to attack. Two more joined them.

K'lrsa finally managed to shove Badru aside. "You go. Take Herin and Garzel and get out of here. Whatever this is, it has nothing to do with you."

"No. I won't leave you."

K'lrsa walked straight up to the nearest Rider—a man who'd been best friends with her brother when they were young. "Here, V'kan. Take me. I won't fight."

"K'lrsa, no." But Badru was too late.

V'kan bound her wrists together, tying the bonds so tight they dug into her flesh. She tried to meet his eyes— she'd known him, known all these people—her whole life, but he wouldn't look at her.

He dragged K'lrsa to her mother whose face was a mask of hatred, her gaze so intense it burned.

As he shoved K'lrsa to her knees, she said, "Mother. Why are you doing this? What have I done?"

"You killed your father." She spat. "Did you forget I had a moon stone, too?" She clutched the stone in her fist. "I *felt* it the moment he died. And I knew it was you. I could feel you on the other side of the knife that you plunged into his heart."

K'lrsa opened her mouth to argue, to explain that he'd asked her to do it. He'd begged her for mercy.

Her mother turned away, calling out, "Trial's tonight. We'll stake her in the desert in the morning."

"Mother. Wait!" K'lrsa tried to go after her, but V'kan held her down.

The crowd followed her mother, a few glancing back as

they dispersed. Not one looked at her with kindness or concern.

Not one.

K'lrsa knelt there weeping as Riders surrounded Herin, Badru, and Garzel and took them away.

They didn't fight.

What choice did they have? The sun had set. It was the Trickster's time. They couldn't leave and had no hope of winning against so many.

K'lrsa felt ill. She had killed her father, but she hadn't murdered him. It wasn't the same thing. It wasn't her fault. He'd asked her to do it.

But would that matter to her mother? A woman so consumed by grief that she'd burned down to her very core, no softness or warmth left in her?

CHAPTER 13

V'kan tossed her in an empty tent near the center of camp. Did they have so many prisoners now that they kept a tent ready for them?

No one offered her food or water and she didn't dare ask even though she was starving and her throat so dry it felt like she'd swallowed the desert.

She paced the confines of the tent, trying to figure out what she should do. She had to make her mother listen. Had to make her understand that she'd only done what her father wanted her to do.

How could they believe otherwise? She'd loved her father. He was her sun, all the warmth and light in her life.

She listened to the people going about their business, the conversations and laughter as families gathered for dinner, and was glad she was too parched to cry.

Finally, it was time.

She heard the expectant hush as everyone gathered in the center of camp and then V'kan came and dragged her through their midst. He threw her to the ground in a cleared space at the center of the crowd.

She knelt there, before the six-member Council. A council she wasn't surprised to see now included both her mother and her brother.

Not that anyone would know they were related to her from their cold expressions.

It seemed everyone in the camp was there, ringing the small space where she knelt, their faces full of anger, disgust, and curiosity.

No kindness. No doubt. No sympathy.

"Bring the slave," K'lrsa's mother ordered.

Two men dragged Lodie forward and held her off to the side.

She was alive, but not well. She clearly hadn't been eating enough; the flesh hung from her bones, her cheeks sunken in wrinkles.

K'lrsa struggled to her feet. "Lodie? Are you okay?"

Lodie glanced at her and nodded once.

"What did you do to her?" K'lrsa turned on her mother. "She's a sister of my blood. You were supposed to take care of her."

"She's alive isn't she?" Her mother turned her attention to Lodie. "When you first arrived, you told us that you could make a sun stone or a moon stone show when someone was telling the truth."

Lodie nodded.

"I want you to do this now."

K'lrsa licked her lips. She might have a chance. All she needed was enough time to tell her whole story.

Lodie frowned. "Why do you care now? She can tell you my story is the truth. You don't need a spelled stone for that."

"I don't care about your story. You came here with the moon stone of a murderer around your neck and though I was bound by the bonds of blood not to kill you, that doesn't mean I have to listen to you."

"Mother!" K'lrsa lurched forward, but V'kan yanked her back.

"Silence!" Her mother turned a look of such pure venom on K'lrsa that she froze. Where had all this hatred come from? They'd disagreed before—they were fundamentally different people, it was bound to happen— but never had her mother looked at her with hatred.

Her mother turned back to Lodie. "So? Will you do it or not?"

Lodie looked to K'lrsa who nodded even as her mother seethed in anger at their exchange.

"Yes. Give me the stones."

Each of the council members passed over their stone and one-by-one, Lodie took them and murmured words over them in a language both familiar and foreign. It had the rhythms of the tongue of the tribes, but the sounds were all shifted just enough to make it incomprehensible.

While she waited, K'lrsa sent a silent plea to the Lady Moon and Father Sun that she be allowed tell her full story and have it believed.

Lodie handed back the last stone and stepped to the side once more. She couldn't blend with the crowd, she was too tall for that, but she made it clear her part in the events was over.

K'lrsa's mother stepped forward and the crowd went silent.

"What is your name?" Her voice shook with emotion.

K'lrsa raised her chin. She was not going to let this crowd cow her. "K'lrsa dan V'na of the White Horse Tribe. You are my mother."

Her mother stared back at her with dead, black eyes as the moon stone in her hand glowed a light silver. The sun stones of the men behind her matched it with their yellow light.

"Tell me a lie."

"I didn't love my father with all my heart." The stones all flashed an angry red and her mother's face contorted with rage, making her almost unrecognizable in her pain.

"Tell me a lie I'll believe."

"I wanted to marry G'van. I thought he was wonderful and a perfect match for me."

Once more the stones flashed red. Her mother's lips twitched with the barest of smiles. She stepped forward, so close her breath puffed a stray strand of hair against K'lrsa's cheek. With a deathly calm, she said, "I have only one question for you, K'lrsa dan V'na of the White Horse Tribe. Did you kill your father?"

K'lrsa licked her lips. She couldn't just answer the one question. She had to explain what had happened.

"I…"

"Answer me! Did you take a knife and shove it into your father's chest?" Spittle flew from her mother's lips.

"Mom, please…Let me explain." She grasped at her mother's arm, but her mother twisted away.

"ANSWER." Her entire body trembled. "DID. YOU. DO. IT?"

Tears ran down K'lrsa's cheeks. She glanced at the crowd, desperate to see even one friendly face, just one person who believed there was more to the story than a yes or no answer.

She saw none.

"ANSWER ME." Her mother loomed before her, practically crackling with rage.

"Yes," she cried. "But it wasn't what you think."

The stone at her mother's throat flared silver, illuminating her pained grin of triumph.

She turned away as the crowd roared forward, shouting and screaming, hands reaching to tear at K'lrsa's hair and clothes.

"It was an act of mercy," she shouted. "He asked me to."

But no one was listening.

CHAPTER 14

Riders surrounded her, keeping the others at bay, but someone still managed to yank out a piece of her hair. As the crowd roared and screamed around them, the Riders escorted K'lrsa back to the same empty tent as before.

They didn't do it out of kindness or some sense of camaraderie. They did it so she'd be alive in the morning when it was time to drag her into the desert and stake her under the midday sun on a fire ant hill, her belly sliced open and eyes gouged out.

K'lrsa didn't care about that. Not now. It wasn't real to her and wouldn't be until she was actually dragged outside.

What she cared about was that her mother actually believed she'd murdered her father. Not killed him as an act of mercy, but murdered him. Her brother believed it, too. Or else why would they have done this to her?

She sat in the center of the tent, shoulders slumped, as the mutter of the angry crowd flowed around her. She flinched as something hit the side of the tent.

How could they do this to her without asking what had happened?

Didn't they know she'd worshiped her father? He was her everything. The one who'd encouraged her to become a Rider. The one who'd given her Fallion. The one who'd believed in her when no one else did.

How could they think she would willingly kill him?

They should know better.

K'lrsa stared through the small slit at the top of the tent where the moon shone silver and wondered why the Lady hadn't intervened on her behalf.

But she knew why.

The gods weren't like that. They didn't just step in and fix a person's life. They might lend guidance on occasion if they were feeling particularly generous, but for the most part they sat back and let people find their own way.

If she wanted out of this situation, she'd have to do it herself.

She was so hungry she could barely think. She hadn't eaten since morning and the heat of the day had drained her dry. And she hurt. She wasn't used to riding anymore. Especially not a day-long frantic race across the plains.

She needed to set aside the demands of her body and focus her mind on the problem.

She crossed her legs and rested her hands on her knees, palms up. Bit by bit she slowed her breathing, shutting out the sounds of the angry crowd, putting aside the hunger and fear that gnawed at her. She repeated the Pattern over and over again, seeking the path to the Core. Seeking that place outside of time where she could rest and refocus.

At first, the sounds of the camp were too loud, pushing in on her, reminding her of what she'd lost and what she faced in the morning.

All those people had once been *her* people. She'd shared meals with them, hunted with them, sang songs with them.

True, she'd always been a bit of a loner—preferring to hunt alone with Fallion rather than spend time in camp— but she hadn't had enemies. At least she hadn't thought she did.

Now all those people hated her. Believed her capable of the worst sort of murder.

She shoved away the anger and sadness that threatened to overwhelm her and focused once more on the Pattern.

But the image of her mother's face twisted in hate kept pushing its way into her awareness.

And her brother, so stony and cold.

She wanted to scream and wail and thrash her hands against the ground.

But she didn't.

Instead she repeated the Pattern, over and over and over, until her mind finally emptied of every thought and worry and sensation.

At last, she succeeded.

She floated inside the Core waiting for morning.

CHAPTER 15

Someone pinched K'lrsa's leg. Hard.

"Ow. What'd you do that for?" she demanded, before she remembered where she was.

She peered into the darkness of early morning. Whoever had pinched her smelled like dirt and sunshine. "M'lara." She grasped her sister's hand tight and leaned forward, desperate for a kind face.

As her eyes adjusted to the dark, she could just make out the large, somber eyes and high cheek bones of her sister. At eight summers old she was already beautiful.

"K'lrsa." Her slender arms wrapped around K'lrsa's neck as hot tears fell down her cheeks.

K'lrsa rocked backward slightly at the force of the hug, laughing softly. Someone still loved her. Someone believed in her.

She leaned her face against M'lara's; their tears mingled.

"Oh it's so good to see you, little one."

"Mom says you killed Dad," M'lara whispered. "How can she believe that? You didn't, did you, K'lrsa? You didn't kill him? Tell me you didn't."

She grabbed M'lara by the shoulders and leaned forward until they were almost nose to nose. "I did."

M'lara tried to pull back, but K'lrsa wouldn't let her. "But." She shook M'lara slightly. "He asked me to. He was already dying. It was an act of mercy."

M'lara stopped struggling, her brow furrowed in confusion. "Couldn't you save him? He wasn't that bad, was he?

K'lrsa shook her head. "No. It was too late for that. He was…They'd…"

She looked into the innocent face of her little sister and the words failed her. How could she tell M'lara what had been done to him? Wasn't it better that M'lara keep her last happy memories of him?

K'lrsa looked away. "I'm sorry. I did everything I could but it was too late."

M'lara sniffled and a tear rolled down her cheek.

"Do you believe me?" K'lrsa held her breath, waiting for the answer.

M'lara thought about it for a long moment and then nodded. "Yes. But…They're going to kill you for it in the morning, K. You and that slave woman. The old one."

"Lodie? Why are they going to kill her?"

M'lara shrugged one shoulder. "Mom doesn't like her. Hasn't since she arrived. I'm not sure what exactly she said, but Mom didn't want to hear it."

"Then why keep her around? Why not just let her go."

M'lara poked at the ground, drawing little patterns in the dirt. "She's kin. Blood sister to you. Can't kill her or else mom'd be a kinslayer. Can't send her away, who knows where she'd go."

"So what's changed? Why keep her alive all this time only to kill her now."

M'lara chewed on her lip until it seemed the whole thing had disappeared into her mouth.

"M'lara?"

"Mom's gonna shun you. Before they kill you."

"What?" K'lrsa sat back, stunned.

A person who was shunned was no longer part of the tribe. Even the desert turned against them.

Once shunned, her only choice would be to go back to the Daliphana.

"Why bother if they're going to kill me anyway."

"So she can kill the old lady, too."

"What is wrong with her?" K'lrsa slapped the ground.

Her mother had always been aloof, but this, this was a disregard for basic human life.

What had Lodie ever done to her?

M'lara shrugged again. "She'd get rid of the one with the *Amalanee* horse, too, if she thought she could get away with it but the wise man won't let her."

"Badru?"

"No. The scarred one that came with the old lady."

"Vedhe? She has really pale skin and hair?"

M'lara nodded. "Yeah. Her."

"She has an *Amalanee* horse? Since when?"

"I don't know. His name's Kriger. He's gray and really nice. He lets me feed him dried apples. Mom doesn't like it, but she's too busy to know what I do most of the time anyway." M'lara hunched her shoulders and focused on the dirt she was still moving this way and that. "She hardly talks to me anymore, K. She's so angry all the time." Her voice broke and she hiccupped back a sob.

"Oh, little one. Come here."

M'lara climbed into her lap and K'lrsa slowly rocked her side-to-side humming an old song she used to sing M'lara when she was just a baby.

Her heart clenched.

In her desire for vengeance, she'd forgotten she was leaving M'lara behind, too. Her mother and F'lia she'd thought about.

They were women, capable of handling their loss.

But M'lara?

M'lara was just a girl. A scared little girl whose father was dead and whose mother had changed beyond recognition.

They sat there like that for a long time. Nearby a guard paced back and forth, his or her feet scuffing the dirt with each step. A wind blew between the tents, a nearby tent snapping back and forth in the breeze. It brought with it the smells of home. Dirt most of all.

K'lrsa rested her cheek against M'lara's. "Can you do me a favor, little one?" she whispered.

M'lara nodded.

"Will you help Lodie escape tonight? Her and the others that came with me?"

M'lara shook her head.

K'lrsa sat back, letting her go. "Why not?"

"Because I'm here to help *you* escape." She looked back at K'lrsa, her eyes wide, serious as could be.

K'lrsa fought the urge to laugh.

What was she going to do now?

CHAPTER 16

K'lrsa pushed M'lara off her lap. "You can't help me escape."

"Why not?"

"It's too dangerous. I won't let you. You could get caught."

M'lara crossed her arms across her chest and jutted her lower lip out. "I didn't get caught coming in here to see you."

"It's not the same. You didn't see them tonight. How angry they all were. M'lara. Please. Go help Lodie."

"No."

"M'lara!"

M'lara glared at her. "I said no. I won't do it."

A guard pulled the tent flap aside, thrusting a torch in before him. It was T'kar, the first boy she'd ever kissed. He stood there frozen, looking back and forth between them.

M'lara glared at him, her cheeks streaked with tears.

"M'lara." He knelt between them, speaking softly. "Come on. You need to go back to your tents now."

"No. I don't want to." She moved away from him.

K'lrsa caught her wrist. "Go, M'lara. I'll be fine."

M'lara glared at her, but K'lrsa didn't let go. Finally, she nodded and K'lrsa released her wrist. As M'lara stormed out of the tent, T'kar cast a quick look of sympathy her way before he followed.

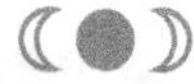

At least one person didn't hate her guts. Maybe even two people.

The day was starting to look up.

Who knew what might happen before it was over?

Maybe she'd live to see sunset.

She tried to find her way back to the Core but finally gave it up as hopeless.

Good thing, too, because it wasn't long before D'lan barged his way in. "M'lara just shook me awake, crying her eyes out, claiming that Dad asked you to kill him."

"He did."

"And why should I believe you?"

"Because it's the truth. You know me. You know how much I loved Dad. I never would've murdered him. I almost couldn't kill him even though he begged me to do it."

The sun stone at his throat shone a very soft yellow. He stroked it absent-mindedly as he studied her. "That slave you sent here. She was on G'van's horse. What was she doing with a horse from the Black Horse Tribe?"

"We stole it."

Again the sun stone shone a soft yellow.

"And those people you came here with? They're from the Toreem Daliphate."

"Yes, but it's not like that. They're not allies of the Black Horse Tribe. At least, not anymore."

The sun stone had dimmed when she said they weren't allies of the Black Horse Tribe but brightened on her last words.

"Please, D'lan. Your stone. It's still truth-spelled. Let me tell you my story. You'll know if I'm lying."

He hesitated.

"What do you have to lose? They're still going to kill me in the morning. Please? Hear me out? You have to know there's more to this."

He still hesitated and she whispered, "Please? For Dad?"

He sighed and seated himself across from her, his face

still a stony mask. "Fine. But only because he would've wanted me to hear you out."

He removed the sun stone from around his neck and held it in his palm so they could both see it. "Go ahead then. No lies."

So she told him.

About going after their father and finding him dying in the desert sands, his eyes gouged out, his belly slit open, his hands staked to the ground. About him begging her to kill him. And how he'd made her promise not to avenge him, but she'd sworn to anyway. And how Father Sun had shown her the slaver's caravan and Lodie was there and guessed the truth but didn't betray her. About how she'd taken Vedhe's place, sealing the woman's fate. How Lodie had said the slavers were going to kill Vedhe in the morning so she'd helped them escape with G'van's stolen horse. And about how G'van was killed the next morning but she'd still made her way to Toreem, taken as a slave to sell in a brothel.

And then she stopped. Because Badru's and Herin's secrets weren't hers to tell. And as much as D'lan was family, she wasn't sure she could trust him with their true identities.

"Well? You got to Toreem? And? What happened next?" he demanded, enthralled with her story despite himself.

"I…um. I was taken into the court of the Daliph." She kept her eyes on the sun stone, willing it to stay yellow. "While I was there, K'var of the Black Horse Tribe came to demand that the Daliph give him more troops so he could kill all his enemies in the tribes."

"K'var did this?" D'lan rocked backward. "And did the Daliph give him the troops?"

She nodded. D'lan lurched to his feet.

She stood, blocking his way. "Wait. There's more you need to know. It was K'var who killed Dad, D'lan. He admitted it. And L'ral is the one who led him there."

"L'ral? That skinny little fool? The one that was supposed to marry F'lia?"

She nodded, tears in her eyes. She still hadn't seen F'lia. And she didn't have it in her to tell her best friend that the love of her life had betrayed the man who'd treated him like a son.

"At least he's dead. What about K'var?" D'lan gripped his dagger.

"He's dead, too."

"How?"

"I killed him."

D'lan nodded. "Good."

"But, D'lan, those troops he asked for?"

"Yeah?"

"They're coming. They're only a few days behind us. That's why we're here. To warn you."

He cussed. "I need to tell the Council."

He raced out of the tent. She started to follow, but T'kar blocked her way. "Sorry, K'lrsa. Orders."

She sat back down in the middle of the cold, empty tent to wait, wondering what would happen now.

CHAPTER 17

K 'lrsa didn't have long to wait until she was once more dragged out of the tent and brought before the Council and the rest of the tribe. The sun was just rising, but the entire tribe had gathered.

She stood alone before them, shivering, her stomach grumbling with hunger as D'lan munched on a piece of dried baru.

She focused on him. Better that than to look around at the sullen anger on the faces of her once-tribe.

Her mother stepped forward, arms crossed. "D'lan says there's more to your story and I should let you tell it."

"And?"

She shrugged, not looking directly at K'lrsa. "I'm not sure I care. You still killed your father." She glanced at K'lrsa, her eyes burning with fury. "Didn't you?"

"To put him out of his misery!" She clenched her hands, trying to control her temper. This was so ridiculous. Bad enough she'd had to do what she had, but for her mother to continue to blame her for it was just too much.

She turned her back on her mother and shouted to the crowd. "I found my father staked to the ground over an ant hill. His belly was sliced open. His eyes were gouged out."

"Liar!" Someone shouted from the back of the crowd.

"No I'm not!" She glared at the crowd, meeting anyone who'd dare's eyes. "I loved my father more than anyone else

in this world. I would've never willingly harmed him. He begged me to take his life. It's the only reason I did. To spare him suffering. There was no hope of saving him. He'd been there most of the day by the time I found him." She choked back the tears, remembering how he'd looked when she found him there with the grel circling his weakening body.

She turned back to her mother and held her gaze. "I killed him, but only as an act of mercy."

K'lrsa's mother turned away. She motioned to one of the Riders in the crowd. "Bring the old one." As the Rider raced away, K'lrsa's mother turned back. "We'll see how much of this is the truth and how much is just a desperate attempt to save yourself."

K'lrsa met her mother's fiery gaze, but didn't bother responding.

A tense silence filled the space as they waited first for the Rider to bring back Lodie and then for Lodie to once more truth-spell the Council's stones.

When they were finally ready, K'lrsa looked straight at her mother and repeated everything she'd already said. Her mother's stone shone with a steady silvery light the whole time, but K'lrsa only cared about what she saw in her mother's eyes.

As she continued, a single tear ran down her mother's cheek, and K'lrsa had to fight not to close the gap between them. "I gave him the last of my water," she said, voice shaking. "Even though he told me it was too late." She bit her lip searching for the strength to continue, to relive those horrible moments. "I freed his hands." She flinched at the memory of how his flesh had torn, melded to the metal stakes. "And then I sat by his side. To keep him company until…until he died. To keep the grel away, and so he wouldn't be alone." Her voice scaled higher with each word as she fought for control, fought her memory and sorrow.

The crowd was absolutely silent. It was just her and her mother.

They stared at one another, tears flowing down their cheeks. "He begged me, Mom. *Begged* me, to kill him."

She finally broke eye contact, the pain too much. "So I did." She sobbed as she remembered that horrible moment. How the knife had sunk into his flesh. How he'd stopped breathing with one little gasp of breath. The way his dried lips were frozen in a small smile.

"And his body? What did you do with it?" her mother demanded, her voice shaking.

K'lrsa sighed. "The sands took him. Swallowed him up. But I left his sun stone for you. In a cave. Didn't anyone find it?"

"No." Her voice shook with so much emotion K'lrsa wasn't sure how she could contain it.

She reached for her mother's hand. "I'm sorry, Mom. I knew I should come back here and tell you what had happened, but..." She lifted her chin, meeting her mother's anguished gaze. "I wanted to avenge him. I wanted someone to pay for what they'd done to him. And I knew you'd never let me go if I came back here first."

Her mother nodded slightly. "And did you? Did you avenge him? Did you kill the person who did this to him?"

K'lrsa nodded. "Yes."

"Good." She turned and walked back to the rest of the Council.

Too much to hope she'd say sorry or hug K'lrsa or even smile.

His death had broken her.

"Are you still going to kill me?" K'lrsa asked, scanning the council members for some sign of what they thought.

K'lrsa's mother turned back. "No. But I do think you should find a new tribe."

"What?" K'lrsa stumbled backward, the emotional blow worse than any physical blow she'd ever felt. "Why?"

Her mother sighed. "I know why you did it now and I forgive you for that. But the truth is, you killed your father. I *felt* it when he died, K'lrsa." She shook her head. "Whatever your reason for what you did, I can't stand to see you every day and be reminded of that." She looked around at the crowd. "I'm sure I'm not the only one."

K'lrsa struggled to breathe, the pain in her chest too

much to bear. She glanced around at the crowd—here or there someone watched her in pity, but too many stared back, indifferent or hostile.

"No!" M'lara pushed her way through the crowd and threw her arms around K'lrsa's legs. K'lrsa bent down and held M'lara close, crying without shame.

She'd been ready to die to avenge her father, but this? This was too much.

Without her tribe, she was nothing.

CHAPTER 18

"No. I can't let this happen." D'lan stepped forward, his voice strong and clear as he stopped at K'lrsa's side.

"Mother, you lost the love of your life. I know that. I know how much it hurt you. And I'm sorry it happened. More sorry than you can know." He squeezed K'lrsa's shoulder. "But we all lost him that day. It wasn't just you. And you would've done the exact same thing K'lrsa did if you'd been the one who found him. I would've, too. You can't blame her for this."

K'lrsa's mother glared at him, her jaw clenching and unclenching.

He continued, undaunted. "K'lrsa isn't the one who killed him. She wielded the knife but it was K'var of the Black Horse Tribe who put him there and wounded him past saving."

A mutter passed through the crowd as he named her father's killer, but D'lan continued. "K'lrsa came back to warn us of a threat from the Black Horse Tribe and the Toreem Daliphate. We need to put the death of my father aside and focus on this new threat."

Her mother glared at them through narrowed eyes.

K'lrsa knew there was no point asking her to change her mind. Not now at least. She focused on Lodie, the only friendly face in the crowd and the only one who'd know how bad the news was. "Aran, the Daliph of the Toreem

Daliphate, has ordered his troops to attack us. They've already gathered on the border and will be here within days. Their orders are to kill all who oppose the Black Horse Tribe, which includes all of us."

The crowd erupted. Someone shouted about sending the children to safety. Someone else asked how many arrows they had and if more could be made. Another person demanded to know if she could be trusted, but all of the sun and moon stones that had been truth-spelled shone silver and gold.

Lodie clutched at her chest and collapsed to the ground.

K'lrsa rushed to her side.

Lodie stared up at her. She looked like she'd aged a decade in a moment. "Aran is still alive? But how? How is that possible? I thought I'd poisoned him. I thought..."

K'lrsa leaned close and whispered, "Death walker magic. It's how Herin saved you, too."

If she hadn't already been collapsed on the ground, Lodie would've collapsed then.

"Silence!" D'lan roared.

The crowd slowly quieted, a few low-voiced conversations continuing here or there.

"We need to decide what we do now. Suggestions?"

"We should make a truce with the Black Horse Tribe," V'kan suggested. "Give them what they want."

K'lrsa's mother sneered at him, her disgust evident to all. "No. They've already shed our blood. There can be no truce."

H'kan, a woman who'd joined the tribe at the last gathering stepped forward. "Then we flee. The Tall Bluff Tribe has a camp in the bluffs we can defend against a larger force."

K'lrsa stepped forward, hesitant to speak again, but knowing she had to. "You can't flee."

"And why not?" H'kan demanded.

"They'll banish you from the tribes if you do."

"Explain," her mother demanded.

"Dad wanted to expel them from the tribes. They know this. So now they'll vote to expel us. And the only way that

doesn't happen is if we're there to vote them down."

A dark muttering passed through the crowd.

"Who says?" H'kan asked. "Maybe if we leave them alone, they'll leave us alone.

"Like they left my father alone?"

"He's the one that started it, isn't he? They didn't come into this camp and kill us. They just killed him."

"So you'd let them do whatever they want? Lead strangers across the desert? Trade in slaves? Kill anyone who stands against them?"

H'kan didn't answer, but it was clear what she believed.

K'lrsa turned to the crowd. "We have to make it to the gathering grounds. All of us. All of the tribes. If we don't, we lose everything. My father saw the truth of the Black Horse Tribe and he stood against them. It cost him his life, but it was the right thing to do." She stared around at the faces, mostly scared now. "I've been to the Daliphate. I've seen what our world looks like if we let this happen. Do you want a future where we keep slaves? Where our women are taken and sold for sex? Where our children are so lost in smokeweed and drink that they can't move?"

She wanted to add something about protecting the Hidden City, but she knew they wouldn't care about that. "We have to act. Now. Or we'll lose who we are forever."

"Even if we make it, the other tribes won't." H'kan crossed her arms, daring K'lrsa to challenge her statement.

H'kan was right, but Herin had been, too. They just had to do what they could and hope for the best. "We'll find a way to get them there. We have to."

K'lrsa's mother shook her head. "What good will it do us if we make it to the gathering grounds? There's still a trained army coming for us."

"We'll be safe there. No one can kill on the gathering grounds."

"Says who?"

K'lrsa turned to the tribe's wise man, a short old man with shifty eyes she'd never particularly liked. "You know, don't you? That it's protected?"

He shrugged one shoulder. "So the legends say."

K'lrsa wanted to slap him. Now was not the time to be cavalier about things.

She turned to Lodie. "Lodie?"

But Lodie wouldn't look at her, too lost in the horror of Aran's return.

K'lrsa's mother stepped forward. "Enough. We need time to think this over. Anyone who wants to have their say, please seek out a council member. We'll gather again in the morning."

"In the morning? That's a whole day! We can't wait that long. We have to go. Now!"

Her mother shook her head slightly.

"Mother!"

"Go. Everyone. Prepare yourselves to leave in the morning. If our Riders confirm that troops are on the way, we'll need to move. Either to the gathering grounds or the Tall Bluff Tribe."

K'lrsa watched the crowd disperse, her mouth hanging open in surprise.

How could they just go about their daily routine? Didn't they understand?

But, no, they didn't.

It was her fault. She'd failed to convince them.

And now they might all die because of it.

CHAPTER 19

K'lrsa found herself alone with Lodie who lurched towards her looking so frail she might break. "Are you sure Aran's alive?"

"Yes."

"You saw him yourself?" Her voice trembled as she looked around wildly as if expecting him to suddenly appear.

"Yes. He…" She lowered her voice so no one else could hear her. "He declared himself in the throne room and ordered his men to kill Badru. Said he was taking back the throne because Badru didn't deserve it. It was chaos. Poradom against poradom. Soldier against soldier." She leaned closer. "One of Badru's *own men* stabbed him in the back."

Lodie clutched at her throat. "So Badru's dead?"

K'lrsa shook her head. "No. He's here with me. Somewhere." She still hadn't seen any sign of them.

"But he's badly hurt?"

"No. He's fine."

"You said he was stabbed." Lodie fixed her gaze on K'lrsa, her face clouded with distrust. "Attacked. How would Aran ever let him live? How did you get here?"

K'lrsa glanced around to make sure no one was close enough to hear them. "Badru was killed in the fighting. But Herin brought him back."

"Brought him back? How?" Lodie's voice sharpened as she stared K'lrsa down.

"The same way she brought you back."

"Death walker magic." Lodie stepped back. "I should've…I should've known. I felt the poison burn through me…I knew I was dead…I thought…How did she learn it?"

"Aran. He had people who knew it. Herin said he used to kill Garzel and then bring him back just to torture her. You never saw?"

"No." She shook her head. "If I'd known…I would've…."

K'lrsa thought she was going to say something about helping Herin and Garzel sooner, but she should've remembered that neither Lodie nor Herin were soft, gentle souls.

"I would've found a better way to kill him. Fire probably. I doubt I could've cut off his head before someone stopped me."

"Lodie!"

Lodie looked at her. "What?"

"Never mind. Look, what's done is done. We need to save as many of the tribes as we can now."

Lodie snorted. "I say everyone for themselves."

"Lodie."

"What? They didn't exactly welcome me with open arms. What do I care what becomes of them?"

K'lrsa rubbed at her face. "They're my family."

"Not a very good one from what I saw."

K'lrsa turned to scan the tents, wondering where they'd put Herin, Garzel, and Badru. "We need the others."

"What others?"

"Badru, Herin, and Garzel. And Vedhe. The gods seem to think she's part of this, too."

"Herin's here? Why didn't you tell me?" Lodie glared around the camp, completely recovered from her earlier defeat. She stood tall, her jaw clenched tight in anger.

A Rider walked past them and Lodie grabbed her arm, pulling her to a halt. "Where are they? The ones who arrived with her?"

The Rider nodded towards the edge of the camp. "With the scarred one."

Lodie released her and stomped towards the far edge of camp, not looking back.

K'lrsa scrambled to follow.

They walked past the horse pickets and across an empty space to where two tents now stood, huddled against the barrier as if trying to escape. A magnificent silver horse was tethered outside with the distinctive white mark of an *Amalanee* on his forehead. Fallion and Midnight stood next to him, munching on dried grass.

Vedhe, the slave woman K'lrsa had helped escape, stood to meet them, her hair so pale it was almost as white as the clouds. Her skin was still covered with shiny red patches where the sun had burned her, but she looked better, more alive than she had in the slaver's camp.

She smiled as they approached, but the scars on her face twisted half of her mouth and K'lrsa had to force herself not to flinch away.

"Herin!" Lodie shouted. "Get out here! I want a word with you."

Herin ducked out of the right-hand tent, Garzel and Badru close behind. She watched Lodie, her face carefully neutral.

K'lrsa turned to see if anyone was nearby, but they were alone. It was just the six of them.

Lodie walked right up to Herin and slapped her, the sound of flesh contacting flesh so loud the horses stopped munching their grass to watch.

"Lodie! Stop it." K'lrsa grabbed her wrist as Lodie raised her hand to slap Herin again.

"You had no right," Lodie hissed.

Herin spoke, her voice firm and even. "I couldn't let you do it. I couldn't let you give your life that way."

"So whose did you give?" Lodie asked. "Who died so I could live, Herin?"

Herin stared back at her in stony silence.

"Who?"

Herin flicked a glance at K'lrsa and away again, probably remembering the conversation they'd had when she'd revived Badru, before Sayel volunteered his own life. "A young slave boy."

"You killed a *child* to save me? Herin."

Herin looked away, uncomfortable for the first time K'lrsa had ever seen. "You're my sister. I couldn't just let you die. Not when I had the power to save you." Herin looked back and there were tears in her eyes.

K'lrsa tried not to gawk at her. It was hard to think that underneath all those layers of power and control, Herin was still just a flesh and blood woman like anyone else.

But Lodie wasn't done. "It was my choice, Herin. I willingly gave my life to kill Aran. You had no right to bring me back."

Herin shrugged one shoulder. "I knew the magic. I wanted to see it do something good for a change. And I wanted you to have another chance at life after you wasted the first one on me."

"Another chance at life? You sold me to slavers. You told them to take me away across the desert and never bring me back."

Herin's face twisted up. "It was the only way, Lodie. Everyone saw you die; you couldn't stay."

Lodie sighed. "It's too late to change what you did, but I want you to promise me."

"What?"

"You will never again use that magic. Ever. No matter what."

Herin hesitated.

"Swear it, Herin, or I'll walk back to the center of camp and declare you a death walker."

Herin pressed her lips together. "Fine. I swear it."

"Good."

K'lrsa glanced past them to Badru.

Was it good? What if Badru was killed again? Or Lodie? Or her? Why give away a powerful tool like that?

But studying Herin's face as she pulled her sister close for a hug, K'lrsa realized something. It didn't matter what she'd told Lodie, because if she had to, Herin would break any vow to protect the ones she loved.

CHAPTER 20

Herin and Lodie walked away, discussing possible ways to kill Aran, Garzel trailing behind them, which left K'lrsa facing Badru.

"You okay?" He pulled her close and she sunk into him, breathing in the spicy scent unique to him.

"If you forget the fact that the people I grew up with were willing to think I'd murdered my father and now they won't listen to me about leaving? Sure, I'm great."

He kissed her on the top of the head. "We heard about it from M'lara. I'm sorry."

She shook her head. Now was not the time to start crying again. "What can you do, right?" She sniffed. "They'll either come around or they won't. And if they don't, well...What can you do."

"I could talk to them. Tell them who I am. Who I...was. It might help."

She pulled away, shaking her head. "No. No one here can ever know that."

"Why not?"

"They don't trust the Daliphate and I don't want to try to explain to them that you're the good Daliph who *probably* didn't want to send troops as opposed to the bad Daliph who actually did."

He grimaced slightly. "Point taken."

"And...At some point someone is going to hear the

story of how you were overthrown. You're dead, remember? You can't be you anymore, Badru."

He frowned, but he knew she was right, she could see it in his eyes.

He nodded towards the horses. "Did you see the other *Amalanee*?"

She nodded. "Vedhe's." The pale woman had moved over to the horses and was now brushing her horse's coat, humming softly to herself.

"Grandmother and Garzel were arguing about it half the night."

"Why?"

"Herin thinks she shouldn't have it since she's not of the tribes."

"But neither are you."

"My mother was."

K'lrsa tilted her head to the side. "And your father. Was he of the tribes?"

"No." He turned away, his shoulders stiff.

"Badru? What is it? What did I say?"

His hands were clenched by his sides. He didn't look at her. "My mother was raped. They never caught the man who did it."

"Oh, Badru. I'm so sorry." She winced, imaging what it must've been like for him growing up the son and grandson of rapists. Of course, in the Daliphate being a rapist likely wasn't the death sentence it was in the tribes.

But still. Her own father had been such a source of strength and support that she couldn't imagine what it must've been like for him.

Badru shook his head. "Don't be. You didn't do it. And you weren't the one that was raped."

He nodded towards Vedhe. "Do you think hers can fly, too?"

K'lrsa shrugged. "Probably. We should have Garzel try to awaken it."

Badru frowned. "Doesn't that seem odd to you?"

"What?"

"That we need *Garzel* to awaken the horses for us? I

mean, Midnight's my horse, but he has to say all those words and use a sun stone to awaken him?"

K'lrsa shrugged. She hadn't thought much about it. "How else would you do it?"

"I don't know. But I think…" He glanced at Herin. "I think my grandmother knows."

"Herin keeping secrets? No…She'd never do that." K'lrsa rolled her eyes.

Badru laughed.

K'lrsa nodded towards Vedhe. "Come on. Let's say hi."

She led the way over to the horses, Badru trailing a few steps behind. He seemed hesitant to get too close to the girl. And she was just a girl. Slight framed, slender. Younger than K'lrsa although how much younger was hard to say with all the scars and the way her experiences had aged her.

As Vedhe watched them, K'lrsa had to admit she felt a certain urge to keep her distance as well. She struggled against her aversion to someone her gut told her was sick and therefore dangerous. In the tribes, illness killed often, so anyone who was sick was avoided. K'lrsa knew the girl's scars weren't contagious, but it took everything she had to step closer.

"Vedhe, yes?"

Vedhe approached them with the lithe grace of a warrior and K'lrsa was reminded how Lodie had said she'd killed six men the night she was taken from her homeland. "You Krissa. You save me." She hugged K'lrsa so tight K'lrsa could barely breathe.

"Yes. Well…" K'lrsa didn't really feel like explaining that she wouldn't have had to save her if she hadn't taken her place in the caravan in the first place. She nodded towards the *Amalanee* horse which was watching them with a level of awareness that was almost disconcerting. "Beautiful horse."

Vedhe nodded. "Kriger."

"Kriger?" The horse snorted and K'lrsa laughed. "Seems he knows his name. Where did you find him?"

"He find me. And Lodie. In the bad land."

"The barren lands? That black area where everything was dead?"

Vedhe nodded. "Black horse tired. Lodie tired. Vedhe tired. Want out. Ride when no sun or moon. Lost. All gray. Walk and walk and walk. Moon never comes. Sun never comes." She stroked Kriger's nose. "Kriger finds us. Leads us out of bad lands. Saves us."

"Huh." K'lrsa studied him and he studied her back. "That's…wonderful. And then he just stayed with you?"

"Yes. Mine. For me." She put her body between Kriger and K'lrsa.

"Of course he is. Anyone can see that."

Vedhe snorted. "Tribe not see. But Kriger show them. Kick and bite until they leave him alone."

K'lrsa laughed. "Well done, Kriger. I hope Fallion would do the same if anyone tried to take him from me."

She wanted to ask more, but just then M'lara came running up with a large bowl full of sour greens, millet, and what looked like hare meat. K'lrsa's stomach grumbled. "Oh, thank you. I haven't eaten for at least a day now."

"I made it myself."

"Did you now?" K'lrsa scooped some into a smaller bowl and took her first bite. She had to fight not to spit it back out. "You used the salt?"

M'lara nodded, grinning from ear to ear. "Uh-huh. I know it's really good stuff and Mom doesn't use it much, but since it was for you…"

"Thank you, M'lara."

K'lrsa forced herself to take another bite and smile.

Salty as it was, it was still food, and at least someone had cared enough to bring it to her even if she was going to need to drink a whole waterskin when she was done.

CHAPTER 21

M'lara settled herself at K'lrsa's feet as the others came to join them outside the two tents. "Hey, K, who are these people?"

"Well, that's Herin and Garzel, and this is Badru, and of course you know Vedhe and Lodie."

M'lara studied Herin, Garzel, and Badru before turning back to K'lrsa. "What happened to her fingers?" She nodded at Herin who waggled the fingers in M'lara face, making her squeal in fright.

Herin cackled, the sound like earth cracked after too much sun. She leaned close. "I asked too many questions when I was younger. My mother took one finger joint for every question I asked." She waved her fingers again, grinning.

"That's not true!"

"No?"

"No." M'lara shook her head. "K, what happened to her fingers?"

K'lrsa choked down another bite of food. "It's rude to ask questions like that, M'lara."

"But you know the answer?"

K'lrsa nodded.

"Tell me, please. Please, please, please."

K'lrsa sighed. Such things weren't for children. Why burden her with that kind of knowledge? But staring

around camp she saw kids laughing and playing and adults chatting as if it were any other day. Maybe if they understood what life outside the tribes was like, they'd see the threat they faced.

"K?"

"A very bad man did that to her, M'lara. The same one who sent soldiers to attack us."

M'lara goggled at Herin. "Is that true?"

Herin nodded. "Yes. He took one joint for every time I tried to kill him." She held up both hands, fingers splayed. "He's very hard to kill."

M'lara leaned against K'lrsa's legs. "Why would you try to kill someone so many times?"

"Because he needed to die. He's a very bad man."

M'lara chewed on her lip, studying Herin's fingers with a sort of rapt fascination, still not grasping the fact that a man had ordered Herin to be maimed like that.

K'lrsa envied her her carefree innocence.

She'd been like that too. Once. Before her father was murdered.

She sighed.

That's what the Daliphana would do to her people. Strip them of their innocence. Bind them, sell them, kill them. They had to be stopped so sweet little girls like her sister could stay that way.

But they weren't going to be stopped if her people kept acting like nothing was wrong.

She stood. "C'mon, M'lara."

"But why? I like it here."

"I need to find D'lan. We can't wait until morning."

((●))

K'lrsa and M'lara threaded their way through the tents looking for D'lan or their mother. K'lrsa saw familiar faces everywhere, but none were friendly. Even knowing why she'd killed her father, they didn't trust her.

M'lara pushed ahead, leading the way to a tent with green flowers painted at the top. F'lia's family's mark.

"Wait. M'lara, come back."

She didn't wait but instead stepped around the edge of the tent. K'lrsa followed to where an older woman, her hair mostly gray, plump for the tribes, sat, a sour expression on her face.

"M'na. How are you today?" she asked.

"Fine. What do you want?"

K'lrsa flinched from the anger in her voice, but forced herself to be kind back. "Do you know where I can find F'lia? Is she around?"

M'na glared at her. "You don't know then."

"Know what?"

M'na sniffed. "She's gone."

"Gone? Where'd she go?"

"Gave herself to the sands."

"What?" K'lrsa crouched down, too breathless to absorb the news and stand at the same time. F'lia had given herself to the sands? Her bright, beautiful friend, so full of life that she practically shone with it, had just let go? Walked into the desert never to return?

So many questions tumbled through her mind—why hadn't they stopped her, when had she done it—but all she could strangle out was one word, "Why?"

"Why? Because L'ral was gone. And you were, too, and there was V'na screaming about how you killed your father. What was she to think? And who did she have left?"

K'lrsa sat back. Her best friend had killed herself because she wasn't there for her. Because she was too selfish to see what the loss of L'ral might do to her. "Are you sure? Maybe she…?"

"What else do you think happened? One day she's here, moping around, crying her eyes out, wailing over L'ral. The next she's gone, all her things still here."

"Maybe she went to another tribe?"

"No."

"But…"

M'na stood and glared at her. "I know my own daughter. And she wouldn't have left to go to some other tribe without telling me. She's dead. And it's all because of you."

She stomped away before K'lrsa could respond.

K'lrsa watched her go before dragging herself to her feet and turning back to find M'lara waiting in the shadows. "We better find D'lan. Lead the way."

K'lrsa stumbled after M'lara, lost in a haze of grief and regret.

If only she'd done things differently.

CHAPTER 22

They finally found D'lan, but he wouldn't listen to her. Neither would her mother who pointed out that almost all of the Riders were gone and there was no point in moving on without them.

K'lrsa was furious. "Why would you send the Riders away after what I told you?"

"Because we'll need more food if we're to spend any amount of time there. We had enough for the five days of the gathering, but no more."

"But..."

"K'lrsa there's no point in going there if we're just going to starve to death."

She tried again. "We could still start moving in that direction. The Riders will catch up with us. They move faster on horse than the tribe does on foot."

Her mother shook her head. "That's not the only thing we're waiting on."

"What else?"

She pressed her lips together. "We sent three Riders out to see if they can confirm your story."

"You still don't believe me! Even with the moon stone telling you it's the truth?"

Her mother clenched her mouth shut.

"Mom."

"We need to know our options. We might be better off

going to the Tall Bluff Tribe instead depending on where the troops are and how many there are."

"But I told you! You need to be at the gathering to vote. If you're not there…"

"You don't know that's what they'll do, K'lrsa. But I know that if we go to the gathering grounds we'll be trapped with no way out. All they have to do is wait until we run out of food."

"But there's a weapon. Once you're safe I can find the weapon and save us."

Her mother raised an eyebrow. "You? You're going to go find a weapon to save us? A weapon that can destroy an entire army?"

"Yes. Herin says it's in the Hidden City. We'll get you to safety and then we'll find it. But if you don't go…and they expel you…I won't be able to find it. You have to give me time."

"Oh, K'lrsa. How many times have I told you that you're just another Rider, not some great hero?"

K'lrsa desperately wanted to tell her about how Fallion could fly, but she didn't. It wouldn't change her mother's mind. She'd just see it as one more reason K'lrsa thought too much of herself.

"Please, Mom. Convince the others. We need to go. As soon as possible."

Her mother shook her head and turned away, dismissing K'lrsa.

Sighing, K'lrsa trudged back to the tents where the others waited.

CHAPTER 23

K 'lrsa sat down outside the tents with the others and took the travel bar Garzel offered her with a nod of thanks. She still hadn't managed to get the salt taste of M'lara's soup out of her mouth.

"Herin."

"Yes."

"Am I right that if they don't go to the gathering and we get voted out that we won't be able to enter the desert to find the Hidden City?"

Herin thought about it for a long moment. "I don't know. It's not safe to enter the desert if you're not part of the tribes or with someone who is."

Lodie spoke softly, "We'll still be members."

Badru leaned forward. "But you three haven't been members of the tribes for thirty years."

"Once a member of the tribes, always a member of the tribes."

Herin grunted. "Until the Black Horse Tribe expels us, too."

"They wouldn't, would they? They think we're all dead."

"Aran's no fool. If he sent troops, he sent orders." She studied Badru, her eyes narrowed. "But Badru might still be able to lead us."

"Me? How?"

Lodie nodded. "You're right. Depends, though, which counts more. His father's blood or who raised him."

"Wait." K'lrsa looked back and forth between Herin and Lodie. "Are you telling me a member of the tribes raped Badru's mother? I don't believe it. I mean, obviously, G'van cared nothing for our ways, but even he hesitated to rape a woman, preferring to take slaves or prostitutes."

Vedhe glared at her. "Still rape even if slave."

"Yes, of course, sorry. I never meant to imply…" K'lrsa looked away from Vedhe's angry gaze. "You're right. It's still rape even for a slave."

Badru turned on Herin. "You know who my father is?"

"Yes. And he didn't rape your mother. Where did you get that idea?"

"That's what everyone said happened."

Herin sighed deeply. "Did it never occur to you that maybe people lied to Aran about certain things? Honestly."

Badru stared at her, shaking his head softly from side to side.

He finally laughed, a small exhalation of sound. "So my father isn't who I thought he was either? He didn't take my mother against her will. He wasn't some stranger. But you just…You just let me believe that because…Because what? It was easier than telling the truth?"

"No. I let you and everyone else believe it because it was the only chance your mother had to live after what she'd done. She was young and foolish, but she didn't deserve to die for it."

Badru sat back, rubbing his face with his hand, still shaking his head. "Then who was he? Where was he from? What actually happened to my mother?"

Herin pursed her lips.

"Herin! Tell me about my father."

Garzel grunted, nudging Herin to speak.

"Pzah. Fine. Your father came to court with his father who was a member of the Black Horse Tribe. He was very young and very bored and while his father was negotiating a trade agreement your father went off and got into things he shouldn't."

K'lrsa winced at Badru's pained expression. "Herin. You could be a little nice about it, you know."

"Why should I? He cost my daughter her life. He was bored and stupid and didn't understand what it meant for a woman of the Daliphana to lie with a man who wasn't her husband. L'ren was the first boy she'd met who wasn't her half-brother and she was young and stupid and just old enough to get into the wrong sort of trouble…"

Herin shook her head. "He knew our ways were different, but he didn't understand what that meant. In the tribes two young kids old enough to be curious can explore without consequence. If something happens, the families are fine with it. All children are treasured, no matter how they're conceived. But in the Daliphana, if a girl *kisses* a man other than her husband she's cast out or sold. To do more than that is death."

K'lrsa shivered. She'd known the Daliphana was twisted, but she'd never understood just how much or how close she'd come to risking her life there.

"So?" Badru asked. "What happened?"

"The same thing that happens to any man and woman who lie together often enough. She got pregnant." Herin's eyes narrowed in remembered anger. "And the fool girl was so scared, she didn't tell anyone until it was too late to do something about it."

Lodie grimaced.

Badru frowned. "Do something about it. What's that mean?" He looked back and forth between Lodie and Herin. Lodie wouldn't meet his eyes.

Herin sighed. "It means she would've been better off to drink a few herbs early on and end the pregnancy rather than let it go until she couldn't deny it anymore."

K'lrsa gasped. "You would've had her lose the child? But you can't…You can't just snuff a life out like that. Children are precious."

Herin glared at her. "In the tribes, maybe. But there it was a choice between the unborn child and Jania. Aran would've killed her the day he found out, but I convinced him to wait and see if it was a boy. As soon as Badru was born, Aran sold her."

"Is she still alive?" K'lrsa asked.

"No. She died within a year of Aran selling her. He…" She grimaced. "He sold her to one of the worst slave owners, a man known for his cruelty."

As Herin's jaw quivered, K'lrsa remembered this was Herin's daughter they were talking about.

Herin's and Garzel's.

Their only child.

"Did my father know?" Badru asked, his voice trembling.

"No. He'd done his damage and left before she started showing."

K'lrsa studied Herin carefully. "So you told Aran she'd been raped?"

"It was her only chance."

K'lrsa shook with anger as she asked softly, "And who did she say did it, Herin? Let me guess. Some nameless slave boy?"

Herin glared at her, but didn't answer.

"Grandmother? Is that what she did? Did she blame it on some innocent man?"

She lifted her chin. "It's what *I* did. To protect my daughter."

K'lrsa stared at her, shocked.

But Herin didn't flinch away from what she'd done. She'd protected her daughter, just like she'd protected her sister and grandson.

After a long moment, Herin added, "Anyway. The point is, your father was a member of the Black Horse Tribe which means there's a chance that even if the White Horse Tribe and the Summer Spring Tribe are banned, you can still lead us to the Hidden City."

K'lrsa shook her head. "But if that happens, where will my people go? Even if we find this weapon and destroy the Daliph's troops, it'll be too late. They won't be able to stay with the tribes."

"I know. But it may be the only path open to us." Herin nodded towards the main camp. "Maybe you should give it one more try. We can still travel by moonlight."

K'lrsa slumped forward, resting her elbows on her knees. "They won't listen to me. Maybe when their scouts return they'll finally see what I was trying to tell them."

She wished she could do more.
But what?

CHAPTER 24

As night fell and nothing happened, K'lrsa paced back and forth, back and forth, back and forth until finally Lodie stood to block her path. "Enough."

K'lrsa couldn't sit down, she just couldn't. And she was too wound up to sleep. They needed to be on the move. Now. Not tomorrow or the next day. Now.

Lodie beckoned Vedhe and Badru over. Herin glowered at them from where she sat by the fire, but made no move to interrupt.

Once they were all there, Lodie said, "If you want to find the Hidden City, you need to be able to awaken your horses. It's the easiest way to get there."

K'lrsa nodded. "We have. Garzel can do it. He uses his sun stone. Although, it would be nice to be able to use my moon stone." She touched the stone at her neck—her own, thankfully. As soon as things had settled she and Lodie had eagerly swapped their stones, both relieved to have their own ancestors back.

Vedhe shook her head. "Awaken? What is awaken?"

"The horses can fly. You know," K'lrsa flapped her arms, "like a bird. They just have to be awakened to their true nature."

"Kriger fly?" Vedhe hopped like a little kid who'd just been given a sweet, reminding K'lrsa how young she truly was.

"Yes. At least, I think so. Fallion and Midnight can." She glanced at Lodie. "Is that true of all the *Amalanee*?"

"Yes. But you shouldn't need Garzel to do it. Not if you're the horses' true riders. You should just be able to ask the horses to transform for you."

K'lrsa glared at Herin who looked like she had an entire mouth full of bitter root. "Did you know that?"

"Know what?" she snapped.

"That we didn't need Garzel and his sun stone to transform the horses?"

Herin shrugged.

"Herin. You knew? Why didn't you ever tell us?"

"It never came up."

K'lrsa tamped down the surge of anger that threatened to overwhelm her. Of course Herin had known. And of course she'd kept it from them. Knowledge was power, after all, and even with her allies Herin would always keep as much power for herself as she could.

K'lrsa turned her back on Herin, wishing that the woman would just go somewhere and die. "So how do we do this?"

Lodie winced. "I don't know. I just know it should be possible."

K'lrsa glanced up at the sky where the moon was just starting to rise. "Was Herin telling us the truth—that we need the moon for them to fly by?"

"Yes. They don't actually travel in this world, they travel through the land of the moon dream. The light of the moon gives them access in and out."

Badru looked to the others. "I say we try it now. We're not accomplishing anything sitting here."

"We can't do it in camp. Someone will see." K'lrsa glanced towards the main camp.

When had she stopped trusting everyone?

"Well, then let's go somewhere we can."

"Okay."

While K'lrsa and Badru saddled up their horses, Vedhe threw herself onto Kriger's back in an awkward but effective scramble, not even bothering with a saddle.

"Are you sure you don't want a blanket or something?" K'lrsa asked her.

"No. Fine."

"Okay." She mounted up with one smooth motion and they rode towards the entrance to camp.

Two sullen Riders stood guard. One tried to stop them, but Badru rode right past, leaving the guard staring after him in surprise. K'lrsa tried not to laugh as she followed.

"We ride?" Vedhe asked as soon as they were clear of the camp.

"We ride," Badru agreed with a wicked smile.

They thundered off into the night at a full gallop, the camp fading away behind them until it was just the three of them racing across the plains, the wind whipping at their hair, the half-moon shining down upon them, the horses stretched out side-by-side, silver and black and gold, moving with ease across the dry ground. The horses' hooves crushed a small brush here or there, releasing that spicy-sweet scent that K'lrsa always thought of as home.

She didn't want to stop. She wanted to ride on and on forever until she'd left the world behind. Left the Daliph and her tribe and everything else in her dust. Moments like this were some of the few times in her life when she was truly happy, when everything just seemed to fit. No danger she'd say the wrong thing or do the wrong thing. She could just be free.

But eventually the horses slowed and came to a stop. K'lrsa sighed, wishing they could continue on forever, even though she knew that, as much as she wanted to sometimes, she would never leave the people she loved behind.

Badru laughed, looking happy for the first time since they'd left Toreem. Vedhe whooped and danced Kriger in a tight circle. K'lrsa laughed, too, unable to resist their joy.

It was nice to finally have others who understood what it was like to ride Fallion. Who could challenge him.

And her.

"Well?" Badru asked. "Should we fly?"

"Fly!" Vedhe shouted, her face shining with happiness. "Yes, fly."

K'lrsa felt all the worries and cares of the last few days melt away. She nodded. It didn't matter what tomorrow might bring because tonight was theirs.

"Yes," she said. "Let's fly."

CHAPTER 25

O f course, saying they should fly and actually accomplishing it were two completely different things. K'lrsa had no idea how to get Fallion to transform without the aid of Garzel and his sun stone.

She slid to the ground and walked around Fallion as he patiently stood there, letting her study him. Finally, she stood before him. He gazed back at her with his sweet brown eyes.

She waited, hoping for some sort of inspiration, but nothing happened.

She looked to Badru who had also dismounted. "Any ideas?"

He shook his head. "Garzel always touched the teardrop mark with his sun stone. But maybe we don't have to do that?"

"Hm. Maybe." She turned back to Fallion and stroked his nose. "What do you think, *micora?* Do you want to fly?"

He whuffed her hair, but didn't change.

Badru tried ordering Midnight to transform, but Midnight just shook his head and shuffled backwards a few steps.

Vedhe watched them, leaning comfortably against Kriger.

"Maybe we do have to touch the mark?" K'lrsa placed her fingertip on the white mark in the middle of Fallion's

forehead, closed her eyes, and thought about what it was like when Fallion transformed. How he seemed to shiver and his coat shone as if it contained the light of a thousand suns. How beautiful and strong his wings were as they swept the air. How wonderful it was to soar above the world, safe on his back.

He whinnied softly. She opened her eyes.

And laughed.

He'd transformed! His wings spread out behind him, looking as if they'd always been there. He watched her with eyes that now shone with a golden brightness to rival the sun.

"Oh, Fallion, you did it. Thank you, *micora*, thank you."

Midnight had transformed, too. He stood there, with the night sky in his coat, a laughing Badru at his side.

"Do you know what to do?" K'lrsa asked Vedhe.

She nodded and touched the white mark in the center of Kriger's forehead. He shook himself and his silver coat seemed to ripple. He didn't shine the way Fallion and Midnight did. Instead he glowed the way clouds do when lit from behind by the moon. His coat seemed to shift and move, shadows swirling and twining together.

He was beautiful. They were all beautiful.

Fallion nudged her shoulder and whickered softly.

"Okay. Okay. We'll go." She mounted up.

Midnight turned to study them, his eyes the silver of the moon.

K'lrsa shivered.

As much as she wanted to pretend the horses were just ordinary horses that could somehow fly, she knew, staring into Midnight's silvery eyes that he was far more than just a horse. That they were all far more than they appeared.

All these years with Fallion and she'd never known…

What else was right there before her that she didn't see?

She studied Badru and Vedhe. One the man of her dreams—former leader of a great land. The other a foreigner so strange as to be incomprehensible, slender and frail but with a will that could conquer the world.

Both chosen, just like her.

But for what?

She shivered. She didn't want to be special. Or chosen.

She suspected that being chosen meant a lot of trouble and sorrow. Look what had already happened to her.

She shoved the thought away. She didn't want to think about that right now.

She didn't want to think about anything right now.

She just wanted to fly Fallion and forget that there was anything else in the world that mattered other than the perfect union of rider and horse.

She smiled at the others. "Let's fly."

She leaned forward and whispered in Fallion's ear. "Fly, *micora*, fly." His beautiful wings beat the air, once, twice, and then they rose from the ground, higher and higher, leaving everything behind.

CHAPTER 26

K'lrsa laughed at the sheer freedom of being alone on Fallion's back, high above the world, free to go anywhere she wanted.

All the other nights they'd flown they'd had a destination, a place they were desperate to reach. And Herin had clung to her back like a succubus she couldn't shake.

But now it was just her and Fallion and the dark blue sky and the stars that seemed so big and close she could reach out and touch one if only she dared.

Vedhe rode Kriger in big swooping arcs, giggling the whole time. It was a wonder she didn't fall off, but K'lrsa didn't have the heart to tell her to stop. She seemed happy for the first time since K'lrsa had met her.

It was a glimpse into the carefree girl she'd been before slavers came and took her from her home and men used her body against her will, leaving internal scars to match the external ones.

Badru and Midnight flew next to her. Badru smiled at K'lrsa with a smile that made her tingle all over, and she wished for a moment they hadn't come to the tribes. That they'd gone somewhere where no one could find them and they'd have the time to explore that spark between them. Time to dance and touch and laugh in the real world the way they had in the moon dream.

She pushed away such sad thoughts and focused on the moment, staring in awe at the plains spread out below them, stretching in all directions.

No sign of the Daliph's troops. But there, on the horizon, was a large herd of baru, clustered together, ever wary of attack. And there, at the edge of the plains, a desert cat stalked through the night, each deliberate step a display of grace.

She soaked it up, filling her soul with the pure, simple pleasure of being home.

But eventually K'lrsa's thoughts turned to the future.

What would the morning bring? What would the Riders the Council had sent say? Would they find the Daliph's troops? They had to, didn't they?

And what choice would her tribe make when they did? Would they listen to her about the safety of the gathering grounds? Or flee to the false hope of the Tall Bluff Tribe?

She turned Fallion towards the gathering grounds and the path the Daliph's troops would take.

How far had the soldiers come? Was it already too late to reach the gathering grounds before them?

Badru and Midnight flew along at her side, silent. Badru must've felt her tension because he, too, scanned the land below them for sight of the enemy.

Vedhe followed, still laughing as Kriger swooped and dove like some sort of oversized hawk. Eventually, she too fell silent as they flew onward with no sign of the Daliph's troops.

The moon made her way across the sky until she was high above them, and then she slowly started to descend, but still there was no sign of the soldiers.

Finally, Badru broke the silence. "K'lrsa, we should turn back."

"No. Not until I see them." She didn't bother to look at him, her eyes scanning from left to right, looking for any sign that an army had passed by.

"What if we don't find them?"

"We will."

Somewhere birds called out—night hunters on the

prowl—but in the world through which they flew there was no sound other than the steady beat of the horse's wings.

She glanced at the moon now just a hand's breadth above the horizon. She didn't want to be caught on the ground where the Daliph's troops could find them, but she had to know where they were.

She had to see them, to prove to herself that the threat was real, that this wasn't all some sort of weird dream.

She was on the verge of calling for them to turn back when she spotted the large rock formation that marked the gathering grounds ahead.

For a moment, she was relieved. No sign of the Daliph's troops. They still had time.

But as the horses flew closer, she saw the dark shapes of tents staining the ground like a pestilence. Not in the gathering grounds themselves, but just outside, ringing the space so no others could enter.

She flew lower, straining to see who it was. Surely not the Daliph's men come so far in so little time.

No. These were tribal tents. And from more than one tribe.

But predominant amongst them were tents with the markings of the Black Horse Tribe.

She reined Fallion up, fighting the fear and anger that raced through her blood.

The Daliph's troops weren't there yet, but it didn't matter, because the Black Horse Tribe was and they were prepared to block any who sought sanctuary here.

"We're too late."

Badru studied the tents below, his jaw clenched tight. "There has to be a way through."

Vedhe and Kriger trailed behind them, silent, as they passed over the camp two more times, studying the camp for any signs of weakness.

All they had to do was reach the center of that space and they'd be safe, but how? And where were the Daliph's troops if they weren't here?

Shoulders slumped, she turned Fallion back towards camp.

CHAPTER 27

The moon set and they had to land before they made it all the way back. They landed in a wide-open space, the wind scurrying along the dry, broken ground. If nothing else, they'd see an attack coming in plenty of time to react.

K'lrsa paced back and forth the entire time trying to find a way through the Black Horse Tribe's barrier, but she couldn't think of one.

Badru couldn't either. All his training in military strategy and none of it was any help. The best he could do was suggest that they form a v-shaped wedge of Riders and punch their way through the weakest spot. But what good would that do the children? Or those on foot?

As soon as the sun lit the horizon with the color of blood, they continued onward, making it back to camp as the sun finally broke free to beat down upon them.

K'lrsa's mother and brother were there at the entrance, waiting.

"You shouldn't have left. We had to send the last few Riders we had after you." Her mother glared at her from behind crossed arms.

K'lrsa raised her chin. "You shouldn't have wasted your Riders. You know a normal horse can't catch an *Amalanee*."

"Where'd you go?"

"Scouting."

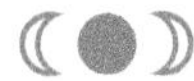

Her brother stepped forward. "Well, then, Rider. Report."

K'lrsa bit her lip. Technically, she wasn't a Rider anymore. She'd forsworn all vows when she vowed to avenge her father. But she didn't really want to get into that right now, so she took a deep breath and said, "We went to the gathering grounds."

"The gathering grounds? How'd you make it that far?" Her brother took a step closer, studying the horses. None were the least bit winded or sweaty.

It was like flying somehow rejuvenated them rather than exhausted them.

"*Amalanee* aren't like other horses." She patted Fallion's neck as he danced away from her brother's inspection.

Her mother scoffed. "You want me to believe you went all the way to the gathering grounds. And let me guess. You came back to tell us it's all perfectly safe and there's plenty of food there for all of us and we should leave immediately."

K'lrsa shook her head at how grief had driven away all her mother's soft spots and left only jagged edges in their place.

"Well? Is that what you found?" D'lan asked.

K'lrsa didn't want to tell them.

She couldn't lie to them, that wasn't who she was. But she knew if she told them about the Black Horse Tribe she'd lose any chance she had of convincing them to go to the gathering grounds.

Badru answered for her. "No, that's not what we found. There's a tribe camped around the perimeter of the gathering grounds. I counted approximately a hundred and fifty tents."

"Around the perimeter? Why?" her mother asked.

Badru glanced at K'lrsa. She shrugged, leaving it to him to answer. "I believe it's so they can attack any who arrive since no blood can be shed on the gathering grounds themselves."

Her mother nodded. "Which tribe?"

"The Black Horse Tribe," K'lrsa forced the words through gritted teeth.

"Well, then that settles it. We're going to the Tall Bluff Tribe."

"Mom, you can't. They'll expel us. And then where will we be."

"You'd rather we fought, tribe against tribe?"

"No, but…"

"K'lrsa. We aren't soldiers. We don't fight."

"But we could. We know how to use bows, we know how to fight hand-to-hand."

"Have you ever killed a man, K'lrsa? Do you know what that's like?"

She nodded.

"Right. I forgot."

"Not Dad. K'var."

"Could you do it again? Now that you know what it's like? Could you do it ten times in a row? Twenty?"

K'lrsa bit her lip.

She wanted to say yes, but she couldn't. She still woke up in a cold sweat some nights at the memory of killing him.

Her mother nodded. "We're hunters but we aren't killers, K'lrsa."

"Neither are they."

But as soon as the words were out of her mouth, she knew that wasn't true anymore.

It had been a member of the Black Horse Tribe who'd killed her father. And a member of the Black Horse Tribe who'd come to Toreem asking for more weapons to attack her people. And it was members of the Black Horse Tribe who now camped around the gathering grounds waiting to slaughter any who opposed them.

Her people weren't killers, but the members of the Black Horse Tribe were.

Her mother turned away and started issuing orders to break camp, sending runners in all directions shouting to awaken the still-sleeping camp.

K'lrsa watched them go, a black wall of despair blurring her vision. Badru touched her arm gently. "We should tell Herin what we saw. See what she thinks we should do next."

He rode Midnight towards their tents and K'lrsa followed, slumped in her saddle as she watched her people prepare to leave.

Why bother?

They might as well stay right where they were. None of it mattered if they didn't reach the gathering grounds.

CHAPTER 28

When they reached the two tents, only Herin and Garzel were outside. Herin was trying to feed herself a bowl of millet with dried fruit in it. She clutched the spoon awkwardly between her maimed fingers, her hand shaking so badly as she raised it towards her mouth that half of the gruel fell off.

Garzel watched intently, his fingers twitching to help.

Herin saw K'lrsa watching and glared, but she scooped up another bite of food and tried again.

K'lrsa slid off Fallion's back, only now feeling the pain of riding for an entire night. She was exhausted. All she wanted to do was sleep, but that wasn't an option.

Badru didn't seem much better as he swung down from Midnight's back, but Vedhe was practically skipping as she moved to the fire and served herself up a bowl of food.

K'lrsa joined her. She'd decided to leave the talking to Badru. She was tired of talking. It never seemed to do much good. She wanted to act, to fight, to strike down her enemies.

Badru smacked the outside of Lodie's tent. "Lodie. Get out here. You'll want to hear this, too."

Lodie crawled out of the tent, her hair sticking out in funny directions, rubbing her eyes clear of sleep. "Have a little respect, would you?" She took the bowl of millet Vedhe handed her and sat down next to Herin.

Side-by-side it was clear they were sisters. They were both taller than almost anyone else in the tribes and shared the same fierce eyes.

Badru glanced back towards the camp, but no one was paying them any attention. Already half the tents were on the ground with people packing them onto the woven frames that could be dragged behind a person or horse.

"We got the horses to fly. All three of them."

Lodie spat out a small rock that she'd found in her food. "You woke me for that?

"No. We tried to find the Daliph's troops. Flew all the way to the gathering grounds looking for them."

Herin set her bowl down. "And? Did you find them?"

"No. But there were people camped at the gathering grounds."

"The Black Horse Tribe," K'lrsa interjected.

He nodded. "The Black Horse Tribe."

"And then some."

"How many?" Herin asked.

"About twice as many as this camp."

Herin ran her tongue over her teeth. "Well, the annual gathering is soon. Maybe they just got there early."

Badru shook his head. "No. This was a camp ready to fight."

"Pzah. The tribes haven't fought each other for four hundred years."

"I saw the weapons stacked outside each tent, ready to use. Bows. Swords. And the way the tents were configured, too."

Herin pursed her lips.

Vedhe added, "Guards. Watching."

Herin frowned. "You're sure it wasn't the Daliph's troops?"

"Positive."

"Then where are they?"

K'lrsa shrugged. "They must be here, we saw them coming, but they aren't headed to the gathering grounds.

"So where are they?"

Badru met her eyes and K'lrsa felt her stomach drop at the certainty and fear she saw there. He turned to Herin.

"They must be circling around, getting behind the tribes. If we go to the Tall Bluff Tribe we'll be walking into a trap." He stood and paced back and forth. "Of course. He's no fool. You said it yourself, Grandmother. And he's not one to accept a stalemate. No, he *has* to win. He *has* to obliterate his opponents. Make them crawl at his feet."

Herin growled. "Badru! Stop pacing and explain yourself."

"Aran's troops. They didn't go to the gathering grounds because they didn't need to. They've spread out along this side of the barren lands. They're going to move forward, driving the tribes towards the Black Horse Tribe. Like herding cattle. They'll be trapped with no choice but to fight."

K'lrsa stood. "Which means our only hope is turning towards the gathering grounds now and fighting our way through before the Daliph's troops arrive."

He nodded.

K'lrsa turned towards the center of camp.

It all made sense, but now she had to convince the Council.

CHAPTER 29

By the time K'lrsa reached her mother—who was standing in the center of the camp issuing orders to everyone she saw—she didn't have to figure out how to convince her to go to the gathering grounds instead. V'kan came riding through the single entrance to camp at the same time, covered in dirt, his horse lathered, slumped in the saddle, his upper arm tied with a strip of baru hide covered in dried blood.

He rode his horse right up to K'lrsa's mother and slid from the saddle.

"V'kan. What happened to you?"

"I was attacked." He paused to take a long drink from a waterskin that someone shoved into his hands.

People gathered around to listen as he continued, "Just a scout, thankfully. But I saw their main camp." He nodded to K'lrsa. "Like she said. Troops from the Daliphate."

"Where?" Her mother asked, her voice sharp.

He grinned. "Near the border with the barren lands. They're behind us and marching south, away from the gathering grounds. We're safe."

A murmur ran through the crowd. V'kan didn't know about the Black Horse Tribe.

K'lrsa pushed forward. "That's what I was coming to tell you. Badru thinks the Daliph's troops are circling around behind the tribes. Once they get there they'll drive us

towards the gathering grounds. We'll be trapped between the two forces."

Her mother stared at her for a long moment, clearly thinking through her options.

"Our only hope is to make a run for the gathering grounds," K'lrsa added, glancing around at the crowd to see if anyone else agreed.

"And then what?" Her mother asked.

K'lrsa shrugged. "Fight our way through to safety."

Her mother scoffed. "Oh, just like that?"

"I'd rather fight another tribe than trained soldiers. And…" She took a deep breath. "If I have to kill again, I'd rather it was one of the people responsible for my father's death than some stranger following orders from a leader he's never met."

Her mother nodded. She turned to the crowd. "Keep packing. We still leave as soon as we can. I'll speak to the Council about which direction we're going."

K'lrsa hovered nearby as the council members gathered to argue back and forth. She knew she'd convinced her mother with the temptation of revenge, but what about the others? Would they see that this was the safest path for the tribe?

D'lan waved her over.

"Yes?" She glanced at the other members of the council, suddenly nervous.

"We think we have a chance," he said. "If we can get the other tribes to the gathering grounds before the Daliph's troops get there we can all band together and force our way through the Black Horse Tribe's guard. But we need the other tribes."

She nodded. It made sense. "How are you going to get them there in time?"

He smiled. "You. As you reminded us just last night, no horse can beat the speed and stamina of an *Amalanee*. You had to've ridden for the entire night and yet your horse doesn't even look winded."

"Okay. I can go to two of the tribes and Vedhe and Badru can go to the others."

"No. They're outsiders. No one will trust them. It has to be you."

She bit her lip. "Okay. I'll do it. And you'll head for the gathering grounds?"

He nodded.

"Do we know if the other tribes are on our side? Dad said the Tall Bluff Tribe…"

Her mother stepped forward. "Things have changed since your father died, K'lrsa. Those who side with the Black Horse Tribe have already gone over to them. Those that remain are on our side."

"Are you sure?"

"I am. Now, go. Get ready. The sooner you reach the other tribes, the more chance we have of surviving this."

D'lan walked her to Fallion, telling her along the way where each of the tribes should be at that moment—none were in their normal camp site.

K'lrsa listened with half an ear, wondering what she was going to tell Badru and the others. She didn't want to leave them behind, but she had to. At least for a few days.

CHAPTER 30

K 'lrsa threw what she needed into a small pack as she explained to the others where she was going and why.

"I'll come with you." Badru grabbed his own pack.

"No." Herin and K'lrsa spoke at once.

"Why not?"

Herin answered. "We need you here."

"Why?"

"The horses. If something happens and we have to flee, they're our only chance of escape."

"But what about K'lrsa? Who will protect her?"

"Pzah. She'll be fine. Or hadn't you noticed that she's perfectly capable of taking care of herself."

"But what if one of the tribes attacks her?"

K'lrsa threw her pack over her shoulder. "I'll take that chance. Badru, please stay here. I need you to help. We aren't trained to think like fighters. You are. Work with D'lan. Come up with a plan in case I fail."

He frowned, but at least he'd set his pack down. "Why should he listen to me?"

"Because you know what you're talking about and he's smart enough to realize it." She gave him a quick kiss on the cheek, waved at the others, and ran to where Fallion stood, waiting for her.

The sooner she left, the sooner she could return.

CHAPTER 31

It took her the better part of a day to reach the Tall Bluff Tribe. Fortunately, they were already on their way towards the gathering grounds and much closer than they normally would've been. She rode into their camp at sunset, demanded to speak to their council, told them what she had to say, emphasized how important it was that they make it to the gathering grounds as soon as possible, and left as soon as the moon peeked above the horizon.

They'd offered her a place to sleep for the night, but she'd refused. She still didn't trust that they were really allies no matter what her mother thought.

She flew Fallion through the night, only stopping to rest when the moon set. She stumbled into the midst of a skinny copse of trees—nothing compared to the actual trees she'd seen in the Daliphate, but enough to provide some shelter from animals or humans out roaming at night—and grabbed a bit of rest until the sun rose and she could continue her journey.

She found the Spring Winds Tribe early the next morning, delivered her message, and continued on.

And so it went until she found the Desert Storm Tribe at sunset on the second day. Again she was offered a place to sleep and again she refused.

She wanted to get back to Badru and the others as soon as she could. Even now they might be reaching the gathering

grounds, facing off against their enemies. What if she was wrong about the plan? What if the Black Horse Tribe attacked them right away?

Fortunately, the path back was much shorter. On the way out she and Fallion had traveled in a gentle arc along the edge of the desert, but going back they were able to cut straight across. It was a more dangerous choice to fly over the desert, but not as bad in the winter months as in the summer months.

As Fallion flew over the sprawling desert dunes, she looked for signs of the Hidden City. She knew from her dreams that it was in the desert, but she didn't know where. And didn't see it as they traveled.

She tried not to worry about what the tribes were doing now. Had they believed her? Would they arrive in time to help her people reach safety?

As she and Fallion flew on through the night, K'lrsa struggled to stay awake. She'd had barely any sleep for three days straight. Even Fallion was showing the signs of exhaustion, his wing beats more labored than usual.

Her stone pulsed a soft silver, urging her towards the ground and the outlines of a small cave. She urged Fallion to land, curious.

It looked familiar. Like the cave where she'd left her father's sun stone and L'ral's bracelet. But it couldn't be the same one. Could it?

Regardless, the pull of the stone was strong enough she knew there was something in that cave she had to see.

Fallion landed outside the cave, his wings disappearing as soon as his hooves touched the sand. She found water and grain stored just inside the cave mouth and scooped them out for him before lighting a torch and stepping into the depths of the cave.

It *was* the same one. There was the scrawling note she'd left in Rider's script and there, her father's sun stone. Why had she left it behind? Why hadn't she kept it?

It was the only thing left of him.

She ran her finger along the colored strings her mother had woven. Knots of protection, strength, and love.

How had she thought someone would just find it and take it back to the tribe?

If they could, most avoided traveling through the desert. Even with the shelters it wasn't safe. Too many tricks and illusions to lead one astray.

She hesitated to grab L'ral's bracelet.

No point now, with F'lia gone. Maybe his mother would want it, but she didn't want to touch it.

He was a traitor. The worst kind.

Finally, she grabbed it just long enough to shove it into the bottom of her pack. Her father's sun stone she wrapped carefully in a small strip of cloth and tucked into the small pouch on Fallion's saddle.

She bedded down in the back of the cave and slept until morning, her dreams haunted by memories of that horrible day.

If only she'd listened to her father…He'd told her not to go to Toreem. But if she had, her whole tribe would be walking into a trap right now. And whether she'd done the right thing or not, it was too late now to turn back.

She'd made her choices, she had to live with the consequences.

CHAPTER 32

She spent the next day awake and restless to continue her journey, hoping she hadn't made a mistake by stopping in the cavern for the night. She could ride Fallion, but she didn't know if the Black Horse Tribe had scouts patrolling the desert. And it would be easier to see the camps from above at night.

She ran her father's sun stone through her fingers, thinking about what he'd tell her to do now.

She wanted to keep it. It was the only thing she had left of him. But she knew he'd want her to give it to her mother. And that D'lan would want it so his future grandson could wear it someday when this was all over.

She'd give it to one of them, eventually. But for now she tucked it back away within easy reach.

As soon as the moon rose, she continued her journey and reached the gathering grounds while the moon was high in the sky.

The Black Horse Tribe was still camped around the perimeter, even on the desert side. There were more tents now. It looked like a few of the Daliph's troops had joined them.

She longed to land in the center of the gathering grounds and take a long drink from the well hidden there in the midst of the curved rock formation, but she didn't.

Just because they couldn't kill her, didn't mean they

couldn't hurt her. And they'd wonder how she'd bypassed them.

Instead, she turned Fallion towards where she'd last seen the White Horse Tribe.

She didn't have far to travel, just out of eyesight of the gathering grounds was their camp, ringed with the baru-hide barrier.

She landed Fallion far enough away no one would see and rode the rest of the way there.

They'd changed things. The barrier was higher. Smaller, too, everyone crammed into much less space than before.

As soon as the Riders at the gate saw it was her, they sent for D'lan. He met her in the center of camp, dark circles under his eyes, stumbling slightly. "D'lan, you look horrible. Are you getting any rest? Eating enough?"

He shook his head. "You sound like K'na."

"Well, you should listen to her."

"I'll rest tomorrow. I wanted to make sure we were secure."

"I noticed the barrier. And the horses are now in the center of camp?"

"Badru suggested it."

"And you listened?"

He nodded. "He was very persuasive. Tomorrow he starts us all on new drills so we'll know how to fight a man with a sword."

"How'd that happen?"

He laughed, smiling for the first time she'd seen since she'd been back. "Challenged our three best fighters to attack him. All at once. Took them out while most of us were settling in to watch."

She smiled. "Good. I'm glad."

"That he took our three best fighters out without any apparent effort?"

"No. That he found a way to convince you to listen to him."

"Good thing, too. I was planning on taking a small group and busting through the Black Horse Tribe line to reach the gathering grounds. He pointed out all the flaws in that plan pretty quick." He narrowed his eyes. "Anything else I should know about him? He seems pretty knowledgeable about all this."

She shrugged. "The Toreem Daliphate is a very different place."

It pained her to lie to him, but Badru deserved her protection. So did Herin and Garzel, as much as she hated to admit it. "Now. Do you want to hear my report or not? Not that there's much to report."

"Did you find all the tribes?"

She nodded. "Didn't stick around to hear what they decided, but they all know now."

"You in love with Badru?"

"What kind of a question is that?"

"A brotherly one."

She shook her head.

"Well? Are you?"

She licked her lips, trying to find the right answer.

"If you have to think about it, the answer is no."

"No...It's not that, it's..."

How much could she tell him? How much did she want to tell him?

She sighed. "The moment I met Badru I knew he was that other half I'd been searching for. But...That doesn't make him perfect. And that doesn't mean it's always easy between us. So, do I love him? Yes. But I'm not sure if that means anything. Not if we can't find a way to live a life together."

"Well, he's welcome here. You know we're always happy to have new blood and a man with his skills is a good addition."

"I know. I'm just not sure he'll want to stay after this is all over."

"Would you go back to Toreem with him?"

"No." She said it sharper than she'd meant to, but it was the truth. She was never going back there. Ever.

"Huh. Well, you'll just have to bring him round to your way of thinking then." He winked. "Knowing you, little sister, you'll do it eventually. Now, I better get some of that sleep you and my wife seem to think I need. Tomorrow's going to be another long day. Your tents are over there." He gestured to where, even in the packed space of the new camp, two tents stood slightly removed on the other side of the horse picket.

"Thanks." She led Fallion away, almost happy.

They were still facing imminent death, but the thought of Badru eliciting that kind of smile from her brother, made K'lrsa's day. And, even though it didn't matter to her what anyone thought of the man she loved, it was nice to know her brother approved.

CHAPTER 33

The next morning, K'lrsa stood in the shadow of a tent and watched Badru walk the Riders through his fighting drills. He was very good at it. Patient, but stern. Capable. At ease.

Even the oldest and most stubborn of the Riders listened to him with respect. Might have something to do with the fact that he could put any of them on their back in the dirt without any apparent effort. And casually demonstrated that fact just as one of the trouble students was about to become really difficult.

He worked his students through the morning, making them repeat a handful of new maneuvers until they could all do them with ease.

He'd tried to get K'lrsa to participate, but she was too tired to learn something new.

Her mother was out there, though, getting thrown and throwing others with a grim determination. She'd been a Rider once and still practiced the hundred and five attacks every day, but it had been years since she was in fighting trim. Still, she was the first to manage a tricky combination of hand and foot attack that had an opponent trip right into the attacker's elbow.

When they finally broke for lunch, Badru threw his arm around K'lrsa's shoulders as they walked back to their tent. "So? What did you think?"

"Very impressive."

He grinned and her heart did a little flip-flop. He was sweaty and grimy but she loved him more in that moment than she ever had.

"I have a plan," he whispered, kissing the spot right above her ear.

"What kind of plan?"

"A plan that will get all your people onto the gathering grounds safely without any need to fight our way through."

"Really?"

He nodded. "I'll tell you about it over lunch."

As soon as they were seated with Lodie and Herin—for once Garzel was nowhere to be seen, neither was Vedhe—K'lrsa asked, "So, what's this plan?"

Herin snorted, but Badru ignored her. "We fly people into the gathering grounds."

"Fly them? How?"

"Easy. Each of us takes a passenger, we fly them into the center of that rock structure—you've noticed it has a u-shape and is hollow in the center?"

"A u-shape?"

"Like this. A curve with only a narrow opening at one end. There's plenty of room in the center for us to land and take off and for people to hide. I scouted it out."

"Did you land there?"

"No. I didn't want to risk capture."

"What if we can't? What if that's part of the protection of the place?"

"Grandmother, Lodie. Do either of you know of any reason the horses can't land in the gathering grounds?"

Lodie shook her head. "None that I know of."

"Doesn't mean it isn't a stupid idea," Herin muttered.

K'lrsa frowned. "Why? It sounds like a great plan to me."

"Until you get shot by one of those soldiers. A flying horse makes a pretty good target, you know. And can we really trust these people? All it takes is one to betray us."

K'lrsa nodded. It was a huge risk. But what other choice did they have?

She leaned forward. "Have you noticed that when the horses fly they don't seem to fly in the normal world?"

The others nodded.

"So maybe no one will be able to shoot us. Because they won't see us."

Herin shrugged. "Doesn't get rid of the risk of betrayal. You can't take this many people in one night."

Badru sat up straighter. "Then it takes us two nights."

"The risk…"

Badru stood, his hands clenched into fists. "It's better than sitting here waiting to die. Look. We'll take the children through first…."

"No, not the children" K'lrsa interrupted.

"What? Why not?"

She nodded at Herin and Lodie. "We need to take them through first."

"Herin and Lodie? Why?"

"And Garzel."

"Pzah. Why waste a trip on us?"

K'lrsa laughed. "You really have to ask why? Because you two are the only ones that know enough about the Hidden City for us to succeed in finding the weapon that'll defeat the Daliph's troops. We can get everyone to safety, but if we don't find that weapon it doesn't matter."

Herin nodded.

Badru turned towards the rest of camp. "Okay. So we take them first and then the children. I'll go tell D'lan our plan."

"No."

"What? Why not?"

She chewed on her lip, hating to say what she was about to say. "Because as soon as you tell D'lan, this whole thing is out of our control. He'll tell my mother, she'll tell the Council, and then we'll spend an entire night debating who should go first and whether we should do it at all. We *will* be betrayed if that happens."

She nodded to herself, thinking it through. "We take Herin, Lodie, and Garzel to safety first. Then we get my sister to round up the children for us."

"K'lrsa…He's not going to like this. I just gained his trust."

"I know. But it's the best way to get as many people to safety without someone betraying us."

Badru nodded, but he didn't look happy. "I hope you're right."

"I hope I am, too."

CHAPTER 34

As they ate dinner that night, K'lrsa couldn't help but stare in the direction of the horizon, wondering if the moon was up yet. She was grateful that the baru-hide barriers shielded them from the Black Horse Tribe, but they also blocked her view of the moon and sun. She'd found herself glancing at the horizon, trying to judge what time it was and running into the stupid barrier at least ten times already.

She wanted to drill a small hole through one of the hides so she could peek through, but instead she tried to force herself to eat another travel bar.

Too bad Garzel hadn't run out of the things yet.

She'd moved the horses next to their tent earlier in the day on the pretext that they wanted to be able to mount up as soon as there was any sign of trouble. D'lan had thought it such a clever idea that he'd had the horse picket split into four and moved to each corner of the camp.

K'lrsa made sure to station the horses between their two tents and the barrier. It wasn't a perfectly hidden spot, but hopefully hidden enough to let them get away without too much attention. Of course, someone was eventually bound to notice a horse that glowed golden like the sun, but it was the best she could do.

Finally, when she figured the moon had to be up, she stood.

"It's time."

Herin followed her behind the tents. They'd debated whether to awaken each horse one at a time or to do them all at once. In the end they'd decided one by one. There just wasn't enough space available for three horses with wings to stand.

K'lrsa stroked the white teardrop mark between Fallion's eyes and willed him to transform. He shook himself and light shivered along his coat as his wings appeared. As always, she felt a wave of awe at how beautiful he was, but that was quickly followed by fear that someone would see him.

"Quickly," she whispered, mounting up and offering Herin her arm.

"As if I didn't know that," Herin muttered, scrambling up behind her.

As soon as Herin seemed settled, K'lrsa whispered, "Okay, *micora*. Let's fly."

With one smooth stroke of his wings, Fallion rose into the air. Immediately, K'lrsa felt a shift. The tents below them looked faded, drained of color. It was a more pronounced difference than she'd experienced before and she wondered if Fallion hadn't sensed their need for safety and shifted into the moon realm sooner than normal.

She clutched his reins as they rose over the camp, waiting for someone to point and shout, but no one noticed the horse flying directly over their heads.

She sagged with relief. She'd thought they'd be alright, but she hadn't been certain. Not until now.

They rode in silence as Fallion's wings beat a steady rhythm through the air. They were probably safe to speak, but she didn't want to risk it, and didn't have much to say to Herin anyway.

As they flew over the Black Horse Tribe camp, K'lrsa studied the sentries walking back and forth along its perimeter, bows in hand. Even though no one in the White Horse Tribe had noticed them flying, she still held her breath, waiting for someone to look up and point, to run after them, bow drawn.

But no one did. Here, too, no one noticed the giant horse flying above them.

Herin pointed to their left and K'lrsa nudged Fallion in that direction. Sure enough, there was the curved rock formation with a hollowed-out center. It wasn't a large space. Definitely not large enough to hold the entire tribe. But it would hold the children, at least.

Fallion spiraled in and landed softly on the dusty soil. As his feet touched the ground she could once more hear the sounds of night—insects chirring and people laughing as if they weren't waiting to kill everyone she loved.

Herin slid off Fallion's back and moved to the side to wait for the others. Soon they were joined by Vedhe with Lodie and Badru with Garzel. Each slipped off silently with a small pack tucked under their arm. Food, water, a blanket, but no more than that.

K'lrsa tried not to think what her people would do if they had to be here for weeks with no tents or stools or any of the niceties of camp.

It was cold in the shadow of the rock, but hopefully they'd have enough warmth if they huddled close together.

She nodded to Badru and they flew back to camp, silent once more.

Three down, a hundred or more to go…

CHAPTER 35

They managed to spirit away twelve of M'lara's friends—two each in two trips—before anyone noticed what they were doing.

When Fallion landed softly back at camp after that third trip, K'lrsa knew they were in trouble.

D'lan stepped out of the shadow of the tent, dragging M'lara by the arm. "How did you do that? You weren't there a moment ago."

K'lrsa slid from Fallion's back and led him forward, out of the way so the others could land. D'lan tried to push past her, but she blocked him. "Wait."

"For what?"

"The others need space to land."

"To land? What are you talking about?"

There was a soft thump and then Badru and Midnight came out from behind the tents, too. D'lan pushed past her, but Badru moved Midnight to block him. "Let Vedhe land and then we'll explain."

D'lan turned back to her. "What's going on here, K'lrsa? Where are the others that were with you?" His voice rose with every word. "And why is my little sister sneaking around camp trying to convince children to follow her here?"

"Do you want me to explain or do you want to wake the whole camp and lose us what little advantage we have?"

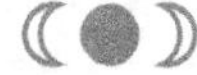

D'lan glanced over his shoulder. Sure enough, a few people had stopped and were looking in their direction. D'lan waved them away, but K'lrsa's mother walked over to them.

"What's this all about?"

"Come with me." K'lrsa led the way back behind the tents. "Vedhe, keep anyone from getting too close."

Vedhe gave a sharp nod and stationed herself next to the tent.

Badru stood at K'lrsa's shoulder as her mother demanded, "So? What are you up to?"

K'lrsa stepped aside. "Badru? Do you want to explain? It was your idea after all."

He seemed surprised, but launched into a quick explanation of what the horses could do, what he'd done the night before, and what his plan was for getting them safe to the gathering grounds.

Her mother looked skeptical, but she didn't interrupt. When he was done, she said, "So you want me to believe your horses can fly?"

K'lrsa nodded.

Her mother rubbed her forehead, a slight smile on her face. "Of course. You father couldn't just get you a nice stallion, he had to get you a horse that could actually fly. "

K'lrsa smiled. For the first time in days her mother looked almost happy. Or at least not bitterly angry.

Her mother glanced towards camp. "We'll have to tell the Council."

"Please don't." K'lrsa almost reached out to physically stop her.

"Why not?"

"I, um…I don't know who we can trust."

"What's that supposed to mean, K'lrsa?" And just like that she was back to the new cold, angry version of herself.

K'lrsa took a deep breath and pulled her shoulders back. This was too important not to fight for. "It means I would never, ever have thought that L'ral was capable of betraying Dad, but he did. I grew up with him. He was going to marry my best friend. If *he* could betray us, then anyone could."

Her mother flinched. "L'ral?"

K'lrsa nodded.

"Why?"

K'lrsa shrugged. She wished she knew.

"Okay. So what do we need to do?"

"I thought we could take the children first. M'lara's rounding them up for us. We've already taken twelve over."

"You don't think their parents will miss them?" Her mother raised one eyebrow.

"I think M'lara's better at sneaking out of tents without being detected than I was at that age and you never caught me at it."

Her mother laughed slightly. "Good point. So children first. And then?"

"Then the adults who don't fight. K'na can go first. She'll know the others we can trust. With three of us going I think we can get most of them out tonight. That leaves the Riders."

"What do we do with them?

"We take them tomorrow night and hold our breath and hope the Black Horse Tribe doesn't discover what we've done until then. The horses can't fly during the day."

"Is that all we need? Two nights?"

K'lrsa glanced at Badru. He shrugged. "I certainly hope so. I don't think we can go more than two nights without them discovering the people we've already taken."

Her mother nodded, knowing as well as they did that whoever didn't make it out on the second night might never make it out.

But they had to try. It was the best chance they had.

"Okay. The others aren't going to like it, but I agree that it's best to keep this quiet until morning when at least the children and non-Riders are safe."

"We should go, then, if we want to get as many to safety as possible."

K'lrsa hesitated.

She felt a desperate urge to hug her mother. She knew she might not hug back, but she had to do it. Who knew what tomorrow would bring?

She stepped forward, threw her arms around her mother, and whispered, "I love you," her voice rough with tears.

Her mother stiffened for a moment, but then she relaxed and hugged K'lrsa back. "I love you, too."

CHAPTER 36

They managed to get almost all of the children to the gathering grounds before they had to inform any other adults. It helped that in the tribes children generally shared a tent of their own rather than sleep with their parents. Only the littlest ones, those under two summers old, or a first child under five summers slept in the same tent as their parents.

M'lara was the last of the older children to leave. She wanted to stay behind and help, but K'lrsa was adamant that she go.

M'lara thrust out her lower lip, her eyes filling with tears. "But I want to stay here with you and Mom and D'lan. I'm old enough to help."

K'lrsa knelt down and took M'lara's hands in hers. "And you are going to help. The children need you. They're over there, alone, scared, with people they don't know. You need to be there to keep them calm. You need to show them how brave you are and how brave they can be. And look? Don't you want to fly? If you stay here too long, you might not get a chance…"

M'lara stared at Fallion, her eyes full of longing as he stretched his golden wings.

"We need you there, M'lara. Come on. We don't have much time before dawn."

She hesitated a moment longer and then broke. "Okay."

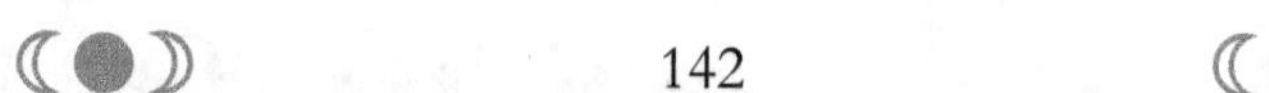

K'lrsa tried to hide her smile as she helped M'lara into the saddle and mounted up herself. They flew to the gathering grounds, M'lara oohing and aahing and pointing out all the things K'lrsa hadn't had time to notice. The way the stars sparkled, the Black Horse sentry with red hair, the tent with a stringed instrument sitting outside instead of a bow.

As K'lrsa flew back towards camp alone she knew those few moments with her sister were moments she'd treasure forever.

Her joy was short-lived.

She landed to find D'lan waiting for her, two unconscious Riders at his feet.

"What happened?" She leapt off Fallion's back, glancing around to see if anyone else was nearby, and led Fallion out of the way so Badru could land when he arrived.

"I caught them sneaking around the tents, trying to watch you. I had to stop them." He glanced towards the main camp, his jaw twitching in anger.

K'lrsa licked her lips—so dry after a night of flying. "So should we take them over? I can take this one, Badru can take the other."

Badru and Midnight landed and Badru came to join them. "What's this?"

"They got a little too curious. D'lan took care of them. I thought we could take them to the gathering grounds." K'lrsa glanced towards the sky. They didn't have time for this. Already the moon was partially blocked by the barricade. They only had time for a few more trips and she wanted at least a few more adults there before dawn.

Lodie had a special gift with animals and children, but even she'd be hard-pressed to keep so many children quiet for an entire day.

"No. We can't." Badru frowned towards camp.

"What? Why not?"

"It's too dangerous. If we take them to the gathering grounds, what's to stop them from telling the Black Horse Tribe what we're doing?"

D'lan nodded. "So what do we do with them?"

"Put them in the tent. We'll continue on with the others." He nodded towards where K'lrsa's mother was approaching, two men and a woman, all crafters, trailing along behind her.

Quickly, D'lan and Badru dragged the bodies towards the nearest tent. One of the men moaned slightly. D'lan waved Badru away. "Go. I'll keep watch on these two."

K'lrsa didn't want to leave, but she had to. She smiled at the woman on the left, G'vina, a woman who'd trained F'lia in pottery when they were younger. "Come on. We don't have much time."

G'vina pulled back. "Where are you taking me?"

"To safety. Please. We don't have time to waste." K'lrsa urged her forward with a gentle but firm hand against her back.

Fallion followed them behind the tent and transformed before K'lrsa could even think to ask him. G'vina gasped as she reached out a tentative hand to touch his wings. "So beautiful..."

K'lrsa smiled. "He is, isn't he?"

Fallion shook his head and pranced slightly as if he knew exactly what they'd said.

"Here. Let me help you up."

G'vina moved as if in a dream, but she didn't resist when K'lrsa boosted her onto Fallion's back.

As they rose over camp, passing Vedhe who was circling above, K'lrsa saw Badru helping one of the men onto Midnight's back. She glanced at the horizon where the moon had dipped so low there was only a slim sliver of it left before it started to disappear.

She shivered. Come morning, everyone would know that they'd found a way to take the children to safety. Some might even guess that the horses had had something to do with it.

And when they did? How long until someone betrayed them?

CHAPTER 37

They managed two more trips before the moon disappeared. K'lrsa and Badru were able to return to camp, but Vedhe was trapped in the gathering grounds. As K'lrsa stared towards where her sister and Vedhe and the others hid, she chewed on her lip, realizing how fragile their plan was.

How had she thought a bunch of children and a handful of adults would be able to hide in the midst of their enemies for an entire day? Surely someone would start crying and they'd all be discovered. And then what?

"It'll be okay." Badru whispered as he pulled her close.

"Will it?" she whispered back.

"Yes."

She buried her face against his chest, letting his assurance comfort her. She didn't really believe it, but she was so tired and scared she needed something to keep her from collapsing.

"Come on." Badru pulled her towards the tent. "Let's rest while we can."

"But the horses…We can't just…"

"D'lan's posted guards. See? And, if things go well, we're going to have to do this all again tonight."

She ducked into the nearest tent, Badru behind her, trying not to think about another night spent flying back and forth, back and forth over and over and over again.

Better that, though, than days spent fighting off attacks from the Black Horse Tribe. Because that's what they'd have to do if their plan was discovered.

As they snuggled down together, K'lrsa so exhausted she barely registered the fact that Badru's strong, lean body was pressed against hers, she asked, "Do you think we've done enough to save them, Badru?"

"I have to."

"But maybe we could've…"

"No. We can only do so much, K'lrsa."

He might be right, but she still wished she'd done more somehow. The difference between success and failure was so close…

One slip and they'd lose it all.

CHAPTER 38

D'lan awoke them around mid-morning with an offering of some dried baru meat and nuts. K'lrsa ate hers with glee. It wasn't fancy, but K'lrsa didn't care. At least it wasn't travel bars.

"So?" she asked as she tore off a chunk of meat with her teeth.

"The camp's swarming like a bee hive. Mother called a meeting first thing. Announced that we'd found a way to get some of the children and non-fighters through to the gathering grounds and that we'd done so last night. Said we'd be taking the rest of the camp through tonight."

"And?"

D'lan's jaw twitched. "And she's had people stopping her all day demanding to know *how* we got them through. The Council's livid. They threatened to take a vote to expel her."

"What?" K'lrsa coughed on the handful of nuts she'd just shoved in her mouth. "They can't do that, can they?"

He shrugged. "They could, but as she pointed out to them, it wouldn't get them any closer to knowing how we did it."

"Has anyone shown signs of betraying us?"

"Yeah." He clearly wasn't surprised. "H'kan tried to leave camp right after the announcement was made. Said she was feeling cramped with all the tents and people around and wanted a walk to clear her head. Almost had one of the guards convinced when I came along and found them."

"What did you do with her?"

"Tied her up and threw her in my tent along with the two from last night. And instructed the guards that no one is allowed to leave for any reason. Added a third guard just to be safe."

"You're sure they were going to betray us?" K'lrsa hated to think they'd come to the point where they were tying up members of their own tribe out of fear.

D'lan shrugged. "No. But we can't take the chance." He stood. "Get what rest you can now. It's going to be a long night for you two."

But she couldn't rest after he'd gone.

At any moment the Black Horse Tribe could discover M'lara and Herin and Lodie and all the others huddled together behind that inadequate rock. (A rock at least as tall as the palace in Toreem and curved to offer them protection from all but one narrow spot, but what she knew about it couldn't overcome her dread.)

She sat in front of the tent and scanned the camp, looking for anyone acting suspicious. She twitched each time a person drifted too close to the baru-hide barrier, stiffened each time someone approached the entrance to camp. All it would take was one person warning the Black Horse Tribe and it would all be over.

Badru at least had something to do with the day.

He gathered all the Riders that weren't on guard duty and ran them through the attacks he'd taught them.

She tried to watch, but her heart wasn't in it.

As she paced and waited and paced and waited she worried what they'd do with the other four tribes. There was no way they could fly them onto the gathering grounds, too. It would take too much time. And require trusting too many people.

She stroked Fallion's nose. Bad enough to risk him for her own tribe.

But if they couldn't fly them to safety, what could they do?

Because if they didn't get them through…None of this mattered.

Worse. Her people would be trapped in the gathering grounds, surrounded by enemies, and no longer protected by the gods. It would be a slaughter.

She shook her head.

She couldn't think about it. She couldn't. There was nothing she could do now and worry would just wear her down.

But she did think about it.

All day.

CHAPTER 39

K'lrsa was lying on her back in her tent, staring at the walls, trying not to go crazy with worry and impatience, when she heard shouting from the entrance to the camp.

She raced outside, dodging around tents and past people too slow to move out of the way, and reached the entrance just as D'lan arrived.

"Who was it?" He demanded.

O'lin—a young Rider who'd only passed the Rider's test the prior summer and still had the bumpy skin of youth— stared back at him, his eyes white with fear. "I tried to stop them. I did. But..." A tear fell down his cheek. "I wasn't strong enough."

"Who?" D'lan's voice was like a boom of thunder.

K'lrsa felt a moment's pity for O'lin, but then she remembered that he'd let someone escape to warn the Black Horse Tribe.

He straightened up. "H'kan. And F'ril. And J'ren and F'len. F'ril was standing guard with us. He pointed to a cloud of dust on the horizon, asked if we thought it was the Black Horse Tribe. He said he had to warn you. When he returned, the others were with him, on horseback. K'don and I tried to fight them, but...We failed. K'don was..."

He nodded towards where K'don lay sprawled, his throat cut.

"Who did that?" D'lan gripped the knife at his belt.

"F'ril."

D'lan shook with anger. K'lrsa grabbed his wrist. "Later. We have to worry about protecting the rest of the tribe now. Look. The horses are too far away to catch now."

Already they were just a speck on the horizon. They'd be at the Black Horse Tribe before anyone could stop them.

She glanced at the sun. If the Black Horse Tribe responded immediately, they could attack before it set.

D'lan's jaw worked. Finally, he turned and gave the high ki-ki-ki of the Rider's call.

From all over the camp, Riders came running. D'lan waited until they were all there and then shouted, "H'kan, F'ril, J'ren, and F'len have gone to the Black Horse Tribe. I expect they'll attack immediately. Prepare yourselves. If we want to live, we have to make it to moon rise."

Without another word, the Riders left to prepare.

K'lrsa didn't have her own bow anymore. She'd lost it when she was taken as a slave. But she could use her father's bow. It was a bit big for her, but better than nothing.

D'lan grabbed her arm. "Go back to your tent. Stay out of the fighting."

"What? No." She tried to wrench her arm free, but he was too strong.

"Only you and Badru can get the rest of us to safety. We can't risk you."

She shook her head. "No. I'm not standing aside. I can't, D'lan."

"You have to! What will we do if you're hurt or killed today?"

"What good will it do for me to stand aside if you're defeated before the moon rises? We all need to fight, D'lan."

He glared at her for a long, long moment. "Fine. But don't get killed."

She smiled. "Wasn't planning on it."

K'lrsa chose one of the prime locations facing directly towards the Black Horse camp. D'lan tried to argue with her again, but her mother overruled him. "She's one of the best shots we have. Let her stay."

K'lrsa *had been* one of the best shots in the tribe. But she hadn't handled a bow in months and could feel the weakness in her arms as she took a practice pull. But she was too stubborn to step aside and let someone else take her place. Especially after her mother chose the spot on the other end of the same barrier.

As they waited for the Black Horse Tribe to arrive, K'lrsa studied her mother. She looked so fierce glaring in the direction of the gathering grounds. So different from the mother who had clothed and fed K'lrsa all these years.

K'lrsa had always known her mother was a Rider before she'd married and that she'd chosen to give that up to raise her family. And her mother had always been strong and confident. But this woman, this fierce warrior ready for blood, was someone K'lrsa had never suspected existed.

K'lrsa wanted to talk to her, to have the time to get to know her better, to know the real her, not just the mother she'd known growing up. But now wasn't the time for it. Maybe later. After this was all over.

She checked the tension in her bow and counted her small pile of arrows.

Fifteen. That's all she had. Just like everyone else.

They hadn't been planning for war.

She had to make each one count. No missing. No hesitation.

She checked the tension in her bow again and arranged her arrows, making sure they were ready for her to fire.

Her mother hissed and K'lrsa looked up. The Black Horse Tribe was approaching. They rode slowly, spread across the horizon in a line three Riders deep.

So many.

Made for easier shooting at least. Miss one, hit another.

Or so she hoped.

Here or there she saw a soldier from the Daliphate, but most were from the tribes. Men for the most part—it seemed the teachings of the Daliphate had already wormed their way in. Either that or no woman was foolish enough to commit herself to such a foul cause.

She recognized men from every tribe, even her own. F'ril rode front and center, a cruel grin on his face.

Hatred flared in her heart. These men were the ones destroying the tribes. The ones who'd killed her father.

She took deep breaths, sinking deeper and deeper into the hunter's version of the Core, until she floated in that place of perfect concentration where nothing existed but the arrow between her fingers and the target.

She chose the third man from the left of center. A man of the Daliphate who rode with an arrogant sneer as if he could barely be bothered to associate with such savages.

As she sunk deeper into the Core, she no longer felt the hot sun beat downing down upon her. No longer smelled the stale scent of too many people in too small a space. No longer heard the sounds of the men riding forward.

Her world was her target.

He stopped just out of bow range, along with the others, his horse prancing slightly, channeling its rider's excitement.

K'lrsa waited, breathing slow and steady.

She waited, and waited, and waited, her attention focused on the chest of the man she'd chosen to kill, willing him to come closer.

As one, the Black Horse line kicked their horses into motion and men and beasts surged towards the camp. Her target raised his arm, brandishing a long sword that flashed in the sunlight.

She didn't hear the roaring shout of their advance. Didn't feel the ground shake under their charge.

In the center of the Core, all that mattered was her target.

She released her arrow and watched it speed towards his heart as she reached for the next arrow. Even as her first target jerked backward, the arrow burying itself in his chest, she chose her next.

Once more, she pulled her bow taut and sighted on a man's chest. Once more, she released a deadly arrow that struck true.

Her next target fell before she could take aim, so she moved on to the man behind him. And then to the woman on his right. And on and on until she had no arrows left to shoot.

Only as she groped for another arrow and came up empty did she realize that she'd know her last target.

B'lina.

They'd played together as children.

She'd had a crush on D'lan.

Cried for days when he married another.

And now she was dead, K'lrsa's arrow buried in her eye.

K'lrsa fell back, shaking. The bow dropped out of her numb hand.

Someone shoved in next to her and started shooting, but she didn't even look at them, just lay there sobbing.

She'd killed B'lina.

Her friend.

She'd killed her friend.

She tried to tell herself it didn't matter who she'd killed. Because every one of those Riders out there was trying to kill her and the ones she loved. For all she knew, B'lina had been there the day her father was murdered. Maybe B'lina had helped drive the stakes into his hands. Maybe she'd been the one to gouge out his eyes.

But, no. She couldn't believe it. She couldn't believe that someone she'd known her whole life was capable of that.

The fight raged on—she could hear the sound of swords clashing from outside the entrance—but she no longer cared.

She stumbled away, blind with sorrow, the scents and sounds of battle overwhelming. Horses and men screamed. The tang of blood filled her nostrils and coated her tongue.

At any moment the Black Horse Tribe would overwhelm their defenses and ride through camp slashing and killing all who remained.

She should turn back, grab a knife or a bow, and keep fighting.

Her tribe needed her.

But she couldn't.

She couldn't bring herself to kill anyone else. Even if it meant her own life and the lives of those she loved.

She stumbled into her tent and collapsed, covering her ears against the sounds of death all around her.

CHAPTER 40

Badru found her at twilight. He was covered in sweat, a bloody gash on one arm and another along his brow that someone had stitched up with more speed than finesse.

"There you are." He pulled her tight, clinging to her, shaking. "I was so worried they'd taken you or you were injured or…"

He held her so close she could barely breathe.

"Are they gone?" she whispered.

He nodded.

"How many dead?" She tried to force away the image of B'lina toppling backwards from her saddle.

"Of ours? Or theirs?" There was a slight laugh in his voice. He was excited, high on the thrill of battle.

She shrunk away from him. "Either. Both."

He released her, frowning. "Not many for us. They didn't challenge the barriers. And the fact that they chose to use swords instead of bows helped a lot." He wiped his face with the back of his arm, but it didn't help remove any dirt. "They retreated just before the sun set, but they'll be back in the morning. If we don't make it out tonight, they'll overwhelm us tomorrow. They aren't foolish enough to make the same mistakes twice. But you should've seen it, K'lrsa. D'lan and I fought side-by-side to protect the entrance. None could get past us."

He grinned, his teeth as white as the moon.

She buried her face against her knees and shook, curled up like a small child.

"Are you okay? What's wrong?" He raised her chin so their eyes met.

Tears ran down her cheeks. "I killed someone I used to know. D'lan used to chase her with desert snakes when we were little. She'd run away squealing but then come right back for more. And, I...I killed her. I put an arrow through her eye."

He held her gaze. "If you hadn't she would've killed you."

K'lrsa shrugged. She didn't care. She'd rather die than kill someone else she knew.

D'lan ducked inside the tent, looking happier than K'lrsa had ever seen him. He pounded Badru on the back. "Our hero."

Badru blushed slightly, but his grin matched D'lan's. "I just fought like everyone else."

"Don't be modest!" He turned to K'lrsa, eyes alight with memory. "He took a sword off one of the first to attack the entrance and then he single-handedly defended the entrance against three fighters. They couldn't get past him. All those moves he'd been trying to teach us? Nothing, compared to what he did. They didn't stand a chance."

Badru shrugged, but he couldn't suppress his glow at D'lan's appraisal. "Most of them didn't know the first thing about holding a sword. If I'd been facing the Daliph's men instead, it would've been a very different story."

K'lrsa bit her lip. How many had he killed? How many were people like B'lina that she'd known?

D'lan didn't notice. He was too happy. "Well, thanks to you, we'll have a chance to get everyone to safety tonight. Let me know when you're ready and I'll send the first Riders your way."

D'lan left, whistling softly to himself.

K'lrsa turned away, shaking her head.

How could they be so happy about this?

"K'lrsa..." Badru touched her shoulder and she flinched away.

"Are you mad at me? What did I do? I thought you'd be happy I'd found a place here."

"No…I just…How can you be *happy* you killed all those people?"

He sat back. "I didn't take pleasure in it, if that's what you think. But I am happy. To be here with you, alive."

She swallowed, trying to understand the mix of emotions she was feeling. "But how were you able to keep going? When you saw them, dead at your feet? When you knew that *you* had done that? That you'd…"

He pulled her close to his chest, wrapping his arms around her as he rested his cheek against hers. "I was trained to fight from the time I could walk. It wasn't a decision I made each time I struck. It was instinct. Someone slashes at you, you counter. And you counter in a way that means he won't strike again. You don't think. You can't think. Not when your life is at risk."

"But now. Now you're laughing and joking and…"

He sighed. "I'm sorry those people had to die, K'lrsa, but I won't apologize or feel bad for what I did. They wanted to kill me. And you. And everyone else here. I did what I had to do to stop them. And I'd do it again if I had to."

She pulled away from him.

"K'lrsa? Are you mad at me?"

She shook her head. "No. I just…Get some rest and some food. I'm going to find my mother."

She left him without a backward glance.

She should be grateful. He'd helped protect her people. He'd risked his own life for theirs, acted as a member of the tribes, and found himself a place amongst her people. It's what she'd wanted him to do.

People smiled at her and thumped her on the back as she passed by because of what he'd done. He'd not only found himself a place, he'd restored her to hers.

She should be grateful.

But she couldn't help wondering how many he'd killed. And how many might still be alive if men like him and his grandfather had just left her people alone.

CHAPTER 41

She stood at the entrance to camp.

The ground was dark, churned into mud by the blood of the men and women who'd fought there. Those who hadn't survived were piled one on top of the other outside the entrance, arms flung here, heads lolling to the side there, eyes open and vacant.

She swallowed the bile that burned the back of her throat, not wanting to add another horrible smell to what was already a terrible scene.

Grel with their greasy gray feathers and fat, waddling bodies had already started to gather, none yet bold enough to approach. O'lin stood between them and the bodies, covered in dirt and blood, a sword in his hand.

He screamed at the grel and his anguish matched her own. The birds glared back at him with their baleful red eyes. She turned away.

So many dead. And more would have to die before the end. At her hand if she used the weapon Herin and the Lady Moon had told her about.

But what other choice did she have?

Ask Badru to do it for her? Let him carry the blood of hundreds on his hands?

She knew he'd do it, but was that any better?

She found her mother at the center of camp, issuing orders. She, too, looked happy, and for a moment K'lrsa

wondered what was wrong with her that she didn't feel the joy of victory like the others seemed to.

She almost turned away, but she couldn't. She had to do this. For M'lara. She stepped forward. "Come on. It's time to go. I'll take you across."

"No. I'm not going until everyone else has made it." Her mother turned to a Rider and nodded as he held out an armful of bloody arrows. "Put them with the others."

K'lrsa grabbed her arm. "You have to come."

"No. I don't."

"But someone has to be there to lead in case they find us."

She nodded. "That's why D'lan is going."

He joined them, not smiling anymore. "You should be the one going."

"I don't have a wife waiting for me at the gathering grounds, pregnant with our first child. You do."

K'lrsa frowned at her. "No, but you do have a child waiting for you."

She shook her head once, sharply.

"Mother. Please." K'lrsa reached for her mother, but her mother drew back.

"We don't have time for this. If you want any chance at getting everyone out tonight, you need to start immediately."

She wanted to argue, but her mother's stony expression told her she'd be wasting her breath. Her mother turned away, pulling two Riders with her.

K'lrsa watched for a long moment.

No point in waiting. Her mother had clearly dismissed them. "Come on, D'lan. Let's go."

D'lan gestured for two more Riders to follow and they made their way back to the horses.

Badru, who'd just emerged from his tent, intercepted her. "What is it? What's wrong?"

"My mother insisted on staying."

D'lan joined them. "She told me she's not leaving until everyone else is out."

Badru nodded. "Then we better hurry."

None of them pointed out that it wasn't going to be possible. That there were too many people still left to get them all out in one night.

K'lrsa gave Fallion a perfunctory kiss on the nose, stroked his teardrop mark to awaken him, and was on his back before his wings had fully formed. "Come on, D'lan. Let's go."

D'lan hopped up behind her without argument, and they took flight before he was fully seated.

As they rose above the camp, K'lrsa tried not to notice the dark stains on the ground, the bodies piled haphazardly outside the shelter, the grel flocking closer, cawing for the dead.

D'lan leaned forward. "You have to convince her to leave, K'lrsa. Even if she isn't the last one."

She snorted. "Like I can make her do anything she doesn't want to do."

"Do you think the horses can carry three at a time?"

"No. There's no room with the wings. And..." She bit her lip as she glanced at the moon, now just a small portion of her full self. "As the moon weakens each night, the horses seem to as well. Fallion isn't flying as fast tonight as he was the night we left Toreem."

D'lan cussed quietly. "Do you think you can get everyone out?"

"I'll try. It's all I can do."

They spent the rest of the flight in silence.

They both knew it was impossible. No need to say it.

CHAPTER 42

When they reached the gathering grounds, they found a very bizarre sight.

Herin, Garzel, and Lodie stood at the mouth of the rock, the children and other adults huddled against the walls farthest from them. At least fifty Riders from the Black Horse Tribe stood on the other side of the entrance, trying to get in. But they couldn't.

As Fallion circled in for landing, K'lrsa saw a Rider run forward and then stumble backward as if he'd hit a wall.

Another threw a rock, but it too was stopped by some invisible protection.

The magic of the place was protecting them.

K'lrsa sighed, relieved that at least something was going their way.

She knew she should just take off and let D'lan deal with it, but she had to know more. "Herin."

Herin turned towards her, but didn't move closer.

"Is that part of this place? Or did you do something? Will it hold?"

Herin shrugged. "Must be part of the place. We didn't do anything." She glanced back at the Riders still trying to break through. "Seems we're protected as long as we're in here."

K'lrsa nodded. "Good. The last few we bring may just have to jump off the horses' backs, but looks like you can all fit."

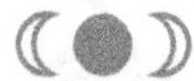

Herin snorted. "Not very comfortable for more than a night or two."

K'lrsa rode Fallion closer so the Riders could see him. She raised her voice to make sure they could hear her. "At least we have the gods on our side."

Herin snorted softly as the Riders backed away. One stepped forward. "Who says?"

Fallion flexed his wings and she nudged him a step closer. The man backed away as she glared down at him. If the barrier did fall, maybe they'd think twice now about attacking.

She turned back to Herin. "I have to go."

She didn't wait for a response. She needed every moment she had if she was going to save her mother.

She, Badru, and Vedhe spent the rest of the night shuttling one Rider after another to the gathering grounds. They barely took time to land before they were off again, dragging a new Rider with them or unceremoniously dumping them at the other end.

All she could think about the whole night was her mother, standing guard at the entrance, refusing to leave until everyone else had made it to safety.

As the moon made its slow way across the sky, they brought thirty then forty-five then sixty Riders across. But still time was against them.

She knew, deep in the pit of her stomach, that it wasn't enough. They wouldn't be able to save everyone.

As the moon finally dove for the distant horizon, K'lrsa landed Fallion back at camp.

The tents had long since been dismantled. Already, some Riders had left, dragging what supplies they could towards the Tall Bluff Tribe.

Another ten Riders remained, standing patiently next to their horses. Her mother's horse was saddled, but it didn't carry supplies.

K'lrsa walked to her mother. "I can make one more trip."

She nodded towards three Riders who stood off to the side. "Then take one of them."

"No. I'm taking you."

She shook her head. "Someone needs to distract the Black Horse Tribe so the others can escape."

"It doesn't have to be you."

Her mother smiled a soft little smile. "No, it doesn't. But I want to do this."

"Why?" The word was pulled out of her throat, taking her heart with it.

"Living without your father is like living without a part of myself. I can't do it anymore, K'lrsa." There were tears in her eyes. "At least this way, my death will have meaning."

"Don't talk like that!" K'lrsa fought the urge to shake her. "I miss him, too, you know. It's like a great big gaping hole opened up inside me the day he died and nothing I can do will fill it."

Her mother touched K'lrsa hand, her calloused fingers rough against K'lrsa's skin. "I know. I know you loved him and you miss him. But a wife's love is different from a daughter's. A wife becomes one with her husband. She entwines her life with his."

K'lrsa opened her mouth to argue, but her mother pressed on. "A daughter is meant to live her life without her father. She's raised to be strong enough to live without him. He's her foundation, not her world."

"That's not true, Mom. I can't do this…Not without him *and* you. Please. I'm not this strong." Tears poured down her cheeks, but she didn't care.

"You are." Her mother hugged her tight. "You're your father's daughter. You can do anything."

K'lrsa hung her head as her mother released her.

"I'm sorry, K'lrsa."

"Then don't do it."

Her mother smiled a sad little smile. "Not for that." She brushed a piece of K'lrsa's hair behind her ear. "For doubting you. For thinking you'd murdered your father. For telling you you weren't special when I knew you were."

"Mom, stop. Don't say these things. Don't…"

Her mother pulled her into a fierce hug and then released her. "Go. Now. Before it's too late."

K'lrsa hesitated for a moment. There were so many things she'd wanted to tell her mother, to ask her, but there wasn't any time left. "I love you."

"I love you, too. And D'lan and M'lara. Now go."

K'lrsa stumbled away, barely able to see through her tears. She threw herself onto Fallion's back and helped the old, grizzled Rider who'd been waiting for her to mount up behind.

As Fallion took to the air, his wings moving so slowly it was if they flew through mud, she saw the last ten Riders racing away towards the Tall Bluff Tribe.

Her mother watched them go, two Riders at her side, and then looked up and waved one last time before turning away.

Even though her mother couldn't see them, K'lrsa waved back before turning her attention towards the gathering grounds.

As the moon slid towards the horizon and Fallion's wing beats slowed even further, K'lrsa wondered if they'd make it back in time. What happened if the moon set before they landed? Would they just fall out of the sky?

They hung over the Black Horse Tribe camp for what seemed like forever as Fallion pushed on, struggling for each wing beat.

"Please, *micora*, you can do it," she whispered as they flew over the edge of the rock formation and down into the center of the people packed tight together, no room to even move as they cleared a small space for her and Fallion to land.

They were almost to the ground when Fallion's wings disappeared and they dropped. Fallion stumbled, but he didn't fall.

They'd made it.

They were safe.

She looked back towards where she'd left her mother.

They'd saved so many, but they hadn't saved them all.

CHAPTER 43

K'lrsa climbed to the top of the rock formation, cutting her hands on the sharp edges, fumbling for places to hold onto as she pushed herself forward, desperate to see, to know what would happen to her mother. She trembled with exhaustion with each move, but she couldn't stop. She had to see.

As the sun colored the distant horizon red and gold and orange, she reached the top and crawled to the edge.

The ten Riders who'd left when K'lrsa did were a smudge on the far horizon—visible for anyone who cared to see. The Black Horse Tribe were all awake, readying themselves to attack once more.

Her mother rode forth, the two other Riders flanking her.

She rode until she was just outside the Black Horse Tribe camp and then stopped. K'lrsa's heart pounded so hard in her chest she couldn't hear anything else

Her mother had a bow hung from her saddle and a full quiver of bloody arrows strapped to her back. So did both of the Riders at her side.

A man strode forward, tall and proud, wearing the brown robes of the Daliphate, a red sash tied at his waist. "What do you want?" he sneered.

"To negotiate surrender."

K'lrsa almost laughed. Anyone who knew her mother would know she wasn't there to surrender.

"Send a man then instead of wasting my time with a woman. Unless you're here as my prize?" He made a crude gesture and turned back towards camp, laughing.

Before anyone could react, K'lrsa's mother had pulled the bow from her saddle, strung an arrow, and shot it through the man's neck.

He collapsed to his knees, blood gushing from his wound, as he choked on his own blood.

The camp buzzed like a hornet's nest after it's been kicked.

Men ran in all directions, shouting. None seemed to think it might be wise to fight back.

K'lrsa's mother took careful aim, shooting one man after another. So did the Riders at her side.

Any person who stopped to issue orders died.

Any person who reached for a bow died.

Bodies lay everywhere and still her mother and the two Riders shot their arrows.

K'lrsa shuddered at the carnage while at the same time taking pride in each and every strike. Her mother wasn't one to die peacefully, to let fate dictate her life. She sat in the midst of chaos and was its master.

But eventually, she had no arrows left to shoot. Same for the Riders at her side.

The enemy moved forward in a huddle, bows at the ready, in groups of at least twenty. They came from the left and the right. Cowards, too afraid to stand and face their foe with honor.

Together they fired.

Arrows blackened the air as they sped towards K'lrsa's mother and her two companions.

Her mother watched them come, unflinching, waiting for the death she'd chosen.

Arrows pierced her chest and her throat and her thigh. Her horse reared, screaming as arrows buried themselves in his chest.

As blood gushed from the wound in her throat, K'lrsa's mother smiled.

She smiled.

And then she, too, fell.
K'lrsa clawed at the ground, completely bereft.

CHAPTER 44

It was cold and windy and miserable on the top of the rock, but she couldn't stand the thought of being around others.

What if they tried to cheer her up? Reminded her that this is what her mother had wanted? That she'd freely chosen to sacrifice herself for others?

Or worse yet, acted like they understood what she was feeling. Had they seen both of their parents die a brutal death? No. Then they didn't have the first clue about how she felt.

Best to just isolate herself.

Plus, the cold and wind fit her mood. She sat on the top of the rock and sulked, glaring down at where her mother's body still lay, untouched. If even one grel dared touch her body...

K'lrsa scanned the skies, full of fury, waiting for a target, wishing she'd brought her bow and arrows with her.

From behind her came the scraping noise of someone climbing.

"Go away. I don't want to talk right now."

It was Badru. It had to be. Who else cared enough about her to climb up here?

But she didn't want to see him right now. He'd gloried in the fight, in killing people she'd known her whole life. What was he to her? A handsome man she'd seen in a dream?

Sure, he'd been kind to her. And she was attracted to him. And they did seem to fit together well.

But…

Really, truly, at the end of the day he was just someone she barely knew.

With a loud oomph the person behind her flung themselves over the last little ledge of rock. It wasn't Badru.

She didn't care.

Whoever it was—a woman by the sound of it—she didn't want them there.

Lodie settled down next to K'lrsa, the ease with which she sat belying her years.

K'lrsa ignored her, choosing to focus instead on her mother's body. At least she'd died quick. Unlike the rest of the tribe that was going to starve to death. Or the other tribes that were going to be slaughtered once the Black Horse Tribe and the Daliph's men attacked.

What had she accomplished? She'd trapped her people here. Kept them from fleeing to safety. Maybe they should've run. They would've lost access to the desert, had to flee their home land, but at least they'd be alive.

Lodie finally spoke. "Badru wanted to come up here. As soon as you started to climb, he tried to follow you. I told him not to."

"Why?"

Lodie sighed. "Because I think there could be something between you, given time. But I thought you might lose that connection if he were here when your mother died."

K'lrsa glared at her. "What makes you say that? How would his being here ruin things between us?"

Lodie smiled, slightly. She actually smiled. It took all of K'lrsa's control not to lunge at her and push her off the rock.

"You forget. I too lost the ones I loved."

"So that makes you an expert in how I feel and how I'll act?"

"No."

They sat there in silence for a long moment as K'lrsa watched two women of the Black Horse Tribe drag her mother's body into the shelter of camp. A man in the Daliph's colors tried to stop them and one of the women shoved him so hard he tripped and fell on his butt.

K'lrsa smirked.

Lodie spoke softly. "Just be glad you saw how they died."

"Be glad?" K'lrsa stared at her. "You see my mother's body down there? You see how many arrows they shot at her? And my father? He was staked to the ground, his eyes gouged out, his belly slit open. You think I should be *glad* I saw that? That my last memory of them was this?" She was shouting by the time she finished, so consumed by anger and bitterness that she couldn't contain it.

"Yes." She pointed down to where the women were tending her mother's body, carefully removing each arrow. "You know your mother chose her end. You saw how she faced her death with calm. And your father. You know he didn't die groveling at some man's feet or screaming in pain."

"You don't understand! The memories of how they looked at the end will be burned in my mind forever. The last memory I have of my father is of his sightless faced turned towards me, begging me to kill him." Tears streamed down her face. She hated it. She hated the memories and the pain and how she couldn't do anything to fight them.

"You know the last time I saw my daughter?" Lodie asked, her voice low and tight. "She was laughing as she chased after her father. Three summers old. Full of life, full of joy, laughter bubbling out of her, the sun shining on her face."

"I'd rather have that as my last memory," K'lrsa muttered.

"But that isn't my last memory of her." Lodie stared straight ahead, her jaw quivering as she looked back on horror. "My last memory of my daughter is a memory of a soldier standing before Aran, telling him exactly what he'd done to her and to my husband. Every single vile thing. Every scream. Every hurt. Every little detail. And Aran laughing about it..."

K'lrsa's skin prickled at the agony in Lodie's voice. "He might've been lying."

She nodded. "He might've been. And I hope he was, for their sakes. But I'll never know. I'll never be free of the nightmares I have imagining their last moments. My husband could've fought back, stood proud, just like your mother did. But I'll never know, because I wasn't there."

K'lrsa bowed her head. It was so easy in the haze of her own grief to forget the pains of others. "I'm sorry, Lodie."

Lodie moved closer and wrapped an arm around her shoulders. "It's okay. I told you, I've lost someone, too. I understand the rawness of your grief even if my loss and yours were different."

K'lrsa closed her eyes and wept, grateful for the woman's steadying presence.

At last, Lodie drew back. "Are you ready? We don't want your mother's sacrifice to have been in vain. We need to decide how we're going to get the rest of the tribes through to safety."

K'lrsa nodded.

She wasn't ready. Not really. But Lodie was right. They needed a plan.

She stood, the chill wind stinging every little bit of exposed skin. The women had taken her mother's body into a tent on the gathering grounds. They were probably washing it right now. But that was just an empty shell.

Her mother was gone forever...

Or was she?

CHAPTER 45

K 'lrsa scrambled down the rocks as fast as she could, scraping her elbows and tearing rents in her pants. She didn't care. They didn't have much time left.

She pushed through the people until she found Herin and Garzel, huddled in a corner, as far away from everyone as they could get—which wasn't very far.

She grabbed Herin's arm as she leaned close. "I need you to bring my mom back."

Herin shook her off. "Pzah. What kind of fool are you?"

Lodie joined them, panting for breath with a few scrapes of her own. "What's wrong? What is it?"

"She can bring my mother back. We still have time." She turned back to Herin. "I saw two women take her body into a tent here on the gathering grounds. We won't be risking our lives if we take her body back."

"No." She flicked a glance at Lodie. "I promised Lodie I wouldn't use that magic again."

"Oh come on, Herin. You and I both know that if it were Badru dead again that you'd use it in a heartbeat. Why won't you do it for my mother?"

"I said no. I won't do it."

"Then give me the knife and candles. I saw what you did. I heard what you said. I'll do it myself."

Lodie grabbed her shoulders and shook her. "Haven't you learned anything, you foolish little girl?"

"Ouch. Let go of me." She struggled and squirmed, but couldn't shake Lodie.

Lodie leaned forward until her nose was almost touching K'lrsa's. "Your mother chose this death. Just like I chose mine. You have no right, NO RIGHT, to take that from her. She wanted to be with her husband in the Promised Plains. Who are you to tell her she can't go? Who are you to make her live a life she doesn't want to live anymore?"

K'lrsa felt the tears blossoming behind her eyes. She didn't want to cry. She didn't want to. But she couldn't help it. "She's my mother. What right did she have to leave me behind? What right did she have to make that choice?"

Lodie pulled her close and held her as she sobbed. "It was her life, K'lrsa. I know it hurts that she chose to leave you, but you have to let her go."

K'lrsa collapsed in Lodie's arms, unable and unwilling to hold herself together anymore. So much had happened since that day she'd found her father and she just couldn't take anymore.

"K'lrsa?" a soft, scared little voice asked.

She looked over to see M'lara standing there, sucking on her thumb, something she hadn't done since she could walk.

"K'lrsa? Are you okay? You're not going to leave me, too, are you? I don't want to lose you, too," she wailed.

"Oh, M'lara. Come here, little one." K'lrsa sat down on the ground and let M'lara crawl into her lap, cradling her tight as M'lara hiccupped and sobbed, her tears wetting the front of K'lrsa's vest.

"You aren't going to go away, too, are you?" M'lara looked up at her with those sad, brown eyes and K'lrsa felt her heart break.

"No. I promise. I'm here for you. I might have to leave for a little bit, to make all these bad people go away, but I will come back to you. I won't abandon you."

"Promise?"

"Promise. I will always come back to you as long as I'm able to."

M'lara nuzzled against K'lrsa and fell asleep, sucking on her thumb once more. K'lrsa pulled her tight, determined not to let her experience another moment of loss or pain.

She looked up to see Herin watching her, worry etched in the corners of her eyes.

"What is it?" she asked, but Herin shook her head and turned away.

CHAPTER 46

The Council, K'lrsa, Badru, Lodie, and Herin debated throughout the rest of the day and into the night how to bring the Tall Bluff Tribe through to safety, but were no closer to an answer by the time they arrived late the next day than they had been when they started.

They couldn't fly that many people to safety.

Not in one night.

And not when the moon was almost gone from the sky.

D'lan wanted to fight their way through, but more of the Daliph's troops arrived just after the Tall Bluff Tribe. Hardened, fierce warriors with the marks of combat etched into their skin, they paced the lines of the Black Horse Tribe camp, itching for a fight.

How could the tribes stand up to men like that?

K'lrsa's only consolation was that her own tribe was safe.

They'd found that they could pass beyond the perimeter of the rock formation and none from the Black Horse Tribe could touch them. But if they didn't find a way to bring the tribes through within the next two days when the moon left the sky and the gathering officially began, it would all be for nothing.

K'lrsa and Badru climbed to the top of the rock formation, ostensibly to study the enemy, but more to escape the tensions of too many people kept together in too small a space.

Vedhe joined them. "New tribe. We rescue, yes?"

K'lrsa shrugged. "As many as we can, I guess. But..." She grimaced. "We have to bring the adults first this time."

Badru paced back and forth, shaking his head. "It won't work. They won't leave their children behind like that."

K'lrsa clenched her fists, wishing she had an enemy right there before her that she could kick and hit. "But we need the votes. If we can only rescue sixty tonight, it has to be those who can vote. Maybe...Maybe the rest can flee with the children?"

Even if they did, though, they'd only be safe for a day or two. The Daliph's men would pursue them.

Vedhe shook her head. She was so young, but her eyes were so old. "Children first."

"I want to rescue them, Vedhe, but we have to think of the future of the tribes. Not just individual lives."

"Children *are* future."

"Yes. Eventually. No children, no future. But...If we're no longer members of the tribes those children might as well be dead anyway. They'll be taken as slaves or have to travel into exile. What kind of future is that?"

Vedhe raised her chin. "Better slaves than dead."

"Is it? Is it really better to be a slave than dead?" she demanded.

Vedhe nodded once. "Yes. Dead is dead. Slave is chance to not be slave. Chance to fight. Chance to be free."

Badru stepped between them. "Enough. We need to decide what we're going to do."

K'lrsa glared at both of them. "Fine. So who are we going to rescue? The children we won't be able to feed and who'll be trapped here after we lose the vote or those who can actually make a difference?"

Badru and Vedhe both replied. "The children."

"But..."

Badru shook his head. "The adults can at least fight. Maybe they'll hold them off another night. If we take the adults and leave the children, the children will be used against the adults. You won't have your votes if the children are left behind to be used as hostages."

Vedhe looked back and forth between them, shaking her head in disgust. "Right thing to do," she said, and walked away.

K'lrsa frowned. If only life were that simple. Black, white. Right, wrong.

CHAPTER 47

That night they managed to bring over half of the children from the Tall Bluff Tribe, twenty-five in total. It wasn't near as many as they'd hoped for, but with the moon so weak, so were the horses.

Each wing beat was now a struggle; they flew so close to the ground, K'lrsa worried they wouldn't even clear the Black Horse Tribe tents.

As she, Badru, and Vedhe huddled together in the early morning chill, K'lrsa sighed. "I don't think we can risk flying them again tomorrow night. And the night after that the moon will be completely gone. That means we can't bring anyone else in for another three nights at least."

Badru nodded.

Vedhe shivered but didn't answer, her gaze focused somewhere that only she could see.

K'lrsa hung her head. "We should rest. I want to…" She swallowed heavily. "I want to be awake to watch when they attack the Tall Bluff Tribe."

She stumbled off to find a blanket she could huddle under. It was colder in the shadow of the rock where the sun didn't reach, but at least there was no wind to slice through her clothing. She missed her tent. Or even one of the dilapidated barns they'd slept in on the way out of Toreem.

Badru didn't follow and she was sort of glad for it.

She didn't know what to do with him. Part of her desperately wanted to latch onto him and have him fill the void in her life left by the loss of her parents. But another part of her was so raw with grief that any human interaction hurt.

K'lrsa fell asleep immediately. She was so emotionally and physically exhausted nothing could keep her awake, not even cold stone and the misery of knowing all their efforts had been for naught.

When she awoke late the next morning, she climbed to the top of the rock formation and waited for the Black Horse Tribe to attack, but they didn't. The Daliph's troops clearly wanted to, but the new leader of the Black Horse Tribe held them back, arguing passionately throughout the day, gesturing towards the distant horizon where K'lrsa knew the remainder of the Daliph's troops were.

The Spring Winds tribe arrived late in the day and camped alongside the Tall Bluff Tribe. K'lrsa shivered to see them so close and yet not be able to do anything to help.

The next day she once again climbed to the top of the rock formation. She paced back and forth, back and forth, back and forth all day, watching as first the Winter Rest tribe arrived and then the Desert Storm tribe arrived.

By sunset all of the tribes were there.

All that was missing were the remainder of the Daliph's troops. And those weren't far behind. From where she stood, K'lrsa could see them, a dark smudge in the distance, less than a day's ride away.

As soon as they arrived, the Black Horse Tribe would attack.

It was going to be a slaughter and there was nothing she could do to stop it.

CHAPTER 48

K'lrsa climbed back down the rock, the weight of a thousand deaths on her shoulders. The sun burned on the horizon, a harbinger of doom, and then disappeared.

As soon as her feet touched the ground, Vedhe grabbed her wrist and dragged her towards the horses. "Come. We go now."

K'lrsa pulled free. She didn't need this right now. "We can't fly. There's no moon tonight. Remember?"

"I know. We ride." She mounted up on Kriger's back.

Badru was already mounted up. When K'lrsa looked at him, he just shrugged.

K'lrsa shook her head. "We can't go anywhere now. It's the Trickster's time. And did you happen to notice the men surrounding us? Do you understand that we can't just ride through them?"

Vedhe narrowed her eyes. "Vedhe not stupid."

K'lrsa buried her face in her hands. "I know. I'm sorry." She took a deep, calming breath. "Let's try this again. Will you please explain to me what we're doing and where we're going?"

Vedhe screwed up her lips, searching for the words. "Man. Little. Fat. Laugh lots. He show me way."

"A little fat man showed you the way? Where is he?"

"Not here. When Vedhe sleep. He talk. In desert."

"The Trickster? You want us to trust the Trickster?"

K'lrsa winced as half the camp turned to look at them.

Herin approached. "What is this? What are you doing?"

"She wants us to ride somewhere. She said the Trickster showed her the way. Like I'm about to trust that little..."

"Actually..."

K'lrsa glared at her. "What?" She rolled her eyes. "Let me guess, there's something else you've known all along and not bothered to tell us."

Herin gave her such a quelling look she stepped back half a step. "No. Not this time. But I do know that the Trickster owns the between times. Twilight, dusk. And also the nights the moon leaves and arrives. And he does have paths that aren't part of this world. How do you think he leads people astray?"

K'lrsa crossed her arms, not wanting to hope. "How can we trust him?"

Herin gestured towards Kriger. "He sent Vedhe the horse didn't he?"

"What are you talking about? Sent her the horse?"

Herin waved the question away. "No time to get into all of that. If Vedhe thinks she can find her way through the Trickster's land, then you should listen to her."

"I don't know..."

"We don't have a choice. If you can't get those people to safety tonight, they all die tomorrow."

K'lrsa sighed. Herin was right, as much as it galled K'lrsa to admit it. "Fine. But you are going to tell me everything you know about these horses and the gods when we get back."

"Of course." From the way Herin's eyes narrowed, K'lrsa knew she wasn't about to give up any of her secrets.

As she scrambled into her saddle, K'lrsa shook her head to think that her life was in the hands of a god who'd let someone die just for sport.

CHAPTER 49

O nce K'lrsa was mounted on Fallion's back, she turned to Vedhe. "So? Now what? Do we wait for a fog to descend or…"

"Follow." Vedhe turned Kriger towards the center of camp. Badru and Midnight followed behind her with K'lrsa and Fallion at the end.

She led them to a clear space outside of the rock formation and then turned Kriger right, after a dozen more steps he turned left, a dozen more then left again, another dozen then left once more until he was basically right back where he'd started, but he just kept going as if this was exactly what Vedhe had intended.

K'lrsa was about to call a halt when she noticed that Vedhe and Kriger were blurring before her eyes. She could actually see through them to the handful of people watching from the Black Horse Tribe camp.

As she and Fallion followed, a gray fog wound its way around Fallion's legs and drifted across the path in front of them, thickening until K'lrsa could barely see Badru and Midnight, the world around her completely gray.

Fallion continued forward until K'lrsa knew they must be walking right through the center of the Black Horse camp. And yet, there were no tents to block their path, no people walking before them.

No sounds of a camp at all.

They continued onward, in that cold, wet, foggy gray nothingness, occasionally twisting and turning and circling back until K'lrsa had no idea where they might be or in what direction they were headed.

She gripped Fallion's reins so hard her fingers ached.

The fog clawed at her skin and clung to her hair and clothes. It shoved its way down her throat until she gasped for breath.

She wanted to run, to turn aside and seek the safety of her familiar world, but it was too late. She had to trust that Fallion knew the path, and that Vedhe was leading them true.

Out of the fog came the sound of cruel laughter, first on her right, then on her left. It echoed all around her.

"Scared?" the Trickster taunted from somewhere in the gloom.

"Go away you vile little brat." She swatted at the air even though she couldn't see him.

He laughed. "Oh ho. Is that any way to talk to a god when you're in his world?" He danced across Fallion's path and then disappeared once more. Fallion continued onward, steady as ever.

The fog thickened to the point that K'lrsa couldn't even see her own hand in front of her face. Badru coughed somewhere ahead and she shivered in relief to know she wasn't alone.

The Trickster pinched her and she flinched, looking left and right, desperate to know where he was, to protect herself from his foul tricks.

He pinched her again, this time on the left, and giggled as he dodged her slapping hand.

And again on the right. And then the left. Twice.

"Stop it!" K'lrsa screamed.

The fog swallowed her words.

It swallowed everything until she could barely feel Fallion moving beneath her.

She tensed, waiting for the Trickster to attack again. God or no, she was going to give him a swift kick in the head if she could manage it.

But as Fallion continued onward, the fog began to thin. Once more they turned right and then left and then left and then left, but this time they spiraled back into the normal world, its dark sky devoid of the moon.

K'lrsa took deep gulps of the crisp, clean air. "Oh, thank you."

She turned her face towards the breeze, letting the wind play with her hair. It carried the scent of horses and fire and people, smells she'd never loved so much in her life.

"K'lrsa?" Badru gestured her forward to where members of the Tall Bluff Tribe stood, arrows trained on Vedhe, muttering to one another about the scarred foreigner who'd just appeared in their midst.

"Coming." She rode forward, waving for their attention. "Please, put your weapons down. We're here to lead you to safety."

She hoped.

She had no desire to journey back through that gray nothingness and no faith that the Trickster wouldn't claim someone for his own.

CHAPTER 50

I t wasn't as hard to convince the tribes to follow them as K'lrsa had thought it would be. They remembered how she'd warned them about the Daliph's troops and the story of how the horses could fly had already spread with the White Horse Tribe Riders who'd fled that final morning.

But it was Badru who tipped the scales.

He was so passionate, authoritative, and certain of what needed to be done that no one could stand against him. A few members tried, but they all fell before his final question: "What other choice do you have?"

Because the truth was, they were out of time and out of choices. They couldn't go back and they couldn't stay where they were.

None wanted to brave the desert. Not without adequate preparation and with a tribe that knew the desert as well as they did waiting for their return.

It was either follow Vedhe into gray nothingness or face the combined might of the Black Horse Tribe and the Toreem Daliphate.

The choice was simple.

In silence, each of the four tribes packed up their tents, staring nervously towards where the Black Horse Tribe was camped. It was too dark to actually see more than a fleck of red here or there where a late-night fire burned. (From the Daliph's men not the Black Horse Tribe. The

Black Horse Tribe hadn't lost all common sense even if they had lost respect for tribal ways.)

Still, everyone was worried that the Black Horse Tribe would discover what they were doing and attack.

They'd never been at war, never had anyone want to kill them before, so every moment in that dark night burned with the frisson of hatred.

By mid-night hundreds of members of the tribes had gathered. They huddled around Vedhe, shifting restlessly, staring out into the blackness.

Badru rode Midnight back and forth down their ranks, stopping and talking to a woman here, a man there, ruffling the head of a young boy who touched Midnight's flank with awe in his eyes. He stopped next to Vedhe. "It's time. Vedhe will lead small groups through. K'lrsa and I will stay here until everyone has made it."

He nodded to Vedhe.

"Children first. Come." She shot K'lrsa a challenging look, daring her to object, but K'lrsa lowered her eyes. Vedhe had led them here, she was in charge.

A group of children—older ones with a few brave young ones who'd pulled away from their parents— gathered before her. "Hold tight." She gripped her hands together to show them. "You lose me. You stay. I come back. I find you. Understand?"

They all nodded, eyes wide with fear, bodies shivering with excitement. She smiled, the scars twisting at her mouth not hiding the tenderness in her eyes, and turned Kriger back towards camp.

They walked forward in a single line then turned right, then left, then left, then left again, the children holding hands as they slowly disappeared, one after the other, swallowed by the black night and a gray fog.

A woman gasped. Another started crying, her husband trying to reassure her that their child was safe. K'lrsa and Badru rode amongst the people, stopping to comfort where they could, arguing where they couldn't.

She tried to hide her own fear, but she couldn't keep herself from looking towards the gathering grounds, wondering if the children had made it through to safety.

She knew the Trickster and his deviant ways; he'd lead Vedhe and the children into the midst of the Black Horse Tribe camp just for a laugh.

Or into a gray nothingness they'd never escape.

How had she ever thought they could trust him?

She talked and cajoled and begged the others to have faith, all the while doubting that Vedhe would ever return.

And then, just as people's voices were starting to grow louder with fear and anger, the high ki-ki-ki of the Rider's call pierced the night.

The first group of children had made it to safety.

They all stared at the place where Vedhe had disappeared, waiting for her return. It seemed to take even longer for her to come back, but at last she did.

People shoved forward, a surge of desperation. Vedhe shook her head and gestured them back. "Mothers. Babies. More children."

A man stood his ground. "Why?"

Vedhe glared down at him. "I say so. And I lead."

Badru rode his horse between them. "We have to work together if we all want to make it through before morning. Sit down."

The man glared at both of them—foreigners, unfamiliar with the ways of the tribes—but he didn't intervene as Vedhe led the rest of the children and the mothers with babies—tied to one another with whatever could be found, blankets, harnesses, ropes—away into nothingness.

Those left behind waited again, flinching at every sound from the darkness, staring into the black of night even though nothing could be seen, until the high ki-ki-ki of the Riders' call rang out once more.

So it went on through the night.

Vedhe looked more and more exhausted each time she returned, but she didn't complain, didn't stop to rest. She just led the next group through. Just kept going like she had when she was a slave forced to walk barefoot through the desert heat.

She took the grandmothers and grandfathers. The artists and crafters.

And finally, the Riders, some from each tribe until only twenty remained with K'lrsa and Badru. As they waited for Vedhe to return one last time, K'lrsa peered into the brightening pre-dawn sky and wondered if it was too late.

And, if it was, should they run? Out into the desert to wait for night to fall once more?

Or fight their way through, using surprise to overwhelm their enemy?

If they ran, there might not be enough votes. If they fought, they might die.

Vedhe and Kriger appeared, Vedhe slumped in the saddle. Kriger stumbled as his feet caught on the flat ground.

K'lrsa rode Fallion closer. "Are you okay? Can we make it through in time?"

Vedhe nodded. She forced herself to sit up and address the remaining Riders. "You lost. You stay. I find you," she sighed.

They nodded. Everyone knew the rules by now.

Vedhe turned Kriger and led the way first to the right, then left, then left, then left. Badru rode in the middle, K'lrsa at the end, Riders between them.

As she stepped into that gray nothingness once more, K'lrsa thought she saw the sun color the horizon.

They'd made it only just in time.

CHAPTER 51

Fallion walked through the gloom, unerring in his confidence as they twisted and turned their way towards safety. K'lrsa slumped forward, too tired to keep her eyes open, a slight smile on her face.

They'd done it. They'd made it through.

They'd brought everyone to safety in one night.

The gods truly were on their side, even the Trickster.

The man in front of her stopped abruptly and Fallion lurched to a halt, almost stepping on him.

"What is it? What's happened?"

Had the Trickster returned? Where was he? She couldn't see anything through the cloying gray fog that surrounded them except for the vague outline of the man stopped ahead.

The muffled sound of words carried up and down the line. Finally, the man in front of her turned so she could see his face. "D'vil says he lost sight of the man in front of him, so he stopped. We have to wait for the scarred one to come back for us."

"Wait?" But the sun had already risen. Vedhe couldn't come back for them. Not until the sun set again.

She shivered as the fog gathered round, creeping through her clothes, pressing its chill tendrils against her skin and tangling in her hair.

"Oh you poor thing." The Trickster laughed from

somewhere to her right. "Are you lost? Stranded here in *my* world?"

He pinched her.

She slapped at his hand, catching him with a hard blow.

"Oh ho. That wasn't very nice, K'lrsa dan V'na. Do you think your pretty little horse can save you from me?" he sneered.

He pinched her again and she flinched as she saw the man in front of her grip his reins tight, his eyes wide with fear.

The Trickster must have pinched Fallion, because he reared, almost throwing her off his back, biting at the air with his teeth.

She leaned forward, stroking his neck. "Calm, *micora*. Calm. Don't let him get to you."

She heard the Trickster move up and down the line, taunting and pinching. The muffled shouts and cries echoed back to her.

They couldn't survive this. Not for a day. Someone would break and run.

"Stay calm," she shouted. "Stay where you are. Don't let him scare you."

But the sounds of panic were rising, the shouts growing more frantic.

They couldn't wait until night. They just couldn't.

What happened when the Trickster grew bored of pinches and slaps?

What happened when one of the Riders tried to run?

When *she* tried to run?

The fog shoved its way down her throat, blanketed her eyes. She couldn't do it. She couldn't spend another moment like this.

She leaned low over Fallion's neck, something Herin had said about the horses prickling in her mind. If Kriger was sent by the Trickster, then…Then maybe Fallion was sent by Father Sun. "*Micora*, somewhere out there the sun is shining. Can you…Can you use it? To banish this fog? Can you shine like you do when you fly?"

She waited, not daring to breathe, hoping she was right as the sounds of panicked men and horses continued.

At first, nothing happened. The fog was as cold and oppressive as ever.

But then, slowly, Fallion started to glow. First, he shone like dawn's gentle golden light. And then brighter like the sun as it just starts to appear, its tentative rays reaching for the sky. And finally like the sun at midday, full and bright and clear, blinding in its brilliance.

The fog tried to fight back, to thicken and attack, but he shone brighter still, like the light of a hundred suns. A thousands suns.

K'lrsa closed her eyes, crying out in pain.

Slowly, the light faded to something gentler.

A man laughed.

She opened her eyes.

They were in the land of the moon dream. She recognized the rolling desert dunes, the clear air and too-blue sky.

It was early morning, the sun barely risen.

Fallion was once more just a normal golden horse. The fog was gone.

Four men on horses before her, still in a line.

"What now?" the closest one asked. They were all looking to her.

"Good question," she answered.

One of the men, grizzled with age, suggested they ride towards the distant mountains, figuring that eventually they'd leave the desert and could find their way to the gathering grounds from there.

The others agreed, deferring to his judgement.

"Wait." K'lrsa swallowed heavily as they all stared at her, clearly surprised that she would try to command them.

The one who'd taken charge crossed his arms. "What?"

She licked her lips as they glared at her. "This isn't our world. We're still on the Trickster's path. The fog is gone, but this isn't our desert. We're in the land of the moon dream."

The man laughed. "The land of the moon dream?" He shook his head and turned away.

"You would've said the same about flying horses a few

days ago. Or about walking a twisted path through fog to bypass your enemies. And yet, here we are."

The man turned back to her. "So what do *you* suggest we do? Sit here and let the sun bake us to death?"

"No." She chewed on her lip as she tried to figure out what to do.

She thought for a moment of calling for Father Sun and asking his help, but then she remembered eyes that burned like banked coals and the way he'd sent her to Toreem without warning or preparation.

He wasn't one to lead lost strays to safety.

Not even the Trickster had done that.

It had been Vedhe.

Vedhe and Kriger.

Which meant…

She leaned low over Fallion's neck and whispered in his ear. "We need to reach the gathering grounds, Fallion. Where Midnight and Kriger are. Can you find them? Can you lead us there? All of us?"

He bowed his head, his golden mane sparkling in the sunlight, but he didn't move.

He pawed the ground and sniffed the air.

He shook his head and whinnied softly.

And then he nudged the horse before him to the side. And the next horse and the next horse until they were at the front of the line next to where D'vil had stopped.

Once more, he pawed the ground and sniffed the air. K'lrsa sat on his back, tensed, waiting for one of the men to laugh, but none did.

Finally, Fallion took a tentative step forward.

"Follow us," K'lrsa called as Fallion took another small step and another.

She didn't turn to see if the men were following. Either they were or they weren't. She just hoped Fallion was able to lead them to safety.

He stopped often to sniff the air or paw at the ground. And he changed direction often, sometimes seeming to double-back on their path. But K'lrsa didn't question him or stop him.

She trusted him.

They continued on until the sun was almost at midday and then Fallion turned right, then left, then left, then left, and they stepped into the center of the gathering grounds.

They were on the stone platform, surrounded by all of the tribes who'd gathered for the initial convocation.

A wall of sound battered them. Some cried out in joy, some in anger.

Badru raced towards her, his arms thrown wide, smiling a smile so large it was a wonder it didn't split his face in two. A young woman with a baby clutched to her breast was right behind him, running towards one of the men.

Row upon row of Black Horse Tribe members glared at them from their side of the dais, muttering and pointing.

A man at the back of the crowd aimed an arrow at her. She watched, frozen, as he pulled his bow taut and then released.

As Badru came closer, the arrow spun through the air. Time slowed.

She could see each and every revolution of the arrow, but was powerless to stop it.

And then, just as Badru reached her and it seemed the arrow would bury itself in his back, it was gone.

Those who'd seen what the man did, drew back in fear, muttering and shouting about dark magics.

She slid off Fallion's back and Badru hugged her, pulling her close, whispering how glad he was to see her.

But K'lrsa didn't care about that or about the man and his bow.

Because there, in the midst of the Black Horse Tribe, was F'lia, the friend she'd thought was dead.

CHAPTER 52

The shouting crowd, Badru trying to pull her back, none of it mattered.

All she cared about was F'lia. Her best friend. A girl who'd always shone like the sun. Someone so gentle and happy and pure that she couldn't imagine her capable of murder or plotting to betray her own people.

But there she was. In the midst of the Black Horse Tribe.

And her face was mottled with rage, her lips twisted into a sneer that made her uglier than anyone K'lrsa had ever seen.

K'lrsa pushed her way through the crowd, shoving aside men and women who glared at her as she went.

She stopped in front of F'lia, unable to breathe all of a sudden, so many conflicting emotions pushing against one another that she felt like she'd burst. Joy that her friend was still alive. Anger that she was here, with these people. Fear that she'd been wrong about her friend all along, that the beautiful surface hid a heart as black as night.

"You're alive," she finally managed, the joy winning out over the anger and fear.

"So are you." F'lia's jaw worked as she glared at K'lrsa. "Where were you?"

"I went to the Daliphate. To…To avenge my father. I thought the Daliph had killed him."

F'lia's eyes filled with tears as she stared at K'lrsa. "My mother said you found L'ral. That he's dead."

"Yes. Didn't you…" But no. No one had found her message. Her mother had only known about her father's death because of her moon stone and his sun stone, but L'ral and F'lia didn't have that. "So this whole time…?"

She looked away. "I thought he'd left me."

"Left you? You were his world."

She shrugged, tears rolling down her cheeks. "It was different after he became a Rider. We spent less time together. And that last year he'd become sort of angry all the time."

"He had?" Why hadn't she noticed?

F'lia shrugged. "You weren't around much to see it. You were always off with Fallion, hunting, or traveling to the other tribes with your dad. You didn't see how he'd changed." She blushed. "I actually thought, that maybe the two of you…"

"Had what? Run away together? After I killed my father, I suppose?"

"No! I knew you hadn't. I mean, I knew if what your mother said was true that there had to be a reason for it. That something must've happened."

K'lrsa felt a weight lift off her shoulders. At least someone she'd known and trusted had believed in her.

Somewhat.

"So why did you leave the tribe? They thought you were dead."

She shook her head. "I don't know. I was angry. And sad. And I…I was going to give myself to the sands. You and L'ral were gone and I didn't know what else to do. I felt so betrayed. But…Then I decided to try and find you guys."

"You left with nothing. Why didn't you just go back?"

She shook her head. "I didn't want to. I couldn't. I ran into J'vin. I wasn't sure what he was doing so far from his lands, but he offered to take me back to his tribe, to give me shelter."

K'lrsa glanced to where a tall dark-haired man at least as

old as D'lan stood watching them with brilliant green eyes. "And?"

F'lia shrugged, but wouldn't meet her eyes.

"F'lia?"

"I was angry. And hurt."

"And? Now?"

She ran a hand over her swelling belly.

"You're pregnant?"

F'lia nodded, a slight smile on her face.

"Oh, F'lia, that's so great! Congratulations!" K'lrsa hugged her, careful not to press too hard. "Does your mother know?"

She shrugged one shoulder and nodded slightly.

"Oh, this is so wonderful."

F'lia wouldn't quite meet K'lrsa's eyes. "J'vin wants me to marry him."

K'lrsa glanced at the man again. He seemed too cold, too intense for her friend. "You don't have to, you know."

"I know. But…"

"F'lia. You're a talented artist. And beautiful. Any tribe would welcome you. If you don't want to go back to the White Horse Tribe, find another. You don't have to marry this man just because he wants you to."

"He is the father. And he…" She leaned closer. "He says the only way my baby will be safe is if we're with his tribe. K'lrsa…" She looked around, her eyes wide with fear.

"I know. That's why I came back. He's wrong. We'll defeat them. And when we do, you'll come back to us?"

F'lia bit her lip with a sideways glance at J'vin, but nodded.

"Good. Now I better go." She hugged F'lia one last time. "I'm glad you're alive."

"Me, too. That you're alive, I mean."

They both laughed and for one more moment K'lrsa was able to forget why they were all there, but then she had to push her way back through the unfriendly faces of the Black Horse Tribe and into the midst of the scared faces of her own tribe.

She stopped at the base of the dais next to Badru and D'lan and turned to face the enemy.

It was time. Time to see if they'd done enough to save the tribes or if F'lia's lover was right and the only safe place to be was with the Black Horse Tribe.

CHAPTER 53

The wise woman of the Black Horse Tribe stepped to the middle of the dais and raised her arms for silence. Her tribe responded, but none of the others did. Some even started talking louder just to make their point.

But then the wise man from the White Horse Tribe joined her.

And the wise men and women from the other four tribes.

Together, united, they raised their arms for silence.

This time the seething mass of people obeyed, turning to watch, their silence a living, breathing thing fraught with anticipation.

In unison, the six wise ones invoked the Lady Moon as they did every annual gathering. They called on her for peace, protection, and prosperity. Next they invoked Father Sun, asking for his mercy and thanking him for his warmth during the cold times. And they invoked the Trickster, begging him to continue to lead their enemies astray, leaving unspoken their wish that he spare the tribes his tricks.

It was the same invocation as every year. Just so many meaningless words. As always, the wise ones completed the invocation with a bow towards the back of the dais, a space where none were allowed to stand. The space K'lrsa and the others had stepped out of just a short while before.

Never before had anything happened.

But this time it did.

A silvery moon beam shone from the back of the dais. The wise ones backed away and the crowd leaned forward as it grew wider, filling the empty space, and, then, out of the ray of light stepped a woman so graceful and beautiful that none could look away.

K'lrsa recognized her at once. It was the Lady Moon. Her features didn't ripple like in the moon dream, but K'lrsa recognized her nonetheless. She was in the guise of the matron—old enough to be wise, but young enough to be alluring.

"Go, my children." The Lady gestured for the wise ones to return to the crowd.

They stumbled down the dais, into the midst of the equally surprised members of the tribes.

The Lady stepped to the center of the dais and studied the crowd. "As you do every year, you have gathered here, members of the tribes, to exchange news, to see friends, to make plans for the new year, to renew the bonds that hold you together as one people with one purpose." Her voice chimed, as beautiful as she was, reaching the far edges of the crowd.

Most stared at her rapt, but a man near the base of the steps in the Black Horse Tribe section sniggered.

The Lady turned her depthless gaze upon him and he quailed before her, shrinking back through the crowd until he was on the outer fringe.

She smiled slightly as she turned back to the crowd. "Unfortunately, as that man and the hearts of many of you here today show, you are no longer unified in a single purpose. Four-hundred years ago my husband, my son, and I brought you together. We gave you a home. We promised you protection. In return we asked for one thing—that you protect the Hidden City and keep the desert safe from those who would exploit it."

The crowd was absolutely silent. Not even the babies held in their mother's arms moved or squirmed.

She turned towards the Black Horse Tribe. "There are some among you who don't believe in us anymore. Who would turn away from the sacred trust we gave you. Who would lead strangers across the desert for profit."

"And why not?" A man stepped forward from their midst, tall and strong and fierce. "Why not trade with our neighbors? They gave me the medicine that saved my wife's life. What have you ever given me?"

The Lady nodded, acknowledging his question.

The man wasn't the only one glaring at the Lady with anger or distrust. K'lrsa shook her head, amazed by their gall. Couldn't they see they were challenging a god?

Maybe they could and just didn't care, but surely they had to know that an angered god was a dangerous god?

The Lady addressed the crowd. "It's true that we don't give you everything you could need or want. That some die that we could save."

The man's gaze darkened further.

The Lady turned to address him, but her words carried throughout the space. "We did that once. Gave everyone everything they asked for. And we learned that they want what they should not. That they ask for what no one should ever ask for. And that times of plenty twist them away from the right path. No matter how much we gave, they were never satisfied." The sorrow in her voice vibrated in the air. "They always wanted more. When we gave everyone all they could want, the world burned." Her eyes flashed silver. "Never again will we be so foolish."

"So what good are you then? If you won't help? If you won't give us what we need?" the man demanded.

The Lady tilted her head to the side, studying him. "We do help. But there is more to life than gold. Or silk. Or fine foods."

"I didn't want gold. I wanted my wife to live." He glared at her, his whole body shaking.

She frowned. "But it was her time. You all must pass to the Promised Plains at some point."

"She was only twenty summers old."

"Life must have balance. Those who are born, must die. And not all can live to old age. There must be uncertainty and challenge and loss."

He shook his head in disgust. "You're worthless. Go away."

K'lrsa stepped forward, but Badru pulled her back and whispered, "She's a god. She doesn't need you to defend her."

But didn't she? Because so far she wasn't doing a very good job of convincing anyone to follow her.

The Lady sighed and turned back to the larger crowd. "We are at a crossroads. Your ancestors swore to protect the desert and the Hidden City. They swore not to reveal its secrets to strangers. But there are those among you who lead trading caravans across the desert and would willingly sell the secrets of the desert to any with gold enough to pay."

She turned towards the Black Horse Tribe, but her voice continued to carry to everyone present. "We will not force you to honor the vow your ancestors made us. That is not our way. But I will say this."

Her eyes flashed silver as she scanned the crowd. "If you choose not to protect the Hidden City. If you decide to lead those who are not part of the tribes across the desert—be they trader or slave—we will remove all protections we have granted you."

She stepped forward, the cold anger on her face more fearsome than a shout. "No longer will there be shelters in the desert. No longer will the barren lands protect you from the greed of the Daliphana. No longer will your moon stones and your sun stones guide you. All of this, we will withdraw."

She glared at the man who'd spoken before. "And any who try to cross the desert—be they of the tribes or foreign—will find that the desert has turned against them. That the sun burns so hot they blister through their clothes. That the sands shift before and around them until they are lost. And that water, once available in enough quantity to help a man live if not thrive, is lost to them."

There were angry mutters and frightened whispers from the crowds.

"So you're abandoning us?" the man demanded.

"No. You have a choice to make. Renew the vow your ancestors took and continue to benefit from our protection. Or turn away from us and live a godless life with all that entails." She raised her chin, a breeze blowing her hair back as her eyes flashed silver once more. "You must decide. As a people. Follow us or go your own way. We will not intervene, but we will enforce your choice."

The wind whipped to a frenzy, spitting dirt and grit into the air. K'lrsa shielded her eyes as those around her cried out.

A moment later, the wind was gone.

And so was the Lady.

CHAPTER 54

The crowd erupted in conversation, people shouting and screaming at one another. Some rushed the dais, looking everywhere for the Lady, but there was no sign she'd ever been there.

K'lrsa covered her ears to stem the noise, but it didn't help.

The man who'd challenged the Lady shouted to anyone who'd listen that he didn't care what protections she removed, he didn't need her or any other god. Look at his wife. Look at the Black Horse Tribe lands, now all desert. Where were the gods when he'd needed them?

Another man from the Black Horse Tribe shouted right back that he was a fool to believe they could trade with the Daliphana if they didn't have access to the desert. It took four days to cross to the northern lands. How would they make it without protection and water and with the sun and sand against them?

Eventually, the wise ones managed to quiet the crowd.

The wise woman for the Black Horse Tribe stepped forward. "You heard the Lady. We have a choice to make, as a people. Either we swear an oath to the gods and accept their protection and their limitations, or we choose to sever our ties with the gods, to make our own way forward."

The man who'd shouted at the Lady opened his mouth to speak, and the wise woman silenced him with a glance and a raised fist that held a carved wooden rod. "All who want their say, will have it."

It was the oath stick that each member of the tribes swore upon when they reached the age of fifteen summers. The paint was flaking from its surface and large chunks looked like they'd been gouged out of it, but it was still solid and whole.

"Only he or she who holds the oath stick may speak." She looked at the man once more. "You want to argue, you wait your turn. Who's first?"

The man yanked the stick from her hand only a moment before the man who'd been arguing with him.

He spoke passionately about all of the benefits he'd seen from trading with the Daliphana and the distant northern lands across the desert. He pointed out his wife in the crowd, fully healed from the summer fever that had almost killed her. He held up an arrow with a metal tip, that glinted in the late day sunlight, and told how that little bit of metal he'd traded for had changed their lives. How they dined on baru almost every night, no longer constrained by poor weapons.

K'lrsa listened with narrowed eyes. Much of what he said was true. But was it worth the sacrifice of everything they were?

Next came the man he'd argued with. He spoke of how the tribes counted on the gods to protect them. How he'd sheltered in the desert more than once, protected by their benevolence. He spoke of the distant Daliphana and how they had never before dared to cross the barren land, but how they might covet the lands of the tribe if there were no barrier to keep them back.

Back and forth it went. First one side, then the other.

Those waiting to speak lined the steps of the dais and wound around the crowd like a gigantic snake.

K'lrsa listened to everyone, Badru at her side.

As the arguments continued, people saying the same thing in different ways, others began to drift away. First the children left. What did they care about some argument they didn't understand? Their friends were there and they wanted to play.

Slowly, others drifted away, one by one, two by two, until only a small core remained.

But that small core argued back and forth, neither side willing to concede. They talked well into the night, long past the point where the moon had shown herself as a sliver in the sky. The same arguments over and over made by the same people.

At last, the wise woman took the oath stick back. "Enough for now. Sleep on what's been said here. We'll continue in the morning."

K'lrsa and Badru made their way back to the White Horse Tribe tents that had been set up near the center of the gathering grounds. (One of the many blessings of taking Vedhe's path into the gathering grounds was they actually had supplies once more, not just what could be carried on a flying horse's back.)

Herin, Lodie, and Garzel were seated a little distance away in front of two tents.

"Why didn't you stay?" K'lrsa sank down on a small stool and took the hunk of baru Garzel offered. She was so hungry she would've eaten one of his travel bars.

Herin shrugged. "The first day is never worth listening to. By mid-day tomorrow it'll have devolved into a handful of arguments. Then I'll listen."

K'lrsa took the drinking skin Badru offered her. It was full of fermented mare's milk. She grimaced at the taste and handed it back. "What do we do if the vote goes against us?"

Herin shrugged.

"We should leave for the Hidden City tomorrow. Maybe we can…"

"It's too late."

"But you said that maybe if Badru's father…"

"He's dead. Died the year after he left the Daliphana. Summer fever."

"Then…"

"If we lose the vote, that's it."

K'lrsa leaned against Badru, taking comfort in his steady presence.

They'd brought everyone here. Now they just had to hope it was enough.

CHAPTER 55

K'lrsa was too worried to eat breakfast the next morning. She sat in the shadow of the rock and watched as the debate raged on. Only a few diehard supporters of each side were left, saying the same things over and over again, neither side willing to budge.

Finally, when she couldn't take it anymore, K'lrsa stepped forward and snatched the oath stick. The next woman in line yelled at her that it was her turn.

"Please. You've spoken three times this morning and haven't said anything you didn't say yesterday." K'lrsa stepped to the center of the dais. She flipped the stick over and over in her hands, trying to find the right words. Finally, she looked up. A few more people had drifted closer, curious to see what someone new might say.

She cleared her throat. "I don't like trade. I don't like what it's done to us. I don't like how men of the tribes who've spent too much time in the Daliphate look at me." A woman on the edge of the crowd nodded agreement. "And I don't like how they treat me. I don't like to see our proud young warriors stumbling around drunk on fire ice or high on smokeweed."

There were a few jeers at this, but she licked her lips and stared over their heads. "Like I said, I don't like trade. And I certainly don't like that we, who believe that all are equal, would participate in the enslavement of others." She pointed at Vedhe. "That woman was taken as a slave and dragged across the desert by traders we led here. Her entire family was murdered and we were part of it if not by action then by assistance. She only lives now because I helped her escape before they killed her, deeming her too scarred to sell."

K'lrsa paused, letting the crowd turn to study Vedhe who faced them with confidence, her chin high and shoulders back.

The next woman in line reached for the oath stick, but K'lrsa moved it away. "I said I don't like trade. But there is nothing in what the Lady Moon said that would prevent us from trading in the north and bringing our goods to the Daliphana." She held up her hand to forestall argument. "*We'd* have to do it. We couldn't just lead traders across the deserts. We'd have to negotiate and pay for the goods and take the risk that no one would buy them, but we could do it if we wanted."

There were some nods from the crowd and a few intense conversations as people debated how they could make that work.

Somehow in all their arguments, neither side had noticed that the Lady hadn't forbidden them to trade. She'd just forbidden them to take others across the desert.

K'lrsa opened her mouth to continue, but the wise woman from the Black Horse Tribe plucked the oath stick out of her hand. "I think that about settles it. We've all had our say. It's time to vote." She nodded to a man nearby who shouted for the tribes to gather. He was louder than anyone K'lrsa had ever heard before.

Slowly, the crowd gathered round, most not looking very interested in the conversation even though this vote would change their lives.

The wise woman stepped forward. "It's time to vote. We must decide whether we swear allegiance to the gods in exchange for their continued protection or whether we choose to go our own way. Your council members have listened to the arguments. They can repeat them for you if you need them. Each Council will take the votes of their members old enough to vote and we will gather here at sunset to give their count. The side with the most total votes will win. Now go."

K'lrsa trudged back towards their camp. Had she done enough? She didn't know and wouldn't until that night.

Badru came up beside her. "We need to plan."

"For what? How to flee when the vote goes against us?"

He shook his head. "No. How we're going to get to the Hidden City once the moon is full enough for us to fly again."

"Badru, we don't even know if we're going to win the vote."

"Better than sitting around sulking all day."

"I wasn't going to sulk," she said, but he was right.

Better to do something than just sit around worrying all day.

CHAPTER 56

K'lrsa and Badru sat down outside the tents. Vedhe, Lodie, Garzel, and Herin were already there, waiting for them.

"So?" K'lrsa asked. "What's the plan?"

Herin pointed to Vedhe. "You'll take Garzel." She pointed to K'lrsa. "And you'll take me. We'll leave as soon as the moon rises, make it as far as the horses can take us, rest until day and then continue for as long as we can until it gets too hot."

"What about me?" Badru asked.

"You and Lodie will stay here."

Lodie glared at her, but didn't say anything.

Badru stood. "No. I'm going with you."

"Pzah, boy. Sit."

"No. Not until you agree that I'm going."

Herin glared at him. "You don't need to go."

"How do you know?"

"Because I know."

K'lrsa looked past them, trying to see if she could tell how the vote was going.

Lodie stood. "I want to go, too."

"No!" Herin said, too harshly, and K'lrsa turned to watch them.

Lodie loomed over her. "It's my choice. And I'm going."

"Who will take you?"

"I will." Vedhe went to stand next to Lodie.

"You're taking Garzel."

Vedhe shook her head. "No. Lodie wants to go. I take her."

Badru smiled. "Then I'll take Garzel."

Herin was so angry her eyes were almost popping out of her skull. She stood, fists clenched. "You don't understand," she hissed at Badru.

"Then explain it to me." Badru firmed his stance, crossing his arms as if readying himself to resist a charge.

Herin leaned forward and whispered in his ear too quietly for K'lrsa to hear what she said.

Badru pulled away, his brow furrowed. "But then…That means you and…" He looked around at the others.

Herin nodded. Badru turned to K'lrsa, but Herin grabbed his arm and dragged him back whispering to him the whole time. He whispered back, clearly furious.

K'lrsa looked at Lodie. "Do you know what that's about?"

Lodie shrugged. "Just Herin trying to make decisions for everyone. As usual."

Herin glared at her, but Lodie just smiled.

Badru took the opportunity to pull free. "I'm going."

"But…"

He glared his grandmother into silence. "I'm going."

For a moment, K'lrsa thought Herin would keep arguing but instead she turned and stormed away.

Badru sat down next to her, with an embarrassed shrug.

"What was that all about?" K'lrsa asked.

"Nothing. She's just trying to protect me is all."

"From what?"

"Life."

CHAPTER 57

At sunset everyone made their way back to the central dais. Even the little children were there. K'lrsa scanned the crowd, wondering what the results would be. To her it was so obvious that the best choice was to choose the protection of the gods, but from all the arguments over the last day she knew not everyone saw what she did.

The members of the Tall Bluff Tribe were standing together but in two distinct and almost equally-sized groups that wouldn't look at each other.

That wasn't good.

Nor was the general feeling of excitement coming from the Black Horse Tribe. She met F'lia's eyes from across the platform and saw her fear. For K'lrsa? Or herself?

The wise woman for the Black Horse Tribe stood on the dais and everyone fell silent. "We are here to vote on whether we obey the god's rules and in return enjoy their protections or whether we go our own way."

Behind her stood six representatives, one from each Council. D'lan was on the far right. She turned to him. "How does the White Horse Tribe vote?"

He held up his counting board with its white stone and black stone markers. "We have one hundred and twenty-three votes for the gods and forty-three against."

K'lrsa glared at him. It would've been a hundred and twenty-seven for the gods, but he'd refused to let Herin,

Lodie, Garzel, or Badru vote even though they had the blood of the tribes. One hundred and twenty-eight if he'd allowed Vedhe's vote.

K'lrsa studied those around her wondering who had voted against the gods.

And why?

She should have spent the day walking amongst them, trying to counter whatever argument had swayed them rather than watching Herin and Badru brood.

She turned back to the dais. She'd missed the counts for the next two tribes. The wise woman turned to the angry man from the day before. "What does the Black Horse Tribe vote?"

"We vote to cast aside the meddling gods and go our own way." There was a loud cheer from his tribe.

The wise woman shook her head. "Your count please."

"Ten to follow the gods and a hundred and eight-two against."

A woman shouted from the crowd. "You don't even have that many adult members."

The man grinned, but didn't answer. K'lrsa tried to count how many adults they did have, but already the wise woman had moved on to the next tribe.

The designee from the Tall Bluff Tribe, a tall, thin woman with stooped shoulders announced a count of seventy five for the gods, seventy-six against.

How could so many want to give up the protection of the gods? What kind of fools were they?

The crowd waited, hushed, as the last tribe, the Desert Storm Tribe gave their numbers. "One hundred seventy-three for the gods. Five against." The woman representing the tribe met K'lrsa's eyes. "We didn't forget that we wouldn't be here now without the help of horses provided by the gods."

Hisses and boos from the Black Horse Tribe met her statement. A man shouted that without the meddling gods the vote would already be over. In their favor.

The wise woman turned to the other wise ones who were gathered together at the base of the dais, each with a counting board. "What's the tally?"

They checked back and forth, one with the other. "It's a tie. Five hundred and twenty-two votes each."

"What?" a man across the way shouted. "How is that possible?"

A little boy flounced to the ground at K'lrsa's feet with an aggrieved sigh. "You mean they still haven't made a decision? This sucks." He rested his chin on his hands with a pout.

K'lrsa agreed.

But she was still reeling from the fact that so many of the tribe would forego the protections of the gods. For what?

The wise woman held up a hand to quiet the crowd, but before she could speak, Herin strode forward. "Not all the tribes have voted."

The wise woman stared at her. She leaned forward. "H'lina?"

Herin nodded. She pointed behind her. "And L'dia and G'zen. And my grandson, Badru. We are the last living members of the Summer Spring Tribe."

"Liar," someone shouted from the crowd and others joined him.

The wise woman stood. She gestured for Herin to join her. "No. I recognize this woman. She was a member of the Summer Spring Tribe. As were her sister and her husband." She nodded towards Lodie and Garzel.

"I recognize them, too," the wise woman for the Tall Bluff Tribe said.

The wise woman for the Black Horse Tribe turned to Herin. "So? What is your vote?"

K'lrsa held her breath. She never knew with Herin what she was thinking and Herin had been furious that Badru and Lodie wanted to go to the Hidden City. But surely she wouldn't vote against the gods just because of that?

Garzel grunted something at her and Herin frowned. "Three for the gods. One against."

The crowd roared, half with excitement, half with anger.

The wise woman shouted over them. "The tribes have spoken. We will continue to follow the ways of the gods and continue to enjoy their protections. Tomorrow all here who are old enough to vote will swear on the oath stick to abide by this decision. Any who cannot, must leave the tribes forever."

She scanned the crowd as it quieted. "Choose wisely. The Daliph's men have surrounded us and any who reject the gods also reject their protection. This matter cannot come up for another vote for five more winters."

Some continued to mutter that Herin and the others shouldn't have been allowed to vote, but it was too late. The vote had been cast, the decision made.

The tribes were safe. At least for now.

CHAPTER 58

By the next morning, most of the Black Horse Tribe had joined the Daliph's troops in surrounding the gathering grounds. They could still cross over easily enough—as they proved rather belligerently when K'lrsa came to study their camp—but they were making it clear that they had no intention of swearing to the gods and that the enemy the tribes would have to fight through was even larger than before.

One Rider, a man her father's age, stepped right up in her face, glaring her down. "This isn't over, you know. Not like you can live on the gathering grounds forever. And when you leave, we'll be here, waiting."

She rolled her eyes. "You don't scare me. We beat you once, didn't we?"

He sneered and lunged at her. She braced for an attack, but he was yanked back at the last moment. She laughed. "You can't hurt us. Not while we're here."

She walked away.

What did she care for the foolish posturing of overgrown boys?

There was one reason she was there. She wanted to find F'lia.

She'd said she'd join them if they won, but like the man had pointed out, they hadn't won yet. Still. The Daliphate wasn't a fit place for any woman.

At last, K'lrsa found her, kneeling on the ground, packing a tent.

"F'lia."

She glanced at K'lrsa and away again. As before, J'vin hovered nearby, watching his prize. "What are you doing here?"

"I came to see if you'd come back with me. You know your mother would welcome you back with open arms. And..." She licked her lips, suddenly awkward. "I miss you. You're my best friend."

F'lia glanced nervously at J'vin. "The Daliph's men have orders to kill any who don't swear allegiance to the Toreem Daliphate."

"And you're going to do that?"

"What choice do I have?" She stroked her belly.

"You could come back to us."

"And starve?"

"No. I'm..." She glanced at J'vin, unsure how much F'lia might tell him. "We're going to find a way out of this, F'lia."

"Let me know when you do." She tied the last knot on the tent tighter than she really needed to. "But until then I have to make the best decision for my child."

K'lrsa wanted to scream at her. Allying herself with the Daliphana was the worst decision she could make for her child. But she didn't. Because she wasn't the one having to make that choice.

She tried again. "You don't understand what that place is like for women." She shivered just remembering.

"I'm sure it's not that bad."

"It is!"

"You seem to have survived it just fine."

"You don't understand. They made me take baths every day and wear these ridiculous outfits of all sorts of different colors and with so many buttons I could've never dressed myself. And they put my hair up in these elaborate hairstyles. And put all this stuff on my face so I couldn't even recognize myself. And they wouldn't even let me feed myself. Everything was done for me. *Everything*."

F'lia grinned at her. "Did you have to wear silk, too? And pretty jewels? Did everyone look at you and admire your beauty?"

"Yes. It was awful."

She laughed. "But, see? That sounds wonderful to me."

"But it wasn't. I..." How could she explain how horrible it all was?

F'lia stood. "We've always wanted different things, K'lrsa. Those silks you rejected so easily? I would've died to have. And now I can have them." She smiled, but it was a smile full of sorrow. She grabbed her pack. "Goodbye. Hopefully we'll meet again under better circumstances."

K'lrsa watched her walk over to J'vin. He threw a possessive arm around her shoulder and led her across the border into the Daliph's camp.

It was wrong.

All of it.

But it was F'lia's choice to make, her life to live. All K'lrsa could do is be there for her friend when she realized her error.

CHAPTER 59

As the sun hovered directly above them, beating with the ferocity of summer even though it was winter, the five remaining wise ones gathered on the central dais.

The wise woman from the Black Horse Tribe had left with her tribe. K'lrsa was sorry to see that even one steeped in the mysteries could turn against the gods, but it was what it was.

Once again, the wise ones invoked the protection of the gods, but this time there was no appearance by the Lady or any other god.

The wise woman for the Tall Bluff Tribe stepped forward and held the oath stick above her head with one steady arm. "All adults who wish to remain a part of the tribes must swear their loyalty to the gods and their willingness to protect the desert and the Hidden City. Any who cannot swear this oath should leave now."

No one moved. The wise woman studied the crowd, pivoting slowly so she could look at each and every person. "I should also warn you that none will be able to swear a false oath. If in your heart you don't intend to abide by your vow, do not attempt to swear on the oath stick."

She turned towards the far left side of the dais. "Shall we begin?"

A young man from the Tall Bluff Tribe took the oath first followed by his mother and sister. The oaths were

quick. Each person grabbed the stick, nodded when asked if they agreed to follow the gods and protect the desert and the Hidden City, and that was it.

No flash of light. No test of faith. Just a simple, straight-forward declaration.

But even with such a simple vow K'lrsa knew it would take the entire day to get through everyone. She considered returning to her tent until most of the crowd had gone, but decided she might as well stand witness.

Not long after, a man from the Black Horse Tribe stepped forward to take his oath. When the wise woman asked him if he agreed to protect the desert and the Hidden City, he nodded just like all of those before him.

But this time, when he went to remove his hand, he couldn't.

He jerked away from the wise woman, the stick still clenched in his hand.

"Get if off me," he screamed as he shook his hand, but the stick remained glued to his flesh.

He started to sweat, muttering desperately as he used his knife to try to pry the stick loose. It wouldn't budge. He swore as the knife slipped and he cut himself.

A heat haze filled the air around him.

He tried harder to remove the stick, digging the knife into the flesh of his palm, but it didn't work.

The haze intensified until the air was wavy with it, the man's shape blurred.

A scream tore from his throat as the light of the sun concentrated itself upon him, glowing brighter and brighter until K'lrsa had to shield her eyes against the glare.

He screamed and screamed and screamed, his voice spiraling upward in agony.

And then…

Silence.

K'lrsa lowered her hand.

The man was gone.

The stick lay on the ground where he'd stood, but there was no sign he'd ever been there.

The wise woman picked the stick up, her hand shaking

so badly she had to press it to her side. She turned to the crowd and said, loudly enough for all to hear, her voice as shaky as her hand, "As I said, do not attempt to swear a false oath. If you can't find it in yourself to follow the ways of the gods, then best to leave now."

K'lrsa shuddered.

The wise woman was right. Better life as an exile than to burn.

A man standing a few rows before her turned and pushed his way through the crowd. His mother called after him, but he didn't stop.

"Who's next?" the wise woman asked.

No one stepped forward.

K'lrsa didn't blame them. What if it hadn't been the man's impure heart? What if the gods were just capricious and cruel, like she knew them to be?

The wise woman tried again. "Who's next? If your heart is pure you have nothing to fear."

But still, no one was willing to take the risk.

Finally, when it was clear that no one else would, K'lrsa forced herself forward. Her throat was so dry she couldn't speak.

The wise woman held out the oath stick.

K'lrsa wiped her sweaty palms on her vest.

She closed her eyes for a moment and then gripped the stick in her hand, waiting for the fire to shoot up her arm, but it was just a plain old stick with some grooves and scratches on its surface.

There was a slight tug on her palm when she agreed to follow the gods, but that was it. She handed the stick back and walked away quickly, just in case.

As others stepped up to take their oaths, she walked back to their tents.

It was time.

Time to find the weapon that would save the tribes.

CHAPTER 60

When K'lrsa reached their tents, she found Badru and Herin screaming at each other with Garzel and Lodie seated nearby watching, Lodie with amusement, Garzel with resignation.

Badru stood toe-to-toe with Herin. "I'm going, Grandmother, and there's nothing you can do to stop me."

She glanced at K'lrsa. "There's one thing I can do."

He followed her gaze. "You wouldn't dare." He clenched his fist as if ready to hit her.

"Wouldn't I? To save you?"

"Stop it. Both of you." K'lrsa pushed between them. "She's your grandmother, Badru. And as annoying and repellant as she may sometimes be..." She glanced at Herin.

"Thanks."

K'lrsa almost smiled. "She deserves your respect. She's very much part of the reason you're alive today."

Herin nodded. "Which is why he should listen to me now."

Badru shook his head. "Not on this."

"Pzah, you foolish boy. Don't you understand what I told you?"

"I do. But I think saving these people is more important."

Lodie stood. "Now that that's settled. The six of us should make sure we're ready to go."

Herin clenched her jaw and rolled her eyes. "Far be it from me to want you two to live out the week." She stalked away.

K'lrsa shook her head. Typical Herin. Worried about Badru and Lodie, but hadn't once thought about K'lrsa being in the exact same danger.

Then again, K'lrsa had always known Herin's priorities: Herself first, Badru, Lodie, and Garzel second, anyone else a distant third.

She turned back to the others. "So? Do we have a plan? Do we know how to find the Hidden City? Is it hard?"

Lodie shook her head. "Should only take about three days to get there. Our stones can guide us if the horses can't."

"If it's so easy to get there, why doesn't everyone go?"

Lodie shrugged. "Ignorance mostly. Most don't believe it exists and if they do they don't know how to find it. But fear, too, for those who know enough."

"What's there to fear?"

"Nothing much." She stepped away. "I better talk to Herin. See if we can't reconcile before I die." She winked at them and left.

"No one's going to die, are they?"

She turned to Badru and Garzel, but neither one acknowledged her question.

"Badru?" She poked him. "I said no one's going to die, are they?"

"Huh?" He chuckled. "What kind of question's that?"

He turned towards the dais. "I better swear my oath before it's too late. Be right back." He kissed her on the cheek and walked away.

She looked at Garzel. He shrugged and turned away, too.

She stood there, alone, wondering what it was that they all seemed to know that she didn't.

CHAPTER 61

As the sun set and twilight fell, the wise ones finished with the last of those in line to swear their oaths and started winding their way through the camps looking for any stragglers.

The wise man for the White Horse Tribe walked up to where they sat eating a meal of dried paste root and millet. It was the worst meal K'lrsa had ever eaten, but still food. He nodded towards Herin. "You haven't sworn."

Herin spat on the ground. "Pzah. And I'm not going to."

He blinked back his surprise. "Then you have to leave."

"I will. As soon as the moon rises." She nodded to their packs.

K'lrsa shook her head. "You didn't swear your oath? But you have to. We can't travel the desert if you don't."

"Why not? You'll be leading us and you swore it."

"Herin. I just swore I wouldn't lead strangers into the desert. If you don't swear your oath, what do you think that makes you?"

Herin blinked once, twice, then she cussed her head off. "Fine. Give me that stick." She yanked it out of the man's hand and muttered that she agreed to follow the god's rules, every line of her face showing how unhappy she was to do so.

K'lrsa held her breath, waiting for the sun to strike her down, but nothing happened.

 225 

The wise man must've been thinking the same thing, because he took his time taking the stick back.

Lodie and Garzel swore their oaths next.

They, too, had no issues.

Next it was Vedhe's turn.

She shook her head. "Not of the tribes."

The man frowned at her. "But you have to be. You have an *Amalanee* horse."

"So do I," Badru said. "And I wasn't one of the tribes when Midnight found me."

"Yes, but as I understand it both of your parents were."

Badru nodded.

"Which makes you of the tribes." He held out the stick. "Here, child. Swear your oath."

Vedhe crossed her arms.

K'lrsa nudged her with her foot. "Vedhe. Just swear your oath. We can't take you to the Hidden City if you don't."

Vedhe laughed. "You not take me. Kriger take me. Not need you. Or tribes."

Herin shrugged. "Her choice."

"But…What will happen to her if she doesn't? And us for taking her with us?"

Cruel, child-like laughter filled the air. The Trickster stepped out of nothing right next to Vedhe.

Herin narrowed her eyes, glaring at him. So did K'lrsa.

"Give me the stick, old man." The Trickster turned to where the wise man cowered.

He handed over the oath stick, his hand shaking badly, and then backed away, careful to keep the Trickster in sight the whole time.

The Trickster held the stick out to Vedhe and she took the other end. "Do you promise, my child of pain and suffering, to protect the secrets of the desert even after you return to your people?"

"Yes."

"Good enough for me. And if it's good enough for me, it's good enough for my parents."

He threw the stick back to the wise man who dropped it, scrabbled around for it, and then fled.

The Trickster turned slowly, smiling at each of them. "So you're going to the desert, are you? Even though you're going to die?" He raised an eyebrow at Herin who glared back at him, full of venom. "Even though you'll never come back?" He turned to Lodie who pretended he wasn't there. "Even though…"

He turned towards Badru and Badru lunged at him. "Go away you vicious little man."

The Trickster jumped backwards. "Oh ho ho. You think to challenge the gods do you, baby Daliph?" He shook his head. "Not a wise choice my boy, not a wise choice." He lunged at Badru and Badru flinched backward.

And then the Trickster was gone as if he'd never been there.

K'lrsa slapped Badru on the arm. "What were you thinking, challenging him like that?"

He shrugged.

Before K'lrsa could say more, Herin stood. "No time for that. We need to leave."

"Fine. Let's go." K'lrsa saddled up Fallion and grabbed her small pack, but she couldn't stop thinking about what the Trickster had said.

Was someone going to die on their trip? And, if so, who?

CHAPTER 62

The horses had transformed and everyone was seated, waiting for K'lrsa, but she found herself hesitant to leave.

"I'll be right back." She didn't wait for a response as she dodged through the rest of the camp past huddles of people tensely talking about what to do now that they'd sworn to the gods but were surrounded by their enemies with no way out and food enough for only another week.

There was a lot of dark muttering about how they should've chosen the other option instead. She didn't blame them. She'd've probably been saying the same if she hadn't had a clear path forward.

She found her brother in the center of the White Horse Tribe camp, surrounded by angry men and women, all shouting at once. He was trying to calm them, but no one seemed to be listening.

She pushed through to the center of the group, ignoring the cries of those she shoved out of her way. "D'lan. We need to talk."

"Can it wait?"

"No. We're leaving."

"What?" He stepped closer and said through gritted teeth, "We need the horses. They're our only chance of keeping everyone fed."

He raised his voice so everyone could hear him. "I was just explaining that we can use the *Amalanee* to carry hunters

so we'll have enough food to wait out the Daliph's troops. Because, as we all *know*," he glared at a man on his right, "we can't use them to leave because the Daliph's men would just follow and attack and we could never stand against them."

He continued, looking to K'lrsa for confirmation. "*We* know that because *we* actually fought the Black Horse Tribe before anyone else arrived. And it wasn't easy."

K'lrsa nodded. "Yes. If we can avoid fighting them, we should."

She glanced around at all the scared and worried faces. They needed a plan.

She raised her voice. "I'm leaving to find a weapon to help us defeat them. Badru and Vedhe are coming with me. While we're gone, you need to train. Badru showed us how to fight these men. Use this time to prepare."

"Why do you get to leave and we have to stay?" the man D'lan had glared at asked.

"Because Fallion is my horse. And he's the only way to find this weapon."

"You could let someone else take him. He's just a horse."

K'lrsa laughed. She turned to D'lan. "I have to go."

He nodded. "When will you be back?"

"Six days? I hope."

He grimaced. "Okay."

D'lan looked at her.

She looked back. Her brother, but a man she barely knew. Still. One of the only two family members she had left. She hugged him.

Neither one of them knew quite where to place their arms—having never really hugged before in their lives—but they managed an awkward pat on each other's backs.

"Hurry back. We'll starve without you."

"No pressure."

She pushed her way back through the crowd, but didn't turn towards where the horses waited.

She had one more goodbye to make.

She found M'lara seated alone at the edge of the White Horse Tribe camp, in the shadow of a tent, staring out at the Daliph's camp.

"M'lara."

"K'lrsa." M'lara jumped to her feet and wrapped her arms around K'lrsa's legs, holding on so tight K'lrsa staggered and almost fell.

K'lrsa let her cling for a long moment as she stroked her sister's long black hair. But then she pushed M'lara back and knelt down in front of her. In the faint light of the moon, tears glistened on M'lara's cheeks, following the path of the many that had gone before them.

K'lrsa brushed one of the tears away, regretting that she had to leave M'lara behind yet again. "I came to say goodbye."

"Don't go." M'lara flung herself at K'lrsa, wrapping her arms around K'lrsa's neck so tight she could barely breathe.

"I have to do this, sweetie. I'm sorry, but we need a weapon to defeat those bad men out there."

"Why does it have to be you? Can't someone else do it?"

K'lrsa almost broke as she stared into those big, brown eyes, so full of loss and need.

She held M'lara close. "I wish. I'll be back. I promise."

M'lara pulled away, glaring at her. "You already promised not to leave me again."

"M'lara. I have to do this."

She sniffed, trying to hold back the tears that filled her eyes once more. "But you will come back? And then you'll never ever leave again?"

"I will."

"Okay."

K'lrsa hugged her sister once more, not wanting to let go.

But she had to.

It was time.

CHAPTER 63

"Took you long enough," Herin muttered as K'lrsa threw herself into Fallion's saddle.

"I had to say goodbye, Herin. And I'm not going to let you make me feel bad about it."

Herin didn't respond, so K'lrsa turned to Badru and Vedhe. "Who wants to lead? How do we do this?"

"I lead." Vedhe turned Kriger towards the desert. With one massive sweep of his wings, Kriger leapt into the sky, Vedhe and Lodie clinging to his back. Midnight followed right after with Badru and Garzel.

As soon as they cleared the ground, they disappeared.

But K'lrsa didn't follow. Not yet.

She took one last look at the camp. She'd promised to come back. And she'd meant it.

But, as simple as it all seemed—find the Hidden City, get the weapon they needed, and return—she'd learned that sometimes what seemed simple wasn't at all.

She *had* to come back. M'lara needed her. She'd have D'lan but he was too distant and he had a child of his own on the way. M'lara needed someone who'd love her unconditionally like K'lrsa's father had loved her.

K'lrsa shook her head. No time to dwell on that now.

"Let's go, *micora*." She patted Fallion's neck and he spread his wings and leapt into the air. They quickly rose above camp and into that place that wasn't part of the real

world, Midnight and Kriger far ahead of them.

As they chased after, K'lrsa flashed back to the Trickster's visit.

Did he know something they didn't?

Or was he just playing another one of his cruel little jokes? Like when he'd showed her all those bodies staked to the ground?

As they rode through the night, K'lrsa wondered what she'd do if one of the others was threatened. She cared for them, even Vedhe with her strange silences, awkward sentences, and scarred face.

She didn't want to see harm come to any of them.

But if it came to it, if it was her life or theirs, who would she choose? Especially knowing that if she died her people might never be saved?

Herin, Garzel, and Lodie had been gone from the tribes so long, what did they care about going back to save them? And Badru wasn't part of the tribes. Would he carry on out of love for her? Or in honor of the new friendships he'd begun to form?

She wasn't sure.

And she didn't think Vedhe would.

K'lrsa's people had never been kind to the girl. They weren't comfortable with difference or weakness. K'lrsa saw that now in a way she never had before.

She cared for her companions, but others needed her more.

It was horrible and selfish, but she realized that if she had to choose, she'd choose to save the tribes over saving the others.

She almost wished they weren't there. That she was all alone like when she'd set out to avenge her father.

Then it had been so simple. Continue or quit. Go forward or fall back.

This…

With so many lives at stake and so many things she didn't know…

This was something entirely different.

And she didn't like it.

CHAPTER 64

The horses seemed to gain strength with each beat of their wings, carrying them farther and farther into the desert.

Soon the gathering grounds and the tribes were left far behind. All K'lrsa could see in any direction were sand dunes, wavy from the winds that continually scoured and shifted them into new shapes.

There were no paths in the desert. No landmarks to follow. Just sand.

But the horses flew on, moving steadily forward with each rhythmic beat of their wings. They at least knew where they were and where they were going.

Around the middle of the night, K'lrsa grew tired of the sound of her thoughts. She turned in her saddle, but could barely see Herin; her face was in shadow, her eyes lost in the wrinkles on her cheeks.

"What can you tell me about the Hidden City?"

In this weird place that wasn't the real world she knew her words were easy to hear with no wind to snatch them away, but Herin didn't answer.

"Herin. I know you can hear me. Tell me about the Hidden City."

Herin sniffed. "Badru shouldn't go there. When we land, tell him and Lodie to go back."

Like either one would listen to her. "Why?"

"It'll be the death of them."

"Why the death of them and not the death of any of the rest of us?" K'lrsa searched for clues in the woman's face, but it was too dark.

"Pzah. Must you always ask so many questions?" Herin muttered.

"I just want to understand. Why shouldn't Badru go but it's fine for the rest of us?"

Herin shook her head.

"Herin."

"Just tell him not to go." She went to cross her arms and then hastily grabbed onto K'lrsa once more.

"You know he won't listen. Why can't you just tell me?"

"I promised him I wouldn't."

K'lrsa sighed. "And you'll keep that promise even if it costs him his life?"

Herin pressed her lips so tight together her face became a mass of wrinkles.

K'lrsa turned back around wondering why she'd even bothered. Up ahead, Badru sat on Midnight, Garzel behind him, staring straight ahead, his jaw firm like he was riding to battle.

Maybe it wasn't worth it, whatever this weapon was. Maybe they could find another way.

She turned so Herin could hear her. "I don't want Badru to die for this, Herin. Is there another way to defeat the Daliph's troops?"

"No. You need a weapon powerful enough to defeat Aran."

"I don't care about Aran. Let him rot in Toreem."

Herin clutched K'lrsa's arm, her fingers digging into K'lrsa's soft flesh. K'lrsa flexed her arm against the grip, realizing how weak she'd become during her time in the Daliphate, her arm as much flesh as muscle now.

Herin leaned close, her breath the familiar stench of death and cinnamon. "Don't be a fool girl. If you don't defeat Aran all is lost."

"All is lost? Please. He's one man. Let him have the Toreem Daliphate as long as he stays away from us."

Herin gripped her arm tighter, the stubs of her fingers pressing painfully. "Aran will never be done with the tribes. Not until he's destroyed them."

K'lrsa shook her head. "How can you say that? It's not like he's ever sent troops against us before."

"Now that he has, he won't stop. He wants the Hidden City." She relaxed her grip.

"Can't the gods do something about him?" K'lrsa rubbed her arm, wincing in pain.

"I don't think so. There's…There are other gods and they don't…No. The gods can't directly stop him."

"Not directly? But indirectly?"

"Mmhm. Through you or Badru or me or Lodie."

"It'd be nice if they told us these things."

Herin shrugged. "It's not their way. Or, at least, not anymore." K'lrsa forced herself not to flinch away as Herin leaned in. "When I was younger, I was sent a moon dream and told to go with Garzel to Toreem. To kill Aran."

"What?" K'lrsa almost unseated herself and Herin trying to turn to look at her.

"He knew somehow. Before we ever met. He used to gloat about it when we were alone. I think…I think maybe our gods acted too directly, which let his gods act as well. I think that's how he got the death walker magic." She shook her head. "I paid for it, too, until you stepped forward on your own with a goal the gods could support."

"They had to wait for me to decide to go after him."

She nodded.

"Well, I promised M'lara I wouldn't leave her again. So if you want Aran dead, you're going to have to do it yourself. I'll give you the weapon, whatever it is, after I use it to save the tribes. Deal?"

Herin didn't answer.

"Herin? Do we have a deal?"

"We'll see how it goes in the Hidden City." She leaned back and ignored any further attempts K'lrsa made to talk until it was finally time to land.

They found a shelter large enough for six people and three horses with enough stored provisions to feed them right next to where they landed. The food was plain—dried meat and nuts and fruits—but better than Garzel's travel bars.

For the first time, K'lrsa wondered what hand the gods had in the creation of the shelters she'd taken for granted her entire life. Of course, if the shelters really were provided by the gods, she didn't see why they couldn't have provided a six-course meal complete with fresh fruit and hot bread. Honestly, if they were going to provide, why not provide well?

But it seemed the gods had their limits.

CHAPTER 65

K'lrsa tried to talk to Badru after they landed, but he somehow managed to avoid her even in the confines of the cave. First he couldn't talk to her because he was helping Garzel start a fire, then he claimed he was so tired he couldn't keep his eyes open, and after he woke up he took Lodie aside for a long, private conversation.

But after he and Lodie just sat there, neither one saying a word for a long time, K'lrsa knew for sure he was just doing it to avoid her. She shook her head in disgust and started across the room, determined to have it out with him.

Lodie scrambled to her feet and quickly intercepted her.

"Move. I need to talk to Badru." She stepped to the side, but so did Lodie and the cave wasn't so big that she could keep going.

Lodie blocked her against the wall. "Not until you've listened to what I have to say."

"Fine. But make it quick."

"Why do you want to talk to him?" Lodie asked.

K'lrsa laughed. "Uh, isn't that obvious? Herin told me going to the Hidden City will kill him. I'm going to convince him not to go."

"Do you trust him?"

K'lrsa frowned. "I don't see what that has to do with anything."

"It has everything to do with this. Do you trust him?"

"Yes."

"And do you trust me?"

"Yes." K'lrsa watched Badru over Lodie's shoulder, determined not to let him slip out of the cave while she was distracted.

"K'lrsa, look at me."

K'lrsa kept her gaze fixed on Badru.

"K'lrsa…Look. At. Me."

K'lrsa sniffed in annoyance, but she turned her attention to Lodie. "Happy? Now that you've distracted me so he can run away again?"

She shook her head. "Badru will still be there when we're done. But I want you to think about something before you go over there." She held K'lrsa's gaze with her own. "Badru is perfectly capable of knowing a situation is dangerous and still facing it. And just as you have every right to choose to risk your life, so does he."

"Is Herin right? Will he die if he goes there?"

"It doesn't matter. What matters is whether you love and trust him enough to let him make his own decision about this."

"Not if he's wrong!"

Lodie stared her down. "Tell me something. If he is going to die there and you only have a couple days left together, is this how you want to spend it? Avoiding each other? Arguing?"

"If it would give us more time together. Yes."

"It won't. You won't change his mind on this." She leaned closer. "I've lived most of my life without the man I loved. And the last few days we spent together we weren't even speaking. I've regretted that every single day since."

K'lrsa let out a deep sigh. She understood what Lodie was saying, but she wasn't sure she could actually listen to her advice.

Lodie smiled as if she could read K'lrsa's mind. "You didn't listen to me when I warned you about going to the Daliphate, at least you could listen to me now."

K'lrsa chewed her lip as she studied Badru.

She wanted to know what the danger was in the Hidden City. And to tell Badru to stay if it really was going to cost him his life.

But Lodie was right.

If the situation were reversed and K'lrsa knew the risks and had made a decision, she wouldn't want Badru telling her not to make it.

She turned back to Lodie. "Okay. I'll listen. This once."

Lodie patted her on the arm and stepped aside.

K'lrsa made her way across the cave and settled down in front of Badru. He was tensed, ready to fight.

She smiled. "Don't worry. I'm not going to ask you to stay behind or ask what this danger is that could kill you but not me. Lodie's right. We shouldn't waste the time we have trying to avoid one another or fighting."

He smiled back. "Good."

"Well, then…Tell me something about yourself that I don't know. Tell me about growing up in Toreem. Who raised you if your mother was gone? Herin?"

"Oh no. Not Herin. And my mother would've never raised me even if she'd lived. The Daliph's children and grandchildren were raised by poradoma, the boys kept separate and trained in combat from the time they could toddle."

"They were?"

"Mmhm."

He launched into a detailed description of the wing of the palace where the children lived, telling her about all his training, his childhood friends, his favorite and most hated poradoma, and the tricks he'd played on them.

It was funny.

But sad, too.

Because Sayel—the man who'd befriended K'lrsa and ultimately given his life to save Badru—had been one of those poradom. And while she smiled to hear Badru tell how he'd snuck his way into the kitchens with Sayel's help, she was also reminded just how fragile life was.

Not only was Sayel dead, but so were all of those children Badru had been raised with. They'd been killed in the lethal competition to see who would succeeded Aran. A fight Aran had encouraged, pitting them one against the other for his own amusement and protection, urging them to worse and worse atrocities to prove themselves his worthy heir.

No doubt, Aran *was* a vile man. She'd already known that from the stories Herin told and the way Badru flinched at his name.

But was it her responsibility to stop him?

Shouldn't his own people do so? Why did it have to be her, a foreigner who'd never been harmed by him?

She pushed those thoughts away and focused on the moment, glad she and Badru had had this chance to deepen the instinctual connection they'd always had into something more real and tangible. She could finally see how they might be together, day-to-day, when this was all over.

And she liked it.

But that night, as they flew closer and closer to their destination, all she could think about was Aran and what Herin had said about needing to stop him.

Because the truth was she didn't want to. She didn't even want to be the one to save her own people.

Before her father was murdered, she'd thought herself a strong warrior, superior to all. She'd dreamed of having enemies to fight and chances to show the world how special she was.

She'd known she could defeat anyone and anything if given the chance.

But now she knew the truth.

She was just a girl. A girl with an amazing horse who could shoot a bow better than most. Who might be smart and attractive but was still just a girl like any other at the end of the day.

A girl who just wanted to go home to her family, what little of it remained. To hunt baru and ride Fallion and never, ever think about anything else again.

That's what she wanted.

But she knew she'd never get it.

CHAPTER 66

The rest of their journey to the Hidden City was uneventful. The horses knew exactly where to go and the weather was perfect. They were able to find a shelter each night with plenty of space, food, and fuel for a fire.

The closer they came with nothing to challenge them, the more nervous K'lrsa felt.

If this city was so secret and contained such terrible weapons why was it so easy to find? Where were the sand storms and guardians to keep them away? Shouldn't the path be twisted and difficult?

When they stopped at the end of the third night of travel, K'lrsa knew they had to be close, but it was too dark to see much more than the shelter the horses lead them to.

The next afternoon when she emerged from the cave, there the Hidden City was, just like in her moon dreams.

It was a large city the color of sand encompassed by a wall that had to be at least two or even three times the height of a man. Buildings thrust into the sky from behind that barrier, blocky shapes fighting one another for the sky.

It wasn't a beautiful city.

It looked built for war.

In the middle of nowhere.

K'lrsa ducked back into the cave. "Let's go. The city's not that far away. We can ride the rest of the distance."

Herin shook her head. "Not until the moon rises. Let

the horses fly us the last little bit. Might as well save our strength for what's ahead."

"And what would that be, exactly?"

Herin snorted. "Pzah, girl. Don't you think I'd tell you if I knew?"

"You know something. You've told Badru…"

She shook her head. "That's something different."

Before K'lrsa could speak, Herin held up her hand. "Leave it. We need to focus on the city now. I don't know what challenges we'll face, but I know we will face them. Rest and prepare. The wisdom of the gods always comes at a price."

K'lrsa returned to studying the city. Always in the moon dream it had stayed out of reach. No matter how long she'd walked, even when she'd walked an entire night, she'd never reached it.

She wondered if the same thing would happen tonight. Would they fly and fly and fly and never get there? Maybe that was the challenge to reaching it.

But, no. Not with these horses.

Restless, she went to find Fallion. He stood in the shade of the cave, off to the side, happily munching on dried grass stored on a perfectly horse-height ledge.

She scratched his nose and he whuffed her hair before returning to his food.

She leaned against him, grateful for his steady presence. The best gift her father had ever given her.

She sighed.

She'd been so busy between going to Toreem and training as a dorana and trying to figure out who to kill and coming back to save her people and everything else that she'd never really had the time to think about the loss of her father.

It was always with her and she'd cried about it and had nightmares about it, but she'd never just stopped to think about what a huge gaping hole he'd left in her life.

But standing there with Fallion, the loss crept over her. She was consumed with a vast feeling of emptiness. Like someone had hollowed her out until there was nothing left inside and she knew she could never fill that gaping void where his steady presence had once lived.

He was gone and he wasn't coming back and there was no one, no one in this world who could ever replace him.

Badru was nice and attractive and kind, but he wasn't her father. He couldn't offer that unconditional love and support her father had given her. No one could. No one could love the way a parent loves.

And the only other parent she'd had was gone, too.

A tear fell down her cheek. And then another and another.

Her mother had been right. Her father had raised her to live without him. But she'd always known deep down that no matter how far she went, no matter what she risked, he'd be there to catch her, to bring her home safe, to comfort her when she failed.

But now…

Now that was gone. She was on her own.

She wanted so much to just talk to him. About Badru and Aran and all of it. He'd know what she should do.

But he was gone.

And he wasn't coming back.

She buried her face in Fallion's mane and cried, silently, so no one would hear. She didn't want to be comforted. She just wanted him back.

Fallion continued chomping his food; the slow, steady rhythm of his heart slowly bringing her back to herself. He was so extraordinary, but yet so normal at the same time. And always there for her.

She wasn't alone. As much as it felt like it sometimes. She had Fallion and Lodie and Herin and Garzel and Vedhe. And Badru.

Badru. A man who was willing to risk his life to stay by her side.

And instead of spending what little time she had left with him she was crying in the corner.

She wiped away her tears, determined to make the most of the time they had left.

CHAPTER 67

K'lrsa found Badru outside, watching the Hidden City. He spoke softly as she joined him. "I thought we'd have another night before we found it. I thought we'd have a chance to…" He shook his head.

"To what?"

"Nothing. It's too late for that now."

"Badru, are you going to die in there?"

He ran his hand down the side of her face, holding her gaze with his gorgeous blue eyes. "I love you, you know."

"And I love you. But you didn't answer my question."

"And I'm not going to. Come on. Let's eat with the others."

They gathered in a circle outside the cave to eat a supper of dried baru meat wrapped in small flat discs made from millet flour, laughing and talking, telling stories of their wildest childhood pranks.

Vedhe told some strange story about swimming in water so cold she almost died just because her brother dared her to. And Badru told a story about sneaking a stallion out of Toreem and riding it across the plain.

Herin almost laughed at that one. She definitely smiled.

The others didn't hold back. Laughing and shouting back and forth in their enthusiasm.

It was the best meal K'lrsa had had in…ever.

But finally they fell into silence, each of them staring at the city in the distance as the moon rose.

"No point in delaying any longer." Herin grabbed her pack and walked to Fallion's side.

The others followed, grabbing their packs, standing, stretching, getting ready to leave.

Impulsively, K'lrsa hugged Garzel. And then Lodie. And Vedhe. They all returned her hug with varying levels of amusement. Vedhe squeezed her back so hard she thought she might break.

K'lrsa turned to Badru. He smiled as he held his arms out for her, so beautiful and strong she almost started crying thinking about what might lie ahead.

She hugged him tight, burying her face against his chest.

He rested his chin on the top of her head. "I wish we'd had more time together to just be."

She nodded. "After. We'll go somewhere in the desert when the moon is full, just the two of us, and we'll dance the Moon Dance for real, in this world."

He stroked her cheek. "I'd like that."

But his eyes were full of such sorrow she knew he didn't think it would ever happen. She pulled away. "Badru...You don't have to come. You can wait here for us. What will six accomplish that five can't?"

He shook his head. "No. Wherever you go, I go."

She closed her eyes. "Don't do this for me, Badru. Please."

"I'm not. I'm doing it for me."

She wanted to argue further, but Lodie was right. She had to let him make this choice.

She turned away. "Okay. Then best get going." She made her way to Fallion's side.

Herin was there, waiting, her arms crossed and a sour frown on her face. "'Bout time."

K'lrsa hugged her.

"Pzah. Get off me." But for a brief moment, she'd leaned into the hug.

K'lrsa pulled back and smiled at her.

Herin shook her head. "Oh, would you just awaken the horse already? We don't have all night."

K'lrsa didn't even have to touch Fallion's forehead this time. As soon as she looked at him, he shook himself and his big, beautiful wings appeared once more.

"Thank you, *micora*." She scratched his nose as Herin scrambled onto his back.

The others were ready. They just needed her.

But she didn't want to leave this place. She didn't want to face whatever was going to happen next.

She knew somehow that this was a cusp moment in her life. A balancing point. After this moment things would change irreparably and she had no way to know whether they'd be for the better or not.

She touched the moon stone at her throat. Was she doing the right thing?

Would everyone survive? And if they didn't, was their sacrifice worth it? Whose lives mattered more? Her friends' or her tribe's?

The stone was warm to the touch, but it didn't offer guidance. She had to do this on her own.

Sighing, she mounted up in front of Herin and urged Fallion to fly.

CHAPTER 68

They landed at the Hidden City when the moon was high above; still only a sliver of her full self, she somehow gave enough light to fully illuminate a large stone archway with markings along the top. The wall of the city continued in a curve on both sides of the archway, completely smooth.

It seemed this was the only entrance.

Beyond the arch stretched a road like the ones in the Daliphate, paved stone laid side-by-side to form a path. The stones were completely clear of sand as if someone had just brushed them clean.

On each side of the road rose buildings, square and squat, the color of the desert.

It was silent. No men, no animals.

Not even a breeze.

K'lrsa was reminded of when they flew. Everything looked like the real world, but there were none of the normal smells or sounds.

The wall, though, was rough under her hand when she touched it.

She pointed to the arch. "Is that writing? What does it say?"

She'd never been taught to read. Why bother? She hadn't needed it to hunt baru.

Herin walked closer. Lodie joined her and they

whispered back and forth, pointing at different spots along the arch.

"Well? What does it say?"

Herin shrugged her pack into a more comfortable position. "It says 'Beware all that enter'. But we already knew it was a dangerous place."

"All those letters for those four simple words?"

Garzel joined Herin and she slipped her hand into his as they faced the arch together.

Herin turned to Lodie. "It's not too late."

Lodie shook her head. "I'm not turning back."

"Why would she turn back? What aren't you telling me?"

But they ignored her.

Herin and Garzel stepped forward, hands still linked. They paused just before the arch and then strode forward, heads held high, and disappeared into a flash of white light.

The road beyond the arch still stretched ahead, as empty as before, no sign of Herin or Garzel.

Lodie stepped up to the arch.

K'lrsa reached for her. "Wait. We don't know what happened to them. You can't just walk through."

But Lodie ignored her and she too stepped under the arch and disappeared in a flash of white light. Once again, the road beyond stretched ahead, completely empty.

K'lrsa turned to Badru. "What happened to them? How do we get them back?"

He held out his hand. "We don't. We follow. It's the only way in. And we need to save your people. And mine."

She swallowed. Was it really the only way in? Maybe they should wait. See if the others came back.

But, no. They weren't coming back, were they?

They'd known exactly what they were walking into.

She looked around, but there was no one to tell her what to do now. She had to decide: continue or go home.

She took a deep breath and put her hand in Badru's and then turned to Vedhe, holding out her other hand. Vedhe gave her twisted smile and placed her hand in K'lrsa's.

They walked forward, the horses trailing behind.

K'lrsa tensed as they reached the arch, waiting for the pain of fire.

She closed her eyes.

They stepped forward.

A flash of white light, but no pain.

K'lrsa stumbled as the noise of hundreds of people, speaking languages she'd never heard before, assaulted her from all sides.

She opened her eyes.

They were on the same street they'd seen from the other side of the arch. But now the street was full of people, walking around talking. It was midday, the sun shining above them.

A man laughed so loudly that she flinched away from him, but he didn't even seem to notice her.

Lodie, Herin, and Garzel were just ahead, waiting for them. The horses stood just behind them.

She took Fallion's reins, stroking his nose. He was calm, not like when they'd been in the crowded cities of the Daliphate. He'd hated it there.

Something was different about this city.

She turned, trying to figure out what it was.

The smell. There was none. A city this size with this many people should reek with the smell of humanity—the combination of sweat and manure and industry. Or at least of baking bread or a woman's perfume.

But there was no smell.

She studied the people around them. Some had the dark skin and hair of the tribes, but others had skin as pale and fair as Vedhe or as dark-skinned as Sayel.

There was more variety in this one crowded street than she'd ever seen in her life, even in Toreem.

And they all carried on as if six strangers and three horses hadn't just appeared in their midst.

Herin didn't seem concerned, so K'lrsa decided to follow her lead. What else could she do?

"Now what?" she asked.

Herin nodded towards the center of the city. "Now we find the labyrinth."

CHAPTER 69

K'lrsa and Badru followed Herin and Garzel and Lodie and Vedhe as they walked along the straight road towards the center of the city. Even though the city was entirely flat they couldn't see that far ahead because of all the people milling in the street, walking back and forth, talking and laughing.

No one seemed to actually be doing anything other than talking. There weren't street vendors like she'd seen in the Daliphana and no one seemed to be headed anywhere important. And, oddly, as many people as there were, K'lrsa and the others never had to step aside to avoid anyone.

K'lrsa wanted to stop someone, ask them who they were and how they'd gotten there, but something kept her from doing it. Maybe it was the look on Herin's face.

She had such focus. Garzel, too.

K'lrsa moved forward to walk next to Lodie who was at least looking around at the people they passed. "What is this place? Who are all these people? And why do Herin and Garzel look like they're walking to their deaths?"

Lodie shook her head, never taking her eyes from the crowd. She was trying to look at every single person they passed, her eyes darting back and forth to make sure she didn't miss anyone.

Did she know someone here? How? And who?

K'lrsa fell back another step until she was walking with Badru once more. "Will you tell me what this is all about? Who are these people? Where did they come from?"

Badru shook his head. "I don't know. I have my guesses, but no answers."

"Well, tell me your guesses then."

He shook his head. "Later."

They walked on through the city past more and more people and more of the same, square buildings. How did anyone know where they were? There were no signs and everything looked the exact same except for all the people. She stared at a woman with hair as red as the sunset and skin as white as milk who was laughing at a joke told by a man even darker skinned than Sayel.

They walked and walked until they should've long-since passed out the other side of the city, but still the road continued onward as straight as ever, the labyrinth somewhere far ahead.

At last, the road they were following ended at another road, this one a curved road that separated them from a large stone wall that stretched into the distance. It looked like the road and the wall might eventually form a circle, but if so it was a very large circle.

The road was empty.

Directly before them, set into that wall, was another arched entrance like the one outside the city.

They stepped onto the circular road and the sounds of the city disappeared.

They were alone. No one to be seen in any direction, even behind them.

As they stepped closer, K'lrsa studied the markings atop the arch. Similar to those on the first arch but different.

Fallion took his reins in his teeth and pulled free of K'lrsa's grip. He turned and walked towards a stable yard a short distance away, Midnight and Kriger following.

K'lrsa would've sworn it wasn't there when she'd first looked that way.

She didn't want Fallion to leave, but it was clear he couldn't come with them and didn't expect to.

"Well." K'lrsa turned to the others. "What now?"

Herin nodded at the lettering. "It says, 'Those who seek knowledge must first overcome.'"

"What's that mean? Overcome what?"

Herin shrugged. "Whatever stands in your path, I'd imagine."

K'lrsa breathed in through her nose as she glared at Herin. Couldn't the woman ever give a straight answer? "You said this was a labyrinth. What else do you know about it?"

She shook her head. "Just that. That at the center of the Hidden City is the labyrinth. Those who find their way to the center of the labyrinth find what they seek."

K'lrsa turned to Lodie. "What do you know about it?"

Lodie raised an eyebrow at K'lrsa's tone, but she answered, "That there are challenges we have to face. Some are physical, and some are challenges of the mind or spirit."

"How many?"

Lodie looked to Herin. Herin shrugged and held up three maimed fingers. Lodie nodded. "We think three. We don't know the order. But one each to test the body, the mind, and the spirit."

"And can we stay together? Or are the challenges individual?"

"Both."

"Both? What does that mean?"

Lodie looked to Herin again. Herin shrugged. "As far as we know we can all enter together, but some may overcome a challenge that others fail. If you want to continue, you'll have to do so without them."

"Can we die in there?"

Herin shrugged as if to say it didn't matter.

"Herin? Can anything in there kill us? If so, I don't think we should all go. Maybe Lodie and Badru and Vedhe can stay here." She knew Herin would insist on going and Garzel with her. This way, though, maybe she could spare the others.

Badru stepped to her side. "We all go. We already made that choice."

"But…"

"It's too late to turn back now." He glanced between Herin and Lodie. "Is there anything else we should know before we enter?"

They both shook their heads.

He drew his sword. "Then let's go."

"Wait." Herin stepped in front of him. "I believe we're allowed to face the challenges as a group, but I'm not sure it will allow us to do so unless we walk through together."

"What is *it*?" K'lrsa asked.

"The labyrinth."

"Is it alive?"

"Pzah, child. Like I know. Something presents the challenges, though, doesn't it?"

K'lrsa wanted to throttle the old grel. Why did she always have to be so infuriating?

Lodie stepped between them. "There are rules we don't understand about how it works. The wise ones of each tribe used to come here. They would make their way through the labyrinth to learn the secrets of the tribes. But it wasn't all of the wise ones. Only those chosen to be the head wise one of each tribe. And before they came the other head wise ones would tell them what to expect."

Herin glared at Lodie, her lips pressed together so tight it was a wonder her face didn't collapse in on itself.

Lodie continued, "But that knowledge died when Aran murdered our tribe and all of the head wise ones. We asked the wise ones at the gathering what they knew of the Hidden City. That's why we know there's a labyrinth and that it contains challenges. And we know that in the past wise ones would come here together. Sometimes a wise one who wanted to step aside would bring their successor and help them make their way through. So we know it's possible to traverse the labyrinth with at least one other."

She looked at everyone in turn. "Deaths were rare then, but they did happen. And this was for those who knew what to expect. We were told that right after the attack on the Summer Spring Tribe a few came here to challenge the labyrinth but they never returned. None have tried since."

Herin snorted. "Now that the history lesson is over. Be prepared for anything."

Lodie added, "And remember, until you reach the center of the labyrinth and are given the knowledge you seek, you have not passed all the challenges even if it seems like you have."

Badru hefted his sword. "Are we ready?"

They all nodded, checking that bows and knives were ready to hand. Badru and Vedhe were the only ones with their weapons already drawn, one to lead, one to bring up the rear. The rest joined hands.

"Ready?" Badru winked at her and K'lrsa couldn't help but smile back even though she felt almost sick with dread.

"Pzah. You foolish children." Herin squeezed K'lrsa's other hand, the stubs of her fingers digging into K'lrsa's palm. "Take this seriously. Lives depend on it."

Garzel gave a small grunt of agreement from where he stood on Herin's other side. Lodie and Vedhe stood, waiting patiently, refusing to join in the bickering.

Badru nodded. "Alright then. Let's go."

They walked through the arch and into the path of fire.

CHAPTER 70

A gust of flame missed Badru and K'lrsa by the narrowest of margins, coming so close it singed K'lrsa's eyebrows. The heat of it blistered her skin as Badru yanked her behind him, shielding her from the source of the flames with his own body as he pushed her behind a tall stone pillar already covered in scorch marks.

Herin's hand jerked free of K'lrsa's as she and Garzel stepped forward.

On the other side, Lodie and Vedhe dashed behind a low stone pedestal, also scored with thick black marks.

Herin raised her voice and let out the high ki-ki-ki of the Riders.

"Grandmother, no!" Badru shouted as she and Garzel took another step forward.

K'lrsa held him back as another gout of flame struck in their direction. She glanced around the other side of the pillar to see what they faced.

It was a dragon.

A dragon? She'd heard of them, of course, but had never thought they were real. Dragons were tales told to children, fantasy beasts out of the age of legends.

But that's what it had to be. Ten times the size of a horse, covered in glistening copper and red scales, each the size of K'lrsa's hand, a long snout, heavy brow ridges, and breathing fire at anything that moved.

The dragon reared back on its hind legs, its tail swishing the ground as it readied itself to breathe fire once more.

"Look out!" K'lrsa screamed, but Herin and Garzel crept forward, studying the great beast.

"The belly," Herin shouted back at them, gesturing to a pale white spot close to the ground. "Cut the belly. Or the eyes. Aim for the eyes."

"Get out of there, Grandmother," Badru shouted.

But it was too late.

The dragon struck. Angry red flames engulfed Herin and Garzel.

Vedhe screamed as they writhed within the flames, holding hands, twin pillars of death.

K'lrsa wanted to scream, but she couldn't find the air to breathe.

The dragon advanced, its sinuous head turned towards the sound of Vedhe's agony.

Vedhe and Lodie fled, seeking shelter behind a larger pillar as the dragon struck, the flames of its breath engulfing the pedestal where they'd been hidden.

K'lrsa gasped, still struggling to get air into her lungs, but she couldn't no matter how hard she tried.

Herin and Garzel were dead.

Just like that.

Had they known?

They hadn't even tried to save themselves. Why do that?

There had to be something she'd missed. They'd sacrificed themselves to find the dragon's weakness. But why?

Why do that when they didn't have to?

She grabbed Badru's arm. "Let's go back. We don't have to do this. There has to be another way."

Badru pulled away, shaking his head, his gaze still fixed on where the dragon stalked Vedhe through tumbled stone pillars.

"Badru."

"No. It's too late."

He was right. The arch was gone.

She spun around, looking to see if she'd somehow been mistaken, if it was somewhere else.

But, no.

There was no arch.

They were in a large circular sand-filled area enclosed with gray stones that led upward, expanding outward every few steps. Pedestals and pillars were scattered everywhere, many with black scorch marks on them, but there was no arch.

The dragon roared its rage as Lodie stabbed at its tail. Before it could turn on her, Vedhe shot an arrow that glanced off the ridge above its right eye. It spewed fire at Vedhe, but she'd already moved on.

K'lrsa knew she should help her friends, but she didn't care about defeating the dragon. She just wanted to go home. Back to where she'd come from.

The spot where Herin and Garzel had died was just a smudge of blackness. All that was left of two people who'd lived and struggled their entire lives and overcome so much.

How was that fair?

What kind of gods did that to people who came to them for help?

Badru dragged her to the side.

Just in time, too.

A burst of fire struck the pillar behind them. It seemed the dragon had turned its attention to an easier target.

Vedhe appeared between a stone pedestal and a pillar that had fallen on its side. She shouted something in her own language and aimed her bow, waiting for the dragon to turn towards her.

It whipped around, faster than it had any right to.

She shot and dodged to the side as it breathed fire at her.

The arrow lodged itself in the corner of the dragon's eye. It screamed so loud a pillar crashed to the ground.

Badru hefted his sword in both hands. "My turn." He waited until the dragon turned to pursue Vedhe and then raced forward, ducking under one of its gigantic, clawed feet.

K'lrsa longed to call him back, but she didn't dare. She watched in breathless fear as he raised his sword and slashed at the dragon's belly.

The sword glanced off its hide, but Badru stayed, moving as it moved, determined to try again.

She shoved her fear aside and reached for her bow.

Her friends needed her help, and even if an arrow was nothing to a creature that size, it was better to try and fail than stand aside and watch her friends die.

She aimed an arrow at its great big, ugly head as Badru readied himself to strike again.

But just as she released, Vedhe shot another arrow. This one went up the dragon's left nostril. The dragon shook its head, trying to dislodge it, and K'lrsa's shot flew wide.

Fire spewed in all directions as the dragon screamed its frustration, clawing at its face.

K'lrsa couldn't see Badru. For all she knew he'd been crushed.

"Here," she screamed. "Come and get me."

The dragon turned, its eyes a malevolent red as it advanced on her. Badru moved with it, sword in hand, waiting for his chance to strike.

The dragon drew a deep breath, readying itself to attack.

K'lrsa tensed.

She wanted to run.

But Badru needed more time.

She fought to stay standing there, in the dragon's path, knowing that at any moment it would attack.

It pulled back, its chest expanding, air filling its lungs. And, then, just as it started to lunge forward, Lodie tackled K'lrsa and they both rolled to the side as flame struck the spot where she'd just been.

The dragon screamed, a sound unlike anything K'lrsa had ever heard before. The sound was almost human in its agony, but primal, too.

The dragon thrashed side-to-side. Fire gushed into the air above it.

K'lrsa stumbled to her feet as Badru broke free of the monster's convulsing body.

His sword was still lodged in the dragon's soft underbelly just below a huge rent in its flesh. The dragon collapsed, curled in on itself, scrabbling to remove the sword that still stuck out from the wound.

Its tail broke the nearest two pillars as it bellowed in pain, thrashing from side to side.

K'lrsa watched, her hands clenched in fists of agony, as each cry and scream pulsed through her.

No creature should have to suffer like that.

She hated what it had done to Herin and Garzel, but whose fault was that?

Not the dragon's. The gods'. They'd placed it here.

"We have to kill it," she said.

"It'll die eventually." Lodie stepped in her path, but she stepped around her.

"No. It doesn't deserve to suffer like that."

She dashed forward, an arrow in her hand, hoping she could reach the creature's eye. Vedhe came forward, too, clutching an arrow like a stake, the same determination on her face.

As they approached, the dragon stilled, watching them with eyes far too intelligent for a mere animal.

It didn't try to attack them, just watched. The wound in its belly was a huge, gaping thing, green-tinged blood oozing out of it. No matter what they did now, the dragon was going to die.

Vedhe held up her arrow and muttered something in her own language, gesturing towards the creature's eye. The dragon lowered its head to the ground, its intelligent eyes wide open.

It didn't move as they came closer.

"Here." Vedhe gestured towards its right eye. They took positions, one on either side of the giant red eye that stared ahead, unblinking.

Vedhe nodded and together they plunged their arrows into the dragon's eye. The dragon twitched, but held steady as they pushed the arrows in further.

It was one of the worst moments of K'lrsa's life. She trembled with sorrow and disgust and anger as the eye finally burst, covering her with viscous fluid. She wanted to stop then, but she pressed the arrow deeper and deeper until the dragon twitched once more and died.

She stumbled away, arms wrapped tight across her stomach, hating the gods more in that moment than she'd hated anyone ever before.

She clutched at the smooth edge of a nearby pedestal as wave after wave of nausea coursed through her.

What was the point?

Herin and Garzel dead.

The dragon dead.

And for what?

To *test* them?

To see if they were *worthy?* What kind of gods did that?

And how did killing a magnificent creature like this dragon make them worthy of anything worth having?

She shook her head.

"K'lrsa?" Badru rubbed the small of her back. "Are you okay?"

She forced herself to stand.

The dragon's body was gone.

A new arch stood in its place, stone like the others, but smaller, wide enough for four instead of six. The writing on top was different, too.

"What does it say?" K'lrsa asked, unable to keep the venom out of her voice.

Lodie answered, "That physical courage isn't enough if you want the knowledge of the gods."

"Is that what that was? Physical courage?" K'lrsa shook her head. "Fine. Let's go. Can't go back now, can we?"

Badru held her back. "I think we should rest here. The arch isn't going anywhere."

He led the way to a pedestal large enough for all four of them to sit together.

Lodie handed around a waterskin full of warm water that tasted of sand but was still refreshing.

"Are they really dead?" K'lrsa asked.

"Who?" Lodie took a swig from the waterskin and passed it on to Vedhe.

"Herin and Garzel. *Who do you think?*"

"Oh." Lodie nodded. "Yes."

"Gee, you seem really broken up about it."

"K'lrsa." Badru chided her.

"Well, honestly. Her own sister is dead and she doesn't even shed a tear."

Lodie took another swig from the waterskin. "Would you prefer I tore my hair out and rent my skin with my nails? Would that make my grief more acceptable to you?"

"No. I'm sorry. I just…I can't believe they're gone."

"They knew the choice they were making when they came here. As did we all."

But had they really? Maybe the others had, but K'lrsa certainly hadn't.

CHAPTER 71

When the others were finally ready, they linked hands once more and stepped through the arch. K'lrsa hoped Herin had been right about the types of challenges they'd face, because Badru no longer had his sword which left them with only some small knives and two bows.

There was a flash of white light as they stepped through the arch and then they found themselves in a cave with no entrance. She could just touch the ceiling with her fingertips. There were no torches or other obvious source of light, but somehow the room was perfectly lit so they could see every single nook and cranny.

She walked forward. It took six steps to reach the opposite wall and would probably take another ten to walk the length of it. Hundreds of small circular holes covered the walls, each with a drawing etched into the stone above.

A flat stone pedestal dominated the center of the space with seventeen long rods in yellow, green, orange, and red sitting on top. There were seven red rods, but only one green.

K'lrsa sniffed, expecting to smell water or dust, but there was no scent to the place.

Again.

Of course. Whatever this place was, it wasn't any more real than the arena.

"So what do we do now?" K'lrsa ran her fingers over

the carved drawing of a sun, trying not to notice how small the room was.

Lodie turned one of the rods over in her hand. "We solve the puzzle. I assume this is the test of the mind." She held the rod up to one of the holes in the wall. It would fit.

But which hole of the hundreds did it belong in?

K'lrsa ran her fingers over another carving, this one of a quarter moon, trying to take deep enough breaths to get air into her lungs. "Do you understand it? Can we solve it?"

She closed her eyes, fighting back an intense urge to claw her way free of the tiny space.

When she opened her eyes again, the walls seemed to be wavering before her. "Do you see that? Are the walls moving?"

"No." Badru put his hand on the wall next to her. "See? Not moving."

She shivered, waiting for the wall to shift under his hand.

"Are you okay?" He took her shoulders in his, trying to meet her eyes.

She shook her head. She needed to get out of there. Now.

"K'lrsa?" His brow furrowed in concern.

She took great, big panting breaths trying to draw more air into her lungs.

She swayed slightly, struggling to stay upright. The walls *were* moving.

"K'lrsa." Badru shook her gently. "Look at me."

She struggled to focus on his bright blue eyes, but she couldn't. Her eyes rolled around trying to see everything at once.

"K'lrsa. I want you to close your eyes and listen to my voice." He spoke strongly, his thumbs rubbing small little circles against her skin.

She closed her eyes and focused on the movement of his thumbs, letting their steady motion bring her back to herself.

"The walls…" she whispered.

"They're not moving." He took her hand and placed it against his chest. "I want you to breathe when I do, okay?"

She nodded.

He took a deep breath in and she did, too, but when he didn't let it out right away, she shook her head and tried to pull away. He held her hand to his chest, making soft noises to calm her.

"Center your breathing, K'lrsa. Find the Core. You know how to do this."

She almost smiled. He'd remembered about the Core.

She took one deep shuddering breath and then another. And another.

Slowly, she matched her breathing to his until finally her pulse slowed and she could hear Vedhe and Lodie's arguing instead of the blood pounding in her ears.

She started to open her eyes, but Badru whispered, "No. Not yet. Keep them closed. Keep breathing. In…and out….and in….and out."

She let her body be guided by the rhythm of his voice, slowly relaxing and letting go of her fear.

Lodie shoved past them. "No, no, no. Not like that. That's all wrong."

K'lrsa opened her eyes. Badru's fingers tightened on her shoulders, but she shook her head slightly. "It's okay. I'm…I'm okay."

Vedhe answered Lodie from somewhere behind her. "But sun, see?"

Badru held K'lrsa's gaze. "Are you sure?"

She nodded.

And she was. Whatever had scared her had passed. The walls were no longer moving. And she could see that they never would.

She turned to where Lodie and Vedhe were arguing, pointing at different spots in the wall, talking about the sun and moon and stars and phases and cycles. She didn't understand a word of it, so she turned to Badru. "Do you know what they're talking about?"

He shook his head. "I just hope they do. Or else we'll be stuck here until the end of time."

"Or until we run out of air." Her breathing quickened at the thought.

"Now, now. Don't do that." Badru grabbed her chin and forced her to look at him. "Calm, deep breaths, remember?"

Right.

She licked her lips. Why were they so dry all of a sudden?

He held her gaze. "Breathe with me. In….out…."

K'lrsa fought the urge to run around the room screaming as she matched her breaths to his and reminded herself she just had to keep calm until Vedhe or Lodie figured out the puzzle.

That's all.

She just hoped they managed it before they all really did run out of air.

Or food.

Or water.

Or patience.

CHAPTER 72

In the same way that light filled the cave even though there were no windows or torches, air seemed to be replaced as well, which eventually allowed K'lrsa to calm down enough to sit on the stone pedestal and watch the others work.

She earned a few dark glares for fiddling with the colored rods, but most of the time the others were too absorbed in trying to decipher the challenge.

After they'd been there what felt like forever, the pedestal K'lrsa was sitting on became so hot she had to jump off. As soon as she did, food appeared. It was simple fare like in the caves, but food nonetheless, and plenty of it. Dried meat, sour greens, and small biscuits made of seeds, berries and fat.

As they ate, the others paced the room. They'd tried everything they could think of, but nothing had worked. There was no meaning to the number seventeen that any of them knew. Nor to the combination of the numbers seven, six, three and one which were the numbers of red, orange, yellow and green rods, respectively.

"What about the symbols? They have to mean something." Badru pointed to a sun, a quarter moon, and what seemed to be a cloud.

Vedhe brought the three yellow rods and placed them into the holes. Nothing happened. Just like with every other attempt they'd made.

"Maybe all seventeen have to be in place before it will work?" Badru asked.

Lodie snorted. "Let's hope not or we're never going to leave this place."

"What are you trying to do?" K'lrsa asked.

Badru pointed to the holes. "I was thinking maybe the yellow rods represent Father Sun, the Lady Moon, and the Trickster."

Lodie rolled her neck, wincing in pain as it made a loud pop. "But then what would the others represent? And how would that be a real challenge? It would just be a test of memorization that any could pass once they'd been told the answer. No. There has to be something more to it."

K'lrsa paced the room, studying all the little symbols. She traced the outline of one in the shape of a hand held out as if to stop someone.

She stepped back, studying the rest of the symbols on the wall. There were two more symbols just like the hand one.

"Lodie, what do you think this symbol means? I understand the sun and the moon, but what about this one with the hand held out?"

Lodie shrugged. "I'm not sure it means anything. It might just be there to make finding the moon and sun symbols harder."

"But what if it does have meaning? What if they all do?"

Badru walked along the wall nearest him, running his finger over different marks with a frown. He paused on a drawing of a long-legged bird. "I've seen something like this before. In my grandfather's study, after he died. There were drawings that used some of these symbols. But they were combined together, not separate."

Lodie nodded as she came to join him. "Yes. Right. That makes sense."

"What does?" K'lrsa asked as she looked over Lodie's shoulder.

"It's possible these are from the old style of writing. If so, then each symbol stands for a sound. You combine the sounds to form words." She touched another example of the outstretched hand symbol. "If so, this one could be stop, which means it stands for the sound 'st'."

K'lrsa touched a small circular mark with an x through it, wondering what sound it represented. "If that's true, then maybe we're supposed to create a word with the rods."

Badru shook his head. "No. There are too many rods for that."

"Then maybe four words, one for each color."

"But what four words?"

K'lrsa glared at him, wishing he would be just a little more enthusiastic about her idea.

Vedhe held up the three yellow rods. "Knowledge. Na-ley-je." She gestured with each rod in turn.

Badru frowned. "But that's only one word. What are the other three?"

K'lrsa glared at him.

Lodie stepped between them. "Why don't we start with that and see what we find? We'll worry about the other words after."

K'lrsa turned back to the wall. "Okay. So what are the symbols to spell knowledge?"

"How should I know?" Badru asked.

But even as K'lrsa turned to glare at him once more, Lodie walked the nearest wall, trailing her fingers along each symbol. Her tongue stuck out slightly as she paused on different ones, studying them with narrowed eyes.

She paused for a long time on a drawing of a triangle inside a circle, but eventually moved on.

Finally, she pointed to one that looked like a squat, fat bird. "This one. I think it's the na-na bird, which makes it the first symbol."

"Great!" K'lrsa glanced at the wall next to her, expecting to see more drawings of the bird, but didn't. It was okay. That just meant it would be easier to find the whole word. "So what's the second symbol?"

Lodie continued on until she came to a small drawing of three wavy lines. She tapped it with her long fingernail.

"This one. Leven is a type of flood that comes only once every hundred years."

Badru peered at it. "And you're sure that's what the symbol represents?"

"It's as good a guess as any."

"And the third symbol?" he asked.

Vedhe shook her head. "Find when find others together." She moved to the opposite wall and started looking for the two symbols together, muttering when she found one or the other but not both.

K'lrsa took the wall to her left. Lodie the one to her right and Badru the one opposite.

They searched in silence, the frustration mounting each time they found one of the symbols but not the other. At last, Vedhe cried out, almost dancing in excitement.

Lodie joined her, but after studying the third symbol, she shook her head. "No. I don't think that's it."

They continued their search, slower this time.

Badru found the next pair, but it wasn't right either.

Still they pushed on, searching, squinting at the symbols, hoping to find a combination that made sense.

K'lrsa was halfway across her wall when she finally found the two symbols next to each other in the very top row. "Lodie?" she called softly, her voice thrumming with excitement.

She didn't want to get her hopes up, but she was sure this was it.

Lodie traced the markings of the next symbol. Her tongue moved along her gums with a soft squelch as she studied it. Finally, she nodded. "Yes. I think that could be it."

K'lrsa laughed. "Ha! We did it. Where are the yellow rods?"

Vedhe handed Lodie the yellow rods. She placed them in the holes—she was the only one tall enough to do it— her hands shaking so badly it took her three tries to place the last one.

They gathered together and waited.

But nothing happened.

Lodie pulled the rods from the wall and threw them on the pedestal with the others. "Keep looking," she growled and stalked back to her wall to resume the search.

But K'lrsa didn't move.

Lodie was wrong.

Those were the three symbols. She knew it.

Badru came to stand next to her. "What is it?"

"Those are the symbols. I know they are."

"Maybe they occur together somewhere else on the wall, too."

K'lrsa shook her head. "No. These are them."

He turned to the pedestal where the rods lay, now arranged by color. One green, seven red. Six orange, three yellow.

He shook his head.

"What is it?" K'lrsa asked.

"I think we were wrong about the colors."

Lodie turned to listen. So did Vedhe.

He pointed at the red rods. "If we use one color per word that means there has to be a word that's seven symbols long and another that's six long. That isn't going to happen. Think about it. Knowledge was only three."

Lodie nodded.

They all stared at the rods for a while, Badru moving them around, trying to make shapes with them, but none knew what to do next.

Lodie gave a small gasp and stepped forward, eagerly rearranging the rods to form groups with one of each color. There were seven piles when she was done, the smallest with only a red rod in it, the biggest with one each of yellow, red, orange, and green.

She pointed to the lone red rod. "A small word." And then to the largest pile. "A larger word."

Badru laughed. "Of course. We're just missing blue." He rearranged each pile so that red was first followed by orange then yellow then green. "See?"

K'lrsa shook her head. "No. What is it?"

"It's the order of a rainbow. And the colors of the Daliphate. Red, orange, yellow, green, blue. With purple

reserved for the gods. But there's no blue because there are no words that long."

Smiling, he took a pile with one red, one orange, and one yellow rod and placed them into the holes they'd tried before.

There was a flash of silver light and the rods disappeared, replaced with the three symbols now joined together to form a larger symbol.

Vedhe clapped like a child and K'lrsa laughed.

"Don't get too excited," Lodie muttered. "We still have fourteen of these things left."

K'lrsa refused to feel defeated. Not when they were so close. "We're getting there. So what phrase includes the word knowledge?"

Lodie pursed her lips. "That phrase on the arch outside the labyrinth."

"Of course! It had the word overcome in it. So what's the symbol for 'ov'? Lodie?"

Lodie scanned the row, her mouth working silently as she moved from symbol to symbol. Six symbols later, she stopped. "Here. Give me a red rod."

K'lrsa handed her a red rod, as well as an orange and a yellow.

"One more. Give me the green one, too."

K'lrsa handed her the green one and Lodie shoved all four into place. As she stood back there was another small flash of light and the rods were once more replaced with the symbols joined into one.

Badru grabbed a red and an orange rod and placed them into the symbols to the left of knowledge. They merged to form a word.

"Seek," he said as he stepped back so the rest of them could study the wall.

K'lrsa took two more rods and put them on the other side of knowledge.

"Must," she told the others as they, too, merged together.

There were only six rods left, but no one moved to place them.

Finally, Vedhe stepped forward with just a red rod in

her hand. She put it on the left side of "seek" and stepped back.

They all held their breath, scared what might happen if she was wrong, but once more there was a light and the rod was replaced with the symbol.

K'lrsa glanced at the five remaining rods. "So we have a word with two in it and a word with three in it."

Lodie grabbed a red, an orange, and a yellow and shoved them into place after the symbols for the word "must".

Badru made as if to stop her, but she shrugged. "It was the only choice once Vedhe did the one-rod word."

So it was. That left the two rods to either go at the start or the end. K'lrsa grabbed them and put them at the beginning. "Whatever the exact words were I know it ended with overcome, because I remember thinking how stupid it was that it didn't say what we had to overcome."

The last rods glowed silver and were replaced by their symbols. All the other holes and symbols in the wall disappeared, replaced by a new arch wide enough for all four of them to pass through together.

They'd done it!

K'lrsa held out her hands. "I'm ready to be done with this room. How about you?"

Vedhe took her right hand and Badru her left. Lodie grabbed Vedhe's hand and they stepped through, ready for the next challenge.

CHAPTER 73

K 'lrsa wasn't sure what to expect on the other side of the arch, but what they found certainly wasn't it.

They stepped into a small clearing in the midst of lush, green plants and trees that towered high above them. Ahead, a narrow white-tiled path disappeared into the greenery. To the right was a green-tiled path and to the left a red-tiled path. Turning, K'lrsa saw a yellow-tiled path and a blue-tiled one as well.

They were inside. A roof above sheltered them from the sun that shone through windows high along each wall. A breeze cooled her skin. Water flowed somewhere nearby, gently cascading down a series of rocks. Birds, hidden in the foliage, trilled in happiness.

"Ama!" A little girl ran towards them from the red path, barefoot, her long brown hair streaming out behind her. She must've been four or five summers old and wore a baru-hide dress that barely reached her chubby little ankles.

Lodie fell to her knees, crying, arms flung wide.

"Lodie? Are you okay?"

"Ama. Come." The little girl tugged on Lodie's hand, leading her away down the path.

"Lodie, wait."

But Lodie didn't even pause.

"We should follow her."

But before they could, a tall young man with skin and

273

hair as pale as Vedhe's stepped off the green-tiled path. Vedhe squealed in excitement and ran towards him.

He laughed as she tackled him with a hug, tears pouring down her cheeks, babbling excitedly in her own language. He enveloped her in a hug and led her away, their heads pressed close together as they too disappeared.

"Badru? What is this? What's happening?" She gripped his hand, scared that someone would come to lead him away next.

"K'lrsa," a voice called softly from behind her.

She shivered as she recognized the voice.

Her father? But how was that possible?

She turned, slowly, letting go of Badru's hand, not daring to breathe lest she shatter the illusion.

But it was him. It was really him standing there, smiling at her, his eyes crinkled in joy.

"Dad?" she whispered.

"Of course. Didn't anyone tell you what this place was?"
"No."

"It's the crossroads between the land of the living and the land of the dead. It's where both can meet."

She didn't want to believe it. But she'd missed him so much…

"But, the labyrinth. We were…"

"You made it through to the center, K'lrsa. I'm here to guide you to a place where you can rest before you receive the wisdom of this place."

She held herself back for another long moment until she couldn't stand it any longer and then flung herself into her father's arms. It was him, it really was. Exactly like she remembered.

"How is this possible? How are you here?"

Her dad laughed. "Come. I'll explain it all. Over some good food."

He always had liked his food, even the simple fare they usually ate.

They walked down the yellow-tiled path, her father with one arm thrown casually around her shoulders, talking the whole time about how wonderful she looked and how she'd have to tell him everything he'd missed since he'd been gone.

He led her to a clearing with a small fire pit and a pair of baru-hide camp stools set around it. A blanket next to the stools was covered with an assortment of her favorite foods—most from the tribes, but some from her time in the Daliphana, too—grilled baru, fresh apples, figs stuffed with goat cheese and drizzled in honey.

Her father sat down. "Eat. I'm sure you're hungry."

She glanced back down the path. Where was Badru? She'd completely forgotten about him in the thrill of seeing her father. "Dad. I…Where are my friends?"

"With their loved ones. Getting some well-deserved food and rest, just like you. Now, come. Eat. I'll explain everything."

"But why couldn't we stay together?" She chewed on her lip, torn between her desire to spend time with her father and her worry for the others.

He smiled. "Because the dead are selfish. We each wanted time alone with our loved ones. Is that such a bad thing? We have so much to catch up on and no one else will want to hear it. Don't worry." He patted the stool next to him. "There will be time later for your friends. I'd like to meet the young man who's captured my daughter's heart. But later. After we've had a chance to talk. I've missed you, K'lrsa. Haven't you missed me?"

"Of course!"

"Then sit and spend a little time with your father, would you?"

She glanced down the path once more. Her father was right. It was just a meal. And she might never have this chance again. She could find the others after.

She lowered herself to the camp stool, looking around at the tall trees and dense bushes, so different from the plains and deserts of home. "What is this place?"

"A sanctuary. A place to revive and recover after the ordeal of the labyrinth." He cut an apple and offered her half.

She took it, delighting in its crunchy tang, something she'd never experienced before she went to the Daliphana. "I can't stay long, you know." She forced the words out even though they were the last words she wanted to say. "The tribes need me. The Black Horse Tribe and the Daliph's men have them trapped in the gathering grounds."

"You have more time than you think. Time flows differently here than it does out there. Hadn't you noticed?"

She nodded. "But I still don't understand. I thought when I reached the center of the labyrinth I'd receive knowledge. Or a weapon. Or knowledge that is a weapon."

He laughed. "Patience. I know it was never your strength, but don't spurn this gift the gods have given us."

She grimaced. "The gods. I'm not very impressed with them right now. That dragon didn't deserve its fate."

"It wasn't real."

"It seemed real enough. And real or not, I'll carry that death with me forever."

He nodded. "But you understand the gods can't just give knowledge to anyone who wants it."

"Why not? Why can't we all know what they have to teach?"

He fixed her with an admonishing look so familiar it almost hurt. "K'lrsa. Think. What would a man like Aran do with the knowledge to create a weapon so powerful it would let one man destroy an army?"

K'lrsa shook her head. "But I don't understand how killing a dragon somehow separates me from him. You'd think a man like that would be more than willing to do it to reach his ends."

Her father shrugged. "I don't know. Ask the gods."

"I want nothing more to do with them."

He laughed. "Ah, my impetuous, opinionated daughter. How about we play a game of tiles and leave the discussion of gods and worthiness for another time?"

K'lrsa shook her head. She wanted more than anything to play a game of tiles and pretend her father was still alive, but she needed answers to at least a few questions first. "How are you here? How is this possible?"

"I told you. The Hidden City is a waypoint between the real world and the Promised Plains. Here alone, the dead and the living can come together as equals."

"Has it always been that way?'"

He nodded. "Ever since it was created."

"How come no one knows that? If I'd known…If Mom had known…"

He smiled. "If you'd known you would've ridden Fallion straight here after I died. Same with your mother."

"Exactly!"

"And what would that have accomplished?"

She blinked. "I don't know. Why does it have to accomplish anything? I could've seen you again. Said goodbye. Said I was sorry I didn't find you sooner."

He squeezed her hand. "You had nothing to apologize for, K'lrsa. And I'm glad you didn't know you could come here. This place is dangerous for the living."

"Why?"

"Because the desire to live here with someone they love is often stronger than the desire to move forward alone. If you'd come here right after I died, with no other purpose or love to drive you forward, would you have been able to leave?"

She stared at him, wondering if she was strong enough to do so now.

He squeezed her hand again, grimacing as if he could read her thoughts. "Enough of this. Tell me everything that's happened since that day. How did you meet that young man? And who were the others who came with you?"

She knew she should press him for more answers, but the temptation to spend a simple meal with him talking about her life just like they used to was too strong.

So she told him about the vision from Father Sun and how she'd almost killed herself trying to find the trading caravan and how he'd been right that the Black Horse Tribe was trading in slaves and how horrible G'van had treated her and about taking Vedhe's place and meeting Lodie and helping them escape and…

Before she knew it the food was all gone and she couldn't stop yawning. It was dark. The sound of night insects filled the air.

It was still pleasantly warm. Perfectly warm. And they didn't need the fire; she could still see her father just fine.

"What is this place? Where did the food come from? How can I see you so easily even though it's dark?"

He shrugged. "It's best not to question how things happen here, but just accept that they do. The laws of the gods are different from the laws of men."

She tilted her head to the side, studying him. Her father had always been the type to want answers, to push for the truth no matter what. Why not now?

She yawned again, fighting an intense desire to curl up right there on the ground and sleep for a bit.

He smiled affectionately. "You should get some rest. And maybe clean up a bit as well." He wrinkled his nose and she laughed.

He pointed to a nearby white-tiled path. "Follow the path. You'll find a place to sleep and bathe."

He stood.

She fought the urge to clutch at him, afraid that if he walked away she'd never see him again. "Where are you going?"

He mussed her hair. "Don't worry. I'll be back in the morning."

"Promise?"

"Promise." He smiled down at her and K'lrsa felt such a surge of love that she almost cried knowing she'd never find someone who loved her like that again.

"Go, K'lrsa. I'll be here waiting for you in the morning."

Reluctantly, K'lrsa made her way down the path he'd indicated, turning back every few steps to make sure he was still there. He waited patiently, waving to her every time she turned around until the path curved and she found herself in a small clearing with two tents and a small stone structure.

Inside the middle tent was a sleeping pallet with a fresh pair of hunting leathers folded on top. The second tent was smaller and when she pulled back the flap a burst of hot air slapped her face. A sweat tent. She could barely make out the bucket of water and ladle waiting inside through the steam.

But, even though she knew she did need to clean up some, she didn't want to be that hot, not on such a perfect night.

She turned to the stone structure.

Inside was a large bath like she'd used in Toreem, already full of water the perfect temperature, with lavender and rose petals floating on top, deep enough to cover her all the way to her chin.

Next to the tub was a bucket with water and a ladle for her to sluice off the worst of the grime before she climbed in.

She stripped out of her dirty, sweaty hunting leathers— grimacing at how stiff they were from the last few weeks of use when they'd been so beautiful once.

It took her a bit to wash off the dirt of travel before she could climb into the tub, but when she did at last she closed her eyes in bliss.

Wouldn't Mistress Hawthorne be so proud of her now? A proper woman taking a proper bath.

She leaned back, breathing in the soothing scents of lavender and rose, feeling the oils in the water soak into her skin.

She should seek out the others. Make plans for their return to the tribes.

Tomorrow.

They all needed to sleep, didn't they? Recover a bit before they raced back. And they all deserved a chance to see their loved ones. To spend some real quality time with them while they could.

One more meal with her father. That's all she wanted.

Then she'd go back to doing what everyone else wanted her to do.

CHAPTER 74

K'lrsa awoke to the sounds of birds singing nearby just as happy as she was. She didn't know what kind of birds they were, because they certainly weren't ones she knew, but she liked their song nonetheless.

As she pulled on her new hunting leathers, she wondered once again what this place was. It couldn't be real. Not this far into the desert. But it *felt* real.

She stretched, luxuriating in the feel of a clean, well-rested body.

Outside, a light breeze brought the smell of meat cooking. She walked down the path, whistling to herself, anticipating more time spent with her father.

She'd only slept a night, but she felt as if she'd slept a lifetime.

He was fixing breakfast over a small fire, humming to himself as he stirred a bowl of millet and flipped a few strips of baru.

She soaked in the sight of him, trying to memorize every single line. All these nights since he'd died she'd never quite managed to picture his face. How had she forgotten those smile lines around his eyes or that small sun mark on his left cheek?

He caught sight of her and smiled. "About time you woke up."

She felt a surge of joy as she walked forward. It was so

good to have him back.

She knew she couldn't stay forever. She had to save the tribes. But maybe just one more day…

She felt her heart break and reform and break again thinking about losing him again.

She could always come back. After.

She hugged him, afraid he might disappear at any moment.

He hugged her back, laughing softly. "Now, now. Enough of that. Have a seat, take some food, and pick up with your story again. I believe you'd just reached Crossroads?"

She took the food he offered. It was simple fare, food she'd had so many times before she barely stopped to think about it, but it was the best meal in the world. Because her father had cooked it and she was sharing it with him.

She looked around. "Is everyone from the tribes here? If so, why didn't I see anyone I knew when we were walking towards the labyrinth?" All those people on the streets talking, all strangers. They must be dead, too."

"Not many stay in the city. Most move on." He smiled, the wrinkles around his eyes and mouth deepening. "The Promised Plains are real, K'lrsa, and much prettier than this place. They're just on the other side of the city."

She laughed as she took a bite of millet. "No they aren't. I saw what was on the other side of the city before we came here. Just more sand."

"Not if you travel through the city first. If you do that, you'll find lush, rolling meadows full of green grass and plenty of water and as much food as you could ever want."

"Then why aren't you there?"

He grimaced. "I couldn't cross over yet."

"Why?"

"Well, first, I was too tied to someone still alive. When that happens you have to wait for them or wait until enough time passes and the tie between you breaks."

"Who?" She asked even though she already knew the answer. Just in case, maybe…

"Your mother, of course."

"Right. Of course. She's here now isn't she?"

She pushed at her food. She'd always known how much her parents loved each other, how deep their bond was. She shouldn't be surprised.

But she was disappointed.

Just a little.

That it hadn't been his love of her that had held him back. It seemed her mother had been right about that, too. The love between a man and a woman was something stronger than the love between a parent and a child.

She wondered how long it would take for her to form that kind of bond with Badru. Surely it was something built between two people over a lifetime not something that should already be there. But she wished…

"Dad?"

"Yes?"

"With Mom…Did you feel that right away? Were you always each other's everything?"

He smiled, his eyes looking somewhere else. "I knew your mother was the one for me the day I met her. Ah, you should've seen your mother when she was still a Rider. She was something to behold." He shook away the memory. "But the bond we have now? No. That we built together. The seeds of it were there from the beginning, but it was like a sapling. It needed time to put its roots down and grow into something that would last. Why?"

She shrugged. "I just…I see what you have or had or whatever and I look at Badru and I wonder why we don't have that yet."

He laughed. "K'lrsa. How long have you known this boy? And how much time have you had together to actually build this connection?"

"I know. I just…The gods put us together."

"And what do the gods know of human love? Maybe they saw that you two were right for one another, but you're the ones that have to take the promise the gods gave you and turn it into something real."

She nodded. "I guess I just wish it were easier than that."

"Ah, K'lrsa. Love's the hardest thing there is. Walking away is so much easier. So much simpler." He leaned forward. "But don't you ever forget…Love is the best thing there is. It's what makes all the other trials worth it."

She didn't want to argue with him, so she changed the subject. "Do people stay here forever? In the Hidden City? Or in the Promised Plains?"

"No. Eventually we all let go."

"Let go. What do you mean?"

"It's the same with the dead as with the living, K'lrsa. We only continue on for as long as we have the will to do so. Some pass right on to whatever's beyond this. Some cling to whatever they can for as long as they can."

"Why would anyone let go not knowing what's beyond this?"

He smiled. "Ah, the certainty of youth. Life is about change, about growth and exploration. Death is…not. We don't age here, we can't have children, we can't build anything. We just…exist. Most who come here hold on for a year or two until they lose the fear of moving on and the longing for what they left behind. It's rare to last longer than that although it does happen."

"You won't let go, though, will you? You'll wait until I come back? I'll bring M'lara and D'lan. They deserve the chance to say goodbye to you, too."

He winced. "It would be better if you spent the time with me now."

"Oh."

She wondered how much longer she could stay before it was too late to save the tribes. If he had to, Fallion could fly at night and walk during the day.

That would give her at least one more day to spend with him.

And he'd said time flowed differently here. Maybe she could take two days. Or even three.

Her father pulled a small baru-hide bag from his belt. "What do you say to a game of tiles? If I recall, you almost beat me last time."

"Okay."

She knew she should leave, but she wanted to spend as much time with him as she could. It was selfish and horrible, but he was her father and she was never going to get this chance again.

When he died, she hadn't known she was going to lose him. She hadn't known it was their last meal together or their last game of tiles.

Now she did.

Now she could store away every detail for later—his laugh, his smile, the way he looked at her with such pride and affection but still tried as hard as he could to win.

It was just one more day. The world could survive without her for that long.

Couldn't it?

CHAPTER 75

The next morning, when her father smiled at her across the fire and asked if she'd like to play another game of tiles, she said yes.

It was just one more day.

And did the tribes really need her to save them? What if she'd died in Toreem? What would they have done then?

Not like she was the only possible person who could change their fates.

They'd find a way through without her.

And she wasn't going to stay forever. Just one more day. Maybe two.

That was all.

She'd just beaten her father at tiles for the third time in a row—a record—when Badru stumbled into the clearing. He was clean and wearing new clothes, but the clothes were torn and he looked like he hadn't slept for at least a day.

"Badru! What are you doing here?" She sprang to her feet, stepping between him and her father, suddenly wary.

"I've been looking everywhere for you. Come on. We have to go." He grabbed her hand and pulled her back towards the path.

"Wait. What are you doing? Let go of me." She tried to pull free, but he wouldn't let her. "Badru. Stop."

Her father was suddenly there, wrestling her free, and shoving Badru to the ground. "Let go of her." His voice was flat and cold in a way she'd never heard before.

Badru scrambled to his feet, his belt knife in his hand. Her father pulled his own knife.

K'lrsa stepped between them. "Don't."

Her father advanced, the knife clutched in his hand.

"Dad. Put the knife away."

Her father darted around her and almost knifed Badru in the side.

"Dad! Stop it."

Badru circled to keep her between them. "He's not your father, K'lrsa."

"What?"

Her father grabbed her wrist and started to pull her away. "Don't listen to him."

"Let go of me." She jerked free of his grip, using a move Badru had taught the tribes.

She backed away from both of them. "What is going on here? Badru, what are you talking about?"

He kept a wary eye on her father as he spoke. "There was supposed to be a third challenge, remember? A challenge of the spirit."

She glanced at her father and her stomach dropped.

No.

Please, not that.

"You think this is the third challenge?"

He nodded. "Can you give up the person you love most in this world to move forward and obtain the knowledge you need?"

She flicked a glance between him and her father. "So this wasn't real? He's not real?" Her voice trembled with tears.

Badru nodded.

"But…" She stared at the man she'd thought was her father. "Are you sure?"

Badru grimaced. "Yes. Think about it. Was your father always perfect? Did he always have time for you and say all the right things and did you always get along?"

She shrugged. "Mostly, yes."

"But *always*, K'lrsa? Every moment of every day? Could you have really spent two straight days with him and been perfectly happy?"

"Well…" She winced, remembering the times her father had really annoyed her with his stupid jokes. "No."

"But you could with this man, right? Because he isn't your real father with all his flaws and imperfections. He's who you remember your father to be. He's the best version of him."

"How do you know that?" She crossed her arms, fighting the urge to run to her father and bury herself in his arms.

"Because the same thing happened to me, K'lrsa. It just took me less time to realize it."

She frowned. "Who did you see?"

His lips quirked into a half-smile. "You."

"What? How's that possible?"

He shrugged, eyeing her father warily. "You walked away with your father and when I followed, there you were. Both of you. We had dinner together and talked and…That night…You and I…" He shook his head. "Look, the details don't matter. But I finally realized it wasn't really you."

"How?"

He laughed. "You were too nice to me. And you didn't care that your father was there because we finally had time to be alone together. It…It wasn't you. It was who I hoped you'd be, but not really. I love how much you love your family. And as much as I'd love to spend all day in bed with you sometime, I know you never would if your family was there, too."

K'lrsa laughed softly.

She turned to the man she'd thought was her father. "So you're not real."

"No. But I do love you and I am proud of you and I know you can do anything…"

"Oh, stop it! If you're built on my memory of him then your love and your pride are, too."

He bowed his head, just like her father had when she'd upset him when he was still alive.

K'lrsa turned away, shaking, fighting the urge to weep. She hated the gods. Hated them! "How do we leave this place?"

"You just have to ask," the man who wasn't her father replied. He waved a hand and a small arch appeared in the center of the clearing, just wide enough for two.

"What about the others?" she asked.

"They have to make it through on their own."

"No." She shook her head. "That's not true. Badru found me. We can find them."

She flinched at the thought of pulling Lodie away from the laughing little girl who must be her daughter, but they had to do it.

Badru turned to her father. "Lead us to the others."

"Very well. Follow me."

K'lrsa grabbed Badru's hand—just in case it was a trick—and followed her father down a green-tiled path that appeared on the edge of the clearing.

CHAPTER 76

They walked in silence, K'lrsa studying the back of the man she'd thought was her father. Even though she now knew it wasn't him she still treasured the time they'd spent together. Badru was right. It had been the best of her father. A condensed version of all her favorite memories brought to life.

Eventually, they reached another clearing.

In the center was a loud, laughing group of people, all as pale-skinned and fair-haired as Vedhe. She sat in their midst laughing so hard she snorted whatever she was drinking up her nose which just made her laugh even more.

She looked so happy.

K'lrsa stood on the edge of the clearing, Badru at her side, and watched as Vedhe talked to the man next to her, her eyes full of light and joy.

Was it fair? To take her from this place?

Did it matter that it wasn't real?

Didn't Vedhe deserve some level of happiness after all she'd lost? Shouldn't she be allowed to believe for as long as she could?

Badru whispered in her ear, "We need to tell her."

"Do we really?"

He nodded.

She sighed. He was probably right.

Vedhe did deserve to know she was being tricked by the

gods. That this was all a cruel lie.

She might still choose to stay anyway…

K'lrsa wouldn't blame her if she did. Of course, how could she stay, knowing the truth?

K'lrsa turned and studied the man who looked just like her father. "I've missed him, you know."

"He's missed you, too." He looked down at her with her father's brown eyes and she trembled at the cruelty of it. That whatever this man was should look and act just like the father she remembered.

She closed her eyes.

"Be well," he said.

When she opened her eyes, he was gone.

She fought the urge to call him back, to go racing down the path to the clearing in hopes of finding him once more.

She had to let go.

Her real father, the flesh and blood man who'd raised her, would want her to carry on. He'd be devastated if he knew she'd sacrificed even one life to spend more time with a memory of him.

She bowed her head for a moment, regretting bitterly how deeply he'd instilled that sense of duty. Had he known then how much it might cost her?

She took Badru's hand and they stepped into the clearing. "Vedhe," she called.

"Krissa. Badru." Vedhe stood, smiling. "My family." She pointed at each one, saying names K'lrsa couldn't possibly pronounce or remember, but K'lrsa nodded each time, allowing her another moment of happiness.

Badru nodded. "It's very nice to meet all of you."

K'lrsa just kept smiling, too torn to speak.

The family immediately turned back to their conversation as if no one else was there. The man next to Vedhe tugged on her arm, pointing at something on the table, but she shook him off and came to join K'lrsa and Badru, dodging a girl and boy who were chasing one another through the clearing, both laughing so hard they could barely stand.

Vedhe smiled, her joy so bright it eclipsed the scars on her face. She nodded towards the children. "My sister. And brother child."

K'lrsa almost turned and left.

What right did she have to destroy that joy? To force Vedhe back into the world that had killed these people.

But she knew even if she didn't, Badru would.

K'lrsa took a deep breath, willing herself to speak, but Vedhe spoke first. "Not real."

"What?" K'lrsa asked.

Vedhe nodded to the people in the clearing. "Not real family. Dream."

"You know?"

Vedhe shrugged one shoulder. "Know. Not care. Still family." Tears filled her eyes.

K'lrsa threw an arm around her shoulder as they watched the children chase one another and the adults raise their glasses with a shout and laughter. "If you want to stay, you can. We'd understand. I know saving my people isn't…That you don't…That they don't matter to you like they do to me. And that's fine, they shouldn't. I…I wouldn't blame you if you wanted to stay here forever."

Vedhe shook her head. "No. Like family. But not family. Time to leave."

"Are you sure?"

Vedhe nodded. "Goodbye first."

She walked back to the group and hugged each one in turn, kissing them on each cheek, whispering a few words. The little girl she saved for last. She swung her through the air and laughed as the girl giggled and shrieked in excitement.

She set the girl down, whispered a few words to her, and then hugged her fiercely. When she let go of the girl at last, they all disappeared.

Vedhe came back to them, looking far more at peace with her decision than K'lrsa was.

"Where now?" Vedhe asked, looking back and forth between them.

"Lodie." K'lrsa gestured to the red-tiled path that had just appeared on the far side of the clearing.

They followed it into the lush green vegetation, walking in silence, weighed down by what they'd left behind.

CHAPTER 77

T he red-tiled path eventually ended in a small grassy clearing next to a pond. The little girl who had toddled up to Lodie when they first arrived was sitting in the pond, splashing in the water, laughing and smiling, as content as any child could be.

Lodie sat on the bank watching her with a handsome young man at her side. Their heads were close together as they talked softly, laughing and touching. It was strange to see a woman as old as Lodie acting like a young woman newly in love.

K'lrsa glanced at the others.

"We have to tell her," Badru said.

Vedhe shrugged one shoulder.

K'lrsa turned to argue with Badru, but he'd already stepped into the clearing. "Lodie."

Lodie tensed, but she didn't look at him.

"Lodie," Badru said once more. He stood behind her, just an arm's reach away.

"Go away." Lodie didn't turn. Her fingers clutched the hand of the man next to her.

Badru moved around in front of her, blocking her view of the little girl. Lodie moved just enough to keep her in view, but still wouldn't look at him.

K'lrsa joined him. "Lodie? We need to talk to you. Why don't you come with us? Just for a bit."

"No. Go away."

"But Lodie...This isn't real." K'lrsa winced to say the words. "This man and this child, they're not the ones you lost. They're..."

"Don't you think I know that, child?" Lodie looked up, her eyes full of tears. "I know more about this city than anyone left in the tribes. I know its secret. I also know that most of the dead only stay for a season, maybe two, waiting for their lost loves before they move on. A few stay longer, but not this long."

She looked out at the child, still laughing and playing in the water. "And children? They never stay. Not even for a season."

"But then, I don't understand. If you know that they aren't real, why won't you leave with us?"

Lodie laughed, a harsh, barking sound. "Because this is all I have left of them. When I step through the next arch, they're gone forever. At least here I can have them as I remember them."

"But what about the tribes? We have to continue if we're going to save them."

"I gave up my real life to save Herin. Wasn't that enough?" K'lrsa fell back before her anger.

Badru knelt down in front of her. "Lodie. You can't stay here forever."

"Why not? I'm fed. I have a place to sleep and bathe."

K'lrsa bit her lip. "But we don't know how long you can stay here before it becomes impossible to return to the real world."

Lodie shook her head. "It's already too late for me."

"What are you talking about?"

Badru stood, blocking Lodie from her view. "Lodie, don't."

"You should tell her."

"Not yet."

K'lrsa moved to the side so she could see both of them. "What are you talking about?"

They ignored her. Lodie nodded towards the center of the clearing where an arch had appeared. "As soon as you step through she'll know."

"Know what?" K'lrsa demanded.

Badru clenched his jaw.

"Tell her now, Badru. If you have any hope, you have to be the one to tell her."

"Badru? What is she talking about?"

He shook his head. "It's already too late. She won't…" He shook his head. A small tear beaded one of his eyelashes.

"Badru! What is it? What haven't you told me?"

He sighed. "You know how Herin said that coming here would be the death of me?"

"Yes. But you're fine. It was…It was Herin and Garzel who died." She swallowed against the memory.

"It wasn't just them."

"What are you talking about? You're fine."

"No. I'm not. I'm already dead."

"What?" She stared at him. "How are you standing here if you're dead? This isn't funny, Badru."

"I know."

"Then explain yourself!" She shouted so loud the little girl in the pool stopped playing and stared at her.

Badru looked around as if searching for the words as K'lrsa glared at him, waiting.

"Remember when we entered the city?"

"Yes."

"And there was writing over the arch?"

"Yes."

"Well, Herin lied about what it said." He glanced at her and away again. "The Hidden City has two entrances, one for the living and one for the dead. The gate we came through said, 'Only those who have not yet tasted death may enter here.' It was the gate of the living."

"And, so? What does that matter?"

Badru crossed his arms. "I've died before, K'lrsa. So has Lodie. So had Herin and Garzel."

"The death walker magic?"

He nodded. "Anyone who has been revived with death walker magic can never leave the Hidden City for the world of the living once they enter."

"But nothing happened to you. You look fine. You

look…normal."

Lodie sighed. "In the Hidden City the living and the dead walk side-by-side, as real to one another as anyone. But the living can never go to the Promised Plains and the dead can never go back to the real world."

K'lrsa narrowed her eyes. "But I thought you said Aran wanted to come here. If he does that means he'll never be able to leave. He'll be stuck here forever."

"He won't care. He can rule from here forever. Over the world of the living and the world of the dead."

"But I thought most of the dead move on."

Lodie shrugged. "Aran isn't like most men."

"But how could he rule the world of the living if he can never go back there?"

"How does any man rule? Through the complicity of others."

K'lrsa looked back and forth between Lodie and Badru. "I don't understand why you came if you knew you were going to die."

"For you." Badru reached for her hand.

"For me?" Fury rushed through her body as she backed away from him. "How dare you?"

"You needed me here. To reach the center of the labyrinth. To save the tribes."

She ground her teeth so hard she thought they might break. "I could've done it alone. I would've rather that than have you give your lives."

Lodie snorted. "Really? You would've defeated that dragon all by yourself? Didn't need Herin and Garzel to distract it while you hid? Didn't need Badru to slice it open?"

K'lrsa glared at her. "I would've found a way."

"And here? Did you free yourself or did you need Badru to bring you back?"

Badru reached for her hand again, but she yanked it away. "K'lrsa, please. You have to understand."

"Understand what? That because of you and the choice you made, I'm going to be alone for the rest of my life? You didn't even ask me, Badru! You could've told me the risks. We could've talked it through. Together. But you just arrogantly chose to…"

"I chose to put my love for you above my self. Is that so bad?"

"When it takes you away forever? Yes! If you'd asked me what I'd rather have…"

"You would've chosen our happiness over the lives of everyone in the tribes. Over M'lara's life? And F'lia's? And D'lan's?"

She glared at him. "You didn't have to come. The others were enough."

He grabbed her hands and stared into her eyes. "I couldn't take that risk, K'lrsa. What if I'd stayed behind and you'd never come back? What then?"

She fought against the tears that threatened to overwhelm her. "At least there would've been a chance that we both survived. But this way…"

She pulled free. "I can't do this," she whispered.

"Yes, you can."

"I'm not that strong, Badru."

"Says the girl who let a slaver caravan take her hostage and who trained to be a dorana just so she could avenge her father."

She shook her head. "I didn't know better then."

"You're still strong enough to do this. And…If you want to, when this is all done, you can come back to me. I'll wait for you. We can be together still."

"I can't go to the Promised Plains with you."

"No. But we can stay here in the City together for as long as you want."

"And M'lara?"

"Bring her."

K'lrsa shook her head.

He pulled her close. "You don't have to decide now. Just know that I'll be here if you still want me. And, see? I'm as real as I ever was."

She shook her head, wondering how real that was.

She turned to Lodie. "So? Are you coming with us?"

"No."

K'lrsa nodded. She knelt down and took Lodie's hands in hers. "I...You helped me when you didn't have to. When you probably shouldn't have. And I'll be forever thankful for that. I'm sorry...I'm sorry my tribe didn't treat you better and I'm sorry it had to end this way."

Lodie patted her on the arm. "Nonsense. I get to spend as much time as I want with my daughter and husband. What could be a better end than that?"

K'lrsa bit back her reply and hugged Lodie instead. "I'll miss you."

"And I, you."

Badru nodded to Lodie. "I'll see you when you're ready to continue your journey."

She harrumphed. "Planning to hang around a long while then?"

Badru nodded. "As long as I need to." He held out a hand to K'lrsa. "Ready?"

"Ready." She took his hand and they walked over to the arch.

Vedhe joined them and they stepped through, hand-in-hand.

CHAPTER 78

There was a flash of white light as they crossed the threshold.

And then pain. More pain than K'lrsa had ever felt before.

She screamed, clutching at her temples. It was like a white-hot knife had been poked through each eye, like someone was taking her head and squeezing it between their hands until it was ready to burst, like they were shoving slivers of wood under every fingernail.

She couldn't see, could barely breathe.

"Stop!" she cried. "Please, make it stop!"

She was vaguely aware of Vedhe screaming somewhere nearby and Badru whispering comforting words as he rubbed her back, but all she cared about was the pain. She curled in on herself, rocking back and forth, the agony too much to bear.

It pulsed through her body from her head to her toes to her fingertips until there wasn't a part of her that didn't hurt. Even her hair hurt.

She whimpered, her throat too raw to scream as the pain went on and on and on.

Finally, just when she'd decided she'd rather die than endure another moment, it ended.

She lay there, gasping, her sides heaving as Vedhe continued to scream.

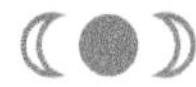

Every part of her throbbed with the memory of agony as she slowly pushed herself to her feet, tensed for the pain to return.

Vedhe's screams ended so suddenly K'lrsa fell forward as if she'd been pushing against some thick wall and it was suddenly gone. She knelt down by Vedhe and pulled the trembling woman into her arms, rocking her and crooning some lullaby she hadn't realized she still knew.

She looked around, trying to identify what it was that had attacked them.

They were in a small circular room with one archway before them and one behind with hallways leading off to either side. White stone everywhere—the floor, the ceiling, the walls. Full of light even though there were no windows or torches.

The Lady Moon watched them impassively from the entrance to one of the hallways.

"Why are you here?" K'lrsa asked.

But even as she asked the question, she knew the answer. Just like she knew that they were in the heart of the labyrinth, at last, and that the archway on the other side of the room led to the Promised Plains.

And she now knew the source of her pain. Knowledge, shoving its way into a mind too small to grasp it. Her "reward" for completing the labyrinth.

Images and words flashed through her mind so fast she couldn't capture them; everything was a jumble, appearing and disappearing too fast to be of any use.

She took a deep breath and turned her attention inward, searching for the hunter's version of the Core where she could center herself and put aside fear and all these unnecessary thoughts. She had to shut out images of how the Core had come to be and what the major practitioners of it had meant by the mantras and all sorts of other information that pushed forward, demanding her attention.

She didn't care about that. Not now. Maybe not ever.

She anchored her thoughts on the Lady Moon. On why she was there and what the place was and why it existed.

The Lady's daughter, the Dawn Maiden, goddess of first kisses and hope, of the eternal promise of love, had created the Hidden City—or at least its precursor—in response to the plea of a young woman, much like F'lia, who had lost the one she loved to tragedy, never able to tell him how much she cared.

The girl begged the goddess to let her see her love just one last time. To let her tell him in death what she'd never told him in life. The Maiden, foolishly, took pity on the girl and created a bridge between the world of the living and the Promised Plains.

It was a city now, but once it had been just a small clearing with a single tent.

The Maiden didn't realize what a terrible mistake she'd made until it was too late.

The young woman came, saw her love, and then refused to leave.

And why should she? When her love seemed as real and alive as he'd ever been? When they could be together day and night like she'd always wanted them to be?

The girl stayed. For days. And then weeks. And then months.

For years.

And she was happy at first. To have her love at last.

But the dead don't age.

And they can't have children.

Each year the girl grew older while her love stayed young.

She pined for the life they could never have, for children and grandchildren, to live in more than just a small clearing. The Maiden turned the tent into a city, but it still wasn't enough for the lovers. They wanted more.

The Maiden tried to fully bridge the two worlds. She, a child of immortality, couldn't see the need for death and separation. But the other gods did.

And they stopped her. Banished her to a cold, dark place, never to return.

But they couldn't undo what she'd already done. The City remained.

Eventually the woman's lover moved on to the Promised Plains. He did it to free her, to let her live the rest of her life. Instead, she chose to join him in death.

It should have ended there, but it didn't.

Others came, somehow aware of what the place was.

The dead came, waiting for the loves they'd lost too soon.

The living came, desperate for another night, another day.

Over and over again they came.

And each time it ended in tragedy.

Years of life wasted.

Those left behind by the living—children, spouses, friends—forgotten.

The pain of one death spread outward by the wounds of loss kept open for too long.

Rare were those who could come, see their loved one, and leave to face the loneliness and emptiness of living alone.

The Lady Moon watched and mourned. For her lost daughter and all the lives frozen in time, unable to move forward.

She moved the City. Hid it away in the middle of the desert and blurred all memory of its existence. Her son created the barren lands. They recruited the poorest of the Daliphana to form the tribes and protect their secrets.

As the gods discovered the mistakes they'd made in answering men's and women's wishes, they placed those weapons and powers and secrets that they couldn't destroy in the Hidden City, at the center of the labyrinth.

Only the wise ones of the tribes knew it existed. Those and the scholars who studied the ancient writings.

Or men like Aran, obsessed with power and eternal life.

K'lrsa shuddered as she turned to Badru.

He'd said he'd wait for her. That she could come back to him. That they could still be together.

But now she knew the truth of that lie. Had seen it play out a thousand times.

She wouldn't do that. She couldn't.

She took his hand, so real, so strong. She stroked his golden-brown cheek and stared into his beautiful blue eyes.

"K'lrsa? Is everything okay?"

She turned away. "Yes. Just a lot to take in." She looked at the Lady, saw the understanding and compassion in her eyes, and hated her anyway. "I could use food. And water."

The Lady nodded, accepting K'lrsa's anger as her due. "Follow me. I can provide both."

K'lrsa took Badru's hand in hers as the Lady led them down the nearest hallway, Vedhe trailing behind.

They stepped into a room with colorful cushions arranged in a circle, much like the sitting area in her room in the Daliphate. Now she understood why. Because once the barren lands hadn't existed and the tribes and the people of the Daliphana had been one.

She shoved the new knowledge that threatened to overwhelm her away. That and her own thoughts and worries.

She didn't want to think anymore.

All she wanted was to eat.

And maybe take a nap.

To sit next to Badru, his foot touching hers, for just a little while.

For as long as she could before duty woke her to her purpose once more.

She'd think again. Later.

Much later.

CHAPTER 79

They ate a delicious meal of meats swimming in gravies, cradled in hot discs of bread. K'lrsa knew to avoid the bright red one, but Vedhe made the mistake of trying it and coughed so hard everyone had to laugh. There were also soft cheeses and fresh fruits.

So many spices. Such delicious flavors.

K'lrsa hated the Daliphana, but she had to admit their food was certainly better than the plain fare of the tribes.

But not worth the cost.

She shoved the thought away as knowledge about people who'd lived so long ago no one remembered their names threatened to overwhelm her. She didn't want to think about trade and how men thought and what they valued and what they fought and died for.

"How do I make it go away?" K'lrsa asked, breathing through her nose as the knowledge pushed for her attention.

"What?" Badru asked.

"All this information." She glared at the Lady. "How do I make it go away?"

"Forever? But you just received it. How do you know you don't want it anymore?"

Vedhe shook her head. "You can't give it back. It's too valuable."

K'lrsa stared at her, her mouth hanging open in surprise. "Vedhe. How did you do that?"

"What?"

"Speak my language like you've always known it?

She tapped her skull. "It's all in here now. I can understand everything you say and tell you anything I want and not sound like a fool." She tilted her head to the side. "Your language is weird. All clicks and clacks. But now I understand. Knowledge. And you can speak my language."

K'lrsa shook her head. "No I can't."

"Yes, you can. Do you understand this?"

K'lrsa gasped. "Yes. How is that possible?"

The Lady chuckled. "Language is just another subject of study. Another form of knowledge."

"But there are things I don't know still. Aren't there?"

"Of course. You didn't last very long. Vedhe lasted longer, so she'll know more. But neither of you will keep all of it. It's too much. The longer you go without using it, the more it will fade."

"So over time we'll forget."

"Yes. Just like I'm sure you've forgotten much of what you learned as a child."

"So what's the point? Why did we go through all that if we're just going to lose it?"

The Lady stared her down with the look of a disappointed mother. "I said you'd lose most of it. Not all of it. You'll keep what you truly need. Like Vedhe." She nodded towards her. "She'll keep your language. And if you practice with her, you'll keep hers."

Vedhe smiled. "Yes. We'll practice every day."

K'lrsa tried to hide her lack of excitement at the idea. "So is that it? Is knowledge the weapon Herin brought us here to find?"

But even as she asked the question, she knew it wasn't.

Somewhere was a room. And in that room were all the weapons the gods had ever created for men that men couldn't handle. Swords that gave the bearer the power to defeat ten men at once. Stones that threw fire. Even a staff that brought water wherever it was driven into the ground.

All of these, the gods had once given men.

And all of them, men had eventually misused.

Not usually the original bearer. But at some point some man (or more rarely, woman) had turned the weapon to evil, to making the world a worse place than it had been before the weapon existed.

"When?"

The Lady shook her head. "In time."

"But how much time do we have? The tribes are surrounded. And it'll take us days to get back to them."

"You have time still."

K'lrsa glared at her. "My father said that, too. But he was a lie. I'm sure his words were as well."

"The man you saw was not your father, but he wasn't a lie. And neither was what he said."

K'lrsa looked away.

She didn't want to think about her father. About how close she'd come to seeing him again.

And then it occurred to her. "My father. Is he...Is he here somewhere? Can...Can I see him?"

But as soon as she asked the question, she wasn't sure she wanted to.

She loved her father. More than anything.

But...This would actually be her father. A man with his own opinions.

A man who might be disappointed with the choices she'd made.

Could she face that?

Could she bear to see him and know he didn't support her completely? That in his eyes she could and had made mistakes?

Before she could take it back, the Lady answered. "Yes. He wants to see you very much. But first there's another who wants to see you."

"My mother?"

"No."

"Then who?"

"You'll see."

K'lrsa set down the rest of the apple she'd been eating. She didn't have an appetite anymore.

CHAPTER 80

After the Lady left to get whomever it was that wanted to see her, K'lrsa started to pace the room. Who could it be?

Not her mother. Not her father.

Then, who?

G'van? Please, no.

K'var? Ugh.

Who else could it be?

The Lady returned and K'lrsa stared, trying to figure out who was behind her. She shifted to the side, but the man was shrouded in shadow.

The Lady stepped forward and revealed the man behind her.

L'ral.

K'lrsa turned away. "I don't want to speak to him."

"Please, K'lrsa. You have to listen to me."

"No. I don't."

He came to stand next to her, but she refused to look at him. "What do you want? Because I'm never going to forgive you for what you did."

"Your father already forgave me for that."

"What?" She turned to glare at him and he backed away, stumbling on a pillow.

"Your father's here. We've talked. Lots. He understands."

"Does he."

"Yes. I…" He took a deep breath, licking his lips nervously. He always had been nervous. She'd never really understood what F'lia saw in him.

She raised her chin. "You know, F'lia's pregnant."

He flinched. "Is she?"

"Mmhm."

"Who…?" He winced, trying to force the words out. "Who's the father?"

"Some older guy from the Black Horse Tribe. J'vin, I think it was."

He nodded, clearly upset.

She glared, glad she'd found a way to hurt him.

"She's why I did it, you know." He wrung his hands together.

"You killed my father for F'lia?"

He flinched. "I didn't kill him."

"Oh, I'm sorry. You led my father to his death because of F'lia?" Her words were like knives she flung at him.

He winced. "You didn't see how much she coveted those things, K'lrsa. The silks and salt. And there was this pigment—this blue color made from the shells of some sort of sea creature. She wanted it so bad. She tried to earn enough to buy it, but…It was so expensive."

"So what? You sold my dad for it?"

"No." He shook his head, no better with his words in death than he'd been in life. "I didn't know they'd kill him. I thought they just wanted to talk to him, to bring him 'round. They told me they'd give me the pigment at the annual gathering. All I had to do is let them know what people were saying."

"You did more than that."

"I know. When I told them that your father was campaigning to expel the Black Horse Tribe, they demanded I bring him to them."

"And you didn't think that was strange?"

"K'lrsa. Would you have? If you'd been me? Would you have really believed they would do that to him?"

She looked away.

"Will you please tell F'lia you saw me? And that I love her? That she could find me here if she wants."

"No."

"Why not?"

"Because she's having a child, L'ral. She needs to look forward, not be stuck here with you."

His jaw worked as he looked at her, tears in his eyes. "Please, K'lrsa. I don't want to hold her here. I just want to say goodbye. Try to make her understand."

"That you brought about someone's death because she wanted pretty things? Spare her."

"Just think about it? Please."

"If I promise to think about it will you leave?"

He nodded.

"Fine. I'll think about it. Go."

He walked away, shoulders slumped.

She turned away, sick. She knew F'lia would want to know she'd seen L'ral, but she also knew that F'lia would want to see him herself. And if she did, she'd never be able to leave.

CHAPTER 81

K'lrsa squeezed Badru's hand so hard she knew it must hurt, but she couldn't help it and he didn't complain, as they followed the Lady down the hallway to another space, this one a grassy area with camp stools set in a circle with soft grass beneath and the sound of water running somewhere nearby like the pitter patter of children's feet. Tall trees and leafy green plants surrounded them.

She felt ill. It was too much like the place she'd been with the man who wasn't really her father. She started to leave, but when she turned around there he was, tall and proud, a soft smile on his face, his eyes more kind than she remembered.

"Dad!" She flung her arms around him, almost knocking them both over.

He laughed, the sound vibrating his chest as she clung to him, afraid to let go and lose him again.

"K'lrsa." He smiled down at her with all the pride and love she'd remembered.

"You don't hate me then?"

"Why would I hate you?"

"For lying to you about going after the Daliph."

He shook his head. "A bit disappointed that you didn't listen. But I could never hate you, K'lrsa."

She sniffed back tears. She hadn't realized until that moment how scared she'd been that he'd turn on her. She knew he'd always loved and supported her, that there'd been nothing she'd ever done that had shaken his love in her.

But in her darkest moments since he'd died, she'd wondered if he'd still feel that way if he'd known that she'd left her family behind to kill a man he'd told her not to kill.

Her father led the way to the camp stools. K'lrsa flinched, the memory of that other man too strong.

She'd thought he was her father, too.

Maybe this just another illusion. Another lie.

Her father studied her. "You've changed since I saw you last. You're…more guarded. More…"

"Damaged? Less confident?" She sat down next to him, trying not to feel the hurt of his words.

He frowned. "Are you okay?"

She shook her head, fighting against the tears. She didn't want him to see her cry. They didn't have that much time together and she wanted to make the most of it. "I'm fine. It's just been hard. The Daliphate wasn't what I expected. And coming home wasn't either."

"Your mother told me."

K'lrsa felt a sharp ache in her chest. "Where is she? Doesn't she want to see me?"

He smiled. "You two. Too alike to know what to do with one another. Yes. She wants to see you. But we thought it best that I see you first. That we have this time."

"Time for what?"

He shrugged. "To talk."

She looked around. Badru and the Lady had left. It was just the two of them now.

"Did she tell you about Badru?"

"The young man that was with you?"

She nodded.

"Only a little bit. That he came with you and seemed to be a strong warrior and to care for you and that you seemed to care for him. Is there more?"

She sighed. "I don't know. He's the one I went to kill you know. He was the Daliph."

"Really? He seems young for that."

"He was. But he was the only one left to inherit." She picked a piece of grass and started to shred it into small strips. "I dreamt of him before we met. In the Moon Dream. We couldn't speak, but we moved together so perfectly. And then when we met there was that same pull, that same spark."

"But?"

She shook her head. "It doesn't matter now."

"Why not?"

"Because he's dead. He was killed and brought back by death walker magic, so when we came here he died for real."

Her father waited, knowing her well enough to know she wasn't done.

"He wants me to come back here after. So we can be together."

"And?"

She frowned and threw the pieces of grass away. "I made a promise to M'lara. That I'd come back and I'd never leave her alone again. I'm all she has."

"She has D'lan, too. And the rest of the tribe. It wouldn't be the first time someone in the tribe raised another's child."

"But I made her a promise."

"Okay. So you made her a promise that you wouldn't leave. But you want to?"

"No. Yes. Maybe?" She shook her head, so angry with Badru that she didn't know what to do with it. "There was potential there for us to be something amazing. But…We weren't there yet. And living in a dead city isn't…What will that get us? We won't be able to have children or build anything together. We'll just be. Here. How long can we last if we aren't creating something that binds us together?"

"You could come for a while. See what it's like."

She bit her lip. "I can't do it again, Dad."

"Do what again?"

"Lose someone I love. First you, then Mom. Now Badru. I can't come back here and try and find out that I lost a chance at something amazing. Better to leave now."

He touched her knee lightly. "K'lrsa. I want you to look at me."

She did, reluctantly.

He continued, "I can't begin to describe for you the depth of love I feel for your mother. It's…It's the thread that bound my life together, that made everything else make sense. Without it I'd just have been some fool Rider who could hunt a baru and tell a good joke. Her love was, is, my foundation. It gave every moment, every choice a meaning it wouldn't have had otherwise."

"Why are you telling me this?" she wailed.

"Because if you think there's a chance that you could have something that powerful with Badru, then I think you should come back here. M'lara will understand."

"No she won't."

"Someday, I hope."

"But what if I'm wrong, Dad? What if it's nothing? Or what if it is this great, amazing love but we can't sustain it. I saw those memories, Dad. I know how it turns out."

"But do you think those people regret the days or weeks or months they had with their loves? Do you think the lives of emptiness they would've had otherwise were better?"

"My life wouldn't be empty."

"But it wouldn't be full, either." He squeezed her knee and sat back. "Take the risk, K'lrsa. Give whatever exists between you the chance it needs to grow."

She nodded her head slightly, but she didn't want to think about Badru and love and loss anymore. "Dad. I'm not sure I can do what they want me to do."

"How so?"

"I'm so tired of death and killing and…" She shivered. "I don't want to kill all those soldiers."

"Then don't."

"But if I don't they'll kill us."

"Who says?"

"That's what they're there for. To kill everyone in the tribes."

"On one man's orders. Do you think they'd make that choice, each of them, given the power to do so?"

She frowned. "Some. But not all."

"And the ones that would, would they still try to if the ones that wouldn't weren't there at their sides? If they didn't have someone else's order to hide behind?"

"No. Probably not. But…I can't get Aran to take back his order."

"No, you can't. But maybe what you can do is find a way to defeat his troops without destroying them."

She nodded. "Maybe."

"Your real problem is the Daliphana not those soldiers."

"Herin and Lodie want me to kill Aran, the current Daliph. If I do that, then the Daliphana will leave us alone."

"No they won't."

"Why not?"

"Because they need the trade the tribes can provide them. Before Aran arranged to have the Black Horse Tribe lead them across the desert the men of the Toreem Daliphate were poor and miserable. Aran isn't the problem. He's part of it, don't get me wrong. He's a cruel, vicious man who delights in pain. But Badru would make the same decisions as Aran. So would any Daliph."

He held up a hand to stop the argument forming on her lips. "The Toreem Daliphate needs trade. If you hadn't been there, by Badru's side, acting as his conscience, he would have sent those troops to attack the tribes himself. Not because he was a hateful man, but because he was a ruler who had to think of the best interests of his people above all else."

K'lrsa wanted to argue with him, but she couldn't. The stupid knowledge she'd gained from the labyrinth kept flashing in her mind, showing her incidents from history going back thousands of years.

Leaders of nations didn't make choices based on sympathy for outsiders. They chose what was in the best interests of their people.

Or they weren't leaders for long.

Like Badru.

Whose people had turned on him because he acted against them.

"So what am I supposed to do? Kill them all? Destroy the Daliphana?"

"It's one choice, but not the only one."

Once again, knowledge of what had happened in the past flooded her mind. If they had a natural barrier like a mountain range or sea, they could hide behind it, confident that it would keep them safe. Or they could fight to a mutual standstill, both equally as powerful and unwilling to continue the conflict. They could surrender to the Daliphana, set their own terms.

All had worked in the past.

The question was, which would she choose?

"What do *you* think I should do?" she asked.

He shook his head. "This choice you have to make on your own, K'lrsa. Take the night. Rest. Think on it. What you want will determine what choices you're given when it comes time to choose your weapon."

He gestured to a small path through the foliage. She could just see the outline of a tent waiting for her.

"I don't want to go yet."

He patted her hand. "Don't worry. I'll be back in the morning. With your mother. Go. Rest."

When she still resisted, he gave her his most stern look and said, "K'lrsa dan V'na, I order you to go to bed." And then he laughed, the sound so rich and happy it warmed her to her toes. "I haven't had to order you around like that since you were little! Now go."

She gave him a quick hug, hoping it wouldn't be their last, and walked down the path, lost in her thoughts, unsure what she'd decide come the morning.

CHAPTER 82

K'lrsa couldn't sleep. She knew the sensible choice was to choose a weapon that would destroy her enemies, but she didn't want to be the person to wield a weapon like that. And the knowledge she'd gained from the labyrinth also let her see how one act of destruction could echo and reverberate through hundreds of years.

Only if she killed every last man, woman, and child in the Daliphana and every single person who had every sympathized with them would she maybe have a chance of avoiding those repercussions. But she couldn't do that.

Badru came to find her at some point in the night. She was tempted, not knowing when or if they'd ever have the chance to be together again, to take things further than they'd ever taken them, but she held back, knowing it would just confuse the decision she ultimately had to make about whether or not to return to the Hidden City to be with him.

The next morning they made their way back to the room where they'd eaten the day before. Her mother was there—they exchanged a fierce hug, both trying not to cry.

"I didn't want to lose you," K'lrsa whispered.

"I know. But I couldn't do it anymore. I'm so much happier now."

K'lrsa flinched away from her joy. She'd given her life, left her children behind, and all for what? Love? If it could

do that to a person, maybe she didn't want it.

She glanced past her mother to where Herin and Garzel sat. "I should say hello to the others."

"K'lrsa…"

"Yes?"

She took a deep breath. "I want you to know I'm proud of you. I always have been."

K'lrsa couldn't speak past the lump in her throat.

"I love you."

"I love you, too."

They hugged, both shaking from the strength of their emotions.

K'lrsa walked over to Herin who sat hunched on a camp stool as grel-like as ever. "Why didn't you tell me? I would've kept him away."

"Pzah. You were no more capable of keeping him away than I was. If you'd tried to leave him behind, he would've just come here himself. At least this way he was able to help you through the labyrinth."

K'lrsa sighed.

Herin smiled. "Plus you know how much I like my secrets."

K'lrsa laughed. She studied Herin's hands, still maimed, each one missing its top joint. "So even in death you carry his mark?"

"What? Oh. Hadn't really thought about it, they're so much a part of me now." Herin held her hands up and narrowed her eyes as she focused on each hand. The air shimmered for a moment and when it was done each finger was whole.

Herin flexed her fingers with a small smile.

K'lrsa reached out to touch one old, wrinkled fingertip, her mouth open in awe.

"Oh, honestly, child. You'd think I'd performed a miracle. I'm dead, remember?"

K'lrsa shook her head. Even in death Herin was still Herin.

Herin gripped her arm. "Promise me you'll stop Aran."

K'lrsa sighed. "If I stop him someone else will just rise to take his place."

"Yes, but no."

"What does that mean?"

"Someone else will rise to lead the Toreem Daliphate. But there's a vast difference between a man like Aran and a man like Badru. A man like Aran always wants more. A man like Badru is content with what he has. He'll only act to maintain that. You can bargain with a man like Badru. You can't bargain with a man like Aran."

"But the Toreem Daliphate won't allow another leader like Badru."

"True. But no one can be as bad as Aran. He brings out the worst in others. Men do things for him they would never do otherwise. He gives them license to indulge the worst part of themselves. I'm not saying they'd be kind and wonderful if he didn't exist, but they wouldn't be what they are with him there."

K'lrsa shook her head. "I just want to save the tribes, Herin. Let someone else deal with Aran."

"Pzah, girl. Think what the world becomes if those who can stand against evil don't."

"There has to be another way. Someone else…"

"Well, there isn't. No one in the Toreem Daliphate will act. They're too scared."

"Badru would."

"Yes, well, Badru's dead, isn't he?"

"Like I needed reminding." She turned to see her father watching from the far side of the room and walked over to him.

"Have you figured out what you're going to do?" he asked.

"No." She leaned against the wall. "Did you ever question whether you should speak out against the Black Horse Tribe? Did you know they might kill you?"

He bowed his head, a line forming between his brows as he searched for an answer. "I knew I was making enemies. I knew some would oppose me. I even suspected they would try to expel me or the White Horse Tribe. But I didn't think they'd kill me. Or turn on us the way they did."

"If you'd known, would you have still done it?"

He nodded. "Yes. Someone has to be the first to stand. You either do what's right, regardless of what others choose, or you accept a life that's less than what it could be. Things might not turn out no matter what you do, but at least if you stand for what you believe in you'll know you tried." He shook his head. "Too many watch in silence and let evil thrive. That's what bad people count on, the silent majority. Don't you think there were those in the Black Horse Tribe who didn't want to see slaves brought across the desert? But did they speak out? No. And look what happened."

"But…How can one person make any difference? You tried and they killed you."

"One person *can't* make a difference. Not alone. But if one person stands against evil and others stand with them, they will make all the difference."

She frowned. "But that first person. What if no one stands with them?"

He smiled, a soft, sad smile. "Maybe by standing and falling they inspire two more to stand next time. And when those two fall they inspire four. Who inspire eight. Until the sheer mass of those who choose to stand is enough to tip the balance."

She nodded. It made sense. But it didn't matter. Because she had to make a choice now.

CHAPTER 83

As K'lrsa stepped away from her father, Badru met her. Wordlessly, he pulled her into a hug. She leaned against him, breathing the sweet scent of his skin for a long moment.

It wasn't fair. That he could feel so real, so alive. It was a cruel thing the Maiden had done all those years ago. To make something lost seem so real.

It was hard enough to move on when someone died, but this…this was intolerable.

She wondered if there was a weapon in that room that would destroy the Hidden City.

She shivered.

If there was, would she use it? Could she forever close herself to the possibility of seeing her loved ones again?

She closed her eyes.

She'd thought she wanted to be someone important, to be that person that everyone looked to to save them. To solve all their problems and rescue them.

But she didn't.

Not now that she'd had a taste of the personal toll it took. Of the uncertainty and doubt that came with having other's lives in her hands.

She just wanted to be left alone to live her life as best she could. To spend her days hunting with Fallion and her nights…

Alone.

She pushed away from Badru. "I should go. We don't have much time left."

He nodded. "Remember, I'll be here for you when you're done. I'll wait as long as I need to."

"Badru…I don't know…I…"

"Shh. Don't make a decision now. I told Lodie I'd wait for her, too. I'm not going anywhere. Not for a long while. And if you decide to come back, I'll be here, waiting."

She kissed him softly on the lips, melting into the soft honey taste of him for a long moment before she pulled away.

"It's time," the Lady said, coming to stand in the entrance to the hallway.

K'lrsa joined her and Vedhe.

She turned to look at all the ones she loved who she would never see again after she left the City.

"Come. You'll be able to say goodbye after you choose."

K'lrsa followed the Lady down the hall, the weight of everyone's hopes weighing on her shoulders, Vedhe keeping pace at her side.

"What will you choose?" she asked Vedhe, realizing she hadn't given much thought to the girl. What was it *she* wanted?

Vedhe shrugged. "I don't know. A part of me wants to raze the Daliphana to the ground until not a single stone is left standing."

K'lrsa stumbled. "Why?"

Vedhe looked at her like she was a fool for not knowing. "They killed my family. They took me as a slave. Their men raped me."

"But it wasn't everyone."

"No. But everyone in the Daliphana benefits from what they do. I wasn't the first they took, nor the last. They all know about it. There are no innocents."

"The children."

Vedhe shrugged one shoulder. "I probably won't do it. I'm not sure I could stop there."

K'lrsa blinked, taken aback by Vedhe's words.

"Who else would you attack?"

Vedhe didn't answer and wouldn't look at her.

"Vedhe? Who else?"

She flashed back to the memory of Vedhe's tent, staked out so far from the others of the tribe. To Lodie, skinny from lack of food.

"I may not make a choice at all."

"What?"

Vedhe smiled, her scarred skin twisting upward. "Remember, every object in that room was deemed too dangerous for men. Maybe it's best we leave them there."

K'lrsa chewed on her lip. Vedhe was right. Maybe nothing in that room was safe.

The Lady stopped outside a door, her hand on the metal handle. "Are you ready?"

Vedhe shrugged. "I confess, I do want to see what there is. I want to know my choices before I turn away. See what the room offers up to me. It's…a test of character."

"But will you be able to walk away after you do?"

"Only one way to know." Vedhe stepped forward and the Lady opened the door, escorting her inside.

K'lrsa was so nervous she couldn't breathe, but she followed after.

Her people needed her.

She had to find something to save them, no matter how dangerous it was.

CHAPTER 84

T he room was small with just a handful of artifacts on each of the floor-to-ceiling shelves that lined the walls, but K'lrsa had the impression that the space was much more vast than she could see.

The Lady stepped into the center of the room, drawing her attention away from a nearby shelf where a hand mirror lay facedown. "K'lrsa dan V'na of the White Horse tribe and Vedhe Kanaatanva, congratulations. You have conquered the labyrinth. And for this you have earned a reward." She gestured at the objects on the shelves. "You may each take one object from this place to use during your lifetime. Be wise in your choice because each of the objects in this room is an object of tremendous power."

K'lrsa frowned. "Why let us take them then?"

The Lady smiled. "Our hope is that the knowledge you gain by coming here will help you to make a wise choice and that only those who truly need one of these objects will take one from here."

K'lrsa scanned the shelves. "So we can choose one item?"

The Lady nodded.

"Or none," Vedhe added.

"Or none," the Lady agreed, "which is the most common choice. Often the knowledge gained by conquering the labyrinth is enough."

"Not for me." K'lrsa looked around, wondering where to start. "How do I know what each one does?"

"You can search your memories. Or ask me."

Vedhe picked up the hand mirror and turned it over. She gasped in surprise, touching her face as she stared into it. A small tear trickled down her cheek and her hand shook.

K'lrsa peered over Vedhe's shoulder.

She saw Vedhe and herself. Vedhe's skin was flawlessly smooth and pale as milk, her hair brilliant in it whiteness, her lips a perfect shade of pink. K'lrsa's skin was a warm, burnished honey, her hair as black as the blackest night, her eyes the green of a mossy bank.

They were the two most beautiful women K'lrsa had ever seen. More beautiful even than the Lady. K'lrsa stared at herself, enraptured, lost in how beautiful they both were.

She tore her gaze from the mirror. "Put that thing back. It's deadly."

Vedhe's hand shook. She continued to stare into its depths, unable to wrest herself free. K'lrsa covered the mirror's surface with her hand. Vedhe hissed and slammed the mirror facedown on the shelf.

Vedhe backed away, shaking. "I never cared before," she whispered, running her fingers over the scars on her face.

K'lrsa hugged her as she continued to stare at the mirror.

The Lady nodded. "There are some who would've taken that mirror and spent the rest of their days staring into its depths. Others would've never even left this place so caught up in what they saw."

K'lrsa studied her with narrowed eyes.

Had the mirror been a trap? A ploy by the gods to distract them from ever leaving this place?

But, no. The knowledge of the labyrinth reminded her that this place presented what each individual desired, even if that was something too dangerous for them to handle. Of course there would be objects not only fatal to others but to the user as well.

K'lrsa nodded at it. "So what was it? Why does it exist?"

The Lady ran a finger along the embossed handle. "Once there was a very powerful woman who coveted the beauty of the gods and demanded that we give it to her. So we did."

"Why do that? Why not tell her no?

"It was easier to give her what she wanted than fight her directly."

"What would've happened if you had fought her?"

"She would've turned her people against us and made it illegal to worship us." She shrugged. "Not all would've followed, but many would have."

"And? What do you care if people don't worship you?" She walked away, running her hands along the shelves.

"Who gave her the mirror?"

"My son, the Trickster, of course." There was a sharpness to her smile as she turned to face K'lrsa once more. "She had her wish."

"And you had yours." K'lrsa glanced at the mirror again, remembering how tempted she'd been by it. "How long did she last after you gave it to her?"

"A month or so. She refused to eat or drink, too enthralled with herself to do more than stare."

"Why didn't someone take it away from her? Like I did for Vedhe?"

The Lady smiled. "She was their ruler. None dared stand against her."

"Even to save her life?"

The Lady nodded.

K'lrsa shivered to think how the woman had died surrounded by those who could've saved her if only they'd dared do so.

She ran her fingers along a smooth wooden walking stick leaning against the wall and it vibrated under her fingers as if alive. "What does this one do?"

K'lrsa fought the urge to hold it, certain that if she succumbed she wouldn't be able to put it back.

"Many things." The Lady watched her closely, tensed as if she wanted to snatch the staff away.

"Such as?" She stroked its smooth surface again, feeling

an answering response.

The Lady shook her head. "It's not for you. Choose something else."

"But it is for me. It's here after all. What does it do?"

The Lady grimaced. "It was created to allow its user to draw water from the ground."

A useful tool in the desert. But it didn't explain her fear. "What else can it do?"

She pressed her lips together, clearly unwilling to speak of the staff's powers. "The last user used it to empty a sea of water so he could walk across it. The one before him used it to collapse the earth and create a great chasm that none could cross."

"Really?" K'lrsa stroked the wood with her fingers, wondering whether she could use it to create a barrier between the tribes and the Daliphana.

If she did, would her people forgive her for isolating them from their source of trade? Did she care? At least they'd still be alive to hate her.

Vedhe picked up a small golden orb. Even from across the room the sight of it made K'lrsa shiver. "Vedhe? What do you have there?"

Vedhe startled and set it back down, stepping back. "The sun."

"The sun?" She laughed.

"The sun. It has the power of the sun."

The Lady nodded. "It was a gift from my husband. It allows the user to start a fire no matter the conditions or to light the way no matter how dark."

"But it could be used to raze an entire kingdom." K'lrsa took a step closer to Vedhe, ready to block her from grasping the orb once more.

Vedhe stared at the orb, her hands twitching slightly.

"Vedhe, you can't do it. Too many innocents would die."

Vedhe turned away. She touched a small round stone and then picked up a wooden box that sat next to it, but it was clear her mind was still on the sun orb.

K'lrsa sighed.

If Vedhe chose the orb, she'd use it to destroy the Daliphana first. But what if she turned it on K'lrsa's people next. K'lrsa would have to stand against her. But how?

She turned to the Lady, speaking quietly so Vedhe wouldn't hear. "If she chooses the orb, is there an object here that can counter it?"

The Lady led her to a small bowl filled with silver liquid. "This. If you place the orb in the liquid, it will extinguish its fire."

"Thank you."

K'lrsa paced the room, looking at the other objects, wondering what other options she had to save her people. But all the while she was watching Vedhe, waiting to see what choice she'd make.

CHAPTER 85

K'lrsa found herself returning to the wooden staff over and over again, picturing how she could use it to flood the barren lands so none could cross them.

"K'lrsa." The Lady's voice was sharp with anger. "I told you that one is dangerous."

"Everything in this room is dangerous. Why this one more so than any other?"

"Because you can't reorder the world like that without consequence."

The knowledge of the labyrinth filled her. K'lrsa could see the effects. Droughts and floods that would last for years. Once prosperous lands now barren. Others gone, buried or abandoned. A wall of water so high it could reach the top of any mountain, slamming down on the coastline.

She shuddered and stepped away.

There had to be a better choice.

She walked the room, looking at each and every object. Some repelled her so much she could barely be near them, weapons of such extreme destruction they stank of evil.

They must be for Vedhe, weapons drawn to the dark anger inside her.

She sighed as she watched Vedhe handle each one, knowing she'd have to be the one that stood against her.

She didn't need a new enemy. Not with the ones she had already.

K'lrsa ran her fingers over the embossed surface of a copper cuff, green with the patina of age, and knew that if she wore this cuff there wasn't a man who could resist her. With it on her wrist, any man would do as she willed. She could ask him to kill himself and he would, gladly, smiling as he plunged a knife through his heart.

Any man would betray everything he was for her. The allure of attraction magnified to the point of lethality.

She could use it to save the tribes.

If she stood before the Daliph's troops and ordered them to kill themselves, they would. To the last man.

And that's the only way she could use it.

Because the cuff only worked while the victim was present. If she ordered the troops home, they'd return as soon as they were free of the sight of her. It was either order them to die or be chained to them forever.

She drew her hand back, disturbed by how easy it would be to destroy so many.

There had to be another choice. There had to be something she could use to save her people that wasn't evil or twisted beyond reason. But what?

CHAPTER 86

K'lrsa didn't know how long they'd been in the room, but she knew it was time to decide. Even if time did flow differently in the labyrinth, it still flowed forward.

In the far corner, on the bottom shelf, was a small silver necklace coiled on a pouch of silk. She knelt down, cautiously touching the silver chain with her fingertips. The necklace had a pendant, wrought in the shape of a double loop, weaving back in upon itself.

"What is this? What does it do?" she asked.

"It can transport the user and those the user chooses across any distance."

"So I could use it to return to the tribes immediately?"

"Yes."

"And I could move the tribes to a place of safety?" She thought about the shelter of the Tall Bluff Tribes. Maybe if she took everyone there, the Daliph's troops would give up and go home.

The Black Horse Tribe had already lost the vote. Surely there was no reason to stay on other than spite?

And if they didn't, she could just move them again, forever keep them out of reach. Or move the Daliph's troops back to the Daliphate.

The Lady shook her head. "No. It's not that simple. The more people you try to move at one time, the more damage you do to them. If you were to move the tribes, not all would survive."

K'lrsa frowned. "How many would die?"

"Hard to say. It depends on the distance and the size of those you move. And what objects stand between where you are and where they go. At least some would die."

K'lrsa sighed and stood back up.

She walked over to the wooden staff and ran her fingers down its length. Of all the objects in the room, this was the one that called to her.

Vedhe had returned to the golden orb. She stroked its shiny surface, mesmerized by its brilliance.

K'lrsa tensed. "Vedhe."

"Yes?" She didn't take her eyes from the orb.

"Do your people have metal? If we didn't have access to the Daliphana, could the tribes trade with you for pots and pans and needles? And fabrics?"

Vedhe nodded. "The metals, yes. The fabrics we trade for, but we could trade those with you, too. They come from the east."

K'lrsa nodded. "Good. So I could raise a barrier between my people and the Daliphana. We'd be safe from them. Your people and mine could trade for what we need."

Vedhe turned to study K'lrsa, still holding the orb. "But what would you give us?"

"What?"

"What would you give us in return for these things you want?"

"I don't know. We…" She frowned. The Daliphana had wanted their trade route, but if she closed access to the Daliphana then the tribes had nothing to offer.

Vedhe stroked the orb's golden surface, her eyes unfocused.

"Vedhe? Please tell me you aren't going to choose that."

"Why?"

"You said it yourself. You're not sure you'd stop with the Daliphana. I can't let you use that. It's…It's too much."

Vedhe glare at her. "Who are you to say?"

K'lrsa stepped forward. "I killed the man who killed my father. And it felt good. For a moment. But it didn't bring my father back. And it didn't change anything. That feeling didn't last. I still feel just as empty now as I did before."

Vedhe raised her chin. "That man you killed will never hurt anyone else ever again. Who knows how many you saved when you killed him."

K'lrsa shook her head. "That thing would kill everyone, Vedhe. The innocent and the guilty. It isn't right to make them all suffer for the sins of the few."

"The innocents of today are the tyrants of tomorrow."

"But they're still innocents. You can't do this. Please. Don't."

Vedhe studied the golden orb. The light that seeped through the cracks in its surface played across the scars on her face, making her look inhuman.

"Please don't, Vedhe."

Vedhe turned away, the orb gripped in her hand as she stepped towards the door.

K'lrsa held her breath, waiting. If Vedhe chose the orb, K'lrsa's hopes and the hopes of the tribes were ruined.

She couldn't let that kind of destruction happen.

Even if it saved the lives of everyone she loved. She couldn't let Vedhe use it.

Vedhe paused in the doorway and turned to look at her.

"Please, Vedhe," she pleaded.

Vedhe turned away.

CHAPTER 87

K 'lrsa called after Vedhe as she moved to leave the room, the sun orb in her hand. "Vedhe. Don't do this. I know how much you want to hurt them. I…I saw what was done to you. I understand."

"No you don't! You saw me go into that tent every night, but you weren't there. You didn't feel it." Tears ran down her cheeks. "You will never understand what that was like. Never!" She came back towards K'lrsa, the orb clenched in her fist. "And that was after they killed my entire family."

The Lady stepped forward, placing her hands over Vedhe's. "Child, you are allowed to take anything from this room that you want. Those are the rules of this place. But do you really want this? Do you want to become like them. They killed your little sister. Would you in turn kill all of their children? Think about those little girls and boys, all dead because they had the misfortune to be born in that place."

Vedhe shook, her whole body trembling with suppressed emotion. Rage, fear, sorrow. Each flitted across her face.

K'lrsa didn't want to move, scared that the slightest distraction would break the impasse and Vedhe would leave with the orb.

"Vedhe, child. Here. Did you see this artifact?" The Lady reached up to the top shelf next to the door and

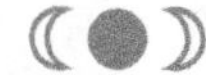

pulled down a circular tube made of onyx stone with glass on each end.

"What is it?"

"It allows you to see the true heart of a person. Whether they are good or bad. You could, if you wanted revenge, you could take this. You could use it to see the truth of people. You could use it to eliminate those who are evil. Just those who are evil."

Vedhe's grip on the sun orb loosened. She set it aside on a nearby shelf and took the black tube from the Lady's hand.

She held it to her eye and turned it on K'lrsa.

K'lrsa trembled under her gaze.

She was a good person, but she wasn't perfect. She was impetuous and selfish and she'd hurt those she loved the most.

"Well?" she asked softly. "Do I pass? Am I good enough to live?"

Vedhe lowed the glass from her eye. "Yes. Just barely." She winked.

K'lrsa laughed and all the tension left the room. "So is that what you're going to take?"

Vedhe nodded.

As K'lrsa hesitated, Vedhe laughed. "You want me to leave with it now? So you know?"

K'lrsa nodded. "Sorry."

"That's okay. I'll wait for you outside." Vedhe walked through the doorway, the onyx tube in her hand, the sun orb still on the shelf by the entrance where she'd left it.

K'lrsa studied the orb for a long moment. It was the easiest way to destroy the Daliph's troops. But that kind of power...

It needed to stay here.

She turned to survey the room. Her eyes lingered for a long, long time on the wooden staff.

And then on the copper cuff.

Both would work. She knew how she could use them to defeat the Daliph's troops.

But both were too dangerous.

Eventually she stooped down and took the silver necklace. She could use it to move the Daliph's troops back to Toreem. And every time they returned, she could move them back to where they belonged.

The Lady nodded, a small smile on her face. K'lrsa didn't miss the fact that she'd placed herself in the path of the wooden staff.

They stepped out of the room and back into the hallway.

It was time.

Time to save the tribes.

CHAPTER 88

The Lady stopped them in the hallway. "K'lrsa dan V'na of the White Horse tribe and Vedhe Kanaatanva, you have chosen your reward for conquering the labyrinth. Now I must tell you that there are conditions on your use of the objects you have chosen."

"What? Why didn't you tell us this before we left the room?" K'lrsa leaned against the wall, arms crossed. She was so tired of there always being one more thing.

The Lady smiled. "Peace, child. The conditions are simple and if you choose not to follow them you may return the object now and never be subject to them."

"Hm. I see. So you let us choose an object, get us outside the room, and then impose conditions we won't want to follow so that we return the object before we get a chance to use it?"

"Ah, K'lrsa, don't you trust us just a little?" Before K'lrsa could answer no, the Lady continued. "The conditions are simple. You will never allow another to use the object you have chosen. It is yours and yours alone. Only you have been deemed worthy to wield it and only you shall."

"And if we violate this?"

"We will take it back. Neither of the objects you chose were so powerful that it would allow you to stand against us."

K'lrsa looked at the now-closed door. "Were there objects in there that would?" K'lrsa thought about it and laughed. "Of course. The wooden staff. That's why you were so scared I'd take it."

"It destroyed an entire people! Isn't that enough?"

"But that wasn't your fear. Your fear was that I'd choose it and be able to stand against you."

The Lady ignored her. "The other condition is that the artifact will return here when you die. It is yours and yours alone."

"What's to prevent someone from coming here after I die and claiming it again?"

"Nothing. But they will have to come here of their own will and make their way through the labyrinth and the object will have to appear to them in the choosing room. If all that happens, they can have it. But I can tell you it's rare. There are some who've stepped through those doors and had no choice at all."

"But I thought it responded to your need?"

"That. And it also responds to your strength. So? Do you agree to these terms?"

Vedhe nodded. K'lrsa shrugged.

"Good. Then it's time to say farewell. Follow me."

She led them back down the hallway to where Badru and the others waited.

CHAPTER 89

K'lrsa wiped her sweaty palms on her pants as they approached the cushioned room where everyone was waiting for them. Her heart pounded in her ears and she couldn't seem to get enough air into her lungs. Why was she so nervous about this when she hadn't been about selecting an object that could save everyone's lives?

As they paused on the threshold to the room, Vedhe held the lens to her eye and studied everyone, but put it away with a disappointed sigh. "It doesn't work on the dead."

The Lady patted her on the shoulder before stepping into the space.

Everyone turned to look at them.

Badru was the first to his feet. "What did you choose?"

Herin joined him. "Was it the orb of fire? That would be the best weapon."

"Only if you were as cruel as Aran." Lodie stepped up next to Herin, shaking her head. "Please tell me you didn't choose the orb of fire."

"I almost did," Vedhe said. Everyone turned to look at her. "But K'lrsa said she'd choose something to counter me if I did."

"Why would you choose that?" Lodie asked.

"To destroy those who hurt me."

Herin turned on K'lrsa. "And you were going to stand against her. Pzah, girl. What kind of fool are you?"

"The kind who doesn't believe in punishing the innocent."

Herin snorted. "Good luck with that. You'll see what happens when you hold back with your enemies. And so will your people."

K'lrsa crossed her arms, trying not to second-guess her choice.

Her father patted her on the arm. "So what did you choose?"

K'lrsa held up the pendant around her neck. "It allows me to go anywhere I want, immediately. And I can take others with me."

"And how is that going to defeat an entire army, you fool?" Herin spat.

"I don't have to defeat them. I just have to move them somewhere the tribes aren't. I'll take them all back to Crossroads and tell them if they return again, I'll leave them in the deepest desert next time."

"And you think that'll be enough to keep them at bay?"

She shrugged. "It'll have to. Because I'm not going to kill men who were just following orders. Or children who have no fault for where they were born."

Herin walked away in disgust, muttering to herself.

Badru turned to Vedhe, his eyes wide with alarm. "And you? What did you bring back from there?"

Vedhe held up the onyx tube. "It allows me to see the truth of someone. If they're good or bad."

"And how do you plan to use that?" Herin called.

"If someone is bad, I'll kill them. If they're good, I won't."

Herin snorted. "So simple is it?"

Badru looked back and forth between them, shaking his head.

"What? Say what it is you want to say." K'lrsa crossed her arms, waiting for the rebuke he so clearly wanted to give.

He opened his mouth and closed it again and then leaned forward, studying her. "So, you went into a room filled with powerful weapons out of legend, and you came back with a necklace that can take you anywhere you want and a viewing tube that lets you see if people are bad?"

K'lrsa's father threw an arm around her shoulders. "Well I, for one, am proud of you. For seeing that not everything requires brute force and open war."

"You're proud of her? Will you be proud of her when she dies like you did because she underestimated her enemy?"

"Badru! That's not fair. And don't you dare speak to my father like that."

"It's the truth. Clearly you don't understand the threat Aran represents if you think this will defeat him."

"I don't want to defeat him, Badru. I just want him to leave us alone."

Badru grabbed his hair in his hands. "You don't get it! Aran won't leave you alone. Ever. Not until he's found this place and made his way to that room and taken the most dangerous, deadly weapon he can. You will never be safe from him until he's destroyed. None of us will."

"You will. You're already dead."

Badru shook his head. "If Aran finds his way here, we won't be safe either."

K'lrsa looked away. "I'm sorry if I didn't pick the weapon any of you would have. But I'm the one that has to live with using it, not you. And I made the choice that worked for me. If that doesn't work for you, well, I'm sorry, but the choice has been made. And it's time for Vedhe and me to leave."

"You'll come back after?" Badru asked, staring at her with those beautiful blue eyes of his.

K'lrsa chewed on her lip.

At last she said, "I don't know. I…I want to, to see what it is between us. But I made a promise to M'lara that I wouldn't leave her again."

He seemed to sink in on himself. "Oh."

"Badru." She grabbed his hand, but he snatched it away.

"No. Go. You're right. I, I understand."

He walked down the hall and out of sight, never looking back.

K'lrsa started to follow, but her father stopped her. "Let him go."

"But…"

"K'lrsa. What could you say to him right now that would change things?"

"But I do love him."

"And he'll be here if you change your mind. I'll talk to him for you. Now come here. Give me a hug." He pulled her into his arms and for one brief moment she let herself pretend that he was alive and she wasn't about to leave him and everyone else she cared about behind forever.

"I love you, Dad."

"I love you, too. And know that whatever you do, I'm proud of you."

She nodded, suddenly scared. "I don't want to lose you again. Will you be here if I come back?"

"You won't lose me. You carry me with you everywhere you go."

It's not the same, she wanted to wail, but she just nodded, too close to tears to speak.

"Trust in yourself, K'lrsa."

She hugged him one last time.

She turned to her mother and hugged her. Her mother tucked a piece of hair back into K'lrsa's braid. "Tell everyone I love them. And take care of them for me."

K'lrsa nodded, too emotional to speak.

Her parents walked away, hands joined.

She pressed her lips tight together, finally letting herself feel just a bit of the anger that threatened to overwhelm her.

It wasn't fair.

They got to go to paradise and she had to return to a life that was barely worth living. A life without Badru or her father or her mother. All because no one else was there to do what needed done.

What had she done to deserve this?

K'lrsa turned to the Lady. "I'm ready. Where are Fallion and Kriger?"

"They can't travel with you, not this way."

"But we will get them back?"

The Lady nodded. "They'll find you again."

K'lrsa gripped the pendant around her neck and held out her hand to Vedhe. "Ready?"

"Ready."

Vedhe put her hand in K'lrsa's and they looked around the room one last time. K'lrsa closed her eyes and pictured the platform in the center of the gathering grounds and willed herself to go there.

Her body was wrenched into nothingness. For one long moment it felt like she was being torn apart, stretched between two impossibly distant points, and then she stumbled forward and fell to her knees in the exact center of the platform.

She gasped, every breath so painful she wanted to scream. She coughed and spat blood. Vedhe huddled next to her, gasping for air.

"Here." K'lrsa offered her a hand and Vedhe took it.

They stood, surveying what they could see of the camp.

It was the middle of the night, the moon hung above them, full and ripe. There were no campfires within the gathering grounds—probably not enough wood to fuel them—but a ring of fires marked the edge of the grounds where the Daliph's troops waited for the tribes to surrender or starve.

K'lrsa touched the necklace at her throat, wondering if maybe she should've chosen the orb of fire or that staff. But it was too late for that now.

CHAPTER 90

No one stirred as K'lrsa and Vedhe walked through the nearest cluster of tents. There were no guards posted, no one watching or waiting for their return. As they stepped out of the space between the Tall Bluff Tribe tents and the White Horse Tribe tents, K'lrsa saw someone sneaking through the night, dodging from the shadow of one tent to the next, coming from the direction of the enemy encampment.

She ran forward, grabbing the person's arm before they spotted her. The woman she'd grabbed cried out in pain, but quickly muffled the sound.

"F'lia?" K'lrsa asked as she dragged the woman into the moonlight.

"Let me go. If they see me, they'll kill me." She struggled to free herself, but she'd never been as physically strong as K'lrsa.

K'lrsa didn't let go but she moved them back into the shadow of another tent. "Who will kill you?"

"The Black Horse Tribe."

"What are you doing?"

"Smuggling food in. I do it each night so the tribes won't starve."

"How long have we been gone?"

She shrugged. "Ten days. D'lan and the others have been talking about fighting their way out."

"Ten days! But…" K'lrsa shook her head. Just one more lie of the gods.

"You have to let me go, K'lrsa. They'll think I've been captured."

She started to release F'lia, but stopped. Shaking, she looked to Vedhe. "Can you look at her? Can you see?"

K'lrsa had never wanted to believe that F'lia might have known about her father. But…She could never be sure. And what if F'lia was lying now? Maybe she wasn't bringing food to the tribes. Maybe she was spying on them.

Vedhe raised the small tube to her eye and studied F'lia. "She wants things too much. And she uses men. Uses her beauty. But she'd never kill for it. Or harm others for it. Or want others to cause harm for her. And she is trying to help."

K'lrsa let go of F'lia. "Can you take us to D'lan?"

F'lia hesitated, but then she nodded. "Keep to the shadows and don't speak."

They darted around the edge of the camp, from the shadow of one tent to the next, in silence.

Eventually, they made their way to the base of the rock formation where the shadows were deep and dark. F'lia whistled softly and someone answered. She crept forward, looking both ways, and a man stepped forward to meet her.

K'lrsa followed.

D'lan reached for the knife at his belt before he recognized her and let his hand fall away again. "You're back."

She nodded.

"And did you bring a weapon to wipe these traitors from the face of the earth?"

"It won't kill them. But it will get rid of them."

He crossed his arms and glared at her. "Not good enough. They'll just come back until we finally kill them all."

Vedhe raised the tube to study D'lan.

"What do you see?" K'lrsa asked.

"A good man." She lowered it and studied him with her own eyes. "Vain. Arrogant. Scared. Angry. But a good man."

D'lan frowned at her. "Who asked you?"

"D'lan, enough. We're back and we have a way to end this."

"How?"

"I can send them back to the Daliphate."

"How? By asking them nicely?"

K'lrsa tilted her head to the side and studied him for a long moment. "You know, I don't have to explain myself to you. I'm the one with the way to save us and I'm going to use it. What you think of that is not my problem. Now, if you'll excuse me, I need rest. So does Vedhe. We'll see you in the morning."

"K'lrsa!"

She ignored him.

She was done letting others tell her what to do or second-guessing her.

CHAPTER 91

K'lrsa was awake at dawn. She paced the small area in front of her tent, worried about what had to happen next. It was simple in theory. She'd go out there and send all those soldiers to Toreem.

But the reality of it was far more frightening. When just she and Vedhe had traveled from the Hidden City, she'd ended up coughing up blood and Vedhe still wasn't breathing quite right.

And that was just the two of them.

What was it going to be like to transport hundreds at once? And across that great a distance?

She'd chosen the necklace because it wouldn't murder hundreds, but she'd been wrong.

She paced the tent, opening and closing her fists, over and over again, thinking, pacing, wondering what to do. For a brief moment she longed for the wooden staff and the ability to just shove a mountain range between the plains and the Daliphana. But that would've never worked either.

Vedhe coughed into her hand as she emerged from the other tent. She had dark circles under her eyes.

"Are you alright? How do you feel?"

She smiled weakly. "I think I'll stay here when you go to Toreem. Traveling that way once was enough for me."

K'lrsa nodded as Vedhe fixed herself a cup of peppermint tea and sat down.

"I'm worried if I try to transport so many it'll kill them."
Vedhe nodded. "Yes. And maybe you as well."
K'lrsa chewed on her lip. Vedhe was right.
Vedhe sipped her tea. "You could make an example."
"How?"
"Take ten through. I'm sure at least one will die."
"If I just take ten?"
Vedhe nodded, taking another sip of the tea. "Take them through. Bring the dead one back. Tell them you'll take more of them through and that more of them will die if you do. Or they can choose to leave peacefully."
"I'm not sure I can survive two more trips."
"Maybe you don't have to go?"
K'lrsa frowned. There was so much she didn't know about the pendant. What it did. How it worked. What she could or couldn't do with it.
The gods. Were all their gifts traps?
Once she'd saved the tribes she wanted nothing more to do with them. Ever.
She paced some more, clutching the pendant, thinking, trying to figure out if Vedhe was right. If she could send the men without going there herself. "Well. It's worth a try at least."
She settled onto a stool next to Vedhe and rooted around in her bag. Just her luck, she still had one of Garzel's travel bars. "Want some?"
Vedhe grimaced, but she took half.

CHAPTER 92

K'lrsa walked to the edge of the gathering grounds, Vedhe trailing along behind her. Others, seeing them, followed.

Word had spread while she was gone that she'd left to find a way to save them.

But here she was. No obvious weapon. Badru no longer by her side. Herin, Garzel, and Lodie gone, too, although K'lrsa wasn't sure anyone had really cared much about them.

"Who is your leader?" K'lrsa shouted towards the men who'd gathered on the other side of the invisible line that separated the safety of the gathering grounds from their camp.

"Why? Gonna shoot him?" one of the men asked, making a rude gesture in her direction.

She felt fury course through her body.

That one gesture reminded her of every single man in the Daliphana who'd treated her like she was nothing, sneered at her, or made her feel dirty as their eyes roved over her body. She grasped the pendant, focused on the man, and willed him to Toreem.

He disappeared and the men nearby backed away, muttering curses. One dropped to his knees, praying.

"Did it hurt?" Vedhe whispered.

"Not at all." K'lrsa smiled and one of the men who'd stepped forward to challenge her, fell back. "Where's your leader? Bring him to me now."

She glared at the men, her hand clutched around the pendant, almost wishing someone would challenge her. All the frustration and fear of the last weeks and of the months she'd spent in Toreem threatened to overwhelm her.

She desperately wanted a target to take it out on.

A man pushed through the crowd, a multi-colored sash tied around his waist. "What do you want, little girl?"

Anger flashed through her like water on a hot pan as the man smiled at her, running his eyes up and down her body.

"I want you to take a message to Aran for me."

"Aran?"

"Your Daliph."

"You will address him as the Most Honored Leader of the Toreem Daliphate."

"No. I will not. He lost that privilege when he died the first time."

"Died?" The man laughed.

"Yes. Died. Or didn't you know that your leader was a death walker?"

There was an angry mutter from the men behind him. Death walkers were hated and feared within the Daliphana. Anyone discovered with the knowledge of death walker magic was immediately killed.

The man laughed easily. "And how would you know?"

K'lrsa shook her head. "It doesn't matter. What does matter is that you will take a message to him for me."

"Will I now? But my orders are to stay here until the Black Horse Tribe is restored to what is rightfully theirs."

"That's never going to happen."

"Why? Because your gods are on your side? Hadn't you noticed, little girl? They can't act directly on this world. They can only act through those who follow them. And as far as I can see, that's pretty little girls like you. Not much to fear, I'm afraid."

K'lrsa breathed through her nose as she glared at the man and fought the urge to send him somewhere so far away he'd never find his way home. Like the middle of those oceans she'd heard about.

Unfortunately, she needed the smug, arrogant little shit.

"As I was saying…I need you to tell Aran something for me."

"Tell him yourself."

"No. I have no desire to set foot in the Toreem Daliphate ever again. Now…"

"Why don't you quit playing at leader, little girl?"

K'lrsa flushed with anger as the men behind him laughed. "Tell Aran I'm sending his troops back to him. And if he wants them to live he'll keep them on his side of the barren lands. We'll send someone to negotiate a new trade deal."

She willed him to the plains in front of Toreem.

The remaining men whispered back and forth, looking around for their leader.

She turned to Vedhe. "Who are the worst of this lot?"

Vedhe looked at them through her viewing tube. "That one. And that one."

She pointed to two men standing towards the back of the crowd.

"I want you all to watch what I do here. I am going to send those men out into the middle of the plains. Far enough away that they have to walk back, but close enough for you to see where they go. I can send them farther, but it might kill them. I can send all of you back to Toreem right now, but it will very likely kill you. I don't want to do that."

She focused on the two men and willed them into the middle of the plains behind the encampment. As they appeared, one stumbled into the other but both were alive.

The men before her muttered darkly, but she was safe, protected by the gathering grounds.

"Leave. Now. Go back to where you came from. Anyone still here tomorrow, I'll send to Toreem myself."

She started to turn away and then turned back, remembering F'lia.

Raising her voice, she said, "Anyone from the tribes who wants to return to us and is willing to vow to follow our ways, may do so."

She didn't care if it wasn't her place to make the offer. It was the right thing to do.

CHAPTER 93

"What now?" Vedhe asked her as they sat on the steps of the central platform and watched the Daliph's men pack up their tents.

"Now we wait and see if anyone wants to return. And if the Daliph's men leave."

"Do you think they will?"

K'lrsa shook her head. "I don't know. Is what I did to those men enough to overcome Aran's orders?"

A man wearing the brown uniform of a Toreem soldier walked towards them, head down as he pushed past curious members of the tribes.

He stopped just out of arm's reach.

"Yes?" K'lrsa asked.

He looked up at her, tensed as if ready to fight. "I want to join the tribes."

"What? Really?" That was the last thing she'd expected him to say. "Why?"

"I don't want to go back there."

"You're a man, it can't be that bad."

He sniffed. "The Daliphana aren't that bad for some men. But for others…I…I've heard you don't care here, what a man does, who a man is, as long as he contributes to the tribe."

She nodded.

"I want that."

"And *can* you contribute?"

"I think so. I can hunt. I can ride."

She chewed on her lip. "We are losing most of the Black Horse Tribe. Their land was almost completely desert, but we'll still need to patrol it."

Vedhe leaned over. "Don't you need to ask D'lan? Or the other tribal leaders?"

"For one man? No."

The man relaxed slightly, smiling.

"I haven't said yes, yet. Vedhe, can you test him? And you'll have to take the same oath the rest of us did."

He nodded as Vedhe raised the tube to her eye and studied him. She looked surprised by whatever she saw, but only said, "He's true. He'll be a strong member of the tribes."

"Then be welcome."

"Thank you! I'll get my things and be back."

"Be careful. If they know what you've done…"

"I will."

He walked away, head held high, a skip to his step. K'lrsa smiled, watching him, glad to have done something positive for the day.

But it turned out that the man wasn't alone in his desire to join the tribes.

By the fifth time it happened, a small crowd had gathered to watch, including M'lara. K'lrsa sent her to fetch D'lan, knowing that if things continued the council leaders were going to want a say.

He arrived just as a sixth and seventh man presented themselves for judgment. Vedhe approved the first one, but spat at the second one. "This one is evil. His mother should've drowned him when he was born."

The man glared at her with pure hatred in his eyes, but turned and left without another word.

"What is this, K'lrsa?" D'lan demanded as the other man took a seat behind them on the pedestal with the others of his fellows who'd already asked for shelter.

"These men wish to join the tribes. They're all trained soldiers, capable of living off the land, and hard workers."

"Who's to say they won't betray us?"

"Vedhe. The object she took from the Hidden City allows her to see into someone's true nature, to judge them."

D'lan harrumphed.

"She was pretty accurate about you last night."

He laughed slightly, acknowledging the point. "What are we going to do with them? Where will they go?"

"Someone will need to patrol the Black Horse Tribe lands. Whatever's left of that tribe can do it, but they'll need more people, especially Riders."

"But this many men and no women. It'll cause problems. And trying to integrate them into our way of life…They don't think like we do, K'lrsa."

She studied the men. "They'll have to learn to if they want to stay. We won't allow what happens in the Daliphana to happen here." She turned back to D'lan. "Two have wives and children. They'd like to bring them here, eventually."

He shook his head. "No. If they want to stay they need to marry someone in the tribes."

"But, D'lan. They have families."

"I'm sorry. We've always accepted outsiders into the tribes, but it's always been through marriage. It's the best way. If they want to come, they have to come alone and marry someone of the tribes."

She winced. "Do we have that many single women to marry them?"

"Some will not want to marry," Vedhe added. "At least two of them so far."

"Oh." K'lrsa looked at the men again, trying to figure out which of the two it was. "Well, that's alright then. As long as they contribute and follow our ways. Isn't it, D'lan?"

He nodded. "I'm fine with it. But I don't speak for all of the councilmembers."

"No. But they'll listen to you. Call a meeting. Tell them

this is the price I demand for rescuing you from the Daliph's troops."

D'lan choked. "The price you demand for rescuing us?"

"Yes."

D'lan looked like he wanted to say more, but two more of the Daliph's soldiers approached, small packs slung over their shoulders.

CHAPTER 94

Of course, just because the men wanted to join the tribes and Vedhe judged them fit to do so didn't mean everyone agreed. As the day wore on, more and more people gathered around to watch the men ask for sanctuary.

By the end of the day, almost a hundred men from the Daliphana were seated behind and around Vedhe and K'lrsa, and over half of the tribes seemed to be gathered in front of them buzzing like a bee hive.

The wise man for the White Horse Tribe came forward, bearing the oath rod. "If they're going to stay, they need to swear the same oath as the rest."

K'lrsa nodded. "They will."

"Who's going to take them on?" a young man from the Tall Bluff tribe asked.

"Whoever wants to. My tribe could use more Riders. And we could use the training they can provide in how to use swords. Isn't that true, D'lan?"

He nodded. "The White Horse Tribe will welcome fifteen of these men. I speak for our Council when I say this."

The men shifted nervously, whispering back and forth, probably doing the math just like K'lrsa was. Fifteen to the White Horse Tribe, but what about the rest?

"These men are strangers to us. They don't understand our ways. They aren't like us," a woman shouted from the crowd.

K'lrsa stood. She was sore and sweaty and tired after a long day sitting outside, but she had to keep going for just a little longer. "We were once one with the Daliphana before the gods took us away and offered us sanctuary. They may not be like us now, but we were all one people once."

She stared down the woman. "We treat all as equal because we know that every man, woman, and child must contribute or we perish. They will learn. Or they will go back to where they came from."

"We can never go back." It was the first man who'd come to her. "If we go back, they'll kill us. If you won't take us now, we'll…"

She rested a hand on his shoulder. They couldn't travel across the desert. They'd die.

"If my people won't take you, I'll send you across the desert to the Northern lands."

She didn't know what the gods would think of that, but she didn't care either.

She turned back to the crowd. "I know there will be adjustments. These men will say the wrong things and do the wrong things. But they will learn and we will be better for having them amongst us. Each generation we benefit from new blood joined to ours. Members of the tribes have always been free to choose mates from outside of our ranks. Why would we deny that now?"

"But there are so many of them," a man protested.

"We will adapt. As we always have."

"What if they change us?"

"Then it will be change for the better. Or why else would we do it?"

K'lrsa chewed on her lip as she watched those in the crowd shift and mutter. It wouldn't be an easy transition, but she knew it was the right choice to make.

She tucked a stray strand of hair, stiff with sweat, back into her braid. "I'm tired. As I'm sure you all are as well. Tomorrow we start the long trek home. These men will take a vow, the same one you took. And once they have, please, welcome them to your fires. Give them shelter for the night. Show that you're better than the men of the Daliphana."

She stepped down from the platform and made her way back to her tent.

In the morning, she hoped they'd be able to leave in peace. Most of the soldiers and members of the Black Horse Tribe had already left.

If the rest weren't gone by morning she'd have to send them away, and she was soul-sick at the thought of such senseless deaths.

CHAPTER 95

It was early morning and K'lrsa lay on her sleeping pallet, staring at the walls of the tent. She could hear people stirring outside. No cook fires. No wood to fuel them nor food to cook. Just the sounds of people starting another day.

Would it be a day of promise? Freedom at last?

Or a day of conflict and death?

She knew she could send the soldiers away with the pendant, but she didn't want to. She detested the thought of so much life wasted.

Maybe the Riders could drive away the rest, spare her having to do it.

But could she ask them to risk their lives like that when she could so easily handle it?

She dragged herself out of bed and splashed her face with cold water. It was nice to be so close to a natural well, a luxury she didn't normally have. That would end today.

Her tribe would return to her lands and she'd go with them.

Or would she?

She could return to the Hidden City. To Badru.

It meant leaving M'lara behind or taking her to a land of the dead where she'd be the only child.

Or she could stay with the men who hadn't been welcomed into one of the tribes. Could work to form them into Riders. Start over. Away from D'lan's influence and all the people who'd known her her whole life.

Find her own way.

It would be good to grow past the girl they still thought she was.

But would M'lara want to come with her?

And what about Vedhe? Would she leave now? Go back home?

Strange to think how the girl had become a friend, the only one who understood her loss.

K'lrsa stepped outside and there was M'lara, crouched in the shadow of a nearby tent.

"Hey there." K'lrsa smiled at the sight of her precocious little sister.

"Hey." M'lara joined her. "Are you ready?"

"For what?"

"To go home?"

K'lrsa sat down next to Vedhe who nodded to a spot behind their tents where Fallion and Kriger stood. "They arrived this morning."

"How did they get here so fast?"

Vedhe shrugged.

"K?" M'lara sat down next to her looking up with those big brown eyes of hers. "We are going home aren't we?"

K'lrsa ruffled her hair and picked a stray twig out of it, smiling to herself at how much M'lara was like she'd been when she was younger.

"I don't know."

M'lara jumped to her feet. "You promised! You promised you'd come back and you'd stay!"

"Shhh. It's okay. Calm down. I did come back, see?"

She crossed her arms. "But you're not going to stay."

"Well…" She glanced at Vedhe. "I thought maybe we should take some of the new soldiers and patrol the border for a while. Help form them into a new tribe."

M'lara's shoulders slumped. "And I have to go live with D'lan?"

"Not if you don't want to. But…M'lara. There probably won't be any other children."

"I don't care. I want to stay with you."

"Okay." She glanced at Vedhe. "What do you think? Are you going to stay with us? Or go back to your people?"

Vedhe was silent for a long time. "I think I'll stay for now. Until you're ready to defeat the Daliphana."

"That's not going to happen."

She shrugged one shoulder.

"It isn't Vedhe. I'm not going back there. I'm not. Let someone else deal with Aran."

"Well, I'll stay regardless. There's nothing for me back home. And one of the recruits from the Daliphana has a nice butt."

"Vedhe!"

Vedhe shrugged. "He does. And there aren't enough women, right? So maybe he'd be willing to look past this." She gestured to her scarred face.

"The right man will."

"Easy to say when you're not disfigured."

K'lrsa bowed her head, acknowledging her point. "So? Ready to see if the Daliph's soldiers have left?"

The others nodded and they made their way together to the edge of camp.

CHAPTER 96

S he walked the perimeter with Vedhe and M'lara by her side enjoying a cool morning breeze. There was a cluster of tents belonging to the Black Horse Tribe at one end and K'lrsa called to them from the safety of the gathering grounds.

"Are you staying with the tribes?"

J'vin stood and came to meet her. "No. We'll leave after breakfast. If that's acceptable to you, oh Ruler of the Tribes."

"Ruler of the Tribes? What are you talking about?"

"Well you certainly seem to have taken charge. Making decisions for everyone. Banishing the Daliph's men without so much as speaking to anyone else."

"Is that why you're leaving?"

"I'm a trader. I'll have better opportunities in the Daliphana."

"The tribes need traders."

"Do they, Ruler of the Tribes?"

She shook her head, looking past his shoulder to where F'lia had just emerged from one of the tents.

"F'lia." She waved her friend closer.

J'vin tensed.

"I just want to say goodbye to her. Is that such a problem?"

"She's mine now," he growled.

K'lrsa raised an eyebrow. Since when was a woman anyone's possession in the tribes? But this was a man who had chosen the Daliphana over the tribes, so maybe he really felt that way.

"Of course. I just want to say goodbye to her."

F'lia came over, her hand stroking her small belly.

"K'lrsa. Good to see you returned."

So J'vin didn't know about her late-night sneaking. He stood there, watching them. K'lrsa stared him down. "A little privacy please?"

F'lia stroked his arm. "Go. I'll be fine."

Vedhe, who'd been studying him with her viewing tube, shook her head. "He's a mean man. Very cruel."

"Oh, he's fine. He just gets upset sometimes."

Vedhe shook her head. "No. It's more than that. Here. Look." She held the tube out to F'lia.

K'lrsa slapped her hand down. "Vedhe you can't do that. Remember? The gods will take it back."

Vedhe shrugged. "I don't care. Let her see. For the child she carries if nothing else."

"Do you want to?"

"What?" F'lia looked back and forth between them, confused.

"If you put the viewer to your eye, it shows you someone's true nature." K'lrsa bit her lip, not sure if she wanted F'lia to use it or not.

Vedhe held it out to her.

Finally, F'lia took it and turned to look at J'vin with it. She flinched at whatever she saw there. "He's never been cruel to me," she whispered as she handed it back to Vedhe. "But I can see now that it was always there, lurking."

"Come with us, then." K'lrsa jerked her across the boundary as J'vin started back towards them.

"What are you doing?" he demanded.

Vedhe blocked his path. "Go pack."

"No." He tried to shove past her, but Vedhe hit him in the throat with the heel of her hand. Not enough to kill, just enough to make him choke and stumble backward.

"Go pack. If she wants to come with you, she will."

F'lia started to walk back towards him, but K'lrsa held her back. "Remember what you saw."

"But he's never been like that with me."

"It's only a matter of time. Think about your child."

F'lia hesitated.

J'vin cussed at Vedhe calling her names that no one in the tribes would ever use.

F'lia turned away. "Okay. I'll stay."

"Good. M'lara, take her to D'lan. Tell him what happened here."

She looked back at J'vin as M'lara and F'lia left. "Let her go."

He glared at her, jaw clenched, and K'lrsa knew she'd made an enemy for life. But she didn't care. She wasn't going to let her best friend be with a man like that.

They waited until M'lara and F'lia were safely away and then K'lrsa nodded to Vedhe. "Come on. Let's go."

Vedhe feinted at J'vin and he flinched back before they continued on their way, both smiling.

CHAPTER 97

Only two tents remained of the Daliph's camp. Eight men sat outside, drinking from bowls that smelled deliciously salty and meaty and warm.

"You didn't leave," K'lrsa said as the men turned to look at her.

A man with a red sash stood. "No point. If we go back, we're dead. And so are our families."

"If you stay, you're dead."

He shrugged. "I'd rather die here than return to my Daliph and have him kill me for disobeying his orders."

She glanced at the others. "You feel the same?"

They each nodded.

The man with the red sash spoke again, "We're the officers. We gave the rest of the men the choice to leave. Although some seem to have joined you instead."

"They did."

The man wiped at his nose. "So now what?"

"You could join us, too. If you want."

He shook his head. "I'd rather die than live like a desert savage the rest of my life."

"And you won't leave?"

"Nope."

She looked to the others. "And the rest of you? Anyone who wants to leave now, can. Anyone who'll swear an oath to the tribes can stay."

 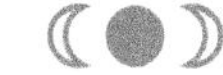

None moved to join her.

"You understand that you're probably going to die when I do this?" Her voice shook and she had to bite her lip to keep control of herself.

The men all stood and lined up before her, hands clasped behind their backs, expressions stoic.

She closed her eyes, seeking inside for the strength she'd need.

It didn't seem like much. Eight lives. Better than hundreds.

But it was still eight men who might have wives and children, a mother and a father. Friends they'd never see again.

She looked at them, wondering what the point was. The death of eight men wouldn't stop Aran.

But she had to be strong. At least the soldiers who'd left the day before would know and maybe think twice before they came against the tribes again.

She should've let Vedhe choose the orb of fire.

Or should've chosen the staff.

Should've raised a mountain range so high no one could pass it. Flooded the barren lands with so much water no one could cross it.

But she hadn't.

And now here she was. Staring at eight men who had no choice but to follow the orders they'd been given.

She touched the necklace. "I'll send you through one at a time. I hope you live. I don't wish you ill. I just don't want you here."

The leader shook his head. "Better to kill us. What Aran will do to us if we live is worse than you can imagine."

"Do you all feel this way?"

They nodded, each in turn.

She swallowed the bile that burned the back of her throat. "Very well." She grasped the pendant and with a thrust of will sent all eight men to Toreem at once.

If they didn't care about living, why should she?

But she did.

She turned away, disgusted, hoping that was the last of it, but knowing it wasn't.

CHAPTER 98

That night they had a great feast. Freed from the gathering grounds, each tribe had sent out a hunting party to find what they could. Some only found a handful of hares or a smattering of birds, but two of the tribes were able to find baru herds and brought back enough baru for everyone to at least have a bite.

It wasn't much, but it was food and it was companionship and it was safety after weeks of fear.

Having been denied their usual socializing, the tribes made up for it with a vengeance, laughing and dancing late into the night.

K'lrsa sat apart, Vedhe by her side. M'lara had run off to join the other children chasing one another and laughing.

"I don't feel part of it now. I'm not sure I ever will again."

Vedhe nodded. "It's why I don't want to go back home. Not yet, at least."

It was so weird to think they'd formed a new tribe. Twenty-five men from the Daliphana, what remained of the Black Horse Tribe, F'lia, M'lara, Vedhe, and her.

And a surprising number of young female Riders or Riders in training drawn by the prospect of mates they hadn't grown up with along with a few of their more determined male suitors who weren't willing to admit defeat to the newcomers so easily.

In the morning they would set out to patrol the border, making sure that all of the Daliph's men had truly returned

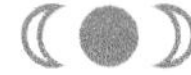

to the Daliphana.

If they found anyone, she could send them back with the pendant.

She flinched at the thought of using it again, but if she had to, she would.

The gods had yet to come for Vedhe's viewing glass. K'lrsa suspected they weren't near as powerful as she'd always thought they were. Oh, sure, they could open a gateway between the land of the living and the dead, but at the same time they seemed powerless to intervene in the actions of ordinary men and women.

"Will you go back to him?" Vedhe asked.

"I don't know. Maybe. When we're sure the Daliph's men are gone and he isn't going to send more. And when I'm sure M'lara will be okay."

"You should kill Aran. Now. Before he has time to gather more strength."

"No. I think he'll leave us alone now."

"He won't."

K'lrsa sighed. "Well, as long as I'm here, the tribes will be safe." She fingered the pendant at her neck. No matter what he threw at them, she could handle it.

Vedhe shook her head. She stood and left.

K'lrsa stayed where she was, watching the others laugh and dance and celebrate.

She felt hollow.

She'd lost so much. Her parents, the man she could've loved. But life went on.

And she still had M'lara and F'lia and Vedhe. And even D'lan.

She didn't know what the future would bring, but she was prepared to face it. And maybe, someday, she'd find a way to move forward, to love again and live a full life.

For now, it was enough to just be back home with the tribes and to know they were safe.

It had to be.

(●)

For the thrilling end to the trilogy, read **Rider's Resolve.**

INDEX OF PRIMARY CHARACTERS

Aran: Current and former Daliph of the Toreem Daliphate. Badru's grandfather. A death walker capable of coming back from the dead. Kidnapped Herin. Cut out Garzel's tongue.

Badru: Former Daliph of the Toreem Daliphate. The man K'lrsa saw in her Moon Dreams as she traveled to Toreem. Rider of the *Amalanee* horse, Midnight.

D'lan: K'lrsa's brother. Rider for the White Horse Tribe. Now a member of the Council.

F'lia: K'lrsa's best friend. Member of the White Horse Tribe. Had intended to wed L'ral before his death.

Garzel: Husband of Herin. Formerly of the tribes. Has been in the Toreem Daliphate serving as Herin's poradom. Has no tongue.

Herin: Grandmother of Badru, wife of Garzel, former captive of Aran's. Honored position in Toreem. Referred to there as Omala. Formerly of the tribes. Missing the top join on each finger as a result of each attempt she made to kill Aran.

K'lrsa: Member of the White Horse Tribe. Sister to D'lan and M'lara. Daughter of V'na and B'nin. Rider of the *Amalanee* horse, Fallion.

Lodie: Herin's sister. Formerly of the tribes. Went to Toreem to save Herin but was made a slave. Poisoned herself to kill Aran, but was brought back by death walker magic. Fled to the White Horse Tribe with the assistance of K'lrsa.

Vedhe: Previously unnamed. Pale-haired and –skinned slave girl brought from the North by a slave caravan. Fled to the White Horse Tribe with the assistance of K'lrsa. Rider of the *Amalanee* horse, Kriger.

V'na: K'lrsa's mother. Former Rider of the White Horse Tribe. Now a member of the Council.

SUMMARY OF RIDER'S REVENGE
(BOOK 1)

K'lrsa loves her life as a Rider for the White Horse Tribe. She spends her days riding her *Amalanee* horse Fallion and her nights avoiding her mother's attempts to settle her down. But there's unrest in the tribes. Trade has brought change and her father is concerned by the way the other tribes have succumbed to the temptations brought from the outside.

When her father finds out that one of the tribes, the Black Horse Tribe, is also helping bring slaves across the desert, he campaigns amongst the tribes to have them expelled.

But before that can happen, the White Horse Tribe is raided by men from the neighboring Toreem Daliphate. Her father rides out to confront them along with his other Riders, but leaves K'lrsa behind.

When her father doesn't return, K'lrsa goes looking for him and finds him dying in the desert, staked to the sand with his eyes gouged out and belly slit open. She swears to avenge him by going to the Toreem Daliphate and killing the Daliph.

Her father doesn't want her to go.

She promises him she won't to appease him, but then secretly vows to do so.

Her father begs her to kill him and put him out of his misery. She does even though it devastates her to do so.

That night she dreams of Father Sun who shows her a trading caravan that will lead her to the Toreem Daliphate.

She lets the caravan capture her, almost killing herself and Fallion in the process.

The healer traveling with the caravan, Lodie, is a slave and former member of the tribes who recognizes that K'lrsa's wounds are self-inflicted. Instead of turning K'lrsa in to the caravan master, Lodie counsels K'lrsa against going to the Daliphate.

One of the slaves in the caravan is a pale-blond woman who they were going to present as a Northern Princess but has been ruined by exposure to the sun. The caravan master, Harley gives K'lrsa the choice to take the woman's place and be sold as a "Desert Princess" or to just be one of the rest of the slaves made to walk across the desert and sold at the earliest opportunity.

K'lrsa chooses to take the woman's place.

After watching how the woman is abused as a result, K'lrsa feels guilty and helps the woman and Lodie escape. In order to do so, K'lrsa makes Lodie a sister of her blood and gives Lodie her moon stone. They steal a horse belonging to G'van of the Black Horse Tribe and flee.

When G'van discovers his horse missing, he attacks K'lrsa. She fights back.

Harley breaks up the fight, but when G'van then threatens Harley, Harley kills him.

Most of the slaves are sold off in Crossroads, but Harley takes K'lrsa and a handful of slaves deeper into the Daliphate.

The Toreem Daliphate is completely foreign to K'lrsa who is used to a nomadic life where all are equal. She struggles to adapt to its different ways.

She befriends one of her captors, Barkley, and eventually confesses to him that her plan is to go to Toreem and kill the Daliph. Barkley arranges for a friend of his in the city to write to Harley offering to purchase K'lrsa if Harley will bring her to Toreem.

On the plains outside of Toreem, their small party— now just Harley, Barkley, Reginald, and K'lrsa—run into a man on a black *Amalanee* horse, Badru. He's the same man K'lrsa has been dreaming about the entire journey.

He's accompanied by an old woman, Herin, who knowns Harley and tells him to leave. She's also Lodie's sister. As they're turning away, K'lrsa calls on their blood connection and demands that Herin help her.

Herin has the party arrested and orders the soldiers to kill anyone who speaks.

They're taken to the dungeons of Toreem where all the others are killed except K'lrsa.

She wakes up in a luxurious room in the palace to find

that she's been chosen as a dorana—an honored concubine—to the Daliph of the Toreem Daliphate. Herin is furious, K'lrsa confused. But it's the best chance K'lrsa has to avenge her father.

K'lrsa finds training to be a dorana incredibly hard. She's not allowed to look at anyone, not supposed to speak. They dress her in ornate costumes that keep her from moving freely. Her fingers are bound with the *meza* so that she can't even feed herself. And, even if she could, she's not supposed to.

Everything she needs is done by her poradoma—Sayel, Tarum, and Morel. Sayel is her head poradom and very fond of her although exasperated by her inability to be a proper dorana. Tarum hates her and takes liberties when he dresses or feeds her. Herin is there to supervise with her constant companion, Garzel.

Weeks later, Badru finally comes to see K'lrsa. She's still been dreaming of him every night and is so grateful to see a friendly face that she confesses to him her plan to kill the Daliph.

He tells her she can't do that and leaves. She waits in her room, certain he'll betray her, but instead Herin and Sayel come the next day and tell her it's time to present her to the Daliph.

She's dressed in even more ornate clothing than normal, including the *tiral*—a full-length coat crocheted of gold that binds her movements to the point she knows she won't be able to attack the Daliph.

Finally, she's brought to the Daliph's throne room. Just outside they run into Badru who is also the Daliph. He's furious she's there and demands that Herin take her back to her rooms. K'lrsa is devastated to realize that the man she loves and the man she wants to kill are the same.

She refuses to continue training as a dorana and is punished by being left alone, unattended with no food or clothing, her fingers still bound by the *meza*.

Eventually, she continues her training and is once more brought to see Badru. This time she enters the throne room, still conflicted about whether to kill Badru or not, but before she can reach him, she overhears a man insult her and turns to confront him, something a dorana is not supposed to do.

Badru sees what happens and declares that an insult to his dorana is an insult to him and has the two men responsible whipped even though they are both senior advisors of his.

After, Herin tries to convince K'lrsa to escape, but K'lrsa refuses, not trusting her.

Badru comes to her rooms and she attacks him, but fails to kill him. He swears to her it wasn't his men who killed her father but she still doubts him.

She asks Badru to free her because she can't possibly be with him if she isn't free to choose to be with him.

The next day he takes her out riding and frees her from slavery and gives her Fallion back. He also declares that any slave owner who chooses to can free their slaves and that any freed slaves can have their property back. His court is in an uproar over the decision.

A courtier insults K'lrsa while on their ride and Badru banishes him even though the man is the son of an important advisor.

When they return, Badru has to leave to attend to an urgent matter and K'lrsa is left alone in the stables where she overhears the arrival of K'var of the Black Horse Tribe who demands more weapons and soldiers to destroy the tribes that oppose him.

She confronts Badru about K'var's demands and he says he'll have no choice but to back the Black Horse Tribe unless K'lrsa can find his people another way across the desert.

K'lrsa throws him out of her room.

In the middle of the night, Tarum comes to kill K'lrsa. She manages to kill him first, but he uses a poisoned blade in his attack and she collapses shortly after.

She awakes to find Herin at her bedside. Her wounds are fully healed and Herin tells her K'lrsa she has been accused by Balor, another poradom, of having an affair with Tarum. Balor claims he's the one who killed Tarum when he found them together.

The penalty for a dorana cheating on the Daliph is death by beheading performed by the Daliph himself. Herin leaves and informs Badru and the others that K'lrsa confessed to the affair.

K'lrsa is able to convince Sayel that she's innocent by showing him the healed scars from the attack. He tells her she was healed by death walkers, those who can also bring back the dead and are feared above all others, and agrees to stand by her side.

At the trial, Badru clearly believes K'lrsa even though the crowd is against her. Since Balor claims he subdued her by force, Badru proposes that they battle to the death to see who is actually telling the truth.

Before the fight, Balor takes a poison that makes him incredibly powerful. K'lrsa shatters her foot and Balor crushes her arm during the fight, but the poison eventually kills Balor and she's declared the winner.

Herin and her husband, Garzel, spirit K'lrsa away immediately after. Sayel follows.

K'lrsa and Sayel learn that Herin was the death walker who healed her wounds the night before in an effort to protect Badru. Herin says she learned the death walker magic from the former Daliph, Aran, who would use it to kill Garzel and bring him back to life again and again in order to torture Herin. She heals K'lrsa again.

Sayel tells Badru that Herin and Garzel are death walkers. Rather than turn them in to the temple where they'd be killed, he banishes them to their quarters.

K'lrsa begs Badru to let her go home and warn them about the threat from the Black Horse Tribe, but Badru asks her to give him three more days. He has her attend court where she learns that K'var was the one who killed her father and that L'ral, who was going to marry her best friend, F'lia, was the one who lured her father to his death.

One of Badru's senior advisors demands K'lrsa's death because he claims she cheated in the trial by combat. Badru replies that there are no rules to such a trial and that if she did poison Balor that was allowed.

Badru frees K'lrsa from being his dorana and brings her

to court dressed as a Rider and places her at his side, something no one approves of. He calls K'var of the Black Horse Tribe forward and accuses him of conspiring against Toreem and sentences him to death.

Before the sentence can be carried out, the former Daliph, Aran, shows himself and demands his throne back. In the chaos of the ensuing fight, Badru is killed by one of his own guards.

Sayel and K'lrsa fight their way to Badru's side and flee with his body through a hidden passage behind the throne. They take Badru to Herin and Garzel to be revived.

All four are trapped in a room and running out of time. Sayel gives his life so Badru can be brought back.

Badru wants to stay and fight to regain his throne, but they convince him they have to flee.

They wait until night and then make their way towards the stables.

K'var is waiting for them. K'lrsa fights and kills him, avenging her father at last.

Herin, Garzel, Badru, and K'lrsa flee Toreem on the two *Amalanee* horses.

They stop outside the city and Garzel uses his sun stone to "awaken" the horses who can now fly. They leave before the guards can reach them, racing to warn the tribes that Aran is sending troops to destroy them.

ABOUT THE AUTHOR

Alessandra Clarke has been losing herself in the worlds of fantasy novels since she was old enough to borrow her first book from the library.

She loves the worlds of Darkover, Valdemar, and Pern, and wishes she could live a hundred lives just so she could read all the books on her to-be-read shelves while still having timeto write, take her pup to the dog park, and see her friends and family.

You can reach her at aclarkewriter@gmail.com or on her website at alessandraclarke.com.